I071284O

Ridge & Root Publishing
West Rutland, Vermont 2025

ISBN 979-8-9898869-8-2

TIES THAT BIND

V. APRILLIANO

THIS BOOK IS DEDICATED TO THE LITTLE VERSION OF ME

You deserved a mom, and not just a mother. You deserved to be cherished, and held, and protected from the bad things. Your life was a display of wild theatrics, and everyone fell for the smoke and mirrors. It was nothing more than props and masks, nothing more than a facade.

When you were trying with all your might to feel whole, you did it alone in a room full of toys, instead of in someone's arms. You learned the hard way that unresolved trauma will lead you into abusive, manipulative, and damaging relationships with people who have failed to tame their own demons.

After years of dragging skeletons out of the closet, opening cans of worms, and letting cats out of bags, I've slayed the demons for both of us, and you have my word that I will protect you, even though your own mother didn't.

Love,
The grown up version of a broken little girl

TIES THAT BIND

V. APRILLIANO

PROLOGUE

I'M DEEPLY TOUCHED that you came back for the second part of my story but I'm not entirely surprised. It's a little like watching a train wreck, but I make up for the train wreck parts with the sarcasm and deep dives into those overfilled filing cabinets in the back of my mind. Most people say I'm witty and tell a good story, and while both of those things are true, I'm also just someone who keeps it real. I don't see any point in lying or spinning a yarn for theatrical effect. In fact, there's no need for any of that, my story is tasty enough without the sprinkles. Looking back, I feel a sense of pride, mixed with a sense of unadulterated fear. I mean, I'm still here, so none of this shit killed me, but even back then, I was skating seriously close to the trap door for the padded party room. I've been through a lot, and I'm not telling you that for some sort of pat on the back or to get your sympathy. I'm telling you that because it's true. I've had people tell me I'm 'resilient' and that I 'bounce back' from things. And maybe the real reason I'm telling this story, is so that I can make some sort of sense out of it. So, let's go back in time.

There I was, just some twenty-something who needed to push the eject button before her ex and his whore had their love child. Just some clueless asshole who wanted desperately for someone to look her in the eyes while they fucked her. An almost-woman, a girl who had 'it' in her, but hadn't had anyone try to get 'it' out. And rest assured, if we're only at the beginning of all of this, and I already told you I murdered a guy, it's safe to say, it gets much worse from here. What would be the point of telling you the rest of this story if I gave the punch line at the end of the first act? Morsels sweetheart, morsels. A little something to make you want a little something more.

So, there I was, about nine months into what was supposed to be a fresh start, and I hadn't figured out that Bunman wouldn't be the place I found peace. Nonetheless, where we're picking up with this whole shit show, it had been a couple weeks since I'd committed my first murder. Looking back at how naive I was at that point, I'm surprised I didn't get myself killed. Just some dumb ass going up against a mob boss. What was I thinking!? I wasn't. My trauma was doing the decision making, especially as I moved on to the next part of this ridiculous adventure, if you want to call it that. As I sit here approaching my thirty-fifth birthday, the state of my life today is a little more 'dark mafia energy,' and a little less 'broken little girl.' I mean, I'm still broken, I've just figured out how to wear better masks. When I feel weak, I pacify myself with sex, drugs, and a place deep within the inner sanctum. Never mind all of that, we'll get to it later.

Not even a year in and I had far more emotional baggage than the day I rolled into Bunman, Vermont, in my twenty-six-year-old piece of Swiss cheese. And it's no surprise that killing a man with a shovel, contributed significantly to my collection of closet skeletons, and the gaggle of demons flying around in my mind. The rage building inside of me at that point was something straight out of hell, a blackened cauldron of bubbling poison, just waiting to slide down the back of someone's throat. A trap door spider, a soul sniper, a quicksand of anguish and despair. I'm not trying to be a martyr here, but if you tried to walk a mile in my dingy white Chuck Taylors, you wouldn't make it past the morning sun porch joint and maple oat latte. You and I have a connection here, maybe we're even friends on some cosmic level. What I'm saying is, I wouldn't wish any of this on my worst enemy.

Surprisingly, it wasn't the murder that fucked with my head, it was the fact that I lost control. I'm not talking like I flipped off some asshole in a Tesla who cut me off in traffic, I'm talking like, I fucking lost it. Bad. I went from never having hurt a soul, to killing a man with a moderately priced garden shovel. In that moment, I was filled with the kind of rage that blinds you. The reality is, it was a case of kill or be killed, but it was so much more than that. The fire inside of me erupted like lava, and landed right on Salvatore Moretti's cranium.

And while we're at it, I guess we should address the sexy, and very powerful, elephant in the room. Giuseppi Moretti was becoming like a big brother to me and I was just hoping I wouldn't let him down. It was the first time in my life that I had known a man with so much power and presence, a man who arouses me just by looking me in the eye. But, even back then, I didn't subscribe to his brand of self-importance most of the time, and I think that's what gave me an in. I listened when most people didn't, and it afforded me a level of protection that most people had to earn the hard way.

I had this little window of time to heal before a whole world of shit hit the fan. I wasn't cut out for any of it, and there I was with a healing gunshot wound, and new scars on the inside and out. I am not saying I'm cut out for that shit in my mid-thirties, either, but something has calloused over for me, I guess. I'm a normal girl, a woman who's trying to be honest with herself about her past. But, in the process of slaying my demons, I've had to make some sacrifices along the way. I don't want to get ahead of myself, so I won't, but if you thought things were nuts before, wait until you hear what happened next. I was feeling sorry for myself about the sling and the stupid exercises I had to do to improve the range of motion in my shoulder. I was depressed and self-medicating, spiraling the drain on the fast track to toaster-bath land. Dwelling on the past, just a broken little girl who wanted her Mommy to love her. I was adjusting to my sister's proximity and new living situation, knocked up, and spending most of her nights in mafia mansion land.

I crawled back into my shell, and wanted to stay there forever, but the next four months would force me to confront some uncomfortable truths about the world I was living in, and who I could trust. Just thinking about it gives me a tightness in my chest that stirs panic of epic proportions. Things were about to take a turn for the worse, if that's even possible. But, at the same time, I was somehow finding myself and becoming a woman. It's hard to explain, like that picture of a kitten looking in the mirror, the reflection of a lion staring back. Because, really, for the next couple of years, I was staring at the reflection of a grown woman who had her shit together. I was just a little girl with a tailored pantsuit, European leather boots, and a Sig Sauer at my hip. I was gazing into a fun house mirror, some catastrophic amalgamation of impostor syndrome and body dysmorphia. Confidently insecure, almost convinced that I was the real deal, even as I hugged my knees to my chest and sobbed. This complete yin and yang of emotions, this pendulum swing of good and evil, suffocating under a weighted blanket of protection. Just a broken little girl in a straitjacket, a solitary confinement cell of demons in cages, some Jekyll and Hyde mind fuck, an absolute acid trip remix of reality.

My feelings were raw, and rough, and out of sorts, I was desperate to feel something besides the pain, to think of something that would bring a smile to my whole damn face. My childhood wounds made me an easy target for the types of people who get off on hurting people. The self-important pieces of shit, the little men with the big key chains, the narcissists. My heart played tricks on me, a perpetual torture chamber of emotions and sensations, but I'd get a little pleasure along with the pain. I wanted so badly to be something, be someone besides a collection of emotional baggage and closet skeletons, a force to be reckoned with. And I guess that was about the time when I decided to ignore the warning signs, the red flags, the obvious lies. Something about trauma does that to you, gives you the ability to compartmentalize things, to rationalize, to store things in tiny boxes in big filing cabinets in the back of your mind. To put up walls that only serve to isolate you from reality, from the darkness and chaos around you, but they also isolate you from the people who love you.

Over time, I figured out how to push people away, especially the people who cared about me the most. I continued to fall into bed with the wrong people, while ignoring what was right in front of my face. I'm not saying I was stupid back then, but sometimes, pretty close. I needed help, and I knew it. I needed to be rescued before my decisions pushed me past the point of no return. But I just racked up more trauma, along with the hangovers and reprimands. This is the point when I started to realize that maybe Bunman wasn't going to be the place I'd get my fresh start. Maybe Bunman was too full of old memories, and new trauma. There was no way I'd catch a break while being chased by my demons. They were hot on my trail, slashing at my back with their blood-red nails as I scurried into the darkness.

Deep down, I have a beautiful soul. I'm full of compassion and empathy, I'm genuine and selfless, to a fault. But I was letting the most broken parts of myself make all the decisions. And when I'm in pain like that, I make decisions like there are no consequences, some knee-jerk reaction to fill my voids. I spent little to no time following my whimsy, and lots of time trying to drown my demons with whiskey and weed. When I was lonely, I'd fall into the bed of any man with a sexy smile and a nice package. And whilst I was doing all that demon-drowning and impulsive-fornicating,

I ignored the pecking order and refused to follow orders. Basically, I ran back to the town that broke me, put myself in the line of fire, and managed to kill a mob boss. Fresh start, my ass.

CHAPTER 1
THE PANIC BUTTON

I OPENED MY EYES that morning, blissfully unaware of what was coming, it seemed like a normal day, considering I had recently committed murder. My newly adopted calico, Indie, stretched next to me, motor running as I scratched under her chin. I wanted to stay in that antique four-poster bed all day, nestled in a cocoon of warmth under the pile of tattered thrifted quilts. After a half assed pep-talk, I pulled on a pair of wool socks to shield my feet from the frigid eighteen hundreds hardwood floor. I peed and padded through the kitchen with Indie at my heels, singing for her supper. As I brewed espresso for my first latte of the day, I made some lame attempt at getting a grip on my current mental state.

A million thoughts and feelings swirled like black smoke in my mind as I steamed the milk. Although I was a seasoned barista at that point, my latte art that morning inadvertently looked like a cock and balls. I shook a bottle of anti-depressants like a rattle, some sort of reassurance the pills were there if I needed them. And if there was ever a time I needed those pills, it was right then, but I returned the bottle to its home on top of the microwave, unwilling to give in. I snagged my thrifted flip-top tin and removed a joint, headed to the sun porch to enjoy coffee with my dear friend, Maryjane.

If we've met before, welcome back. If you're new here, let me get you up to speed. My name is Amelia Birch, and at this point in the story, I was twenty-three and a half, and almost completely healed from a gunshot wound to my left shoulder. My brown shoulder-length ringlets were smashed into a frantic wad on top of my head. My outfit of choice was ratty vintage overalls and a pair of dingy white Chuck Taylors. I was still curvy but had recently lost some weight after the coincidental abandonment of my anti-depressants, and a severe bout of depression. That was about the time I started wearing more flattering clothes, but I didn't like feeling vulnerable, or like I was drawing attention to myself. I have hazel eyes and full lips. My magnificent dimples allowed me to get away with almost anything, and I was just starting to figure that out.

That Friday morning, Giuseppi Moretti had summoned me to his home office. If you aren't familiar with Giuseppi, he was the new mob boss in town. I was acquainted with him by then, but I had no idea what to expect and wasn't really in the mood for whatever he had to say. I hadn't returned to Bunman, Vermont, for all of whatever you call all of that, and I was kind of over the whole thing. With my crazy hair looking even more haphazard than usual, I buttoned myself into a pair of overalls so ratty that I had to wear a pair of black leggings underneath. In the full-length mirror hanging on the bathroom door, I looked as unhinged as I felt. I didn't care, who did I have to impress? And anyway, I'm one of those 'heart on your' sleeve kind of girls so I had no intention of dusting off one of my old masks or in pretending I was fine. What you see is what you get with me.

After fiddling with the key to find the sweet spot, I fired up my twenty-six-year-old Subaru wagon, and you'll be happy to know, it only took me three tries to get her into reverse. I nosed my way up the alley between Muddy Waters and the lot of Giuseppi's Italian Ristorante, with the rotted muffler echoing in my wake. I felt anxious going to mafia mansion land, anxious it was a trap. My ancient station wagon ground to a halt at an official-looking booth. The window slid open and the man stared at my front end, which was giving off a stream of smoke. I cranked my window down, a song skipping on the CD player.

Smacking the dash,

"Amelia Birch, for Giuseppi Moretti."

I gestured aggressively at my front end and then through the gate,

"The caliper's stuck, I'll knock it loose on that speed bump. Just ignore it."

The man nodded like his car did about the same thing, checked a clipboard, and motioned me into the world of rich people with luxury cars that don't look like Swiss cheese. The ornate metal gate swung open in some grand display and I rolled into the type of housing development you see in movies. I didn't even know there was anything like that in Bunman, it was like a different world, and I wondered what the people did for work. I wondered if people at Hidden Hills Estates were peering through their blinds at the woman with crazy hair, as she rolled by in a rusted-out shit-box with a loud exhaust and something dragging. They probably thought I was casing the joint, or 'the help,' heading to my job as a servant for one of the rich powerful assholes who lived in a place like that.

I imagined security systems being activated one by one as I made my way up the street. I slowed in front of a sprawling mansion with tall white pillars, a manicured lawn and fenced in yard. Parking behind my sister's champagne colored Volvo XC90, I wrenched the door open and tried not to slam it shut any louder than necessary. Besides my sister's car, Giuseppi's black Escalade was parked behind a sporty black sedan. There was a Lincoln Navigator and a Porsche 911 somewhere, probably in the four-bay garage. A bungee cord was holding my hatch shut and I had a pair of locking pliers as my turn signal lever, I couldn't relate.

My sister, Opal, swung the front door open and motioned me in, waving like she was happy to see me. Her dark curly hair and bright blue eyes shined, but she was dealing with something deep under the surface. Opal was a gypsy at heart, and I was surprised she had stayed put for this long, I didn't mention it. Right at the very core of Opal Birch is the spirit of a bird, or a creature that needs to be in perpetual motion. Eventually, the mafia mansion life wouldn't sustain her. But maybe she had changed, maybe knowing she was having a baby had caused her priorities to shift.

Opal had been in mama-hen mode since the night I'd been shot. There she was, giving me a once-over with her hands on her hips, but I made sure I looked good on the outside. The black eye was completely healed. For her sake, I left my sling in the car even though my shoulder throbbed without it. I looked okay, she had to see that I was okay, I was fine, on the outside. The whole thing reminded me of my mother's curtains. My 'curtains' looked good from the outside, so she had to know I was okay. But as she looked at me that way, I knew what she was thinking. She wasn't comfortable with all the mob bullshit, and she wasn't willing to get used to it. I knew it, I just pretended I was wrong. She hugged me and kissed my cheek before pointing me down the hall.

When I found Giuseppi he was on the phone, his loafers resting on the edge of a hardwood desk. He gestured me in and I plopped in the leather armchair across the desk from him. There was an empty espresso mug on his desk, and he was rolling the remnants of some whiskey around the bottom of a rocks glass. It was eight thirty-nine in the morning, it must be serious, unless people like that always chase their espresso with well-aged Scottish liquor.

Giuseppi Moretti, or Seppi to friends, was almost thirty-seven, hot as fuck, and could kill you without batting an eyelash. He's six inches taller than me and was sporting a dark pompadour with salt and pepper five o'clock shadow. I'd noticed a little gray at his temples too. Seppi was stocky but in good shape and had a Tony Soprano vibe that intimidated me when I met him. His dark eyes smoldered, and he had white teeth that were probably crowns. He puffed on cigars often enough that there was no way his teeth were that white. Seppi was an Italian chef and 'entrepreneur,' or at least that's what it said on paper. And if I forgot to mention it already, he was the new patriarch of a mob family.

Seppi spoke with his associate on the phone, he was strong, intimidating, and demanding. He was ruthless, powerful, and elusive. But my relationship with him was less of that and more of something else entirely. My relationship with him was this weird dance of some sort. For some reason, Seppi let himself be more vulnerable with me than with anyone else, including my sister. And of everyone in my life, he was the one who knew if I was lying about my current mental state.

I got bored waiting for him to get off the phone, so I took a lap around his office and soaked up the smells of expensive whiskey, old cigar smoke and Tom Ford Tobacco Vanille. I wandered into his bathroom, peed, and used his expensive soap. He had plush towels, and I took a swig of bourbon from a crystal bottle on the vanity. When I swung the door open, he was off the phone. He watched as I disregarded any urgency he may have had to get on with his day, and I continued to snoop around his office like a little kid in a candy store. I ran my fingers over an expensive looking figurine and he gestured toward the chair across the desk from his. In a magisterial voice,

"Dimples."

I rolled my eyes and plopped in the fancy leather chair with my arms folded across my chest like a child having a tantrum. It's not like I'd been avoiding him, per se, I just hadn't answered any of his texts or calls. Oh, and whenever I saw him at the construction site for his new restaurant, I'd hide in my apartment until he left. Opal worked hard to convince me to meet with Seppi that morning. I glanced across the desk and talked with my hands, always the charmer,

"You might wanna alert your neighborhood watch that I'm not some good-for-nothing here to ransack mafia mansion land."

Seppi leaned forward and made a tent with his hands. He squinted at me and I couldn't figure out what he was doing with his mouth. There was a long enough silence that I squirmed, and then he asked an impossible question,

"How are you, Dimples?"

I scrunched up my nose and picked at the stitching on the expensive leather armchair. Shrugging, I fibbed as my eyes fell to my lap,

"I'm fine."

Seppi appeared to be scanning me like a lie detector. I met his eyes and could tell he was trying to climb in and look around, so I looked away. He knew as well as I did that I was full of shit. But besides a deep and very passionate kiss that made my panties wet, our relationship had been nothing but platonic. I mean, as far as Seppi was concerned. I'll admit, my head was full of fantasy fuel I enjoyed while double-clicking my mouse, if you know what I mean. But at that point, our connection wasn't physical, and when it was, it was because of intimate gestures like what he did next, and nothing sexual.

Seppi pulled me to my feet, hooked his finger under my chin and tilted my face so he could look me in the eyes. He wasn't rough, but he controlled the situation, and being controlled ignited the anger and bubbling instability deep inside of me. Seppi's eyes met mine and I swallowed the lump of anger and tears in my throat. He leaned in and I smelled a hint of espresso and expensive whiskey on his breath. The longer he looked in my eyes, the more he knew about what was going on in there, and I didn't like it. There was a storm of caring, guilt, and anger in his eyes, and I realized I could look inside of his soul while he was looking inside of mine. I fought the rage-tears forming, but Seppi sensed the shift, backed off a little and released my chin.

When our eyes met again, I was disarmed, my anger morphing into something else, a tear rolling down my cheek. Once the dam broke, all bets were off. The other thing you need to know about me is that when I'm emotional and mentally unstable, I make hasty decisions; put that in your pipe and smoke it. The darkness in his eyes shifted and I could tell he wanted to fix me. Seppi carried major guilt on his shoulders for leaving me alone in the woods with his father, even if it had been my fault for getting out of the car. And I think he felt guilty for giving up so quickly when I refused to get in the panic room. Sometimes I felt big brother vibes, but usually I felt something else entirely. Seppi got into his 'I mean business' position, but his voice was soft, intimate, and I watched his mouth as he spoke,

"I'm going to help you."

I didn't bother to tell him I was fine again, because he knew I wasn't. I brought some vintage emotional baggage with me when I came back here but killing a man with a shovel had contributed considerably to my collection of closet skeletons. Seppi worked the stopper out of a bottle and poured two whiskies over perfectly square ice cubes. My eyes followed his hand as he slid one of the glasses to my side of the desk. I eyeballed him skeptically, I had no idea why he was feeding me liquor at nine in the morning. He said,

"I insist you meet with my family's psychiatrist."

I moved my eyes to his, he had my attention.

"She's professional, easy to talk to, and she'll help you get your head on straight."

I wanted to be offended but I wasn't, right then, my head was most definitely not on straight, and I knew it. I'd been spiraling and self-medicating. I'd been stashing all my trauma in figurative 'filing cabinets' in the back of my mind, and it was time to get out the shredder. I felt like crying, but also felt like a weight had been lifted.

"Her name is Isabella Rossi, she's agreed to meet with you on Monday afternoons."

I met Seppi's eyes, nodded in agreement and thought we were done, so I went for the door,

"Sounds good."

Fuck that shit, I wasn't in the mood to talk about my feelings. He reprimanded,

"Dimples."

I glanced dismissively over my shoulder at him and rolled my eyes as I reached for the door handle; I didn't have to stay if I didn't want to. He didn't have time for my crap and whipped out his mob boss voice, stern and powerful, barking,

"Sit!"

I dramatically retraced my steps and plopped in the chair across the desk from his, arms crossed again. Seppi always managed to make the pendulum of emotions swing. His face was tense, but I didn't care, I wasn't interested in what he had to say. I had already agreed to meet with his psychiatrist, what else could he possibly want!?

"You might be in danger."

I blinked up at him, I was over his hyper-vigilant bullshit, always so dramatic,

"Excuse me!?"

"Who knows what kind of loose ends my father left behind."

My stomach gurgled and I felt like I was going to shit my ratty vintage overalls in Giuseppi Moretti's fancy leather chair. I got the sweats and felt sparkly like I was going to pass out, so I bent and put my head between my knees. Seppi spun his chair, retrieved a bottle of bubbly water from the glass-front mini fridge, and unscrewed the cap before sliding it across the desk to me. He continued,

"Vinny had to dump the body, you know, since his skull was smashed in with a shovel. Did you forget about that, huh?"

I leveled my eyes at him and squinted,

"No, I was there, did *you* forget about *that*, huh?"

I guzzled the bubbly water and burped violently. His eyes went wide but I didn't excuse myself. I waved him away,

"Everything blew over, it's been weeks."

Seppi put his glass down and made eye contact with me again, a mob boss right then, not a friend and I knew it.

"People like that aren't in a hurry, they sit back and surveil, they send goons to tail you. They sit in the back of a cafe and read a newspaper, they're the stranger you run into all over town."

He was right and deep down, I knew all of this was a possibility. He continued,

"You know I want to keep you safe. But your sister is adding another level to this whole thing, she will cut and run if anything else happens to you. I'm on thin ice here, after the fiasco with my father, Opal has made it clear that if anyone so much as touches a hair on your head, she's out."

Deep down, I knew she was out either way. I flailed my arms around as I talked, raising my voice,

"Okay, so what does that mean!? You gonna fit me with an ankle monitor so you can follow me around on an app? You gonna lock me up in a big cage like one of those fancy exotic birds, so you can keep track of me every second of the day!?

I crossed my arms for a third time, sighed, and shook my head. I was sick of his mafia bullshit a long time ago, and wondered when I was going to get that fresh start I was looking for. He talked with his hands but wasn't loud like me, he stayed calm and in control. Seppi commanded respect without raising his voice,

"You'll tell me if you see anyone who doesn't belong here. You'll tell me if you keep running into the same person while you're out, things like that."

I was just about as unamused as one could be. So, to the patriarch of a mob family, I rolled my eyes again and said,

"Whatever."

Seppi retrieved something from his drawer and slid it across the desk. I snagged a key ring with my pointer finger and two fobs dangled in front of my face. A round black fob about an inch and a half wide, with a large red button in the center, and a Cadillac fob like the one for his Escalade. My deductive reasoning skills are usually pretty good, but I had no idea why he was handing me his keys. Maybe he needed a ride somewhere and wouldn't be caught dead in my bungeed-shut twenty-six-year-old piece of Swiss cheese.

Over it a long time ago,

"Do you need to get dropped off somewhere, or something? Are you too good to ride in Holey Holly?"

I gestured out the front window at the Escalade,

"Jesus Christ, I'll look like some mafia asshole driving that thing."

I moved my eyes to his, and flapped my hand in his direction,

"No offense."

Seppi's eyes smiled a little before he rose from his seat and gestured toward the door. Standing on the front stoop with my arms crossed, he put his hand out for the Cadillac fob and I dropped it into his palm. He pushed a button and the lights of the sporty black sedan flashed. Was I supposed to be impressed that he bought another car? I went palms up and shook my head,

"Yeah, I get it, you're rich. Get over yourself."

Seppi grabbed my arm and dragged me to the back of the car. I stopped in my tracks when I saw that the license plate on the sexy new mini mafia sedan said, 'DIMPLES.' I'm sure I had a shit eating grin on my face when I gestured to my rusted-out collection of duct tape and zip ties,

"That's really nice, but I already have a car."

He shook his head and handed me the keys. I slid into the driver's seat and played with nobs and seat adjustments while he moved the Escalade from behind my new car. When Seppi took his place in the passenger seat, he brought with him a waft of his cologne.

"Opal said your car is a manual, so when I saw this sporty five speed, I thought you'd enjoy it. It's all-wheel drive too, so it's practical."

He winked and I felt it in places I shouldn't, he smiled,

"You deserve to have a little fun, Dimples."

I pushed in the clutch and fired her up, the engine roaring to life when I revved the engine. I looked over at him and pointed at the key chain as it sat in the cup holder,

"What's that other thing for?"

Seppi retrieved the round fob and explained that it was a panic button. It's just what it sounds like. If I was in trouble, I could push the panic button for three seconds. Once Seppi acknowledged the notification on his phone, he'd be able to hear me, and whoever I was with, through a one-way speaker. I panicked he would hear me get raped or murdered, or strung up by my toenails,

"Keep it with you."

Turns out, I wasn't too far off with my comment about the ankle monitor, but who was I to complain that he was trying to protect me from myself. I pushed away the catastrophic thoughts and thanked him. He said,

"Well, come on then, let's take it for a spin, see how you like it."

It was black metallic, sexy as hell, and smelled like leather, I liked it before I even drove it. It had duel exhausts, an ass-warmer, and a built in GPS. It didn't have bungee cords or locking pliers, and I hadn't checked, but I was pretty sure there wasn't any duct tape. I wound my way out of mafia mansion land and the man at the booth nodded as Seppi gave him a low wave, the gate swinging open,

"Take it on the highway, let's see what this thing can do."

I did as I was told, and it was nice to feel safe going ninety on the highway. Not safe as in playing it safe, but safe like I had protection, someone making an attempt to keep me out of harm's way. For the first time in my life, someone was willing to come to my rescue if the worst should happen. I exited the highway and nosed the Caddy into the access lot of a pond. I wasn't ready to go back to reality, but I had no idea that little sliver of time would be so important. Seppi broke the silence,

"I owe you an apology."

I glanced over with my eyebrows scrunched into question marks,

"For what!?"

He shook his head and shrugged,

"I don't know, I just feel like I need to apologize to you."

I shook my head and went palms up,

"I don't understand, shouldn't I be apologizing to *you* for causing this mess?"

I gestured at my shoulder and then pointed at my head,

"All of this is my own doing, you have nothing to apologize for."

He got lost in a thousand-yard stare,

"You shouldn't have been caught up in any of this in the first place. And now that this has happened, you need to get as far from it as possible. Distance yourself from me, Dimples, I'm serious."

I gestured at the panic button,

"You want me on a pretty short leash for someone who doesn't want me around."

He shook his head and talked with his hands,

"I want you around, it isn't that."

He gestured at the fob,

"If I'm going to come to your aid, I need to know where to find you. But you need to separate yourself from this situation until things settle."

I wondered if this was some fancy word-salad he was tossing at me, some kind of maneuver to snare me in a roundabout way. Distance yourself, but I'll know where you are, every second of every day. I admit I'm not one to see things at face value, but I pushed all of the doubts aside because of my relationship with him, and I trusted that he knew best. Seppi glanced at the water again and I wondered what was going on in his mind. He said,

"I'm familiar with the head games this shit plays with your conscience, so I'm offering you a life-line."

He pointed at my head, and continued,

"I have a feeling you're going to need rescuing once you start diving into what's going on up there."

"Do you have people in your life you can talk to?"

I was sure Seppi wouldn't set me up with a shrink who couldn't handle the reality of the situation. But I could never be completely honest with someone like that, someone who paid for a Mercedes with the money she made from the tears of broken little girls like me. Cans of worms exploding, cats running free from their ragged bags, skeletons lurching from their closets, all in the name of 'healing.' His question hit me like a ton of bricks, and tears wrestled in the back of my throat, I swallowed hard. Shit would hit the fan with me once I started wading through a lifetime of emotional baggage that was bursting at the seams. As I stared at the shiny emblem on the steering wheel, I realized the weight of the question, and the answer.

The walls closed in, and I was just beginning to realize I was trapped, but it came in waves over the next few months. It's one thing to have emotional baggage from childhood or some shitty ex-boyfriend, but I had murdered someone, a mob boss, no less. I sucked in a deep breath and let it out, slow and controlled, in some attempt to wrangle my racing heart. I was terrified at the prospect of it all, the number of clowns that would spring forth from that Volkswagen when I finally opened the door. But then, on top of it all, I had killed someone. Yes, I know the man was horrible and needed to die, but that's not how I was wired back then. It was some frantic trauma response, a loss of rational thought, a churning of acid so vile it burned the back of my throat. I lost Seppi's question in the tornado of thoughts flying around in my head so I glanced over at him,

"What?"

He asked again,

"Do you have anyone to talk to? Someone you can trust with things like this?"

After a silence that stretched on forever, I met his gaze, my eyes brimming with the tears I couldn't catch before they ran away,

"Just you."

I should have known right then, but I didn't. I was in a purgatory of sorts, a pocket of time before I realized I was at the threshold of the inner sanctum, whether I liked it or not. Before I realized I could do evil things without the torment of staring at the ceiling. I should have known right then that I was being tested. Was I willing to be tracked twenty-four hours a day under the guise of protection? Yup. Was I dumb enough to accept a sixty-five-thousand-dollar gift from Giuseppi Moretti without thinking there would be strings attached? Absolutely. Was I ready to sort through the contents of the Pandora's box I opened the night I killed that haggard, leather-faced sixty-year-old asshole? Absolutely not.

I made my way back to mafia mansion land with the smells of new car and mob boss swirling together like a well-aged liquor, my body responding in a way I'd never felt before, an arousal that bordered on orgasmic. I was blissfully unaware of the strings that were busy threading themselves through the cracks in my broken soul, like a ravenous snake in a constriction coil.

CHAPTER 2
THIS IS ME NOT TALKING TO STRANGERS

I OVERSLEPT, woke to find that I'd gotten my period, bled all over my favorite pajamas, and destroyed my flannel sheets. Sweet. I threw the covers back and stripped the bed before stripping myself and hopping in the shower. Indie batted at the shower curtain and screamed for me to feed her. It was freezing, I was crampy, and Kane would be playing Halloween music. Listen, I don't have anything against Halloween, it's my favorite holiday. But if I had to hear the same twenty songs on repeat for the next week, I was going to kill someone. My aunt Maggie decided life was 'too short for this bullshit,' and set off in an RV with her new boyfriend, Clem. Her gift shop had been absorbed by the cafe, and that meant there were displays of artisan items drawing in shoppers, in addition to the caffeine addicts. I really wasn't in the mood. Whatever. I didn't bother to shave my legs, and fifteen minutes later I was throwing my towel-dried curls into an extremely messy, messy bun. I wore black jeans, a black V-neck Muddy Waters T-shirt and my dingy white Chuck Taylors. I spritzed on some Alien Elixir, slapped on some lip gloss, and tossed an edible down the hatch before kissing Indie and heading down the stairs to hell.

I grabbed my apron off a hook near the back door and was happy to see Marlaina buzzing around behind the counter, making lattes and gourmet hot chocolate. Marlaina Bernardi was a college-aged hippie chick with olive skin and big brown eyes. Her dark hair was in a French braid, and her smile was like actual sunshine. Kane came around the counter with a bar rag over his shoulder and kissed me on the cheek before greeting a customer. I made myself a pumpkin spice latte and sprinkled the steamed milk with nutmeg. The PSL makes me seem like a basic bitch, but I'm more of an absolute lunatic. I hoped it would turn out to be a good day.

Muddy Waters was one of those rustic coffee houses with dark shiplap walls and trailing plants in the big windows, vines on hooks along the ceiling. It was the kind of place with a gift shop and a place to read. The coffee bar was a long slice of shellacked maple, a row of stools facing the bakery case and espresso machine. There was a small stage where local jazz or folk bands would play sometimes. Muddy Waters is exactly what you imagine when you think of a place like that. A place with impressive coffee and cozy ambiance.

At about nine o'clock that morning, an extremely attractive man strolled through the door. I eyeballed him as he eyeballed the menu and easel of specials. I made a low noise in my throat and looked around to make sure no one heard me. That guy was hot, and I could tell he wasn't a local. We were in the lull between foliage season and the influx of skiers, so we weren't seeing a lot of tourists. I made sure I wasn't doing anything when the handsome stranger was ready to order and I made a beeline to the counter.

Lance Arnault was thirty-four when I met him. He was wearing medium wash Levi's that displayed his ample package, a white dress shirt that was open at the top, and a navy-blue sports jacket. He was wearing a nice watch and smelled expensive. He had a gravelly voice that matched his look, hot and mysterious. My eyes followed his hand as he pulled out his wallet and paid with an American Express black card. When he moved his jacket to put his wallet away, I noticed the butt of a holstered handgun on his hip, and wondered if he was a detective or something, my interest was piqued. There was something about him that made me want to jump his bones in the storeroom. I stuttered,

"It...it won't take long. Your order I mean."

He winked and went to the semi-circle of leather couches in front of the realistic-looking fake fireplace. But instead of calling Lance to the counter to retrieve his order, I delivered it to him. I placed the mug on the coffee table in front of the couch. I'm not sure what I was doing, or what I was thinking, but I was intrigued by the handsome stranger at Muddy Waters. I perched on the arm of the couch and swung my foot like a school girl,

"What brings you to Bunman?"

The man took a sip of his latte and glanced up at me with a line of steamed milk on his upper lip, I wanted to lick it off. He had a Jersey accent,

"I've been dealing with some challenges in the past couple months, and I needed to get away."

I could certainly relate to that and wondered if his challenges included being squirreled away by the mafia, killing a man, or being gifted a panic button. He leaned forward, and put his hand out,

"I'm Lance, and you are?"

I blushed and looked down at my apron, realizing I didn't have my name tag. I wiped my clammy palm on my pants and put it in his,

"I'm Amelia, it's nice to meet you."

Lance did something sexy with his eyebrows,

"Nice to meet you, Amelia. That's a beautiful name, it suits you."

He held my hand for a little too long, but I didn't mind. I wasn't sure what to do with myself, so I retrieved my hand, and bailed,

"Well, I hope you have a relaxing visit and return home with a new lease on life."

I turned and made a face at myself, what an idiot. What was I saying? New lease on life? Was I a seventy-five-year-old man with butterscotch candy wrappers in my pocket? I waved awkwardly, went behind the counter and pretended to blow my brains out. Kane eyeballed me,

"Who's that guy? You know him or something?"

I shrugged,

"I just brought him his coffee, and he introduced himself, that's all. He seems nice."

Kane appeared to be sizing him up. I was hoping Kane wasn't planning on having a dick swinging contest, because I could tell by the bulge in Lance's jeans, that he would win. Unless maybe Lance just had freakishly large balls. I shrugged to myself, I didn't really care either way at that point. Kane threw the bar rag over his shoulder as his way of ending the conversation and went back to work. Shit like that triggered his insecurity and kicked his jealousy into overdrive.

My face was hot, and I felt like I needed to justify why I delivered the handsome stranger's coffee. I was getting ready to explain myself but wasn't entirely sure why. Kane and I weren't currently together or screwing, or spending time together outside of work, but I felt some sort of gut reaction. Right then, I didn't realize the gut reaction was in response to having been warned by Seppi to be on high alert for random strangers. Instead of yielding to the red flags, I'd flirtatiously made fuck-me eyes at some guy who was clearly not from around Bunman. Aforementioned stranger also had a gun on his hip and I didn't give a single shit, thought it was hot. As I was ringing up a basic bitch's scone and fancy latte, Mary Moretti crossed the threshold with her eyes smiling. Mary was in her late fifties and a dark blonde shag framed her face. She was sweet and warm, and it made me happy to see her. I moved around the counter and she kissed me on both cheeks. She sang,

"Amelia, darling!"

Mary was the widow of Salvatore Moretti, and the mother of Giuseppi and Vincenzo. Since I was the one who killed Mary's husband of several decades, you might be wondering a couple things. First, you might be wondering why she wasn't mad at me. Second, you might be wondering why I wasn't in jail. By killing Sal, I freed a lot of people from the perpetual evil he contributed to the world. That included freeing Mary from the prison of being married to a narcissist and tyrant who treated her like a piece of dog shit. As far as any jail time, it wasn't going to happen. Sal's sons cleaned up the mess and the people who knew what happened weren't going to say anything. That didn't mean I wasn't currently battling with my conscience, but I'd be working through that soon enough in therapy.

I made Mary's order as we chatted. After what happened earlier that month, my bond with her had grown. Before Sal died, I'd been sharing lattes with her on Sunday mornings, but our relationship had become deeper after 'the incident.' If you're wondering whether I had a mother of my own, the answer is, it's complicated. My birth mother was a cold selfish bitch who seemed to find nothing more pleasurable than rubbing my face in every bad decision I ever made. She was the kind of person who'd relish any opportunity to rub a puppy's nose in shit. If Mama Moretti was willing to take me under her wing, I was more than happy to crawl under there. She glanced at Lance and I thought there was a flicker of recognition. Mary kissed the air at me, a white paper cup in each hand,

"Sunday for lattes, see you then, darling!"

Mary pushed the door open with her petite backside and went on her way. I gathered up Lance's empty mug and saucer before tending to the rush of late morning caffeine addicts. I tossed an edible down the hatch in the bathroom before starting on sandwiches and paninis. Somewhere along the way, the handsome stranger went on his merry way. I was standing at the espresso machine daydreaming when I caught Kane's eye, and could tell his dormant feelings for me had been aroused by the notion I might be attracted to the handsome stranger.

People are complicated. We have so many feelings, and we all have baggage. We have relationships in the process of growing, and usually also in the process of dying. Sometimes people come into our lives for no good reason at all, and sometimes people come into our lives to shake things up or give us something we didn't know we needed. The door swung open and that time it was Giuseppi Moretti. He motioned for me to come. I moved around the counter and stood in front of him, a look of concern on his face. I tried to figure out what he was thinking about and the way he was looking at me was giving me the shits,

"Did something happen to my sister?"

Seppi flicked his eyes to the back door and followed me to the parking lot with his hand on my lower back. We stood behind my shiny new car and I should admit I was preoccupied with the car, and wasn't really listening to anything he was saying,

Seppi took a long inhale and clenched his jaw, he leaned in, his voice low,

"Have you seen a woman with dark red hair and a pantsuit?"

I thought back through the customers I'd seen in the cafe, and shook my head. I shrugged,

"Nope. Why?"

"Okay, well if you see someone like that, you need to let me know, immediately, it's important. And try to get a picture of her if you can do it without getting caught."

Seppi didn't give me any more information. I made a scribbly mental note on a wrinkled piece of paper in the back of my mind, to take a picture if a red-headed lady in a pantsuit came into the cafe. I wondered if the red-headed lady was his ex-wife or something, maybe she heard he was having a baby with a hippie and wanted to cause trouble. The rest of the day was uneventful, I managed to survive the Halloween music, didn't bleed through my pants and didn't make any huge messes during my shift. When I got home, I changed into sweats and smoked half a joint on the sun porch. My mind was spinning, and I wondered what it would be like to rub shoulders with powerful men. I made a lame attempt at carving a pumpkin, and spread the seeds on a cookie sheet with some butter, garlic salt, and other miscellaneous things before throwing them in the oven.

While I laid in bed that night, I stared at the ceiling and got anxious about my upcoming appointment with Isabella Rossi. I took stock of the lifetime of shit I needed to sort through, like a cauldron of bubbling tar that beckoned me like poison. The absolute truth that I was broken in so many ways, and I was going to be examining all of it under a magnifying glass. There was a creeping dread in the pit of my gut. I tried not to think about it on Sunday but it was a chore. I spent longer than usual with Mary when we met for lattes and scones. I stayed high as a kite and distracted myself by baking crusty bread and sugar cookies. While I was excited to wade through my bullshit, I was also dreading it. If Isabella Rossi knew anything about anything, she wouldn't let me stray too far into the weeds, she would keep me in the hot seat. My old therapist was a train wreck and a complete waste of time, but I had a feeling if Giuseppi Moretti trusted this woman, she was going to know what she was doing.

CHAPTER 3
COFFEE CUP POWER PISS

I WAS AWAKE bright and early Monday morning, in plenty of time to get bubble-gut and the shits before my first therapy session. I retrieved one of Kane's maple oat lattes and curled up in my pajamas by the realistic looking fake fireplace. I was so lost in my own head, I didn't even care that I was sitting around in my pajamas during the early morning rush of caffeine addicts. It was six-thirty when I went down, and I wasn't working until eight, but I stayed on that leather couch until I barely had time to get ready. Less than a half hour before I needed to be aproned up and grinding beans at Muddy Waters, I set off up the stairs to prepare for my day. It took extra time because I decided to take care of my curls instead of slamming them into a wad on top of my head. I went through the motions with the caffeine addicts and basic bitches with their fancy fall lattes, but I was preoccupied with what I should wear to meet Dr. Rossi. She was most likely sophisticated and I should probably dress like I belonged there.

I texted Seppi and asked what I should wear to my appointment. His reply was, 'Not ripped overalls and dirty sneakers.' I made a face and rolled my eyes, but knew he was right. I threw my closet open and stood there taking inventory. Wanna know what I was looking at? About a dozen pairs of ripped overalls in various states of dishevel, and a couple dozen shirts of various sizes and styles. There was a white eyelet dress, a dark green vintage velvet dress, a couple of sweaters, and half a dozen pairs of jeans. I unearthed three pairs of black Lululemons and a pair of Crocs. After digging through the duffle bag of stuff I never unpacked when I moved, I tossed a pair of khakis and a button up shirt in the dryer to get the wrinkles out. I dug out a pair of expensive suede loafers with tassels, that belonged to a lady who got whacked by Salvatore Moretti, it's a long story. I put on eyeliner and mascara, lipstick, and a couple spritzes of Alien Elixir on my pulse points. After kissing Indie on the head, I sauntered out the door like I knew what I was doing.

I bounced down the stairs to Muddy Waters, grabbed a latte to go, and went out the back door with my head held high. I almost got in my old car but detoured to the driver's side of the brand new black

Cadillac CT4. I took in the smell of the leather interior, and for as long as I had that car, I never smoked a joint in it. I fired her up and plugged Dr. Rossi's address into the GPS. I was dazzled by the fact that I didn't have to suction cup my ten-year-old Garmin to the windshield. Fancy. I made my way up the alley onto Maple Street. Twenty minutes later, I was sitting in the lot behind an impressive office building that looked like it was expensive to construct, and was probably filled with people who made a million dollars a year. I scanned the lot and was glad I drove the Cadillac.

I glanced in the rear-view mirror and made sure I didn't have a booger hanging out of my nose, or lipstick on my teeth. I took time for a little pep talk, but it basically boiled down to 'love yourself you piece of shit.' After a couple deep breaths, I got out and started toward the entrance. My phone buzzed and it was Seppi, 'Good luck, Dimples.' I got a lump in my throat and my eyes filled with tears; I was off to a great start. Sometimes it's easier when no one gives a shit about you. I took one more deep breath before pulling the glass door open and standing in front of the directory in the lobby. Isabella Rossi MD was on the sixth floor, so I hopped on the elevator and listened to my guts gurgle as I rode up to her luxury office in the sky.

The receptionist, a pleasant looking middle-aged woman named Elaine, was kind, and didn't make me feel like a nut-job. I fingered through a magazine about home decor, and used the restroom. I looked at my phone, and then put it in my purse, and then pulled it out and looked at it again. I almost bailed, but just as I was about to stand up and walk out, Isabella Rossi opened the door to her office and gestured me in. I was expecting an elaborate pedestal facing a kindergarten-sized folding chair, or some other lop-sided power dynamic. After all, my last therapist would leave me standing in the hallway with her waiting room locked, or forget about me altogether, so I was expecting some form of psychological sabotage.

When I crossed the threshold, I smelled vanilla, and noticed that Dr. Rossi had three options for her patients: a comfy couch, a gigantic Love Sac, and an overstuffed chair. Eventually, I would work my way into the Love Sac, but in the beginning, I sat in the overstuffed chair. Isabella Rossi was probably thirty-six or seven, since she went to high school with Seppi. She was about five foot seven, had an athletic build, and wore a wheat-colored pantsuit with a blush-colored camisole underneath. Isabella Rossi had wavy dark hair that was styled in long layers that fell over her shoulders. She had big brown eyes that were accented with winged eyeliner and just the right amount of mascara. She wore a couple of gold rings and a nice watch. Her black leather heels looked expensive. I stared at her face, she seemed approachable, and like she wouldn't judge me. I wondered what happened to Dr. Rossi that made her want to be a shrink.

I wondered how long she'd been the psychiatrist for the Moretti family. I wondered if she was a psychiatrist for regular people, or if Seppi sent me to her because she helped mobsters process all the death and destruction. I wondered if Giuseppi Moretti ever sat in that chair, or if he preferred the Love Sac. I wondered if she knew I killed Sal. I felt like I was going to need to excuse myself to destroy the bathroom but managed to hold myself together. Dr. Rossi asked me some questions that felt like small talk, but she made notes as I spoke. I explained that I was molested when I was little, that my mother was horrible, and that my most recent ex cheated on me and knocked-up some whore. At the end of the list, I threw in that I killed Salvatore Moretti. Seppi told me to be honest and that nothing would shock her, he was right. When she responded, she didn't start with the murder, it didn't even seem to faze her,

"I think we should start from the beginning."

I didn't really want to, but I described how it started and how it ended at the neighbor's house. I told her that when my mother found out about it, she didn't do anything. I talked about how my mother swept everything under the carpet, and then shined a light on every bad decision I ever made, every asshole I dated, every failure, every situation where a person needs their mother to love them and not judge them. I never had any of that. Even though I didn't dig too deeply into either of those things before I shifted gears, she knew enough to get the point. I sped over the shit with my ex, his whore, and their love child. I didn't bring up Richard, the narcissistic ex I had before the one with the whore. I told her the meds make me gain weight, but that the weed and whiskey help. I mentioned that I make stupid decisions when I'm struggling.

Dr. Rossi sat silent and I could tell she was thinking about what to say. Maybe I was too far gone, maybe she was trying to find the words to tell me she wouldn't be able to help me. Maybe Dr. Rossi was going to call the orderlies to come out of the closet in their white coats and take me off to the funny farm in a straitjacket. Maybe she'd call the cops and they'd cart me off to jail for murder. I squirmed in the silence, she leaned forward and looked me in the eye,

"Do you think the world's a better place without Salvatore Moretti?"

I swallowed the lump in my throat, my voice weak but I meant what I said,

"Yes."

She paused,

"Then you did the world a favor, didn't you?"

Say what now!? Was she joking? Was this a trap? What the fuck was going on here? I looked at her blankly,

"What!?"

She sat back in the chair and put her pen down, talking with her hands like she was conducting a symphony,

"If the world is a better place without him, then you didn't do anything wrong, that's how it works. You didn't kill a kitten or a kid, you didn't derail a train full of newlyweds or burn down a church. You eliminated someone who did nothing but destroy the lives of everyone around him, I'd say you did the world a favor."

With that, Dr. Rossi casually glanced at her classy wristwatch and told me it was time to wrap up our first session. I had no idea what the fuck was going on. Was this real? I thanked her and went out to the receptionist to make my next appointment. A smiling Elaine slid the appointment card to me, and I went into the hallway with question marks over my head. You're thinking, okay, that wasn't so bad. Yeah, well, buckle up. I was already kind of a confused mess and then I paced around the area outside of the elevator, waiting until it was empty. I knew I was going to start bawling at any minute and didn't need an audience. A seventy-year-old grandmother-type got on, and instead of riding down with her, I stood there picking at the skin next to my thumbnail. When the doors opened again and the elevator was empty, I stepped on with my almost empty to-go cup, my emotional baggage, and my demons.

I pushed the button for the lobby and as soon as the doors closed, I melted down but tried to hold it together since I'd have to walk through the lobby. What was that back there? Had Seppi really sent me to a psychiatrist who tried to convince me that murdering an old man with a shovel had been a good deed? You know, instead of a reason for me to worry I'd be going to jail, or to the bottom of Clover Lake with a bullet in my forehead. I shook it off, I was almost out of there and could sit in the heated leather seats of my fancy new mini mafia sedan. I'd make my way back to the land of self-medicating with weed, and an epic case of the munchies. And then the elevator stopped. Shit. I hadn't taken into consideration that someone on a lower floor would push the down button. Crap. Wait, phew, the doors didn't open. I shrugged. OK, good. But the elevator didn't start moving again, it just sat there. I was suspended there with my thoughts and my panic, my guilt and my shame, just dangling by a thread.

I pounded the button for the lobby an ungodly number of times, in rapid succession, but nothing happened. A split second later, the lights flickered and went out. Fuck. Okay, it was fine, that type of thing happened all the time, and someone would be coming to fix it. Someone would notice the elevator wasn't working, people would be getting out of work and want to ride it down to the lobby. For a minute or two, I was thinking like a rational person, and knew I wasn't going to starve to death in there. But what if? What if I died in there and a month later, someone retrieved my bloated, rotting carcass full of maggots? I shook my head and rolled my eyes. All I wanted to do was get in my car, have a mental breakdown, and drive home, was that too much to ask? And then I realized I had to pee. Bad.

So, there I was with my demons and full bladder, in the pitch darkness of that elevator. No big deal, right? I used my phone to light my way and pounded the red button that had a bell on it, I assumed it was for moments like that. I pounded the button about a million times. I had no signal in there, of course. Once I knew I was trapped in there, I really had to pee. I was oddly calm, considering the situation, but that didn't mean I wasn't also panicking, and on the verge of thrashing against the walls like a caged animal. No problem though, someone would find me soon. The people waiting in the lobby would realize the elevator never made it to the bottom.

Within an hour, someone in a dark blue jumpsuit with an embroidered name tag would be coming to fix the elevator, the rational part of me knew that. I wished the elevator hadn't been in the center of the building, maybe if it had been on an outside wall, I'd have had cell service, and I could have called someone, maybe Elaine, to tell her I was stuck in the elevator. Eventually, as I sat there with my back against the wall, I realized I was going to need to pee in the white paper cup from Muddy Waters. I swigged the last of my maple oat latte and pulled down my pants. I put the cup on the floor and made sure I was lined up properly before letting her rip. The cup was filled just about to the brim when the lights flicked on, and the elevator started to move.

There I was, pants and underwear around my ankles, power-pissing into a paper cup and the elevator started moving again. I yanked everything up and slapped the lid on the cup. I'm not kidding when I tell you the doors opened like two seconds later. A man in dark blue coveralls and an embroidered name tag apologized and told me I'd have to take the stairs the rest of the way down. Fine by me. In a lapse in judgment, I tossed the paper cup full of hot piss in the garbage can, and really hoped there wasn't a hole in the bag. Pushing through the door to the stairs, I made my way to the lobby, grateful I'd handled the situation without completely falling apart. But once I was out of my cage, the edges blurred, and my protective coating started to crack.

I pushed through the glass door to the street and made my way to the mini mafia sedan. Either the session, or the brief elevator entrapment, had triggered me, and I was freaking out. I slid behind the wheel and completely lost my mind. I sat there crying, at first, and then it turned into sobs. For the first time in my life, I had been validated. I wasn't shushed, shamed, or told I was a disappointment. While all of that was swirling around in my noggin, I managed to make it out of that broken elevator without becoming a bloated, rotting corpse. And maybe I wasn't going to jail or the funny farm that night.

I was sort of fine again when I pulled out of the parking lot, but once I was on the highway, I started to crumble again. My mind raced, I had a million things swirling a million miles an hour, and I didn't know what to do. There was too much traffic for the mood I was in, and I was falling apart for so many reasons. I was a little girl peering over the steering wheel, trying to keep it between the lines. I was panicking, truly panicking, and then I remembered I had a panic button. So, like anyone with a panic button who's having an epic panic attack, I pushed it for three seconds. If Seppi was with anyone, they would be able to hear me and I didn't care, I was losing it. At one point I was crying so hard I had to pull over. The one-sided conversation went something like this, quiet and unsure of myself,

"Seppi?"

Through tears, and in the most squeaky and pathetic way possible,

"I need you."

That's all I said. Seconds later my phone rang and the big screen on the dash lit up. There was a hint of panic in his voice, along with a little bit of something else,

"Amelia!?"

I was crying so hard I couldn't speak, he rescued me from the sound of my own sobs,

"Get off at the next exit, take a right and go to the park with the gazebo. I'm coming."

The call ended. The panic button provided Seppi with my location and I later found out there was also a tracker on the car. I did what he told me and pulled into a spot facing the park with the gazebo. I was where I was supposed to be, I was safe, and sat there sobbing as I waited for Seppi. I felt claustrophobic in the car, so I sat on my trunk and slid a joint from my thrifted flip-top tin. A wave of self-medication fell over me and I thought maybe I'd be okay, maybe I could handle dismantling my horrible collection of broken pieces.

I finished the joint and hopped off the trunk, pacing around on the sidewalk, picking at the skin next to my thumbnail. Seppi angled the Escalade into the spot next to mine and when he slid from the driver's seat, I made an involuntary sound low in my throat. There he was in his mob boss aesthetic, sleeves rolled up a couple times, top buttons open to reveal a gold chain. He'd run out without his leather jacket. I knew what he smelled like and what his five o'clock shadow would feel like when he kissed me on both cheeks. But he didn't kiss me on both cheeks, the situation was more serious than that. Seeing him made me feel things. Things in my mind and things in my body, but I didn't mention it.

I met Seppi between the cars and leaned into him, the right side of my face against his chest, my curls getting caught up in his stubble. He held my head against the warmth of his body as I cried. I hadn't told him what was wrong and he hadn't asked, it didn't matter. And in a way, things were okay for the first time in decades. I wasn't the bad guy, the failure, the one who did something wrong. We stayed like that for a long time and maybe we stayed like that for a little too long. There was another shift, it was small, but I felt it. I looked up at him with my red face and wet cheeks, a spot from my tears and runny mascara on his shirt,

"She said I did the world a favor."

Seppi took in a deep breath and exhaled slowly as he sheltered me in his arms. It was the first time in a while I felt truly safe. I'm not talking in the way Kane made me feel safe, that was something else entirely. Right then, there wasn't any part of me that was reading into it or feeling things I shouldn't. When my crying slowed, Seppi hooked my chin with his finger and tilted my face up to his. He bent to me and I could feel his breath, hot in the cold, a hint of whiskey and a cigar.

"Tell me what you need so I can give it to you."

I didn't say anything, I just let myself feel whole for a second, even if I wasn't. No lines were crossed, no questionable decisions were made, everything was above board. Seppi casually kissed me right on the lips and said,

"I'll follow you, make sure you get home okay."

And then he got in the Escalade as I just stood there like an idiot. He'd kissed me on the damn lips! I'm not talking like he slipped me the tongue; I'm talking about a closed-mouth peck that was intended to be a gesture of affection. And, I'd seen Giuseppi Moretti kiss a hundred people on the lips, it was no big deal, he was a kisser. But when our lips touched, there was something tender about it and it made me feel the things I was trying not to feel. That kiss had been innocent, but in the two seconds Giuseppi Moretti was close to me, my nipples got hard and my panties got wet. Crap.

CHAPTER 4
CLIPPED WINGS CAN'T FLY

AFTER A BAD BREAKUP, my big sister set off on a solo trip in her converted VW Van. Opal is a couple years older than me and a couple inches shorter. She has a full head of dark ringlets and bright blue eyes. She doesn't have dimples, but she makes up for it with her devil may care attitude. She's a free spirit who loves nothing more than living spontaneously, with frequent stops to sit with her toes in the water while she smokes a big fat joint. Opal is one of those people who will eventually have a hundred bird feeders and a coop full of chickens. She's the kind of person who doesn't follow rules, doesn't care what people think, and doesn't measure herself by someone else's ruler. My sister is one of my biggest role models when it comes to most things, but staying put is not one of them.

Last summer, after meeting up with some old friends along the way, Opal found her way back to Bunman. The day she got there; she met Giuseppi Moretti in the hallway of a hibachi restaurant on the mountain. Things moved quickly, and a month later, she walked out of my bathroom with a positive pregnancy test. I wondered how she was going to deal with it, but she seemed excited, and when she told Seppi, he picked her up off the floor and spun her around. Things seemed to be moving in the right direction. She'd been staying at his mafia mansion, and for the last month or two, Opal had kind of been playing the part of a mob wife.

Deep down, I was pretty sure Opal was getting ready to bail, even before I had been shot by Salvatore Moretti, twice in one week. She and Seppi talked about sticking it out, but even then, I could tell that's not what either of them wanted. Sometimes I wished they would have realized they loved each other, and maybe they had, maybe that's what Opal wanted to tell me. Seppi bought her a fancy new car, and she worked at his restaurant until it burned down. She was adjusting to being with a mob boss, after living fun and fancy free for half a year. She was helping me maneuver the guilt I had over committing murder, but like when we were little kids, from the outside, things looked perfect. There was a tiny part of me that wondered if any of what was going on would trigger her to run away.

She called me the day after my therapy session and wanted to get together for lunch. Immediately, my stomach started gurgling, but I guess it wasn't so much that Seppi kissed me like that, Italians give a lot of kisses. The problem was how it made me feel to be that close to him. I've admitted from the get-go that I find him attractive, but this wasn't about that. And I would never jeopardize my friendship with him by crossing that line. I never had anyone in my life care for me the way he did. I had never felt protected or like someone was watching out for me the way he did. I'd rather die than jeopardize that.

The closer I got to Seppi, the surer I was that we accepted each other without the masks or armor. Before I met him, I thought he was some rich, intimidating, Tony Soprano type and I was scared to death of him. When I met him though, I felt like we had some of the same broken pieces, I could see it in his eyes. And then when my sister found out she was pregnant, he had already been battling with his life-long facade and daddy issues. He was acting tough, and carrying out Sal's orders, because if he didn't, he would lose the ristorante. During our first heart-to-heart conversation, Seppi confided that having a baby was the motivation he needed to stop living under his father's thumb. Seppi didn't want his future child to be involved in Salvatore's manipulation, threats, or intimidation. Seppi also knew, if that was ever going to happen, his father needed to go.

Now that Sal was gone, Seppi felt as if he was going to be able to reinvent himself and start a normal life that included a family. He didn't stop to think about the fact that with his father out of the picture, he would be the new patriarch of the Moretti mob family, whether he liked it or not. Seppi also hadn't anticipated the depths to which I would be involved in all of this, and Opal made it clear she wouldn't tolerate anything that put me in the line of fire, no pun intended. And by then, that ship had sailed.

Opal said she would pick me up and we could go to Maple Grove, a quaint little town about a half hour away. I showered and removed my favorite pair of overalls from the closet. I pulled them on over a long-sleeved shirt and finished the look with my black Docs and a cream-colored cable-knit cardigan. I did my normal messy bun, lip gloss, Alien Elixir routine, and tossed an edible down the hatch before bouncing down the stairs to Muddy Waters. After grabbing one of Kane's maple oat lattes, I sat by the window waiting for Opal to pull up in her brand-new Volvo SUV. When I saw her coming, I slid out of the booth and pushed through the door. When I stepped off the curb, I slammed right into Lance Arnault. Lance was dressed in another pair of well-fitting jeans, a button-up shirt, and different sports jacket. He smelled nice and winked at me. We made small talk, and I excused myself to get in Opal's car, after telling him where I was going and who I was going with.

The drive was quiet, and I almost apologized for what happened with Seppi, but didn't. I knew he hadn't meant his kiss to be sexual, he kissed people all the time, I was the one having the inappropriate thoughts. The bottom line was that I wasn't trying to encroach on her territory, her life, or her baby-daddy. When I glanced over, Opal was crying silently, tears rolling down her cheeks onto her sweater. I wondered if it was something or if it was hormones. Either way, I would share lunch with her and listen until she felt better. Maybe she had spoken to our mother on the phone, or maybe Seppi had said something that hurt her because she was all sensitive and pregnant. I got teary knowing she was sad or upset about something, and put my hand on her shoulder as she drove.

I didn't make small talk or try to make her laugh. I didn't crank the radio or tell witty quips. I just sat with her as she drove to Maple Grove in her fancy soccer mom car. There was a gold and diamond tennis bracelet on her wrist and a designer bag on the back seat. She wasn't wearing thrifted patchwork or something she up-cycled from a man's suit jacket. Opal looked lost and sad, and I couldn't take it, it made me hurt deep down inside, it seemed like she was drowning even before she told me. Watching a person as they drive can tell you a lot about what's going on in their head. Cars are like this little box of solitude you ride around in, and in the safety of those four walls, she let herself fall apart a little. She nosed into a space along main street and slung a Louis Vuitton Neverfull over her shoulder. We strolled along the block of historic brick buildings and found a quiet little deli with booths that had shellacked slices of maple as the tables. The smells of homemade soup and bread swirled in the air with a hint of baked apples and cinnamon. Once we were seated at a booth in the corner, she started to unload,

"I need to talk to you, and I need you to promise it will stay between us."

I put my hand on hers and a single tear rolled down her cheek, she tried to compose herself as the waitress approached. We ordered, and then sat there looking at each other across the table. I had never known Opal to struggle with words. She's the one who has the quick retort, the smart remark that most of us think of five hours later. Opal always knew what she wanted, what she felt, and what she wanted to say. What I was looking at was a pregnant mess who appeared completely out of control and helpless.

"Of course, everything you say will stay between us, I promise."

After chewing an ice cube to buy herself some time, she took a deep breath and unloaded her mental burden,

"I can't do this."

I wasn't sure which thing she was talking about, but I sat in silence and waited for her to continue. She seemed both conflicted and completely sure of what she was about to say. I tried to decipher what her face was doing but couldn't. I waited as she found the words she was looking for. She swallowed the lump in her throat, blinked away tears and stared out the window,

"When have you ever known me to sit still like this?"

I shrugged and went palms up. She moved her eyes to mine,

"After a year with Chad, I knew he was getting serious."

She glanced at her hands briefly,

"He would try to talk about getting a place together, he mentioned wanting to marry me. And when most girls would be beaming from ear to ear, I had major panic, and that lead to a shitty breakup. It wasn't him; it was me, there was nothing wrong with what he wanted, or that he was thinking about our future."

Our eyes met,

"For some reason, even though things with him were good, I felt empty and like I was going through the motions."

Opal fidgeted with her napkin and dabbed at her eyes,

"The time alone was life changing, I proved to myself that I can do whatever I want, I can be whoever I want. I drove across the entire country without getting murdered in my sleep. Do you understand what a big deal that is for me? I proved to myself that I don't need a man to be happy, it made me realize I never want to be tied down. And it made me realize all the stuff mom said to me over the years was complete bullshit. She was wrong, I'm not a failure."

She was right about everything she said and I had an idea I knew where this was going. She'd been with Chad for a year and didn't want to talk about their future, and here she was with someone she knew for a month before she found out she was pregnant. My stomach churned and I braced myself for what was coming.

"I came to Bunman for a visit, I wanted to see you and Maggie but never intended to stay for long, maybe a month or two, not a lifetime."

She shrugged and threw her hands around as she talked,

"There are old wounds here, you know that as well as I do. I don't need the reminder."

I nodded and told her I understood that part, it was hard for me sometimes too, when I got triggered by childhood wounds in the town where I experienced most of my trauma. Her relationship with our mother was just as bad, just a different flavor. Opal was born a free spirit and had no use for our mother's pretension or materialistic bullshit. Opal never made her bed and didn't care if her curtains looked good from the outside. She'd get in a bikini and sun herself on the roof outside her window, she'd smoke cigarettes and weed and make out with boys in the garage. Because of that, she and our mother didn't see eye to eye. One of them full of pretension and superiority, the other one full of piss and vinegar. The two of them went head-to-head since the day Opal popped out of the womb, and as much as our dad tried to make up for it, she grew up without a bond to our mother. She never felt strong or capable, and never once thought she belonged.

Opal didn't see herself the way I saw her, I always looked up to her as someone who could do anything she wanted. Despite our mother's attempts to extinguish her flame, Opal grew up to become a spitfire who knew herself, and what she wanted. She was the little girl who ran away from home at eight-years-old and made it the whole night alone in an abandoned house before going back. She grew into a teenager who wasn't afraid of cemeteries at night or of walking alone in the seedy part of town. She wore flowy skirts, spent time by the water, and never wanted to forget the feeling of grass under her feet, or the ocean rolling over her toes. She knew how to take care of herself, and could do it alone. And never once had Opal Birch dreamt of playing house with a mob boss, in Bunman, Vermont.

"You took me out for dinner with friends, and I was in the wrong place at the wrong time."

She shook her head,

"I feel bad saying that about him."

She waved her words away, started over,

"Seppi's a great guy, I just don't love him like that."

She stared out the window and shrugged,

"I'd driven something like six-thousand miles on my own, I was full of myself, and feeling confident, so I took his number. Maybe, I'd have a fling with a rich guy while I was here."

She looked across the table at me and went palms up, talking too fast,

"But that's all it was supposed to be, not whatever this is that we're doing. I mean, we get along, I'm just not sure what we're doing. I never intended to stay. I don't really feel that way for him and he doesn't feel that way for me, I don't know what we're doing."

She rubbed her growing belly,

"I feel like I'm caught in a trap and it's closing a little tighter each day."

Opal was spiraling, her volume rising as she spoke, pissed and resentful,

"I bump into a guy at a hibachi place and have to spend the rest of my fucking life with him!?"

I gestured to maybe keep her voice down a little, but she disregarded it completely. She got all hands on hips about the whole thing, her voice went even louder,

"What the hell is that!? I know some women go around trying to land a sugar daddy..."

Two older women glanced over disapprovingly, Opal lowered her voice and put her hands on the table, leaning in a little,

"What I'm saying is that some women want to trap a rich man into being their meal ticket. That isn't me, I don't want any of this. He isn't even my type, and you know it."

Opal was right, she always went for mountain man hippie types with a full beard, and not some executive level bullshit with twelve-hundred dollar loafers. The waitress came around to top off our waters, and when she was out of earshot,

"I rescue baby birds who fall out of the nest and move spiders outside instead of smashing them. He has whacked more people than I even know, he's dark and ruthless, and does things I don't want to know about. Remember the night by the fire when I told you I was in love with him?"

I nodded.

"As soon as I said it out loud, I knew I was lying to myself. I'd planned to tell you I was hitting the road again, but that morning, I took a pregnancy test, and it was positive."

I scrunched my eyebrows together. Opal sipped her water and paused for a long time,

"So, I decided maybe I could make it work, stick it out with him. I mean, he's nice, and I'd never want for anything, and maybe I would grow to love him, people say that happens."

She waved it away,

"The test I took that night was because I was hoping the other one had been wrong. I don't really want to get into it."

She looked away,

"There's a lot to it, but the timing couldn't have been worse."

I nodded. She continued,

"Things happened fast. My pregnancy pushed Seppi to evaluate what kind of dad he wants to be. It motivated him to create distance from the dark parts of his family. Maggie was living in the storeroom of the restaurant, you were breaking into garages, and getting high-speed car-chased by Sal. The restaurant was burnt to the ground, you got shot, and killed Sal. I didn't sign up for any of this shit, I was just here for a visit."

There was something else I knew about my sister; she didn't give a shit about power or money. That woman's entire wardrobe came from thrift stores and consignment shops. She was the poster child for a sixties nomadic hippie. She was a free spirit, a bird in flight and her wings had been clipped. In that moment, I knew exactly what she was saying.

"I don't give a shit about the money or the mansions or the cars, so many fucking cars. I don't give a shit about the diamonds or the designer handbags. Do you see what I've become?"

Opal gestured toward the street with tears in her voice,

"That car!?"

I looked out the window, she continued,

"Are you fucking kidding me!? That is the official car of label-whores and young moms who desperately need you to know they have money to burn. Give me a fucking break."

She lifted her arm, the volume of her voice went up again, she scoffed,

"A fucking tennis bracelet!?"

She pretended to gag a couple times, and then pretended to vomit,

"It's like I'm playing a part, and you want to know what that makes me think of!? Our mother. I'm living in a mansion-sized dollhouse, all I need is a box of wine, and a set of crooked curtains to straighten. Fuck."

Opal blinked away tears and picked at her napkin. I was listening but I didn't want to believe what she was saying. I knew she was right about how things happened, who she was, and that she wasn't cut out to be a mob wife. I nodded,

"I understand."

We sat in silence as we ate our sandwiches and soup. But the silence let me get lost in my mind, just swimming in my thoughts while I ate my cream of broccoli soup and half a reuben. I took a step back mentally and tried to assess the situation. I remembered the time Opal joked about going on a date with Seppi, even though he wasn't her type. She had said, flippantly, it wasn't like she had to spend her life with the guy. And here we were.

When we were done with lunch, she wasn't ready to go back yet, so we strolled around town. We walked along in silence, window shopped, and even did a lap around a cute little second hand store, but she didn't get anything. It was almost as if being in that store was a reminder of the life she was leaving behind. The energy she was giving off made me nervous, and I was worried any sudden movements would spook her. We looped back to where we started and sat on the wide marble steps of the library. After staring at the park across the street, Opal put her head in her hands, and wept,

"What am I going to do, Amelia? I'm drowning."

CHAPTER 5
A LANCE ENCOUNTER

I HAD A HEADACHE from a little too much whiskey, and my eyes ached from crying. I promised my childhood best friend, Sunny, I would meet her for the annual Bunman Halloween Parade. It was the biggest parade in the state, and I hadn't spent time with her since the shit went down with Sal. To back up a little, Sunny had been in a volatile relationship with Seppi's younger brother, Vinny. Vinny found out he impregnated the wife of a family associate, and despite being tied to a chair and threatened, he thought he'd try his hand at being the father he never had. He broke it off with Sunny, and then found out the woman had lied about being pregnant. She was retaliating against her husband for something, and focused on the fact that he was unable to father children. She wasn't pregnant, she was playing games.

Amid all of that, shit went down with Salvatore, and the Moretti family was adjusting to life without the puppet master. Once his father was out of the picture, Vinny experienced some major breakthroughs about who he is, and what kind of person he wants to be. He came crawling back to Sunny, and begged her to give him one more chance. I told her she should kick him to the curb, but she took him back. That time around, Vincenzo Moretti was not preoccupied with his father's orders, other women, or acting like a douche bag. That night, Vinny was going to dinner with Seppi and Mary, so Sunny planned to watch the parade.

As I was trying to sort out my current mental state, I got lost in replaying the whole kissing me goodbye situation. I wasn't sure what to make of it, and while it made me feel safe and protected, and aroused me, it had not been meant to be sexual. It was me, not him. Giuseppi Moretti was the most powerful person I knew, and the weak and broken parts of me longed to be sheltered. Seppi was the one person in my life who had the ability to solve all my problems, all I had to do was ask. He would kill someone to protect me, and I knew it. But something else inside of me shifted when he became the boss, it made him even more attractive to me. He was untouchable, and maybe if I was close to him, I would be untouchable too. Feeling safe was a huge turn on for the adult version of a lost little girl who longed to be protected.

I was sorting through my conversation with Opal, and knew she was going to leave sooner or later, but I didn't want to think about it. Maybe she would realize she wanted that life, the one with the mansion and luxury cars and expensive jewelry. I loved my sister more than anything, and hated myself for maybe having feelings for Seppi. Our relationships with him were completely different. She said there wasn't any depth or connection between them, they were living separate lives within the same walls. An alcohol and loneliness-fueled decision brought her to this figurative life-sentence of sorts. At this point, they were only a couple months into this whole thing. I'm no relationship expert, but that's not a great start. Maybe Seppi cared enough about being a dad that it would bring them together, maybe she would find her way to the parts of him that he had shared with me. The thought of that hurt my heart even more than the thought of her leaving.

Seppi was preoccupied with his new role in the family, and managing the construction of his new ristorante. Seppi was trying to keep me safe, for his sake, and to keep my sister from leaving, which she was probably going to do, either way. Instead of having Salvatore's actual voice barking orders at him like before, he was trying desperately to block out the echoes that accompanied his own daddy issues. He felt far away, and I knew it would be like that sometimes. I shook it off and took a shot of whiskey.

And since I'm the worst at planning a fucking Halloween costume, I dug through my closet and threw together a sexy scarecrow. I wore a push-up bra and put braids in my hair. Then it was a pair of black tights and a ratty denim mini skirt with a fitted plaid flannel shirt, top buttons popped open to show a little cleave. I was happy with how I looked, with my cute hair and fake stitches, borderline-whorish eyeliner, mascara, and lip stick. I spritzed on some Alien Elixir and washed an edible down the hatch with one more swig of whiskey. After adding brown boots to complete the look, I was satisfied with my spur of the moment costume. I was feeling squirrelly and unstable, and hoped the weed and whiskey would help, but I'm pretty sure all it did was get me into trouble.

When I got to Sunny's apartment, she swung the door open with a smile,

"What's up, fucker?"

I crossed the threshold, and Vinny kissed me on both cheeks before shrugging into a beat-up leather jacket. Vincenzo Moretti, Vinny or Vin to friends, is a younger, baby-faced version of Seppi. He smells expensive, dresses well, and has classic Italian good looks. He kissed Sunny, and as soon as he was out the door, I could tell from her face that things with him were better. There was no tension or pain under the surface, there was no evidence of tears or a recent argument. Sunny seemed happy and I was looking forward to catching up. I'd been healing from my Sal-inflicted gunshot wound, while wallowing in self-pity over killing him. I hadn't spent much energy staying connected to anyone over the last couple weeks. By Halloween, I was healed on the outside, even if the wounds deep inside of me were gaping open. Thankfully, Sunny and I had a history, so the dead spots didn't cause any damage or hurt feelings. We were life-long friends, so as adults, the years fell away, and we picked up right where we left off. Sunny looked me up and down approvingly,

"Damn, fucker, you look GOOD!"

She lifted me off the ground with a hug. Abigail 'Sunny' Solomon was a strawberry blonde bad-ass. She was the girl with the dark eye makeup and hand-rolled cigarettes, the girl with soft lips and rough edges. Sunny was a girl who could bring boys to their knees, and wasn't afraid of anything. She grabbed the hat to her slutty witch costume, and we went into the night. Forgetting I had tossed an edible down the hatch, I sat on the porch steps with Sunny and shared a joint with her. I closed my eyes and let the feeling of self-medication fall over me. My eye lids were heavy, and my body tingled as the weed set in. She fished a silver flask from her thrifted wool cloak, and we swallowed fire before heading toward the park.

We found a spot on the curb across from Muddy Waters, as night fell and the crowd grew. We people-watched while the parade-goers and darkness closed in around us. As the joint started to ebb, the edible started to flow. We watched the floats move by as children yelled for candy, and cheered for superheroes. Music on flat-bed floats as school bands marched by in my haze of alcohol and marijuana. That was the biggest crowd I'd ever seen at that parade, and I realized I hadn't watched it since I was ten years old. I was swaying back and forth to a high school band playing Lady Gaga when I bumped into the person next to me. I turned my head to apologize profusely, and my eyes landed on Lance Arnault.

His face lit up,

"Amelia, right!? How's it going?"

We made small talk, but I was high as a kite and a little tipsy, and wanted to lick his face. As we watched the rest of the parade, Sunny leaned over to me,

"Who's that hottie? Holy shit! I bet you want to sniff his neck and lick his face."

I giggled and smacked her. I whispered,

"He's the handsome stranger from the café."

As the parade ended and people dispersed, Lance invited us to one of the bars in town, he said there was a Halloween party. We were already dressed up, but I was mentally scrolling through my usual excuses to see if any of them would fit the occasion. Sunny leaned forward, looked around me at Lance, and smacked me,

"We'd love to!"

I glared at Sunny, but wasn't really mad at her. We made our way through the remaining parade crowd to the other end of the block, where the door of Paducci's Pub stood open. Monster Mash flowed out into the street as we made our way through the group of slutty nurses and sexy goblins, smoking cigarettes on the sidewalk. The place was packed, and Lance grabbed my hand as we weaved through the crowd on the dance floor, I grabbed Sunny and dragged her along. Lance raised his hand to signal the bartender and ordered three shots of Fireball. We clinked our glasses and tossed back the cinnamon flavored fire. I closed my eyes and felt the heat rising in my cheeks, I wasn't sure if I was feeling the effects of the alcohol, or the handsome stranger by my side.

While Sunny was chatting with a woman she knew, Lance led me onto the dance floor. He put his hand on my lower back, and we swayed to the music, I caught him looking at my boobs. Our eyes locked and electricity shot between us, as fifty other people danced in their costumes and drowned their sorrows with alcohol. I put my arms around his waist and felt the butt of his gun against my sleeve. Somewhere deep in the back of my subconscious, I was turned on by the thought of a man taking me. Hypnotizing me with his eyes and his words, and then mesmerizing me with his fingers, or any other part of him for that matter.

I was already thinking naughty thoughts when he ordered another round. We clinked shot glasses and swallowed the second-round of fire, making eye contact again. That night, I wasn't a broken bitch, I was in a costume, I could be whoever I wanted, and I was pretending I wasn't broken. That night, I wanted to be someone else, someone stable, and sexy, someone who took a risk now and then. I wanted to be someone who had a story to tell. We moved to the music, our bodies coming together here and there. He was probably just lonely too, but I didn't care. I pulled him into the dim hallway and backed him against the wall. I stood with my left leg in between his and glanced up at him, he closed the gap, and our mouths came together. Our tongues touched and we kissed like we were racing somewhere. He lifted me off the ground and spun me around, my back against the wall, my legs around his waist, skirt riding up.

We didn't spend the night together that night, and we didn't exchange numbers. But if Lance had pushed me into the bathroom, I would have been there with bells on (and nothing else). Neither of us made any promises, and there were no expectations, that night we were whoever we wanted to be. Walking home with a buzz, I told Sunny, I would have screwed the handsome stranger in the vomit and piss covered bathroom of that bar.

CHAPTER 6
OPEN UP MY HEAD AND LET ME OUT

I WOKE UP the following Monday and rolled my eyes when I realized my second therapy session was that afternoon. I got up and enjoyed my usual latte and half a joint on the sun porch, even though it was cold out. I found another nice outfit to wear to my appointment, before showering and getting ready for Muddy Waters. I went through the motions with the basic bitches and their Pumpkin Spice Lattes, and wondered if I was going to see Lance again. I spoke to Seppi, but he was all business, asked if I'd seen the red-headed lady in the pantsuit. He asked if I'd crossed paths with anyone new. And because I'm a fucking idiot, I said no. Do you think I realized at that point that Seppi was trying to warn me about people like the handsome stranger? Nope, not even a little bit. The only reason I didn't tell him about Lance, was because I didn't want another, 'you deserve better' lecture, blah blah blah. I get it, I'm an idiot.

I finished up with the caffeine addicts, made it through the lunch rush of paninis and wraps, and went to my apartment to get ready for therapy. I pulled on a pair of dark gray slacks, a cream-colored button up, and a houndstooth sports jacket that belonged to someone the Morettis whacked. Don't worry, I got the blood out. I slapped on lipstick and mascara before spritzing on some Alien Elixir, kissing Indie, and heading out the door. I sat in the car, staring at the fire pit. I was lost in thought when Kane tapped on the window and I jumped out of my skin. Jesus. I rolled the window down as Kane laughed at me, and my extreme startle response. He leaned against the car swinging his rag, I knew what he was going to say before he said it,

"Wanna hang out later?"

I knew he was going to start with that kind of shit as soon as he saw me interacting with Lance that time. But you know what? At that point, I was out of my goddamn mind, and about to open a huge can of worms with Isabella Rossi, my sister was thinking about leaving, I was off my meds, and I had killed a guy, so what did it matter if I had dinner with Kane Buchanan? What did it matter if I did more than that?

"I can probably do that, I'm on my way to an appointment, but I'll be back in a couple hours. Want me to pick something up on my way back?"

His dark chocolate eyes locked with mine and I swallowed a ball of nerves. I watched him contemplate his next move before leaning in the window and winking,

"I'll take care of dinner, see you when you get back."

Kane whipped out my kryptonite when he tucked a loose curl behind my ear, leaning in a little more to kiss me on the cheek. I watched as he retreated to the world of coffee beans and steamed milk, swinging his rag like he thought he was going to get lucky later. I sat there after Kane disappeared inside. What the hell was that? Old feelings flooded in, and I remembered the day we met, our first kiss, falling for him. It would feel good to sleep with him again, he was always so gentle. And then I remembered finding out about Alex, finding out he loved her, and finding her hair tie and perfume in his nightstand. I closed my eyes and pinched the bridge of my nose before pushing in the clutch and firing up the mini mafia sedan. Buckle up, my little dinner date with Kane never happened.

I blasted Jerry Cantrell as I drove into the city, parked in the lot behind the impressive office building, amongst the other expensive cars. I had ten minutes before I needed to go inside, so I got out of the car and smoked half a joint in the parking lot. Feelings were starting to bubble to the surface, and I didn't like it. I felt the walls closing in on me, and I was outside. The world started spinning, I had a flash of being pinned to the bathroom floor at my neighbor's house when I was little, the panties with the day of the week embroidered on them.

I had a flash of the moment the repressed memories flooded in, sixth grade health class when the school nurse talked about good touch, bad touch. The day I realized I had been a little girl lost, sucked into a place of darkness and shame. Curled up in my walk-in closet hugging my knees as I watered down the pain with tears. Right then, I almost got back in the Caddy and drove far away from there, far enough that my demons couldn't find me. I almost called it quits. In that moment, the pain and darkness almost won. I flicked the joint, wiped my tears, and made a lap around the parking lot before going through the glass doors into the lobby.

I rode the elevator to the luxury office in the sky and had to push myself to go into the waiting room. I had tears in my eyes when I checked in with Elaine. She brought me a bottle of water and a box of Kleenex. My phone buzzed, and it was Seppi, 'Good luck, Dimples.' I wondered if I was going to leave there like I did the week before. I had no idea if my evening was going to include dinner with Kane Buchanan, or another frantic 'Giuseppi Moretti panic button rescue,' somewhere between point A and point B. I glanced up when Isabella Rossi opened her door and gestured me into her office.

I took my place in the overstuffed chair and pulled a Kleenex out of the box Elaine had given me. I was already a mess, and we hadn't even started. I'm not sure why I was bothering with the eye makeup at that point, since it all ended up on a tear-soaked Kleenex. Dr. Rossi sat and waited patiently as I fell apart. She didn't try to change the subject or make me feel better. She didn't distract me from my pain or start taking notes, she just let me sit in my shit and feel it. I don't know how long it took me, but eventually I blew my nose and made eye contact with her. She said,

"It looks like you're having a lot of feelings."

I nodded and looked at my lap.

"What would you like to talk about today?"

I shrugged. She didn't speak. We sat there together in silence until I was ready. I took a deep breath and looked up at her,

"I'm broken, and I don't think you're going to be able to fix me."

Her eyes softened,

"I don't think you're broken, Amelia. I think you've been hurt, betrayed, and shamed, and you're struggling to manage all of that without a little help."

And once again, I felt validated instead of feeling shamed, or shushed, or told I was a disappointment. The dam broke and my eyes overflowed again, I pulled it back and cleared my throat,

"I'm not okay, and I know that."

I twisted the soggy, mascara-covered tissue in my hands,

"Right now, I'm confused about just about everything in my life, except getting high and keeping a steady stream of whiskey in my system. There's so much going on that I don't even know where to start. And I'm not even here to deal with new shit, I'm here to deal with the old shit that broke me in the first place."

She leaned forward and met my eyes,

"There are no rules for this process, you can deal with old shit, *and* new shit."

I smiled a little because she said 'shit.' I didn't know where to start, was I supposed to pick up where we left off last time? Was I supposed to have something I wanted to talk about? Was I supposed to tell her everything, or only some of the things? Was she sitting there judging me for being broken?

"I feel like I'm losing my mind most of the time."

"What does that mean to you, losing your mind?"

I thought for a minute, and she wrote something down on her pad, it made me feel uncomfortable.

"To me, it means I've lost control of my thoughts and feelings. My emotional baggage is popping open and I'm trying like hell to jam things back in but it's creeping out the seams like poison. I lay in bed at night and wonder if the police are going to break down the

72

door. And maybe you're taking notes on your little pad there, so you can justify it when you ship me off to the nuthouse in a straitjacket. You're asking me what I'm feeling, and I have no idea, because I'm feeling everything at once."

"Let's slow down and focus on one thing. How are you feeling about what we discussed last week? Are you feeling better about what you did?"

What the fuck was that!? I wasn't even thinking about that old narcissistic fuck. But I guess I did feel better about it, now that she mentioned I had done the world a favor. Maybe she was right, maybe if you're ridding the world of something evil, it's OK to hurt someone, it's like taking out the trash.

"I'm feeling better about that. I haven't thought about it as much, or had as much anxiety about it. I think you're right, if I hadn't killed him, he would have killed me. And, like you said, I'm a good person. He wasn't."

I realize how fucked up that sounded since I was justifying the fact that I murdered someone, but she had a point.

"I think you were triggered by your trauma, and the fact that you felt like your world was spinning out of control, but the result would have been the same regardless. If you were just out there with some random person who was going to kill you, you would have done the same thing."

I shrugged,

"You're right."

"I think you would feel safer if you learned how to use a gun."

What!? I swung my eyeballs from the window to Isabella Rossi's eyes,

"I have a Sig Sauer and a holster, but I don't feel comfortable carrying it, or shooting it. I do timed drills sometimes to see how long it would take me to draw, aim and fire, but besides a couple times, I haven't practiced shooting it. I was going to take a concealed carry course but then everything happened. I was healing from a gunshot wound and couldn't take the class."

Dr. Rossi leaned forward again, her voice sounded like she cared and wanted me to be okay, or like she would say the same thing to a close friend,

"I have a friend named Cal who can work with you, she's a great teacher and will make sure you're comfortable handling a firearm. It's intimidating to take firearm courses from a man. Men always get their balls involved, and I think half of them get hard just thinking about how powerful they are with a gun in their hands. You need someone who's going to show you how to get comfortable and confident carrying a handgun."

Isabella Rossi pulled the suit jacket away from her waist, and I glimpsed the butt of a cute little handgun. I have to say, I was kind of impressed. The fact that she was carrying, made her a bad-ass, which increased her property value in my eyes. Deep down, I was excited about getting comfortable with a gun. I was looking forward to not needing to push my panic button or run to Seppi if I got myself into trouble. I looked forward to a time when I could defend myself, or someone else, with something besides a shovel. I couldn't imagine feeling safe alone,

"That sounds really nice, thank you."

We moved on to my current quandary with men. I mentioned that I had kissed, or been kissed by, three men over the last week, and I wasn't mad about it. Even as I told her about Lance, not one part of me threw up a red flag or realized he might be trouble. I didn't really care if I saw him again, but he was hot, and I'd fuck him if I had the chance. I felt something for Seppi but kept it behind a wall, I would never jeopardize my relationship with him or cross that line, and I'd never do that to my sister. As far as Kane, I still cared about him, but my hackles went up whenever I thought about Alex, her perky breasts, her hair tie, and her fruity perfume.

"Do you want to work toward feeling deep connections, or do you prefer chasing sexual arousal and jealousy?"

What was it with this woman!? How rude to poke around in my business like that. I didn't have an answer right, away and squirmed around while I tried to figure it out. And then I got pissed off,

"What kind of question is that!?"

She didn't seem upset that I pushed back at her,

"I'm trying to help you figure out why you are having superficial encounters with people, and not building any real connections."

Well, wasn't that some bullshit. I sat there looking at my hands again and picked at a loose thread on the sports jacket. I realized the only person in the world who really knew me was Giuseppi Moretti, and I had real feelings for him, even though I pushed them down deep inside,

"I do have someone."

Dr. Rossi looked like she was waiting for me to say more, but I didn't. What I did was sit there realizing that Seppi was the only person on the face of the earth who wasn't a part of past trauma, hadn't betrayed me, and wasn't family. I blinked away tears again and swallowed my feelings.

Our session ended. I made another appointment with Elaine, and she handed me a reminder card before I went into the hall and locked myself in the restroom. I threw cold water at my face and patted it with a nonabsorbent paper towel. When I was somewhat composed, I made my way to the lobby and out to the sidewalk. I already knew my evening wasn't going to involve dinner with Kane. Fifteen minutes later, I sat in my car in front of the gazebo, facing the rock wall and water, and pushed my panic button.

CHAPTER 7
ANOTHER DAY ANOTHER DEMON

TIME WENT ON. I had been spending time with Kane but wasn't sure what was going on. We hadn't had sex, but we cuddled and made out a couple times, with a little down the pants stuff thrown in for good measure. There was something holding me back, things with him were more of a band-aid than anything. Kane was comfortable and safe, and I knew he cared about me. Spending time with him was effortless, and things came naturally, but I felt like if I kept going down that road, I would fall back into his bed. At that point, I didn't think I could handle another trip to the Bermuda Love Triangle with Kane and Alex.

I got to know Lance, but for some reason, I kept it on the down low, I hadn't even told Sunny I'd seen him again after Halloween. I still hadn't told Seppi about Lance, because he would just tell me I deserved better than some hot, probably Private Detective, with a nice package. Speak for yourself. Seppi knew about my on-again, off-again relationship with Kane, the one that was a little too comfortable for my liking. Seppi would ask here and there if I'd met anyone, and I'd tell him no. Liar, liar, ratty vintage overalls on fire.

So, there I was, gearing up for my fifth session with Dr. Isabella Rossi, doing whatever I was doing with Kane, doing whatever I was doing with Lance, having whatever kind of feelings I was having for Seppi, trying to convince my free spirit sister to slow her role, and being emotionally destroyed by losing control enough to kill a narcissistic fuck with a shovel. You know, just your run of the mill, everyday shit, that everyone does. I still wasn't taking my meds, but I was high most of the time unless I was driving somewhere, and I usually accompanied the weed with some whiskey. I was living life like there were no consequences. If someone told me that some major shit was going to hit the fan in three months, I would have told them to mind their own fucking business. I'd tell them to turn that negative energy right around, and don't let the door hit you in the ass on your way out. Idiot.

The more I spoke with Dr. Rossi, the more I thought about getting a gun for personal protection. Just in case I was ever in a situation like the one with Sal, or if I was in trouble and Seppi wasn't around to bail me out. Kane's ex-military buddy, Mike, had given me a couple shooting lessons over the summer, but they were casual, and I wasn't mentally ready to take it seriously. I wasn't mentally ready that November either, but I thought it would be a good idea to learn. I would feel less anxious if I could defend myself, even if the threat was dead and buried, no pun intended. I had an old can of pepper spray and a pocketknife, but who am I kidding, I'd spray myself in the face and cut my finger off. Then I'd get sparkly, pass out, and vomit all over the place. Using a gun had to be better than that.

And since I was impressionable and easy to manipulate, I had Isabella Rossi's words swirling around in my head. I did the world a favor. I should be prepared to protect myself with something besides a shovel. I shouldn't have to rely on Seppi to bail me out of sticky situations. I told her about the panic button, and it was the first time I saw a flicker of something in her eyes. As if she was wondering why someone like that would care about someone like me. It was the first time I felt like I was lesser, or like I had no business with someone like Seppi. My heart hurt when I thought about how much my relationship with him had changed. My mind would swirl and do kart wheels, I would both plummet into deep dark places, and do tricks on a tightrope over the crowd. Emotionally, I was on the fast-track to straitjacket-land, even if I was denying it.

If this part seems like it was all over the place, that's because it was. I'd lay in bed and think about how I moved there for a fresh start. What really happened was that in my attempt to start over, get away from my ex, his whore and their love child, and the bullshit with my mother, I ended up involved in something so much worse. Instead of healing the wounds I already had, I ended up with new ones. Instead of finding myself, I committed murder. And whether I did the world a favor or not, murdering someone does not qualify as a fresh start. I was broken and out of control. I was having inappropriate thoughts about the one person in the world who understood me. I was lonely and broken and needed to be loved. I was self-medicating and spiraling and lying and had no idea how badly it was going to bite me in the dimple.

And because I make stupid decisions when I'm in that deep dark place, I started pushing Kane away by picking fights and being distant. I had fallen into the regular company of Lance Arnault at his rental condo on the mountain. Lance was dark and mysterious, and where Seppi was soft somewhere deep inside, Lance was not. He was hard and rough. I thought he was a P.I. or something, so I wrote off any odd conversations I heard, or any classified looking shit I found as I snooped around while he was in the shower. Mostly, I just wanted to know if he was married. He seemed like someone who would have a beautiful wife and a couple beautiful kids back in Jersey. Yet here he was, hours from home, living in a condo twenty minutes from Bunman, Vermont. When I heard Lance talking on the phone, he seemed to be speaking with business associates, and not family or friends. It seemed like he was talking in code, but I didn't care. Maybe I could learn how to do covert ops with him. Or maybe he was a rich, handsome criminal, and I could be the Bonnie to his Clyde. It turned me on to think about it. Maybe I'd be the bait. Maybe I'd be the hook.

And if you're wondering, yes, we messed around a little, and I was right about his package. I wasn't sure if I was catching feels, riding the wave of sexual attraction, or just being reckless, but I was enjoying myself. I didn't really care if he had someone back home, I didn't know about them, so it wasn't my problem. Lance was charismatic, we had a good time, and even though he was this incredibly attractive man who wore the typical uniform of a douche bag most days, he had been nothing but nice to me. Do you think that raised any red flags? Nope.

Stupid little me didn't have a care in the world that I was with a handsome stranger I met less than twenty-four hours after Seppi told me to watch out for strangers. And maybe Lance was the real thing, but with my luck, I should have known he had bad intentions. Times like that, I cursed my trauma for never letting me see someone at face value. Never letting myself have feelings without either proceeding with extreme caution or going full steam ahead in the wrong direction. At that point, it could have gone either way, and to be honest, I didn't really care which way it went.

I mashed my ringlets into an extremely messy, messy bun. I needed things to feel safe and familiar and was sick of playing games. That day, my outfit of choice was ratty vintage overalls, dingy white Chuck Taylors, and a sage green cable knit cardigan with leather patches on the elbows. I spritzed my throat and pulse points with Alien Elixir, and used the lip balm I found in Kane's nightstand. After kissing Indie on the head, I bounced down the stairs to Muddy Waters. Kane handed over a maple oat latte and waved like he hoped he'd see me later. I fired up the mini mafia sedan and made my way to the impressive office building of Isabella Rossi. Fuck it. Fuck the pretension, fuck the facade.

As I merged into traffic on the highway, I smiled to myself that the mask was off, let's see what that smarty pants psychiatrist did with me now. Maybe she'd push a button that summoned 'white coats' from the closet with a straitjacket. Maybe they would drag me away to a padded party room in some mental hospital far, far away. Maybe Isabella Rossi would tell me I was too broken, and that I'd never be fixed. I leaned against my car and smoked half a joint before heading toward the glass doors to the lobby. I knew what I was doing at that point. Checked in with Elaine, took a seat and fingered through the outdated magazines about shit I didn't care about. When Dr. Rossi swung her door open and saw me sitting there, I could tell she appreciated the honesty.

Things changed with her that day, at least she knew what she was dealing with. My previous business casual costume, if you will, was my way of hiding the truth. So even though she'd made me feel like I wasn't someone Giuseppi Moretti would give a shit about, Isabella Rossi was now looking at me in a way that told me we were finally on a level playing field. I told her I'd met someone but didn't give away too much, in case Lance really was a private detective, or in the F.B.I. on a stealth mission. Anyway, if he was up to anything nefarious, I'd know it, wouldn't I? Dr. Rossi continued to encourage me to carry a gun for protection. She asked how I was feeling, and I told her. She suggested prescribing meds for my depression, and I told her I had plenty of meds in a basket on top of my microwave. Screw that. And then she hit me in the head with a figurative shovel,

"Are you still struggling with killing Salvatore?

I just sat there and looked at her, why did she have to do me like that? Every. Fucking. Time.

"What!?"

"I'm just wondering if you're still feeling guilty about the night at the refuge."

I thought we had already discussed it. But that woman was clever, she didn't throw out the word 'murder' all willy nilly, she sugar-coated that shit and made it sound like...are you still tormented about losing your crystal slipper at the ball? Are you still sad about losing your jacket at the fair? I shrugged,

"Not really. I smoke a lot of weed and keep myself pretty-well self-medicated, I'm not losing any sleep over it."

I was lying to her, but she uncrossed her legs and leaned forward,

"Good, guilt can eat a person alive and you have no reason to feel guilty for what you did, you didn't have a choice. Like you said, it was a kill or be-killed situation. I'm sorry you were in that position, but that's what happened, and you're going to drive yourself insane if you carry guilt about it."

I found it interesting she used the word insane, I looked her in the eye and replied, flatly,

"I did the world a favor."

I didn't know if I was trying to convince her, or myself. She continued,

"I want you to be able to heal your old wounds, and your new ones. Maybe even find yourself, and have that fresh start you're hoping for."

Boy, she was really poking at my last nerve with a chop stick, and she wasn't done yet,

"I know you were trying to escape the dysfunction with your ex and your mother, and you thought Bunman was going to be the ticket. I understand nothing went as planned, and that being involved with a mob family, is not best-case scenario."

I swallowed the lump in my throat. I didn't know whether she was being genuine or being a bitch, but I wasn't going to give her the satisfaction of my tears.

"Once we clean up all the recent trauma, I'd like to discuss your mother and what happened with those boys when you were little. You've said you struggle with your self-worth and don't think you deserve to be loved. You carry the belief that most of the people in your life will never genuinely care about or accept the version of you without the mask."

With that, my session ended, and I made my next appointment with Elaine before pushing into the hall. I locked myself in the restroom and threw cold water at my eyes before using a non-absorbent paper towel to pat my face. Shit was swirling. Shit was bubbling. Shit was about to explode when I put my foot on the clutch and pushed the ignition. I didn't make it to the gazebo with the rock wall near the water before I pushed my panic button and held it for three seconds. When Scppi called, he told me to get off at the next exit, and park in the lot of a place called Bongiovanni's. He said it would be on the right, and that there would be a big sign with a fat Italian chef. When I pulled in the parking lot, I could tell Bongiovanni's was more of a ten dollar pizza special kind of place, than an authentic Italian Ristorante with dark mafia energy. I leaned against the car in the waning light and smoked the rest of a joint while I waited, ever vigilant of my surroundings as my body began to tingle.

My head was full of gobbledygook, panic was setting in. I had the realization that maybe no one would ever love me, and wondered if everyone who'd ever said they loved me, had been lying. What if I wasn't valuable, what if I wasn't worthy of being protected like a precious treasure? I talked myself out of hyperventilating, a wave of nausea creeping in as I flicked my butt and got back in the car. I needed someone to love me, I desperately needed to feel something besides pain, something deep inside, some kind of connection. I was suffocating and needed to feel like I was more than just a million broken pieces, stuffed into a pair of ratty vintage overalls and dingy white Chuck Taylors. There was a part of me that longed to feel loved and protected, and that part of me was in the fetal position, crying out for attention. I was crumbling into dust when my phone vibrated with a text from Seppi, 'Almost,' and it made my body do something, butterflies danced in my stomach and a rush of heat rose to my cheeks.

I closed my eyes and cried the way you do when you're desperate, I was numb while feeling all the pain. I wanted to turn into nothingness and float away, a broken little bitch, and my own mother didn't love me. My heart was beating in my ears, my stomach doing somersaults. I was ugly crying into my hands when a set of headlights pulled up beside me. I climbed into the passenger seat of the Escalade, Seppi wordlessly looped around the parking lot and drove. I took in the scent of him, a combination of whiskey, a Cuban, Tobacco Vanille. I smelled like tears and weed and Alien Elixir. Back and forth between sobbing and staring straight out the windshield as the lines went by. It was dark by then, and I had no idea where we were going. It didn't matter where he took me, even Giuseppi Moretti couldn't get me far enough away from my demons.

My head was stuck, and that might have been my lowest point in all of this, but who knows. I felt like acting out, just some broken, loveless, worthless, rejected, shamed, shushed, killer. By the light of the dash, I watched as Seppi moved his right hand from the steering wheel. He patted my knee, and I made a noise low in my throat, my juices flowing as tears dripped into my cleavage. I put my hand on his, briefly, but pulled it away, because I felt things I shouldn't. I tried to just let him care about me, without my mind making it into something it wasn't. I tried to accept that he acccpted me, and all my broken pieces, without letting myself feel something more.

Seppi pulled the Escalade into the parking area of a reservoir with access to the Long Trail, and we were the only ones there. He cut the engine and the interior lights came on for a minute before fading to black. We sat in silence in the dark. The next time I started to sob, he moved his hand to the back of my neck and rubbed the base of my skull with his thumb. He was making things difficult, given the way I was feeling, with all my broken pieces and desperate need to feel whole. I wanted Seppi to kiss me deeply and put his hand down my ratty vintage overalls. His voice was gentle and breathy, he was making it worse, instead of better,

"What do you need, Dimples?"

Goosebumps traveled over every inch of my body, my breath caught, and I tried to find my words. I just stared at my hands for a while, and noticed I was picking at the skin next to my thumbnail, even though I would regret it later,

"I'm so incredibly broken."

With that, my voice crumbled, and my words were washed away in a tidal wave of tears. Seppi leaned closer and seemed to be swallowing his emotions when he replied, trying to be strong where I was concerned. His voice was lower, and gentler, maybe he was trying to keep me from running back into my shell,

"Tell me what you need and I will give it to you."

He didn't really mean that, because I needed him to make me feel something. I needed him to make me feel wanted and valued and loved, even if it wasn't his job. I pushed it away, I let it come back. I wanted him. No, like, I needed him. I needed this man who seemed to accept me with all my broken pieces. I needed him to show me I deserved to be loved, even if I wasn't worthy of being loved by my own mother. I closed my eyes and had a decision to make, was I going to beg him to make me feel whole? Was I going to climb over the console and straddle his lap, sob with my head on his shoulder? I wanted to fall apart in his arms, so he could hold all my broken pieces together. And because I was making decisions as if there were no consequences, I unbuckled my seatbelt.

I sat there for a little longer, frozen, before I opened my door and slid out. Seppi probably thought I was going to smoke a joint, because he didn't follow me right away. I had no idea where I was, or where I was going, but there was enough moonlight to see the path. By the time Seppi opened his door, I was beating feet on a trail that led deep into the woods. It was just me out there, with my dimples and the demons in my head. As I ran, the tears slid sideways instead of into my cleavage. The cold air was burning my throat, and it felt like my soul left my body when Seppi's hand clamped around my right forearm. I came to a halt and spun around to release the tension. His hands moved to my shoulders as he stood in front of me. He hooked my chin with his finger and tilted my face toward his. I could feel the condensation from his exhales as he caught his breath,

"Stop."

Ever the sarcastic bitch, I put my hands on my hips,

"Are you a fucking idiot? Does it look like I'm still running!?"

Seppi held me against his chest, and I felt him crying. What the fuck was this? I was the one who needed a shoulder to cry on. It was silent as I let him sit in his shit. When he spoke,

"This is all my fault, the way you're struggling, the panic you feel when you leave your sessions with Isabella."

He didn't know the half of it, but he felt responsible for whatever trauma I had from being shot and committing murder. He didn't know anything about how my mother was, or about what happened when I was little. Seppi was mistaken if he thought all of this is what broke me. He had no idea that this had nothing to do with that, I yelled at him,

"You have no idea what you're talking about, Giuseppi!"

His breath caught in his throat, I had never once called him by his real name. My voice changed as I filled with rage, twisting away from his hands, making my way further into the woods. He followed, matching my pace, what the fuck was his deal? I turned around and got in his face, pointing a finger at his chest,

"You can stop following me, I'm fine! And thanks a bunch for signing me up with your shrink, she thinks it's a real knee-slapper that you give a shit about someone like me!"

He was completely caught off guard,

"What!?"

I put my hands on my hips again, pissed,

"Do you know how she looked at me when I told her about the panic button!? Like, why the *fuck* would Giuseppi Moretti give a shit about someone like *you*?"

Seppi's voice had feelings in it,

"Dimples."

I was having too many feelings, I was panicking, another switch flipped, and I needed to push him away so I could pull the trap door closed. I got close and shoved him back with both hands, yelling as tears streamed down my cheeks,

"And last I checked; you have no idea what it's like to be thrown to the wolves by your own mother!"

Desperately, he pleaded, probably so he could get home to my sister,

"Amelia."

He reached for me and I swatted him away, my voice squeaking at the end,

"My own mother doesn't love me, so why the fuck should I expect anyone else to give a shit!? Huh!?"

I shoved him again, screaming in his face as I cried, but what I really wanted was to feel his body against mine, his arms around me as we lay together. Seppi didn't protest, he just let me rage at him if that's what I needed,

"You have an answer for that Mister Mob Boss!? You have some goon who's gonna make my mother love me!? No!?"

I got close and shoved him a third time, but it was a lie, and I was running out of steam,

"And stop acting like killing your father is the reason I'm fucked up; I was fucked up in the first place!"

I opened my eyes wide and tapped my temple repeatedly,

"I'm fucked up in here, Seppi! None of this is your fault, or your problem!"

He wasn't walking away or pushing back, and it pissed me off. I leaned in and leveled my eyes at him,

"I don't understand why you come when I push that button, it's fucking stupid! For Christ's sake, you're like Pavlov's dog with that thing, some fucked up call and response!"

Right in his face, almost nose to nose, because I needed to feel the heat of his breath. I screamed,

"You can't fix what's wrong with me, so stop trying, you're wasting your time!"

I was done with that bullshit day and wanted to go home. Pushing passed Seppi, I stomped toward the Escalade, his hand gently gripping my right shoulder. I stopped, took a deep breath, and wanted to spin around and punch him in the face. He pulled me into his chest, and I stood there in the woods, wrapped up in the arms of a good man who did bad things. I knew people had died at his hand, but I had never felt more protected. I deescalated, sobbing as he kissed the top of my head, my curls getting caught up in his stubble. I could feel his heart pounding, and as I relaxed in his arms, his pulse slowed along with mine. Seppi held my head against the warmth of his body, he spoke into the top of my head, the heat from his breath on my scalp,

"I need you to be okay."

I wriggled out of his arms, away from the warmth of his body,

"Wow! *You* need me to be, okay!?"

Seppi looked back at me like a deer in the headlights,

"Did you give me that bullshit button so that when I'm panicking or losing my mind, you can come tell me what *you* need!? Fuck that, I'm not interested, you can have it back!"

Seppi was at a loss for words, but I wasn't,

"You can have your car back too, for all I fucking care. You don't need to worry about me, I don't need you!"

The level of pain I felt when those words left my lips is something I can't even describe, because the truth is, I needed him like I needed oxygen. I spun around and marched toward the Escalade. He grabbed for me again but missed, I felt the wind from his hand. He tried again and caught me. That time, I'd reached my limit of Giuseppi Moretti's bullshit, even though he had dropped everything to come rescue me from myself. My face burned with tears and the cold, my heart was beating in my ears, I couldn't have been further from okay. I screamed,

"LET ME GO!"

But he didn't, and that time, my tears were made of fire. I clenched my teeth and twisted my arm free. I stared into the face of a mob boss, and didn't care in the slightest who he was to anyone else, mocking,

"When I tell you to let me go, you let me go! Capiche!?"

Seppi reached for me again, his voice pleading, tears under the surface. Somewhere along the way, he had dropped his armor out there on that moonlit path, his heart on his sleeve,

"Please, stop."

I swatted his hand away and he tried one more time. I squared up and shoved him again, but he was ready for it and tried to pull me closer. Seppi's voice revealed something about his feelings, he was invested in me,

"Dimples."

I felt every ounce of the full-grown woman as she left my body, like the devil during an exorcism. Without the safety of my masks, or the parts of my demons that protected me, a broken little girl was trying to come up for air. I screamed like a child having a tantrum, sobbing,

"WHY DOESN'T SHE LOVE ME!?"

Seppi's face reflected my pain, his hand gently resting on my arm instead of grabbing it, his voice had none of what I heard when he spoke with his associates, there was a desperate quality to it, pleading,

"Please tell me what you need, so I can give it to you."

I met his eyes, and he rubbed his thumb over the inside of my wrist. I didn't look away that time and I saw something else in his eyes,

"What I'm saying to you, Dimples, is that I care for you very much, and it's important to me that you are okay. If you tell me what you need, I will give it to you. Anything you need, it's yours."

I could have said a lot of things, but I said,

"I need *you*."

He could have said a lot of things, but he said,

"I'm right here."

He was eye to eye with me, his voice reassuring and safe, a last-ditch effort for a smile, he winked,

"Capiche?"

I blinked away my tears and smiled a little, "Capiche."

I had no idea what we were doing, this thing between the two of us. I started to cry again, but that time, any sense of feeling whole had left the building. I was this bag of jagged shards and tears, just completely lost and desperate to feel loved. Seppi hugged me again, but that time, I realized he needed me to be okay for his own sake, and not my sister's. I let him take care of me instead of throwing him away, even though there was a part of me that needed more. A part of me that needed to feel his body close to mine. But that moment between us was about something else entirely. Seppi accomplished his mission. I'd been panicking and ready to run for the hills, but he hadn't given up on me, and I could finally feel my body relaxing.

We didn't say much on the way back to Bongiovanni's, he was back in his corner and I was back in mine. I was crying but not as much, I think that's when I realized Seppi cared about me on a personal level. We parted ways and I held it together on the way home. As I laid in bed that night, I realized Seppi's cage had shielded me from the bad things swirling around in the periphery. And as we stood there in the cold darkness of the woods that night, Seppi held all my broken pieces together.

CHAPTER 8
CANNED WHIPPED CREAM

I WOKE ON THANKSGIVING and shuffled to my kitchen with Indie trailing behind me, her thrifted ceramic bowl on the floor, purring as she devoured breakfast. I pulled the fridge open and took stock of the inventory: squash casserole, cranberry orange relish, sliced cheese and fresh berries for the charcuterie board. I made a latte and sat on the sun porch watching my breath after each sip. I waved to Kane as he stood there in his pajama bottoms and a t-shirt waiting for his Staffordshire Terrier, Lola, to do her business. I blared music and got high while I worked with flour and instant yeast. I started dough for dinner rolls and a crusty loaf, before making pumpkin and apple pies.

I got a Happy Thanksgiving text from Marco and glanced at my bedroom door, longingly. I went across the hall to wish Kane a Happy Thanksgiving and when his door swung open, Alex gave me a finger wave from behind the island. She was wearing Kane's robe as she squeezed orange juice. Kane kissed me on the cheek and invited me in for a latte. Was he kidding? I declined nicely (I swear), wished them both a Happy Thanksgiving, and waved at Alex with my whole hand before I turned around. As soon as I was inside of my apartment with the door closed, I lost it. Whatever. I tossed an edible down the hatch and poured a shot of Fireball into the remnants of my latte. The Fireball made me think of the night with Lance at Paducci's Pub. My sister texted to bring extra because a couple more people were joining us. Sunny texted me, 'What's up fucker? Happy Gobble Day, see you soon.'

I was already done with Thanksgiving, and now there were extra people!? I pinched the bridge of my nose and clenched my jaw. I tossed the baggie of edibles in my purse because I was going to need to be good and high for this shit show. The Moretti family was huge and their associates were everywhere. I imagined Mary inviting a ragtag bunch of mobsters that would have otherwise been alone on Thanksgiving. People dressed like Seppi, crowded around the dining room table, expensive whiskey and Cuban Cigars. I'd be nestled in between two rough looking men who had definitely whacked people, as they went to blows over the wish bone, or last piece of pumpkin pie. Fine. I had the stuff to make a chocolate cream pie and a cheese ball.

After I showered and made myself look presentable, I dug through my closet for a decent outfit. Most of my pants were too big, but I had recently thrifted a gorgeous pair of Burberry trousers with the iconic tan, white and black plaid. I tucked in a fitted white button up shirt, left the top button open, and worked a leather belt through the loops. The belt buckle was Aztec style silver and turquoise. A waist length cardigan and chunky heeled boots pulled it all together. My makeup looked nice for a change; my pulse points and throat, spritzed with Alien Elixir. I kissed Indie before I loaded my car and headed to the land of mafia mansions and charcuterie boards made with expensive local uncured meats and fancy cheeses. I rolled to a stop at the booth and handed over the fresh loaf of crusty bread, the middle-aged man winked at me as I rolled through the gate in my mini mafia aesthetic. He leaned out the window of his booth,

"Thank you, Dimples!"

I gave the guy a wave and wondered if he knew my real name. I wound my way through mafia mansion land, I looked good, I felt good and it scratched an itch for me to cook for people. Maybe this was going to be a nice Thanksgiving after all. When the house came into view, I saw a couple of extra cars but didn't think anything of it, I made sure not to block anyone in and parked behind Opal's Volvo. Seppi came out in his slippers to help me carry things in, but first hugged me and kissed both cheeks. He followed me up the marble walkway to the steps and I stopped dead when my eyes landed on a Toyota Corolla with Massachusetts license plates. Seppi slammed into the back of me and our bags filled with casserole dishes, rolls, and pies swung into each other. I scoffed,

"Nope."

I put my bags down, weaved around Seppi, and went for the car. He put his bags down and tried to stop me,

"It's gonna be okay."

I spun around, spitting venom,

"Oh, really? Is my dad here to tell me that my mother fell off a cliff?"

I continued toward the car,

"Enjoy the food, Happy Thanksgiving."

"Amelia."

Without turning around,

I mumbled,

"Fuck this."

Seppi appeared helpless and threw his hands around in the air. Opal threw the front door open as I was unlocking my car. She ran into the driveway in an apron and slippers, and yelled at me like I was a child,

"Amelia!"

I froze, and took a deep breath; I knew I was

going to need it when I told my sister to go fuck herself. I spun around and yelled back,

"What the fuck are they doing here!?"

Keep in mind that we're doing all of this in front of a mafia mansion in a gated community, like absolute trash. Opal blubbered,

"I'm having a baby."

That wasn't news, I threw my hands up,

"And!?"

She crossed her arms and seemed offended,

"And I want them to be involved."

I scrunched up my face and threw my hands toward the front door, didn't give a shit who could hear me,

"You've got to be kidding me."

The climate in her eyes changed, she was pissed and hurt. What was going on? She didn't even want to be with Seppi. She bristled and took a step closer, pointing at my chest,

"Maybe you need to leave."

I put my hands on my hips and raised my voice,

"Excuse me!?"

Opal put her hands on her hips,

"If you can't have a nice meal with our parents than maybe you should leave."

We were standing in the driveway shoving each other like children when my dad and Seppi jogged over to break up the fight. Well, that Thanksgiving dinner was off to a good start. My dad wrapped his arms around me and kissed the top of my head,

"Hi Boo-Boo Bear."

I melted in my dad's arms like I did when I was a child. And then, just like when we were kids, he made his two girls hug, what an asshole. I took my sister's hands and apologized. I didn't know what it felt like to be her right then, and our parents came as a package deal. If she wanted our dad there, our mother would come with him. My dad squeezed my shoulders, kissed the top of my head and steered me toward the house. I shook the cobwebs off the mask and pulled it over my head like a trash bag before we got to the door. I kissed my mother on the cheek and returned her half-hearted floppy-fish hug. She told me I hadn't come to visit lately. The road goes both ways, bitch. Seppi attempted to diffuse the situation by escorting my mother to the climate-controlled wine cellar. It seemed a lot like he was rewarding her bad behavior, but what do I know. Maybe he'd lock her down there or maybe there was a dungeon with a trap door pit filled with alligators. A girl can dream.

Before I set the table, I tossed an edible down the hatch and washed it down with a shot of vodka from the bar. Forks on the left, spoons on the right. Cloth napkins pulled through heavy sterling napkin rings. My mother passed back through the kitchen and dining room on her way to the sitting room in the front of the house. I buzzed back and forth and tried to stay distracted. Sunny and Vincenzo arrived with some of his homemade tiramisu, and an expensive bottle of bourbon. Mary Moretti arrived, and did not, in fact, have a gaggle of stray mobsters in tow. The Morettis were a little less turkey and stuffing, and a little more steak and lobster tails. I wandered into Seppi's office and poured two whiskies over perfectly square ice cubes. I retrieved a Cuban from the humidor, and pocketed the cutter and lighter in Seppi's top drawer before grabbing my thrifted flip-top tin.

I exited the sliding door and held up the glasses, Seppi nodded and smiled from the grill. He leaned down and kissed my cheek when I approached, nodding his head at the counter. I hopped up on the stainless-steel counter of the mob mansion's three-season outdoor kitchen and swung my legs. We clinked glasses and stood there grilling steaks as we watched everyone else move around inside. I liked it better this way and I think he did to, we left our masks inside. Just a broken little girl and broken little boy, self-medicating as our families indulged on fancy appetizers and expensive Cabernet Sauvignon. Everyone was in the kitchen eating crackers and cheeses and fancy nuts, I bet Seppi had fancy nuts. He lit the Cuban and I lit a joint, he glanced over at me,

"Sometimes you need to do the phony smiles and fake hellos."

He flicked his eyebrows as he blew out rings of cigar smoke like a bad-ass, he winked,

"You know, to keep the peace."

That wink went straight to my panties, so I crossed my legs, rolled my eyes, and pretended I was throwing up.

"Listen, Dimples, you're getting ready to have a nice meal in a nice house with people who love you, stop fighting it."

Someone there loved me? That was news. I rolled my eyes again. I wasn't sure if he was actively trying to get kicked in the balls or what. But he had a point, most of the people inside were people who loved me, and I loved them. Whatever,

"Fine."

I managed to hold my tongue through the insults and subtle criticisms. I kicked my sister under the table and made sure to keep my wine glass filled. Sunny helped Opal clear the table and I followed Seppi to get the pies out of the fridge in the garage. Before Seppi pulled the fridge open, he turned to me, I was trapped. At the time, I didn't realize he was asking a different question entirely,

"Has your sister told you she doesn't want to be with me?"

My eyes bugged out of my head before I could pull it back and play dumb, my voice went up an octave,

"Why would she do *that*!?"

He put his finger up and went back in the house for a second, returning with our coats and the keys to the Escalade, he gestured,

"Come on, we don't have any canned whipped cream for the pies."

I put my finger up and ran inside to retrieve a plate of food before joining Seppi in the Escalade. He glanced over at me,

"Still hungry, Dimples?"

I shook my head,

"No."

He shrugged and wound his way down the hill to the gate. Seppi came to a stop at the booth and gave the man a wave,

"Happy Thanksgiving, Gary."

The man leaned out and waved,

"Thank you, Mr. Moretti."

And to me, the man smiled with his eyes,

"The bread is delicious; I've already eaten half of it, but I'm going to bring the rest home; my boys and I don't get to enjoy homemade cooking very often."

Seppi glanced over at me and smiled. I put my finger up and he put the Escalade in park. I slid out and approached the booth with the tin foil wrapped plate of food. I had a cloth napkin wrapped bundle of silverware, and can of soda in my coat pocket,

"I thought you might be hungry, so I made you a plate."

Gary teared up as he peeled back the foil, I felt I needed to explain,

"I'm sorry, there isn't any turkey or stuffing, but

I put some steak on there, and a lobster tail. I made the squash casserole, the rolls, and orange cranberry sauce."

Gary swallowed his tears and asked,

"What's your name, young lady?"

"Amelia."

The man put his hand through the window,

"It's nice to meet you, Amelia, I'm Gary. You're an angel."

I teared up and returned his hearty handshake,

"It's nice to meet you Gary, can I give you a hug?"

Gary stepped out of the booth, and we hugged like two people who used to be strangers. We didn't say anything else; I think we were both choked up and trying not to cry. I gave Gary a low wave and he gave one back. I climbed in the Escalade and put on my seatbelt. Seppi sighed and cleared his throat as he rolled through the gate,

"And that is what I love about you, Dimples."

I shrugged again,

"I like to put myself in other people's shoes. I think it would be lonely to work all alone in a booth on Thanksgiving."

He reached over and patted my knee but didn't leave it there, which was a good thing because it made things warm in certain places. Seppi pulled into the parking lot of a gas station with a little grocery store. We didn't get out right away; we sat in silence for a minute, he turned to me,

"Can I tell you something?"

I nodded,

"Of course."

And just so you know, I wasn't thinking with my lady bits, I meant it, and I was happy he felt safe with me. I knew who he was talking about when he said,

"We're nothing alike, don't have anything in common, and we don't have any real connection. We get along but I think it's because neither of us are invested. I'm busy and distracted, but I can tell she's getting restless. I don't know if she's told you, but she sleeps on the other side of the house. And sometimes when I can't find her, she's sitting in the van listening to music. When she comes inside, I can tell she's been crying. She's not interested in talking about our relationship, and to be honest..."

Seppi set aside all his masks and swords and armor. It was just the two of us, the broken little girl and the broken little boy. His voice was quiet, intimate, he was sharing a part of himself with me, and I knew it,

"I'm telling you this in confidence."

I held up two fingers,

"Scout's honor."

He paused, maybe he was deciding if he could trust me with the information,

"I think sometimes two people have a baby and think that's a reason to spend their lives together."

Seppi was agonizing over the situation,

"We talk about it sometimes, think we could go through the motions as a family, but that isn't what either of us want."

He waved his words away. And in case you've lost track of what's going on here, I'll remind you. My sister and Seppi were both confiding in me, that they didn't love each other, that they didn't want to talk about a future together. That might have been the first time in my life that I handle things like a mature adult. Looking back now, I realize how much restraint I had as they figured things out. I was there for both of them, unconditionally, and never in any of it did I allow my feelings for Seppi to cloud my advice or mold my replies. I just listened to two people I cared for deeply, as they realized they didn't want to spend the rest of their lives together. No big deal. Seppi turned the car off,

"I've said too much, please don't tell her any of this."

I rubbed the back of his hand with my thumb,

"I promise."

Our eyes met and he looked at me differently that time. That might have been when I realized I was Seppi's best friend. I accepted him with all his broken pieces and gave him a safe place to hide when he wanted to take off his armor. I was the only one in the world who reciprocated. With that, he smiled a little and we went in the store to get canned whipped cream for the pies.

CHAPTER 9
SECRETS, SECRETS

WITH THE HOLIDAYS in full swing, Muddy Waters was busy with caffeine addicts, basic bitches, Christmas shoppers, and skiers. I kind of liked putting myself in autopilot as I ground espresso beans, tamped baskets, steamed milk, poured fancy leaves on the tops of lattes. Two weeks until Christmas and I'd been spending time with Lance. Not as in, sleeping at his condo every night, but we'd meet for lunch on the mountain or sometimes we'd get Chinese, and hang out at his place. Sometimes we'd do other things, if you know what I mean. We were starting to get to know each other better. That's when Lance confided the real reason he was in Vermont. As we sat against the headboard holding shots of vodka, he glanced over at me,

"Can I tell you something?"

I shrugged,

"Sure."

"I'm not here to get away from anything, I'm here to find my uncle."

He slid a picture out of his wallet, and I took it from him. I glanced at the picture and it was a candid shot of Salvatore Moretti. Surprisingly, I controlled my breathing, nodded my head and handed the picture back. My voice was steady but my hand was shaking slightly although I don't think he noticed,

"He looks like a nice man, when was the last time you saw him?"

I had a heart palpitation and my guts gurgled. Shit, no pun intended. I took a sip of vodka and a deep breath before morphing into someone who had no idea what happened to Salvatore Moretti. He said,

"Probably late-September, my uncle would come visit me in Jersey sometimes."

Like I'd flipped a switch, I nodded and smiled, went somewhere else in my head, and pulled on a mask,

"That sounds nice."

"I don't usually come here, my aunt forbids me to visit their house. It was better for him to come see me anyway. He used the trips as an excuse to get away from his nag of a wife for a while."

I would have shat my pantaloons, if I was wearing any. What was I supposed to say to that? Mary wasn't the asshole and it took immense restraint not to defend her. Is that why they hadn't acknowledged each other at Muddy Waters? It made sense now, I'd seen recognition in her eyes when she saw him and now I understood why, or at least I thought I did. But maybe he wasn't anybody to Mary, or to Sal, and maybe he was just a goon whose boss sent him to see if he could tie up Salvatore Moretti's loose ends.

"I really hope you find him."

I left out the part about Sal swimming with the fishes and put my finger up like a light bulb went off,

"Have you thought about hiring someone to help you find him?"

What was I saying!? Yes, please hire someone to find him. Quick tip, he's at the bottom of the ocean, wearing cinder block slippers. Idiot. Me, not him.

"I want to see if I can find him myself. My uncle's a private person, and I don't want to worry people. I think he had some risky gambling habits and maybe he skipped town to avoid a debt, who knows."

That made sense. I told Lance I would help him if he needed it, and I'm not sure how I managed to sleep that night, because I did end up staying, and I did manage to sleep. I made drip coffee in a semi-decent coffee maker while Lance sat at the counter fidgeting restlessly with my keys. I laid strips of bacon on a foil covered cookie sheet, rooted around until I found pancake mix and pure Vermont Maple Syrup. I was stirring batter when Lance pressed the button,

"What's this thing do, is it a garage door opener?"

I threw the spoon, batter splattering the wall behind the stove, waving my hands,

"NO!"

He threw the entire pile of keys on the counter like they were poison and threw his hands up. I put my finger to my lips and both of us froze. I waited, each second ticking by like an eternity, I wouldn't know if he'd pushed the button for three seconds until my phone either rang, or didn't. I held my breath and it rang. I answered,

"You, okay, Dimples?"

"I'm okay, it was an accident."

The call ended and let out a big sigh, Lance inquired,

"Who was that?"

No big deal, think, Amelia, think. I pulled an explanation out of my ass,

"It's a button I can push if I get in trouble, like a home security system or that app where you can hold your finger on the screen when you're in an Uber."

I moved his focus to technical things, opened the app on my phone so he could see how it followed my location. Lance noticed the rest of the activations occurred around five o'clock on Monday evenings, so I thought quick and told him it was a weekly test.

I told him I had some stuff from way back, and felt better having a lifeline. I moved the subject back to his missing uncle, and he seemed satisfied. I dodged that bullet by the skin of my teeth. I took the panic button off the key ring and slid it into one of the pockets in my purse.

I didn't tell anyone anything about anything at that point. I did a lot of nodding and listening. Opal was constantly texting me about wanting to leave, Seppi was worried he wouldn't see the baby, Lance was acting like he wanted to tell me something else, and I was sick of seeing Alex in the hallway. I did my job and put a smile on my face. Yes, sir. Yes, ma'am. Whatever you say. Painted a big fat smile on my fucking face and went through the motions with everyone, including Isabella Rossi, or at least I tried.

I checked in with Elaine, strolled into the waiting room like I owned the place, and fingered through the shitty magazines. When she gestured me in, I plopped in the Love Sac and put my hands behind my head. Said nothing. Screw this.

"You seem to be feeling better."

What a stupid fucking bitch,

"Yup, I guess I'm fixed. Thanks, doc."

I sat up,

"Are you fucking kidding me!? I seem to be feeling better!?"

I locked eyes with her,

"Did you get your license out of a gumball machine?"

She didn't appear ruffled, but shifted gears and I wasn't sure if she was going to try to rein me in or encourage me to continue escalating,

"Can you tell me what you're feeling?"

I rolled my eyes,

"Like you give a shit."

I chuckled to myself but seconds later I was hugging my knees as I cried. She said,

"Why don't you come sit in the chair so we can be on the same level."

I rolled my eyes again and dragged myself dramatically into the overstuffed chair. My insides were angry, my outsides were sad. I've always hated drudging up the past, rubbing salt in the wounds. She said,

"Have I given you the idea that I don't care about you?"

"Not exactly, but you found it pretty funny that I have a panic button that makes Giuseppi Moretti come running."

"Amelia, I was caught off guard, I've never heard of that before. It had nothing to do with you or who you are or whether you are worthy of being loved."

Well, look at me being the asshole. I moved my eyes to hers and noticed her winged eyeliner was perfect that day,

"Well, it felt like you didn't think I was worthy of Seppi's friendship."

She sat forward,

"Then there was a misunderstanding. You're a kind and compassionate person and you deserve to be cared for."

I stared at my lap as the seconds ticked and tocked, we sat there in silence. None of this mattered.

"Have you contacted the woman I mentioned, the one with the concealed carry classes for women?"

I shook my head. She picked up the phone and dialed a number. By the end of my session, I had another therapy appointment, a reminder card, and directions to the homestead of Calliope Cromwell. That woman sounded like a Halloweentown amusement park ride. That was the first Monday I didn't push my panic button and hold it for three seconds. Screw it. I went home and got high while I ate Kraft mac and cheese and an entire box of Swiss Rolls.

The next morning, my aunt Maggie stopped by the cafe to give me her perishables, and said she was setting off in her new RV for the Grand Canyon with Clem. She held me close and slid a card and a zipper baggie of weed into the pocket of my apron. She waved and went through the door, leaving a trail of guaiac wood and weed. Something in the way she hugged me had remorse in it, like she felt bad for talking me into coming back to Bunman, especially now that she was leaving indefinitely, again. I had to push my feelings away so I could sling coffees to the basic bitches and caffeine addicts with a big smile on my face instead of big fat tears rolling down my cheeks. If I had let the dam break, it would have been ugly crying, not suitable for manning an espresso machine and tending to the basic bitches.

That night, I asked Lance if he could teach me how to shoot a gun for self-defense. I was going to meet Calliope in three days, but this guy seemed to know his way around a gun, so I figured, why not? I didn't tell him about the hippie woman with the goat farm shooting range. He drove his rental Mercedes out to a warehouse on the edge of town, the parking lot was dark and gave me the creeps, I was glad I was with Lance. I watched as he pushed open a tall industrial looking door, it made a metal-on-metal screech as wheels moved along a rusted track. Lance flipped on fluorescent lights, there was a lot of scrap metal, rusty ramps and crowbars, rusty chains and equipment. I didn't like it.

There was a desk and a vinyl couch from the seventies in one of the side rooms, the entire place smelled like stale cigarettes and gasoline. I wondered how he knew about that place, and wondered if bad things happened there. The place looked like a chop shop or somewhere where men would go to have underground poker games or cock fights, with their actual cocks. There was no heat in there, and I could see my breath. I held his hand and trailed along behind him like a puppy. He opened a safe in an office with an ugly vinyl couch, there were several guns in the safe, big ones, small ones, take your pick. Lance chose a Sig Sauer just like mine, I didn't mention it.

He slid the loaded gun into the waistband of his jeans, and we went behind the warehouse. We were far enough from the center of town that no one would bother us out there, I wasn't even sure anyone would hear us shooting. If I was ever going to kill someone, that would be the place to do it. Lance stood with his arms around me, demonstrating how to hold a gun. He explained the safety, and how to use the sight. I felt the front of his body against the back of mine as I emptied the clip into a bag of cement. I did a shitty job of hitting the target in the middle, and wondered if shooting a bag of cement was the same as shooting an actual person. Lance seemed to enjoy showing me around a gun. Once we were back in his car, we made out hard, something about the guns and the things we didn't know about each other, did something for me. I never told him I had used a gun before, or that I had a class with Calliope at the end of the week. For the record, Lance never took me shooting again, but he told me guns are dangerous. He told me my pepper spray was outdated, threw it out, and got me a new one.

I didn't tell Seppi about my meetup with the gun lady. He asked why I hadn't been pushing my panic button on Mondays and I told him I was feeling better. To be honest, I'd been pushing it for the wrong reasons and there was enough drama around there without me making any more decisions like there were no consequences. I was perseverating on the fact that Seppi didn't want to spend his life with my sister any more than she wanted to spend her life with him. The fact that she was sleeping in a different room, and hadn't told me yet. Seppi's restaurant was going to be reopening in February, so Seppi was tense and stressed and distant. I felt like everyone in my life was circling their own orbits and everyone was moving away from the sun.

When I woke, I made myself a latte and sat on the sun porch with my flip-top tin. Most times, that was my favorite part of the day but when I got out there, Alex was in the back yard with Lola. I don't know why, but in that moment, I felt the world crashing down around me. I remembered the day I found the hair tie and perfume in Kane's nightstand. I wanted to lock her outside so I could run to his place and make love to him. I wanted to go back to the day when our picture was on his fridge, before I pushed him away. My mind went to the day I laid my eyes on him for the first time. His dark chocolate eyes and dark chocolate voice, all the times he tucked loose curls behind my ear.

"Morning, Amelia!"

I acted like I hadn't seen her. Whore. I matched her energy,

"Hi, Alex!"

She waved at me and I waved at her. I wondered how someone could be that bubbly and I wanted to put my finger down my throat. I assessed Alex long and hard, and realized it wasn't her, it was me. I was the third wheel. She was there first; he was hers first. I realized that's what was happening with Seppi too, I had no place in that equation, either. Lance was probably married and had two beautiful kids back in Jersey. I thought about my ex and his whore and their love child, as they got ready to celebrate baby's first Christmas. I even thought about Richard, the one who did more damage than anyone else, and wondered if he was being better to someone else. I contemplated the state of my life for a little while, the state of my heart and what was inside. I wanted to run away or self-medicate my demons into submission.

Was I destined to one relationship after another where I was the third wheel? The complication? The afterthought? I shifted gears and remembered my aunt's card. I padded back to my bedroom and retrieved the envelope and zipper bag from my nightstand. My eyes landed on the front of the envelope, it was just my name, but Maggie's handwriting made me feel things, and sometimes it brought tears to my eyes. Cards from Maggie were my favorite and I saved every letter or card she ever gave me. I mentally prepared for something sentimental or mushy. Her words had the power to motivate me and make me feel loved. I knew it would be some sort of pep talk about my failed attempt at a fresh start and I knew whatever she had said would make me feel a little better.

> Amelia,
> This was supposed to be your fresh start, and it wasn't. I know you're trying to find yourself and your people. You're safe here and this is your home. I am having the service center remodeled into a community studio space with an apartment on the second floor. Construction will begin shortly, and you are the new owner. Merry Christmas & here's to a better next year.
> Love, Maggie

To say I was on overload would be an understatement. My head was racing as I enabled the caffeine addicts and rang out the rich tourists who snatched up expensive artisan items in the gift shop. I didn't cry in the corner when I saw Kane, but I noticed he seemed sad. I swear that I glanced up from making a Cortado and he was looking at me. Part of me wanted to go to his office and kiss him like I used to, make out with him like we were racing somewhere. But part of me wanted to get in the car and drive away from that place, away from Kane, away from Lance, away from Giuseppi Moretti. I heard the door and took my place behind the counter. In came a worried looking Lance Arnault. I motioned to Kane, who flung a bar rag over his shoulder and rolled his eyes. I rounded the counter and Lance gestured for me to come outside with him, so I did. He gestured for me to lean in, so I did. He spoke quietly.

"I think someone whacked my uncle."

I swallowed the fist of panic in my throat and did my best to pretend. Focus, Amelia, focus. I hugged him for a long time to give myself a while to think. My eyes were tearing up but not for the right reason,

"Oh my God, what happened?"

He shrugged and shook his head and then told me something that gave me bubble-gut,

"I don't know, but I've heard rumblings that he got whacked, maybe it was a professional hit. What if he had big gambling debts and someone killed him?"

Well, that was it, I was screwed. I put my hand on his forearm,

"Listen, you can't just go around believing rumors."

I took a deep breath and counted to eight as I exhaled, in an attempt to slow my pulse, my heart beating in my ears.

"I think you should ask your aunt where he went? I know you said she didn't want you at the house but I'm sure she would understand in this case."

Made sense to me. Sure, Amelia, send Lance Arnault to Mary Moretti's house with a gun on his hip. Smart. But I smelled something fishy, didn't think Lance was going to talk to Mary, and wondered who he was working for. I didn't think he was related to the Morettis. And since I'm a complete lunatic, I kept seeing him. Just to be clear, Lance didn't speak to Mary, Giuseppi, Vincenzo, or anyone else for that matter. That led me to believe he was not who he said he was, and unless I had seen the name on his credit card the day I met him, I wouldn't have believed his name was Lance Arnault.

I was walking a fine line between certain death and finally getting that fresh start I was looking for. It seems dramatic but it's the truth, I was dancing with fire in more ways than one but the Morettis had been whacking people for a hundred years, so what was I worried about? Vinny did his job and did it well. There was no trace of that haggard, leather-faced sixty-year old asshole. Right? Everyone in that family knew what was at stake and those boys knew the rules more absolutely than anyone. But then, who was Lance, what did he want, and why had I gone this long without mentioning it to Seppi?

I met Calliope Cromwell at her bohemian goat farm in the middle of nowhere. She was a spunky fifty-something with a gray pixie cut and turquoise framed glasses, her friends called her Cal. Our first time together was a consultation about my goals and why I wanted to learn about firearms. She had a ton of plants, and stained glass sun-catchers filtered the sun into rainbows as it came through the windows. I filled out applications and signed on dotted lines. There were background check forms and releases. Cal looked at my Sig Sauer and measured me for a belly holster to wear inside of my ratty vintage overalls or under a chunky sweater. At first, the gun would be unloaded so I could get used to the feel of it. And then we would move on to some tactical stuff and target shooting, both stationary and mobile. Over time, she assured me I would be comfortable carrying a gun. I felt a little more in control when I left that day, and I got to pet a really cool rescued goat named Minerva Morganstein.

My next appointment with Isabella Rossi was an emotional roller coaster. I had moved beyond the feeling I did something wrong when I killed Sal, but now I was worried about getting caught. Telling her why I was worried, would mean coming clean about meeting Lance, and I was scared to death she would tell Seppi. After a long silence, she put her pen down and leaned forward,

"Everything you say in here stays between us, everything. You confessed murder and I didn't break your confidence, so I think I've earned your trust. Are you worried I'll run back to Giuseppi if you tell me something salacious or inappropriate?"

I looked at her but didn't say anything.

"You have my word, personally and professionally, that everything you say in here stays between us."

I felt completely safe in that room from that moment on, depending on the day. I knew everything I said would be kept between us so I kicked my shoes off and hugged my knees as I cried. I could go back to the beginning and do it over without hiding any of it. From that moment, I felt different about her, and knew she was on my team. I had never had a team. That intelligent, professional woman respected me, and didn't think I was broken. She gave me a safe place to poke at my demons while I stared out the window at pigeons on roofs. Being honest probably made it easier for her to get inside my head, but it was worth it if it was going to make it easier for me to get out.

CHAPTER 10
VINTAGE VELVET DRESS

I WORKED AT the cafe on the morning of Christmas Eve. Kane presented me with a ribbon-wrapped envelope, I presented him with a confused look and may have rolled my eyes. When I was alone in the storeroom, I opened the envelope to find a twenty-dollar gift card to the food co-op, Kane gave the same thing to all the baristas, it was nothing personal. Some of my regulars gave me big tips and some gave me cards. That day, I felt like I belonged, even if life was zigging and zagging and I was in a perpetual state of upheaval.

I was on my tippy toes putting something away on the high shelf in the storeroom when I felt someone behind me. I spun around and there was no one there. I swore I could feel someone watching me, and thought

I felt someone standing behind me. I peeked around the corner and in every nook and cranny, there was no one there. I shrugged, and when I bounced out of the storeroom, I slammed into Kane's chest. I screamed,

"Jesus!"

He looked at me in a strange way, swinging his rag like he meant business,

"Can we talk in my office?"

I shrugged,

"Sure."

I couldn't wait to see what this was all about. Had someone complained that I hadn't served them with a big enough bullshit smile on my face? Whatever, who cares? I followed Kane through the kitchen and dining room, into his office. He pushed the door closed and sat on the corner of his desk. I took a glass of old water off the desk and poured it into the severely thirsty plant in the window, glancing over my shoulder at him,

"If you're not careful, you're going to kill this plant."

I was anxious and couldn't stand still, Kane gestured for me to sit in his chair. It looked like the weight of the world was on his shoulders. I brought the glass to the bubbler and filled it halfway, sat, and as I was taking a sip, he blurted it out before he lost the courage,

"Did you kill Salvatore Moretti?"

I spit the water onto his desk calendar and screeched,

"What!?"

He said it again, exactly like he said it the first time,

"Did you kill Salvatore Moretti?"

Okay, so I had two choices here, I could be honest, or I could lie. I chose something somewhere in between,

"It's complicated."

He got up and paced, ran a hand through his hair. What the hell was he worried about? And who the hell told him? It was making me anxious that he was anxious,

"Kane, calm down. Of course I didn't kill Salvatore Moretti. Do I look like a cold-blooded killer to you?"

I made my complete disaster of a messy bun dance a little, flashed my dimples and winked at him. Nothing. He didn't even smile. Shit. How did he find out? Well, anyway, that's ridiculous.

"I'm not stupid, Amelia. Things happened fast, and I could see it in your eyes when you came back. I saw it. The light in your eyes was gone, and Giuseppi Moretti was in your apartment. The way he and Opal acted; I knew something happened."

I had an answer that was the truth, and he knew it,

"What happened is, I got shot."

Kane gestured toward my left shoulder and was animated as he spoke,

"By who!?"

"You mean, by whom."

He scoffed and crossed his arms and then it was quiet for a while. Eventually, I mumbled my answer and picked at the skin next to my thumbnail,

"It's complicated."

Kane stood in front of me, his eyes wide as he gasped,

"Amelia!"

I responded in the same tone,

"Kane!"

I was anxious so I started to laugh, but he didn't. He clenched his jaw and seemed disappointed in me. I reached out and touched his hand, I wanted to close the gap between us so I wouldn't have to feel his eyes. He stepped back,

"It's none of my business, forget I said anything."

Kane threw the bar rag over his shoulder and left the room, conversation over. Guts gurgling, palms sweating, I needed to get the hell out of there, pronto. I snagged my things, speed-walked to the mini mafia sedan and five minutes later I was on the highway. I dug around in the back pocket of my purse and pushed the panic button for three seconds. It was three-thirty-seven on Christmas Eve, and I was summoning the all-powerful Giuseppi Moretti from the land of mafia mansions, to the parking lot of a place with a ten-dollar pizza special. I leaned against my car as snow fell and smoked half a joint as diamonds landed in my hair. I was in a deep, dark place, on the verge of a break-down that night.

The most broken and needy parts of me needed to be saved. I was just a little girl in a grown-woman's body, getting high as I waited for my lifeline. And while we're at it, what do you make of the panic button? I'm not gonna lie, it has saved my life on more occasions than I can count, but I guess I'm ashamed of how I used it back then. You know as well as I do that this situation might have warranted a phone call to Seppi, you know, to ease my mind. What it didn't warrant, was pushing the big red plunger, pulling the trap door lever, signaling the Bat Cave. But right then, I didn't care about that, and I desperately needed to be rescued from myself. Mini-vans, SUVs and beat up sedans came in and out of the parking lot, filled with mothers and fathers, couples, and groups of high schoolers. A constant flow of people coming to get their cheap, mediocre, one topping pizza and two-liter bottle of soda. Apparently, nobody wanted to cook on Christmas Eve. The little girl inside of me glanced at the sky, looking for Rudolph.

When the Escalade swung in the lot, I was scrolling through Bongiovanni's menu online, deciding whether or not to order a mediocre one topping pizza for myself. I had the munchies and felt like eating my feelings. I climbed into the passenger seat of the Escalade and jammed my gloves into the cup holder, the scent of him offering up some comfort in the storm. Seppi wordlessly drove to a twenty-four-hour truck-stop diner ten minutes away and I could tell he was annoyed or stressed out. We sat in the back and Seppi faced the door. Once the waitress had poured our coffees, he moved his eyes to mine, waiting. I blurted out,

"Kane asked me if I, you know, your father."

I made a slicing motion across my throat, gnarled up my hands like a zombie, closed my eyes, and stuck my tongue to the side for effect. Seppi made a face like I was wasting his time and grumbled,

"I'll handle it."

He slid out of the booth, and scolded,

"It's Christmas Eve and we're hosting dinner. Give me a fucking break here, what's the matter with you, huh!?"

I made a face and narrowed my eyes as he shrugged into his coat. I was being rejected, which immediately turned me into a petty bitch. Seppi put his hand up to tell the waitress we were leaving. He spoke to me like I was a child, his tone and cadence wrought with exhaustion and overwhelm, pinching the bridge of his nose,

"For Christ's sake, have you ever heard of picking up the goddamn phone?"

He motioned toward the door, reprimanding,

"Get up, we're leaving, this was not an emergency."

Seppi retrieved his wallet, tossed a ten on the table to cover the coffees plus a tip, and swaggered toward the door. He glanced at his watch, the wool trench trailing behind him, snowflakes sticking to his stupid hair. He looked like a fucking douche bag in that coat, and I had a mind to tell him to go fuck himself. What was his problem? I finished the last gulp of my burnt coffee and slid out of the booth, following behind Giuseppi Moretti like a puppy. I couldn't believe I ever thought he cared about me, he didn't seem at all concerned with what I was concerned about. We drove back to Bongiovanni's in silence and Seppi was breathing in a way that made me think he was mad at me. He threw it in park aggressively and waited for me to get out, but I didn't, I wanted to hit rewind and get a re-do. He sighed and glanced over, a little less anger in his voice, a little more reassuring,

"I'll handle it, capiche?"

He gestured toward my door,

"Your sister's waiting."

I didn't even look up at him, I just slithered from the seat and shut the door. There he was, off to the land of mafia mansions and playing house with my pregnant sister, he even spit up a little gravel with his tires, whatever. He took a left out of the parking lot toward home. To Opal. Who didn't want to be with him. Fuck. Lance had gone back home for the holidays, probably to see his wife and kids. Kane was celebrating with Alex's family. Marco was in New Hampshire. I pictured my ex and his whore with their lovechild, in a red onesie that said, 'Baby's 1st Christmas.' I pretended to gag, fuck my life.

I bought a slice of pepperoni pizza and sat in my car, people-watching people with people in their lives. I felt empty and abandoned and guilty. A family came out with their leftovers, and I wondered if they would leave some for Santa. The two little kids were giggling and singing Christmas carols, the father kissed the mother and had his hand on her lower back like he loved her. They buckled the kids into their seats in a regular looking SUV with some rust. His beard needed a trim and her roots needed a touch-up, I watched a happy family who didn't put on airs. And then I watched their taillights leave. I bet that family didn't live in a doll house like I did when I was little. I bet that mom didn't care what the curtains looked like from the outside, as long as her babies were safe. And I bet those kids didn't have a mountain of shame swept under their carpets or a starter set of closet skeletons.

As I was wiping pepperoni grease from my lips with a shitty paper napkin, I didn't have any idea how I'd make it through another Moretti family dinner. All the loud Italian voices, fancy linens and expensive liquor. My world was spinning out of control, and I felt like I was going to lose my mind. The guilt was winning, the fear was winning, the self-doubt and second-guessing was winning. Seppi was busy worrying about whatever he was worrying about, but he wasn't worried about what I was worried about. I sat there for another fifteen minutes, watching people who had people in their lives. A high school-aged couple pulled up in a rusty sedan. The boy was a jock, good-looking and he opened the car door for the girl. She was athletic-looking and had shiny hair, I bet she smelled like something from Bath & Body Works. She was wearing skinny jeans, Uggs, and the boy's letter jacket.

I remembered a time when I was young and went to ten-dollar pizza special places on dates. Back then, I had my entire life ahead of me, and I could be whatever I wanted. That broken little bitch could have been anything she wanted. Yet, here I was, satiating the munchies with cheese, grease, and processed meat, alone on Christmas Eve. Perfect. And in the end, I was just some broken, loveless, worthless, rejected, shamed, shushed, killer. I brushed cobwebs from the mask I'd been trying to destroy, a mask that felt like a trash bag when I pulled it over my head. Just this broken woman who had filing cabinets in the back of her mind, filled with stuff she didn't want to think about. I almost didn't go to dinner in mafia mansion land that night, I almost told Opal I had the creeping craps and wouldn't be able to make it, for fear of shitting myself at the dinner table.

While I was in the shower, I contemplated leaving town to start over somewhere else, ready to run away from my new life, but that time I didn't act on the impulse. I tamped that shit down with whiskey, weed, and grocery store Moscato. I finished all the things I had to finish before loading the mini mafia sedan. I prayed my parents' car wasn't in the driveway when I got to Seppi's. If it was, I would go home and tell everyone I had the shits. But then I'd get high and eat an entire frozen lasagna and a pint of Ben & Jerry's. I didn't have it in me to deal with my mother or her bullshit. And anyway, Giuseppi Moretti didn't have boxed chardonnay with a spigot in his climate-controlled wine cellar.

I worked curl cream through my hair and brought my ringlets to life. I did my makeup, including the winged eyeliner, mascara, and lipstick. I pulled on tights and zipped myself into a dark green vintage velvet dress before spritzing on some Alien Elixir. Off I went with my rolls, pies, and charcuterie board. I stopped at the booth and handed Gary a basket of homemade Christmas cookies, he leaned out the window to retrieve them, getting a little misty,

"Thank you, Amelia! My boys are going to love these!"

I smiled and winked,

"Make sure you save some for Santa!"

Gary smiled with his eyes and that made me happy, deep inside. I made my way up the winding drive to Seppi's house, and my parents' car wasn't there, so I stayed. I managed to get everything inside in one trip and let myself in. I hung my coat, and put my Uggs on the mat next to the door. I caught my reflection in the mirror and admired my beaded earrings, they pulled everything together and peeked out through my curls.

Opal was talking to herself in the kitchen, so I went in and put my contributions on the counter. She was buzzing around, going through a mental checklist. She was five months pregnant and glowing, even if she was frazzled and looked exhausted. I kissed her on the cheek before unpacking rolls, and pies, and the stuff for the fancy charcuterie board. I folded my bags and put them by the door, looping through the hall so I could glance in Seppi's office, it was dark and I was a little disappointed.

I helped Opal set the table and put the charcuterie board together, we made a fancy display of gourmet finger foods. Even though she had access to an actual wine cellar, she retrieved a bottle of Barefoot Moscato from the fridge, I didn't even need a corkscrew. I cracked the cap and tossed it to the counter, pouring cheap wine into an expensive glass over perfectly square ice cubes. I was working on my second glass and had an edible or two on board. We danced and snacked on well-aged cheddar, fancy olives, and uncured local pepperoni. My cheeks flushed from the wine as I let go of the day. I left behind the conversation with Kane, and the reprimand from Seppi. I was letting go of the tension and the weight of the world, I was trying to be okay that I was alone, I was safe, and I was going to have one hell of a dinner.

I was leaning against the counter when Seppi made his way down the back stairs, fresh shave, hair damp from a shower. I glanced up, and things seemed to move in slow motion. He dropped his loafers on the kitchen floor and worked a black leather belt through the loops of his expensive tailored pants. Seppi came around the island and put his hands on my shoulders. He kissed me on both cheeks and didn't seem mad anymore. I took in the scent of him during that moment of closeness, nothing but the scent of clean skin and Tobacco Vanille, it did something to my insides. He flicked an eyebrow,

"You clean up nice."

Jesus.

He winked and adrenaline exploded through my veins as I swallowed the nerves in my throat,

"You're not too shabby yourself."

Seppi touched my forearm and slid his fingers across the inside of my wrist as he walked away, sending electricity to unmentionable places. He moved to my sister and kissed her on top of the head, it was obvious they were going through the motions,

"Go shower, I got this."

Opal untied her apron and gave me a wave before she disappeared up the stairs. I heard her in the room above the kitchen, and not in the master bath. Once the shower was running, Seppi told me he 'took care of things' with Kane. I chose to believe him because I had a buzz, and was a little high, and liked that we were alone together. I put the rolls in the oven, set the timer, and followed Seppi to his office. He poured whiskies and brought one of them to me.

When I took it from him, he clinked his glass against mine like it was no big deal,

"Cheers, Dimples."

I mumbled, tripping over my tongue,

"Umm, cheers."

I imagined we were the only ones in the mafia mansion. Things were complicated, I'm not gonna lie, that entire situation was a mess. The two of us had a deep connection like I'd never had with anyone before, and I trusted him with my life. And while that was freeing, it was also a turn on that someone cared enough to protect me, my own mother didn't do that. To this day, I think Seppi likes that I'm a loose cannon, a grenade without a pin, a sassy, dimpled mess, if you will. But right then, it was like Russian roulette, it was like betting it all, an exquisite dance of feelings and thoughts, and sometimes the electricity was palpable.

He drained his glass and left it on the bar before eyeing a shelf of vintage vinyl. He slid a record from its sleeve and situated it on a beautiful antique record player. He plucked the glass from my fingers, sat it next to his, and put his hand out to me so we could dance as the rolls baked in the oven. Seppi hummed along as Frank Sinatra sang about the way someone looked tonight and I blushed. I, in my fancy vintage velvet dress, and Seppi, in his mob boss aesthetic, top buttons open, gold chain, sleeves rolled up a couple times. Our bodies touched as we danced, and I felt like a queen. My right hand in his, his other hand on my lower back, I was in heaven as I followed his lead and I guess nothing has changed. Our eyes met as we danced, I was content and safe, and every bad thing in my head was locked away in its filing cabinet. Seppi leaned in, softly,

"It's nice to see you happy."

His eyes fell to my lips,

"You have a beautiful smile."

I wanted to remember that moment for the rest of my life, the moment Giuseppi Moretti told me I had a beautiful smile. I wondered what my narcissistic ex would think about that, as he strung along yet another broken little girl in a woman's body, desperate to maintain control. There was another shift between me and Seppi that night, and it started when I pressed my panic button. A month earlier, I was pushing it because I needed to know for sure I had a safety net, someone to pull me from my pit of despair before I got sucked under by the weight of my emotional baggage. But lately, it was something different than that, even though I didn't realize it at the time. I don't know, maybe it was the dress and the extra layer of mascara, but I felt like a woman that night, and maybe he could tell. I didn't say anything, what was there to say? He broke the silence,

"No one else in my life smiles with their eyes. But you? You smile with your whole damn face."

When the song ended, he hooked my chin with his finger and tilted my face up to his, emotional and intimate,

"I know you think you're just a bunch of broken pieces, but that's not what I see when I look at you."

I stopped breathing and time stood still as Frank Sinatra sang about having someone under his skin. Miles from that ten dollar one-topping pizza special place, my vintage velvet dress swaying at my sides as I followed his lead. Seppi firmed his grip on me and our bodies touched in the middle. I had only pushed the panic button that afternoon because I knew he would come running. And even though I never put Seppi on a pedestal the way everyone else does, this wasn't about that. Aside from the money, the power and the mob boss aesthetic. Aside from the guns, the cars and the well-aged whiskey. I didn't care about any of that, I cared about how I felt when I was with him.

Even if he was stripped of his status, just some guy with salt and pepper stubble and a second-hand t-shirt about fishing, I just wanted to share space with Giuseppi Moretti. He was my safe place, and right then, we were the only two people on earth. I think that was the first time I wondered if I would ever be anything more than some wounded bird he took under his wing. I closed my eyes and let the whiskey carry me away in his arms. And at that point, it was easily the most intimate moment I had ever experienced. The people I had slept with had never even made me feel like that. The side of my face against his chest, I wasn't strong enough to look him in the eye, for fear of some glimmer of disapproval,

"Thank you for rescuing me from myself."

I paused, but had more to say, choking on my words,

"I don't know what I would do without you."

Tears came, but I held them back the best I could,

"I have unconditional access to you and I abused that privilege today, I won't do it again. I'm just really struggling right now and you're the only one who makes me feel better."

Our eyes met, and my insides ignited. Seppi cupped the left side of my face in his palm and ran his thumb over my dimple,

"I'll come whenever you need me."

From such a powerful man with so many responsibilities, I was deeply honored to be one of them. Our foreheads met and my eyes closed as we swayed. I imagined kissing him and could feel the heat from his breath on my lips when the timer went off.

CHAPTER 11
JOLLIEST BUNCH OF ASSHOLES

OPAL WAS BACK in the kitchen in an adorable red dress with a black sash tied under her boobs, she looked a little like if Mrs. Santa Clause was a pregnant hippie chick. Sunny and Vincenzo, Opal and Seppi, Mary Moretti and I, sat down for a Christmas Eve feast. To say that I was both high and drunk at that point would be an understatement. I finished off the bottle of Moscato, three shots of whiskey, and three edibles. I was sitting at the opposite end of the table from Giuseppi Moretti with a girl boner and wet pants, more than a buzz, more than a little high. He told me I had a beautiful smile, and I wasn't just a bunch of broken pieces. In the middle of dinner, I stood, picked up my glass, and clinked it with my spoon. Imagine this entire train-wreck in an extremely slurred drunk-girl voice,

"Cheers, everybody cheers, this calls for a toast."

Opal gave me the hairy eyeball from the other end of the table. And then Seppi did the same thing and I made a face of self-assuredness as I shook my head,

"You guys..."

I drunkenly pointed between my sister and Seppi. Sunny tugged on my dress and gestured to cut it off and sit the fuck down. She whispered, "Don't do it." I swatted her hand away and smoothed my dress like a lady,

"You two...man...what were the chances?"

Sunny kicked my foot under the table and everyone else was holding their breath, I pointed at my sister again,

"I mean you came into town in the midst of your whirlwind hot girl summer free-spirit trip cross-country."

Opal looked pissed, but I ignored it, she was just jealous she couldn't drink that Christmas. I pointed at Seppi and raised my eyebrow at him,

"And you, Mr. Mob Boss..."

Seppi stood. I'm not sure what the hell he thought he was going to do about it but he sprang into action. Everyone at that table was watching a slow motion train wreck and I couldn't leave my audience waiting. I continued to point in Seppi's general direction,

"And you..."

Luckily, that's when I projectile vomited greasy pepperoni pizza, a bottle of Moscato, three shots of whiskey, and whatever the fuck I ate. No idea, but it smelled horrible, probably some sort of expensive aged cheese. That in turn caused my sister to throw up which then caused Vincenzo to gag. You know, just a good old-fashioned Christmas down on the farm. So, after my obnoxious drunk girl toast, or whatever you want to call, whatever the fuck that was, my pissed off sister took me to her bathroom over the kitchen, not the one in the master bath. Opal sat on the lid of the toilet as I dried off, her presence less angry and more maternal,

"This time of year, gets me too, I get it."

She came over and kissed me on the cheek before tossing me a pair of Seppi's sweatpants and a UVM t-shirt. I rolled the waistband over a couple times, pulled on the t-shirt and pawed around in Opal's underwear drawer for a pair of socks. She sat on the end of the bed and I sat next to her. She said,

"Listen, I get it, but you need to try to hold it together."

I acted as if she had offended me, but she was right, I was off the rails and I knew it. What had I planned to do if I hadn't been silenced by the projectile vomiting? Would I have told the world that I'm confused, and lonely, and broken, and that Giuseppi Moretti was the only one who makes it better? Doubtful. But was I thanking my lucky stars that the big bottle of Moscato didn't agree with me? Absolutely. I made the walk of shame down the stairs and the mess had been picked up. Luckily, the puke stayed on the table, and that's where thick expensive table linens are a saving grace. That should be in the advertisement, absorbs a ton of regurgitated alcohol! A stack of white dessert plates and an expensive looking silver pie server joined the fresh table linens. It was as if what I had done had been erased, just like when I killed Salvatore Moretti.

Opal lit my favorite Christmas candle, and Seppi delivered a steaming mug of tea to the breakfast nook. He kissed the top of my head, jogged up the back stairs and came back down with a Giuseppi's Italian Ristorante hoodie. He passed through the kitchen on his way to eat pie,

"Dimples."

I glanced over at him, still mortified. Seppi winked and gently tossed the hoodie in my direction,

"Catch."

So, I did.

Seppi disappeared into the dining room to eat pie and I held the sweatshirt to my nose. It smelled like him. I squeaked out loud before burying my nose into the neck of the hoodie. Oh my God. And just so you know, I never gave it back, I still have it, over a decade later. I think it was the best thing I got that Christmas, the thing I cherished the most. That was the first night I slept with a part of him, but it wasn't the last. Most nights, I slept with that hoodie next to my pillow. When I was scared, I'd hug it like a teddy bear. Sometimes, I'd cry myself to sleep while Seppi's hoodie held all my broken pieces together.

I drank half the tea then rummaged through the cupboards, and finished it while devouring most of a box of Westminster crackers. When Sunny, Vincenzo and Mary left, I was curled up on the gigantic leather sofa in the living room, under the most amazing blanket I've ever felt. I could see the Christmas tree in the yard and the taillights as people left. When everyone was gone, Opal cuddled up next to me in my little cocoon of expensive luxury blanket. We held each other, looked at the tree and didn't talk about the fact that we were both thinking about our mother and what a complete shit show Christmases always were.

In that moment, I was grateful for my life in Bunman. I hoped my sister wouldn't run too far away when she left. Sometimes, I'd see Opal daydreaming and I knew she was imagining the open road or having her toes in the water. I was grateful for Seppi, and knew there was no one else like him. I didn't allow myself to think about anything else, I kept it kosher, above board, kid friendly. I thought about Lance and even though he was around to find Sal, I had just enough faith in Vincenzo that I wasn't worried. Everyone who knew I killed Sal was in my inner circle, and quite honestly, had more to lose than I did. So, if I kept playing it like I was playing it, everything would remain cool. I was grateful I could see Sunny a couple times a week and sometimes we'd run into each other at the grocery store.

Things weren't so bad. I had a good job at Muddy Waters, I had a shit load of rental income in comparison to my bills. I was in therapy and was going to learn how to use a gun. Come spring, I'd have a community studio space and an apartment to make my own if I wanted to. I had a Giuseppi Moretti panic button. I had a narcissistic ex, an ex with a whore and a lovechild, and a sometimes ex who lived across the hall with his pretty blonde girlfriend. I realized the depth of my feelings for, and dependence on, Seppi was going to become a problem. I fell asleep with my head on Opal's shoulder that night and woke up alone as the sun came up. Merry Christmas. The tree was unplugged, party-poopers.

After making a latte for myself and a cup of tea for Opal, I brought the mugs upstairs on a fancy tray. Opal's room was flooded with sunlight, and I was surprised she was still asleep. I placed the tray on her nightstand and crawled into bed next to her. I spooned her and she put my hand on my little niece or nephew. The baby kicked and I was flooded with emotions as I fully realized we can create life. Every being on this planet, every mouse, bug and bear, everyone is somebody's baby. And two people, two tiny pieces of two people, come together to create life. A beautiful, precious life. Maybe that day would be a new beginning. Opal fell back to sleep so I took my latte and followed the smells of bacon, eggs and home fries with sauteed onions. I padded down the stairs in sweatpants and the Giuseppi's Italian Ristorante hoodie and hopped up on a stool. Seppi came over and kissed the top of my head. He kept his lips there and my crazy morning curls got caught up in his stubble,

"Merry Christmas, Dimples, I hope Santa was good to you."

I closed my eyes and breathed in the scent of him. It didn't matter if I opened a single present that year, I hadn't even eaten breakfast yet and it was the best Christmas I'd ever had,

"Merry Christmas, Seppi."

He winked and retreated to the world of bacon flipping and making cinnamon buns from scratch in his pajama pants like it's no big deal. My eyes followed his ass back to the stove and my attention was pulled away when Opal bounced down the stairs and kissed me on the cheek. I patted her belly, and she moved over to Seppi and kissed him on the cheek. He handed her the bottle of Tylenol and she brought it over to me with a glass of water. I felt like shit and was still mortified about puking on the table. I abstained from substances that day to prevent any more bad decisions.

That was the year I was in Seppi's sweats in all the Christmas pictures. It was affectionately referred to as 'the Christmas Amelia puked on the table.' I wasn't even wearing underwear. Fancy. I sat on a leather sofa with a latte, under that heavenly blanket, with my skin 'down there' touching the inside of Giuseppi Moretti's sweatpants. The same crew gathered, and I observed as they exchange gifts. Opal was bashing against the bars of her cage; it wouldn't be long until she broke free. I had tears in my eyes when it was my turn to open a present.

The rest of the day I went through the motions. I knew without any words that Opal was leaving. I tried to freeze time, burn the day into my brain for when she was parked at the ocean in her van. Part of me was happy and the other part was sad. If Opal left, that baby wouldn't have to be a part of the bullshit. It wouldn't be as easy as that, but I pictured her walking with her baby. Taking its first steps on a beach somewhere warm while holding her fingers. A wave of panic crashed down around me, it wouldn't be as easy as all of that. If that baby was a boy, there was going to be a problem. Boys in a mafia family are born into the mob, born into the power and the protection. Boys in the mob come out of the womb commanding respect and authority. A little baby with Italian eyebrows and a pompadour, that comes into this world blessed, or doomed, to be a mobster.

When we'd finished lunch, I cornered Vinny in the dining room,

"Hey!"

He went palms up, like I was wasting his time,

"What?"

I leaned in and flicked my eyebrows at him,

"Where did you put him?"

He scrunched up his face and moved half a chewed-up cookie into his cheek,

"Who!?"

I made a smashing a skull with a shovel motion, and then went palms up,

"You know, where did you put him?"

Vinny waved me away,

"I took care of it, stop worrying about it, I know what I'm doing."

I leaned in a little more, but I'm not sure why, none of this was a secret to anyone in that house,

"Kane asked me if I killed him, and I told him no, so I'd like to be sure his dented ass doesn't contaminate a well or stink up a landfill. Where the fuck did you put him!?"

Vinny popped the rest of the cookie into his mouth, casually, and put his hand up in a 'chill, everything is cool' kind of way. I pinched the bridge of my nose and turned to walk away,

"Whatever."

He responded,

"Alright, I'm sorry, wait."

I spun around and stood there with my hands on my hips, staring up at him. With a weed-addled nonchalance that infuriated me, Vincenzo Moretti took a drag from an invisible cigar, blew out invisible smoke, and did something nasally and ridiculous with his voice,

"He's schwimmin' with the fishes, schweetheart. Capiche?"

Vinny winked and walked away.

That was the entire exchange. He went into the other room to drink alcohol and eat more of his mother's cookies. The rest of the day was normal, for a girl who was naked inside of Giuseppi Moretti's sweatpants.

All day, Opal was being secretive with her phone. Before dinner, I helped her set the table, and we made a gigantic Italian salad. She seemed happier, lighter, like she had a plan. The doorbell rang and she hollered that she'd get it. Her phone lit up and I glanced down to see who it was. The preview of the message was from someone named Auggie. Something about that name was familiar but I couldn't put my finger on it. I slid onto the deck an joined Seppi and Vincenzo as they tended to the brick oven. The two of them sipped whiskey, Seppi puffed on a cigar and Vinny smoked a cigarette. I sipped my bubbly water.

I cold see through the windows that Opal returned to the kitchen with Mary's father, Nunzio Russo, and his much younger girlfriend, Lucy. The more the merrier, and since I wasn't shit faced or baked, it was going to be a nice dinner. And for the record, Nunzio Russo is a hoot and a half, Mary is an apple who didn't fall too far from the tree. It felt intimate to be that close to the Morettis. I was sitting at a table with Giuseppi, Vincenzo and Mary Moretti, and her father, Nunzio Russo. It felt surreal, or like a scene out of an episode of The Sopranos. Seppi rose at the head of the table and gestured with his wine glass,

"Grab your glasses everyone, I want to say a toast."

Everyone else grabbed their red wine and I grabbed my bottle of fancy bottle of bubbly water.

"Thank you all for coming."

Seppi went around the table and said something nice about everyone, including Lucy. And then he got to me.

"Last but not least."

Without the alcohol or the marijuana, I couldn't run away from my feelings. Our eyes met and he gestured with his glass in my direction,

"To my best friend. Salute!"

Everyone said, "Salute" and drank their wine. I sipped my bubbly water and stared at him, holding my breath for some reason. No one batted an eyelash about what he said, that I was his best friend. He caught my eye for a split second and then just went about his business like it was no big deal. Stone cold sober, I was almost able to keep the tears in their bottles. Almost. I excused myself and hid in the bathroom so I could cry. I should have known then that I loved him, but I didn't. I sat on the lid and soaked the sleeve of that hoodie. I returned as Grandpa Russo was saying he'd be in Italy on opening night. He presented Seppi with a pair of cuff links he inherited from his own grandfather,

"Wear these on opening night, I will be with you in spirit, my boy."

Nunzio hugged Seppi and kissed him on both cheeks,

"Ti amo, Bambino."

Seppi gazed up at Nunzio, two men with pinky rings and gold chains. I pictured Seppi as a child, beaming up at Nunzio,

"Ti amo, Nonno."

That one hit me in the feels.

It was upsetting to me in a backward way that families could be like that. Generations of people could love each other. People who had done bad things, stupid things, things they regretted, and none of it came up at the dinner table. And even if there were bodies everywhere, there weren't any lumps under the their carpet. I served pies, cakes and cream puffs. I refilled glasses while I drank my bubbly water. I refilled Seppi's wine and he casually winked at me before returning to a conversation with his Nonno. I curled up on the couch in front of the fireplace, with a cup of gourmet hot chocolate and the expensive blanket I liked so much. And that was the way I ended my first Christmas with the Moretti family.

CHAPTER 12
CLARITY

I MADE MY WAY HOME, got into the Pajamagram onesie my sister gifted me, and settled onto the couch with one of Maggie's joints. It had been a strange couple days and my mind was on overload. Then, somewhere during the high, I remembered who Auggie was. I sprung off the couch and tripped toward the closet, my feet tangled up in the quilt. I slammed against the wall and scurried down the hall. A couple lidded plastic totes of Opal's personal belongings were neatly stacked inside the closet door. I pulled on my Sherlock Holmes hat, and after a miss, I hit the jackpot. There were receipts, pictures, movie stubs and all that other nonsense people keep for no good reason. Stuff that just collects dust in a closet until it gets thrown out after we die.

I dug out a stack of pictures and traveled down memory lane. Ninth grade slumber party, fifteenth birthday, school dance, license day, first car, prom. And then I found what I was looking for, a stack of old pictures tied with twine. I undid the twine and turned over the top picture. It said, 'I love you, Ope.' There was a heart, and then it said, 'Auggie.' I sifted through the pile and grabbed Opal's senior yearbook from Roundelay High School, scanning the pages for Auggie's picture amongst all the other nonsense.

Under August Sage Ricard's senior picture were his future plans: Attend UVM, hike the Long Trail, work at his uncle's farm-to-table restaurant and market in Cortland, Vermont. I flipped to the back pages where people signed their names or left obnoxious notes about inside jokes. There, on a half-page written in high school boy handwriting, was a proclamation of love from August, more affectionately known as Auggie. He wrote about how they'd live in a converted van and travel to all the national parks, save dolphins and turtles and bees. They could put their toes in every ocean and leave footprints on every beach. Why had I thought she'd ever be content with Giuseppi Moretti?

I discarded the book and Googled farm to table restaurants in the area. On my third try, I found it, Ricard's Eco-Eats, locations in Cortland, Burlington, and Maple Grove. I went to the Facebook page and looked at any picture that had a person in it. Found the guy, same guy as in the old pictures. I navigated to his personal page and scrolled back to the previous summer like a stalker. There it was, a picture of Opal and Auggie at a lake, all over each other, holding sparklers while the moon glistened off the ripples in the water. I zoomed in and took a good look at Opal, there was a calm contentedness in her eyes, one I hadn't seen since her arrival in Bunman, and she was beaming up at him.

It made me sick to my stomach when I realized her life had quickly turned into the opposite of what I saw in that picture. I scrolled back to the present, and while there hadn't been anything for a long time, Opal had reconnected with Auggie for a week or two before she came to Bunman. All of a sudden, her pregnancy made more sense, and she'd said the timing couldn't be worse. Was I groping at nothing or was I on to something? I wondered if she knew something I didn't, and maybe that's why she was halfway out the door the entire time. I snapped the lids on the totes and pushed them back into the closet. I returned to the couch and asked my sister if she wanted to go to lunch the next day. She replied almost immediately, 'Sure.' So, Opal had reunited with her high school sweetheart, and by the way she was looking at him in one of the pictures, I knew they had slept together. There was a chance that kid wasn't Seppi's.

I worked a three-hour rush shift at the cafe the next morning. Then I showered and brought my curls to life before prettying myself up. At my closet, in my bra and panties, I pulled on a pair of skinny jeans and a slouchy brown cable knit sweater before slipping into my Uggs. Lip stick, earrings, Alien Elixir. I was out the door to pick Opal up with a brick in my gut, what if the baby wasn't Seppi's? What if Opal was free to live the way she wanted, with that little life she created? What if it was okay that I wanted to kiss Seppi? I waved at Opal as she bounced down the steps to my car. Seppi waved from the door and I waved back before he closed it. I wondered when Opal would tell Seppi the baby might not be his and I wondered how he would feel about it. She was quiet as I drove, and I could see her wiping tears out of the corner of my eye. I took the highway and drove until we got to the ocean.

Opal sat her pregnant ass in that heated seat and sobbed. I held her hand and sat with her as she cried. She was thinking and feeling and processing and making decisions. It was cold but we got out and walked on the beach, sat on a bench and watched the winter waves. The ocean air unlocked something inside of her and before we made our way back to the car, she unloaded,

"I was coming to see you and Maggie, so I reached out to some old friends who ended up in Vermont for one reason or another. One of my college roommates asked if I planned to see Auggie. I had forgotten he stayed here after college. So, I sent him a message on Facebook and he replied. We met for coffee and that turned into spending time together. For two weeks, we sat with our feet in the water, sharing good weed, talking about life, making love in my van."

She paused,

"We were careful but one of them broke."

Opal looked out the window like when I stare at pigeons on roofs. She brought her eyes back to mine,

"He's the one that got away, Amelia, my first love. Auggie and I share the same dreams and have some of the same broken pieces, his family is a mess too. When he left Roundelay for college, I was devastated. He'd come home occasionally and I thought maybe we had a chance. But at that age, distance seems far and time seems slow."

I knew what she meant. I remembered who she was talking about. He was the kid who would come over to watch scary movies or read with her or go out into the woods and chant with her. August Ricard was the male version of my sister. Seppi gave her a pretentious Volvo XC90 and a meaningless tennis bracelet. Auggie would probably make her a present out of sticks and leaves he collected in the forest. I propped my chin up on my hand and gave her my undivided attention.

"Without the distance between us, it was like we were kids again. We kissed for hours and everything felt right. I'd forgotten how Auggie's hand felt in mine."

She glanced at her hand,

"They fit together perfectly, even now that we're grown."

She waved it away,

"Auggie was leaving for Colorado to help on his brother's ranch for a while, but the two of us had some time together. I was going to be traveling and he was leaving, so we didn't commit to a relationship. I got to Bunman, and before long, I found out I was pregnant."

I was on the edge of my seat.

"There's a chance this baby is Auggie's. Actually, I'm sure of it, and the entire thing has been a mind fuck."

She paused,

"If Seppi took the time to look at a fucking calendar, he'd know the baby isn't his. We didn't even do it until a week before I found out I was pregnant. It just happened so fast. I was scared to raise a baby alone in my van and I made some hasty decisions."

I pictured a grown up version of the gangly pimple-faced dweeb she dated in high school and did a side-by-side comparison in my mind. That baby either belonged to a tall dirty blonde with dreads and freckles; or to a stocky Italian man with black lashes, a dark pompadour, black-brown eyes and dark mafia energy. I put my hand on hers as I computed and tallied and made sense of things. I lied,

"Everything will be okay."

Opal nodded, but I could see she felt trapped. We started our journey back home and stopped for pancakes at a hole in the wall diner that felt like we'd gone back in time.

"Auggie and I decided not to make any promises or guarantees about a relationship. I told him, maybe I would find my way to Colorado and we could meet up again. It was casual but comfortable and we felt our old feelings again. There's something there. With him, things were always safe and gentle, and we understand each other."

I nodded. She continued,

"I got here and started spending time with Giuseppi. To me, it was just some no strings attached fling, nothing serious. It's more like companionship than anything, we don't have sexual chemistry or some deep emotional connection. For months, I'd been living in my van, taking showers at Planet Fitness, my entire life contained to that compact metal box. It felt claustrophobic and made me panic a little that my entire life boiled down to that. If my van caught on fire or got stolen, I'd lose everything I own. That's a daunting reality, especially with a kid."

She caught her breath and I thought she was done, but she wasn't,

"At first, seeing Seppi's house excited me, so much space, I could fit a hundred vans in that place, just so much wide-open space. Everything is nice, all the comforts of home and then some. I can take long baths and hide away by myself in the guest house, reading or just isolating from the world. But then it was those cars, those boats, those diamonds, and I knew I'd made a mistake. I don't have anything in common with him, I don't care about any of those things, and you know it. I appreciate him, and I appreciate all he's done for me, but you know as well as I do that isn't my life. When Seppi wasn't home one day, I called Auggie, and we talked for hours. It didn't scare Auggie away, he said everything happens for a reason and he knew there would be a sign. I'm going to take a test so we know for sure. But Auggie's coming back to Vermont pretty soon and if the baby's his, we're gonna get back together."

I was listening, but I was also thinking how Seppi would be heartbroken if that kid wasn't his. My sister wouldn't put down roots in a place with so many bad memories, and Seppi didn't love her any more than she loved him. But finding out he was having a baby was the whole reason he got serious about getting rid of his father in the first place. Seppi's feelings for Opal were different than his feelings for me, and not in a good way. Seppi's feelings for me would have caught up with us eventually.

For everyone's sake, I hoped that kid wasn't a Moretti. There was no way it would go well, especially if she popped out the future head of the Moretti mob family. Opal is 'make peace not war.' She's 'do hugs not drugs,' well minus the weed, you don't count the weed. She's all 'protect the bees and save the trees.' She's not baby-momma material for the patriarch of the Moretti mob family. As much as I'd been praying the kid wasn't his, it still broke my heart a little.

I was conflicted deep down inside; the situation was a double-edged sword. You're probably thinking I was relieved since now I'd be able to feel however I wanted for Seppi. Here's the thing, someone like Giuseppi Moretti would never want to be with someone like me. It seemed more logical that Seppi had been protecting me so Opal wouldn't leave. Seppi dropped everything to rescue me, more times than I can count. And, most of the time, I was having what amounted to a panic attack, and wasn't in some sort of life-or-death situation.

Things were spicing up around there and I was feeling a little left out of all the major life decisions being made by the people around me. So, I waited. Opal was emotionally checked out by New Years and a week later, she had one foot out the door. Seppi's restaurant was in the process of its reconstruction and he was preoccupied with menus, seating, and paint colors. He had his own shit to worry about. Opal said it was only a matter of time before she'd know if the baby was Seppi's. The entire situation took all the emotional energy I would have used to deal with my own shit.

Before long, Opal and Seppi went away for the weekend and it gave me a sense of panic. That's when she would tell him. Opal didn't like to crap on her own doorstep, she didn't want to sniff her own dirty laundry. She wanted neutral ground. And so, they drove off into the sunset. I knew what was going to happen and it made me sick. I wasn't thinking with the part of my heart that wanted him, or the part that had wished all along the baby wasn't his. I curled into a ball and sobbed into a pillow because Giuseppi Moretti was driving far away to get his heart broken, and it just about killed me.

Before I went lights out for the night, I sent my sister a heart and sent Seppi, 'Be safe.' I couldn't bring myself to say, 'have fun,' because he wasn't going to have fun, he was going to have his heart ripped out. Having a baby had created this deep, personal epiphany for Seppi, a sense of purpose that he could be all the things his father wasn't. My strong, intimidating protector, my second-best friend in the whole world, was going to be reduced to rubble, and there wasn't anything I could do about it.

CHAPTER 13
GOING THROUGH THE MOTIONS

THAT MONDAY, I worked at Muddy Waters and didn't even change between work and therapy. Whatever. I got to the impressive office building of Isabella Rossi and smoked half a joint in the parking lot before going inside. I rode the stupid elevator to the luxury office in the sky, checked in with Elaine, sat on the couch and fingered the stupid magazines about home decor, haute cuisine and trips to exotic places. I picked at something crusty on my jeans and there were grease spots on the black Muddy Waters T-shirt. What was the point of the fucking apron? Dr. Rossi opened the door and we made eye contact briefly as I passed her in the doorway. I went to the overstuffed chair and she situated herself, adjusting the notebook and pen.

I sat there quiet but my mind was screaming. Stoic on the outside, my mind raced, my demons close at my heels. Dr. Rossi crossed her legs and put her hands in her lap. She waited. I appreciated the silence but began to feel wildly uncomfortable, like I should be saying something. Eventually, the discomfort of the silence was more than I could bare, I met her eyes,

"I'm not great."

She thought that was a good time to say,

"If you feel like you're drowning, we can discuss medications again."

I clenched my jaw and she said,

"It's not forever, Amelia, just to get you through if you need it."

I shrugged and picked at a loose thread on the hem of my shirt,

"They make me fat."

She waited for more but at that point, I wasn't willing to give in. I was a respectable size twelve, a ten on good days, and I'd been there before, those pills would make me gain thirty pounds. My anxiety and depression would be better but I'd feel like shit about my body, and my ratty vintage overalls wouldn't fit anymore. It isn't lost on me that I was drowning and someone was throwing me a life line. I was too stupid to accept, I was too worried about gaining a couple pounds, too worried about being a failure at therapy. I sniffled to myself but she was right there so she obviously saw it, even if I didn't look at her.

I entertained the bliss of a clear mind and a nervous system that wasn't in fight or flight mode twenty-four seven. I couldn't imagine, it had been so long. It would be like a vacation from myself, in the wise words of Bob Wiley, a 'vacation from my problems.' Dr. Rossi observed me like her subject but I guess that was her job, and she knew enough not to push it. I said,

"Everyone in my life is orbiting away from me and I can't do anything about it. I feel claustrophobic when the people around me fain concern, and I feel abandoned when they're busy with their own shit."

She said,

"I'm sure the people in your life are concerned because they see you struggling, not out of some obligation."

I clenched my jaw, disregarding that she had said anything,

"I don't know what you write with that fancy pen on that pad of yours, but I'm all over the place. I'm surprised you haven't sent me away."

I shook my head at myself,

"When I started coming here, I'd pretend to have my shit together, hell, I'd agonize over choosing the right outfit. And now? I'm sitting here with my hair a frantic mess and there's a grease spot on my jeans."

I yanked at the front of my shirt aggressively and threw my hands up,

"Coming here with the same clothes I wore to work."

I picked at the crusty spot,

"I have no idea what this is."

I gestured at my hair, even though it had looked like that a million times, made a mental note to get a six inches cut off,

"And what the fuck is this?"

I pinched the bridge of my nose and shook my head at myself,

"I'm a fucking disaster."

Isabella reined me in,

"I'm not concerned with what you're wearing. You feel deserted by the people you love. Do you think that's causing these thoughts?"

I stared at my lap then looked up at her, our eyes connecting. Something told me she was safe and wouldn't tell Seppi I had feelings for him, or that I'd been messing with Lance. I fidgeted a little before I started, it felt like I was inside and outside of my body at the same time. Feelings smashed together in there, pendulums swung, and I had so many feelings at once.

"I'm not sure which thing is causing which feelings, but I'm feeling a lot of things and I don't like it."

She uncrossed her legs and leaned forward,

"If you could pick the thing that's taking up the biggest amount of your mental energy, what would it be?"

I considered keeping it to myself but I was about to explode. I imagined my body splitting at the seams from the pressure of the trauma, gobs of innards dripping from the light fixture above my head. If I said it out loud then the world would know about my stupid feelings for Giuseppi Moretti. But, if I was going to tell anyone, it would be Dr. Rossi. On the other hand, what good would it do to say it out loud? It would just make the whole thing worse, wouldn't it? To collect all those swirling feelings and verbal vomit it in Dr. Rossi's general direction. But then, without meaning to, my mouth started talking,

"I have feelings for someone and if I ever do anything with those feelings, it'll jeopardize what I have with him."

I stared out the window at pigeons on roofs, and blinked away tears, I pictured Opal telling Seppi the baby, maybe, wasn't his. But maybe she had miscalculated, or maybe she'd have the test and find out she was wrong, and the baby really *was* Seppi's. Or, maybe she knew one way or the other. I was trying not to pry and was avoiding reality, so I didn't ask. I pictured the pain Seppi would feel inside his heart, and his body, if he found out he had to let go of all those imaginary Halloweens and Christmas mornings. If he had to let go of all the birthdays and milestones and baseball games and ballet classes. I imagined Opal telling him the truth. What if the baby wasn't his, and what if she told him she was leaving. I completely fell apart and moved my eyes back to Dr. Rossi,

"This is the first time I've felt this much pain about someone else's pain. Like, I can't physically handle knowing this person is hurting, mentally or physically. I can't handle it."

"It sounds like you're describing love."

It felt like I had been hit in the head with a shovel. My breath caught and I'm sure my eyes bugged out of my head. I don't know why I hadn't realized it sooner, and maybe I had. Maybe I knew it all along. But really, who cares, it would never work out, and telling Seppi I liked him would ruin everything, even if he wasn't with my sister anymore. I ended up stuffing the idea way down deep inside and didn't allow it to come back for a while. I deflected,

"No. I mean, I just really care about this person in a way I've never cared about anyone else. I don't have to hide my broken parts or sugar coat things. I can be ugly with him and he can be ugly with me."

I swallowed hard and stared at my lap. That might have been when I first wondered if I was screwed. It's that old thing of the heart wanting what the heart wants, but that couldn't be the case with Seppi. When the world felt harsh and critical, he didn't judge me or wish I was different.

"I would rather die than risk losing him. He's the one who saves me from myself, keeps the darkness from swallowing me whole. And sometimes I wonder if he feels the same, but it doesn't matter, and that's not the point."

"It isn't?"

Why did she have to be like that? No, that wasn't the point...I didn't know what the point was, but it wasn't that Seppi might feel something for someone like me. My mind raced, filling with snapshots in time. The first time he held me to his chest as I cried. The first time I knew he cared about me. The way I felt when I was with him. The way his hand felt on my lower back the night we danced, like he completed an electrical circuit. I pushed him away with my words and my body, and he was the only one who didn't take it personally. Even back then, Seppi was the one who knew what I needed even when I didn't.

Out in the woods when I was desperate, he was exactly what I needed, even though I didn't know it. I didn't need him to put his hand down my ratty vintage overalls or push me up against the Escalade and kiss me, I needed him to reassure me, give me a safe place to battle my demons. The night in his office when the rolls were in the oven, the way he danced with me. There was something in his eyes that night, right before the timer went off. The way he almost kissed me, and if he had, it would have spoken volumes about this thing between us. There was something there, even if I didn't think we'd ever in a million years do anything about it. I forgot the question,

"What?"

"What's the point then? You're saying this person makes you feel like you can be yourself, and you think he has feelings for you. I think you should talk to him, be honest, tell him how you feel."

I took a sip of water to buy myself some time. She glanced at her wedding rings,

"You never know, maybe you two will get married someday."

I spit the water out in a violent half-choke, half-laugh. I wiped my mouth and swiped at my dirty clothes. I rolled a mental film reel of Seppi returning with a broken heart. I swooped in and mended it with a needle and thread. I shook it off, stuffed it down and pushed away any thought of acknowledging my feelings for him or his feelings for me,

"It's complicated."

She gave me a skeptical side-eye before moving on to her next question,

"Okay, we can circle back to that, what's the next thing that's taking up emotional space?"

That was easy,

"My sister's planning on leaving and it's only a matter of time before she does it. She's a bit of a free spirit. She came back to Vermont last summer but hadn't planned on staying. She's ready to head out again, and I'm feeling a lot of guilt about the time I wanted to spend with her. My life kept getting in the way. I'm selfish, she's been miserable for a while, and I just keep telling her to give it time."

"You're not selfish. You're entitled to have things that require your emotional energy, things that take your time away from other people. Have you told Opal how you're feeling?"

I looked down at my hands,

"No, because I told myself she wouldn't leave. It's a long story but Opal got together with someone and she thought she could handle settling down here, but she can't. She's going insane. She's this bohemian wanderer who can't survive if she isn't in motion. It's this weird oxymoron, she can't thrive if she has roots holding her down, the roots act like a noose. It turns out the relationship she's in is complicated. If she stays, she'll be miserable, and she has had one foot out the door the entire time. I just kept telling her to give it time. She has her own demons and I know that, Bunman is a constant reminder."

Isabella nodded,

"How are you feeling about encouraging your sister to stay with someone so she won't leave?"

I hadn't thought about it like that, what a selfish bitch I was. Opal had been miserable for a while at that point and I just kept telling her to give it time. My eyes overflowed about five seconds later and it dawned on me that I was the problem in the equation,

"I don't feel great about it. I didn't realize that's what I was doing but, as usual, I was thinking about myself before anyone else."

Dr. Rossi furrowed her brows,

"I don't think you should be so hard on yourself. This is one of those situations where you can learn from your actions, and adjust your sails."

Disgusted with myself,

"I feel horrible, I didn't even think about my sister's feelings, I just said what I needed to say so she wouldn't leave. Like a fucking car salesman."

I put my head in my hands,

"Oh my God, I'm such an asshole!"

I stared out the window again and it was starting to get dark. My mind flashed to the end of my session, driving home, and not pushing my panic button. I was a selfish, self-centered asshole and Seppi was going through his own shit. Why was I so dependent on him, that wasn't right. Or what if that baby really *was* his and the two of them got married? What if I had to live the rest of my life, maneuvering a relationship with him that didn't cross any lines? You know, while watching them have Christmas mornings, go on family vacations, and make memories together. I'd have to move far away from there, my palms were sweating and I wanted to vomit.

I was really in a jam but I was feeling a little better when I left therapy. I have my own orbit and sometimes it doesn't line up with someone else's. I made another appointment, got my reminder card, used the restroom, and got on the elevator. I sat in my car and cried. It's not that I hadn't realize I had feelings for Seppi, it's that, if that's what love felt like,

I'd never loved anyone before. I'd wanted to marry one of my exes and I hadn't even loved him. That's a lot to handle, so I stuffed it into a filing cabinet in the back of my mind. That was the first time in my life I felt physical pain over the anticipation of someone else's heartbreak. It was frighteningly exhausting to care about someone like that. I went home and got in my fleece onesie, curled up on the couch with Indie, and ate garbage while I cried.

Guilt crept in around the seams and all of a sudden, I didn't want to break the seal with either of them. Maybe she'd changed her mind and didn't tell him. And as I lit a joint under the stove vent, there was a knock at my kitchen door. Kane? Alex looking to borrow a cup of sugar so she could make herself even sweeter? Whatever. I swung the door open to my pregnant sister. She shouldered her designer bag and made a face at herself for carrying such a thing,

"Honey, I'm home. Can I stay here tonight? I'm on overload."

Opal crossed the threshold without waiting for my answer. She kicked her Birkenstocks onto the mat next to the door and zombie-walked to the couch.

"Would you go down and grab my backpack? I wasn't sure you'd be home so I didn't bother lugging it up."

I strolled down the hall with a joint in my hand and retrieved Opal's backpack. There was my twenty-six-year-old Subaru with the mini mafia sedan on one side and my sister's well-aged VW van on the other. I returned to my apartment unsure what any of it meant, glad to see her but anxious just the same. I put out the joint and turned on the kettle to make her some tea. She got into oversized sweats and thick socks, we curled up with the vintage thrifted quilt and the string of fairy lights. We sat there in silence, eating homemade chocolate chip cookies right out of the oven. She didn't offer and I didn't ask. I soaked up every second Opal was eating junk with me under that quilt.

I left the fairy lights plugged in when I went to bed and kissed her on the cheek before retreating to the world of sleepless nights and ceiling tiles. But, that night, I slept. Knowing my sister was asleep on my futon, did something to soothe my soul. When I woke, Opal was making eggs and had retrieved a maple oat latte for me from the cafe. She was sipping one of Marlaina's fancy tea concoctions and seemed to feel better than she had in a long time. I hadn't been paying much attention when she met Seppi. I sipped the latte and felt guilty for being wrapped up in my own shit with Marco and Kane, and trying not to get killed by Salvatore Moretti. I hadn't paid much attention to how she changed once she decided to stay. I had a pang in my gut about how Opal's energy had been jammed up.

I hadn't spoken to Seppi since their trip and didn't want to break the seal. I had a pit in my gut but ate some of Opal's scrambled eggs because maybe it would be my last breakfast with her for a while. She had a twinkle in her eyes, she seemed lighter and her light seemed brighter. Opal buzzed around cooking breakfast and doing dishes and lip syncing to Cyndi Lauper. I sat on the sun porch with my latte and half a joint, contemplating life while she was in the shower.

When I went in, Opal was working curl cream through her dark ringlets. She stood naked in the middle of the living room, open backpack on the coffee table, her body building a human. She swiped on natural deodorant before putting on a long denim dress and thick cable knit sweater. She looked up at me, a storm of emotions swirling around behind her eyes. Once upon a time, she'd be zipping around refilling waters, taking reservations. She'd be memorizing the dinner, dessert, and wine specials. She'd seemed happy in her black pants, white button up shirt, and neat ponytail. She'd been playing a part, spending a little time having a fling with a rich guy who didn't live in a van. A little time working as a hostess at an Italian Ristorante before hitting the open road for the sea.

"It felt nice to stop for a while, to set down stakes, think about building a life somewhere. I met Seppi. It was flattering, and I didn't even realize how powerful he was. I felt special and fancy, like a girl who is nothing like me, and it felt good. It was flattering to be on his arm, in his cars, in his bed."

I cringed a little. She added,

"Everything happened too fast and I had no idea you were wrapped up in all that shit until it was too late. Then I thought, if I'm around, I can make sure Seppi keeps you safe."

There was pain in her eyes,

"Amelia, come sit down."

I was afraid she was going to tell me that she never wanted to see me again, or that she didn't love me anymore. I sat.

"I'm not leaving yet, but I can't guarantee how long I'm gonna stay. Seppi and I talked and he said he could feel it."

I exhaled,

"But, you're staying?"

I teared up and she put her hand on mine,

"For now, yes. I'm not going to do anything until the restaurant opens, He has a lot on his mind and I'm not looking to make things more complicated."

She was going to leave eventually, but I didn't have to think about it for the time being, not until after opening night. I continued to keep my feelings to myself, the last thing I wanted was to complicate things.

CHAPTER 14
I'M GOING TO ASK YOU ONCE

OPAL INVITED ME for dinner, so I drove to the land of mafia mansions and babies that hopefully didn't belong to mob bosses. I waved at the guy who opened the gate, it was someone other than Gary. I sat in the car for a minute to collect my thoughts before making my way to the house. Was I going to get a chance to be alone with Seppi? Would he dance with me? Would I puke on the dining room table? I paired my boots neatly on the mat next to the door, stuffed my hat in my coat sleeve, and hung it next to Seppi's leather jacket. I leaned in and buried my face in the folds of black leather, inhaling a lifetime of his essence as it mingled with Tobacco Vanille and cigar smoke. My nippled pressed against my bra and I tried to hold it together for everyone's sake. But, I wondered if he'd ever killed anyone while wearing that jacket and I wanted to shrug into it like a new identity, let it hold all my broken pieces together. I longed to be a bad bitch, in control, untouchable, someone who didn't need a panic button. Hanging my coat next to his felt intimate and made it more difficult to keep my feelings in check. I was sharing his space, I was becoming familiar, I was a regular guest and I didn't need to knock before entering.

Opal and Seppi were in the kitchen, she was making tea and he was finishing his fourth espresso of the day. He nodded and I nodded back and he winked. I imagined standing between his legs, my face nuzzled into the crook of his neck, his arms around me, kissing the Tobacco Vanille from his skin. I shook it off and sat on the stool next to his, sipping a mug of steaming herbal tea. Just as I was getting my shit under control, Opal kissed Seppi on the cheek in a swirl of patchouli and sage, and shrugged into her wool pea coat. As she shoved her feet into my Uggs,

"I need to run to Hannaford, I forgot cilantro."

Opal went out the door and then leaned in, hollering to me,

"You're parked behind me, keys in your coat?"

"Yeah."

But I said it more like a question than an answer.

I was surprisingly possessive over the car, as if she had him to herself, so why couldn't I have something of my own? Out the door she went, into the night. Shit. My feelings for him were bubbling to the surface and I was panicked. I hadn't seen Seppi since their trip and I didn't want to talk about it, I didn't want to be a part of that conversation. If the kid was his, all my feelings for him would have to be stored in those filing cabinets I keep talking about. Would I be able to handle it? Absolutely not, so I crammed it in with the other things and slammed the drawer shut.

I finished my tea and stared out the sliding glass door at the pool. Maybe if I didn't make eye contact with him, everything would be alright. I didn't break the silence for fear I would cry. Goosebumps spread over every inch of my body when he got up from his stool. Seppi moved to the bar and poured two whiskies, I followed his hand with my eyes as he slid one of the glasses across the counter. Our eyes met and I swallowed the nerves in my throat before nervously looking away. My cheeks were hot and I squeezed my thighs together because other things were getting hot. He sipped his whiskey, I sipped mine. He said,

"She told me."

I nodded, my eyes wide. He swirled the whiskey with the ice,

"I'm going to be okay, Dimples. This wasn't out of left field, I know how pregnancy tests work. She found out about five days after we slept together, I guess it was what I needed at the time, to think I was going to be a father."

For a while, I thought Seppi was happy, and I thought Opal was happy, and the whole thing was bullshit. What if the baby was his and they decided to spend their lives together, it would just about kill me. I was angry and felt betrayed and confused. He sipped his whiskey, I sipped mine. I didn't know what to say. I could tell he was choosing his words,

"I mean no disrespect to your sister when I say this."

I put my hand up, nodded like I understood, and listened to it from his perspective,

"My life was in upheaval because of my father and I desperately needed something good."

I wondered if even with all of the people in his life, if he was lonely sometimes. He continued,

"I'd been dealing with some..."

Seppi glanced in my direction,

"Complications."

I made a face and sipped my whiskey. He continued,

"She was a nice distraction, and I don't mean that in a bad way, but we do not have a connection."

I didn't want to think about it, but I wanted to be there for him, so I listened,

"Like when you know immediately that you're so completely different from someone that it would never work. The night we slept together, we'd been drinking. It was clumsy and disconnected, and something about it made me feel more alone."

I bit my bottom lip and didn't know what to say, had they only slept together once? I didn't want to know. I was pretty sure I'd sleep with him more than once in one night and they had been together for months. I grasped onto the thought that their time together was nothing, it didn't mean anything, it was just some drunken decision. Thinking that, made me feel better. I countered,

"You're just going through the motions?"

Seppi leaned on the counter,

"I care about her, but she's daydreaming about the road and the water and spreading her wings. I want you to know, even if the baby isn't mine, which I don't think it is, I'll be there for her financially for as long as she needs. Either way, she doesn't plan to stay."

It hurt that Seppi knew more about Opal's plans than I did, and I wondered where that left me in the equation. Seppi abandoned his empty glass and came to my side of the island, close enough that I could feel the heat from his body. He hooked my chin with his finger and spoke softly, intimately, our eyes meeting in a tortuous, forbidden purgatory,

"Sometimes, feelings complicate things."

I thought Seppi was talking about his feelings for Opal, but as we stood there like that, I realized he was talking about his feelings for me. Seppi released my chin and his hand fell to his side. I instinctively reached out and gripped a couple of his fingers, the wall between us crumbling at its foundation. The barriers we reinforced, the shields we hid behind were falling away while my sister was at Hannaford getting cilantro. Our foreheads touched, and I held his face in my hands, the warmth of his skin, the scratch of his five o'clock shadow. Our eyes met again and Seppi made a sound low in his throat, the heat from his breath sending my body into overdrive. I held his gaze, and in a whisper of everything I couldn't tell him yet, I swallowed the nerves in my throat,

"I hope someday things aren't as complicated."

Seppi stepped away and sat on his stool, maybe he was creating distance, or maybe conversations like that made him weak in the knees. I nestled into Seppi's neck, and when he slid his arms around my waist, it felt like he was holding on for dear life. When he squeezed me, I made an involuntary sound as the air escaped, and I wished he would never let go. A deep perpetual need for him ached deep in my belly. There was a profound need to be near him and it had nothing to do with his money or power. I needed him because when I was in a million pieces, he would make me feel whole. Maybe Dr. Rossi was right about my feelings for him, what if that was what love felt like? What if when everything was said and done, I'd admit that I felt things for him that I'd never felt for anyone else.

For the moment, I was free in his arms, even if it wasn't time yet. His nooks fit into my crannies, and I wondered what it would be like to make love to a man like that. Would he be gentle, or would he ravage me with the same vicious thirst I had for him. Fuck it. My lips hovered over his neck and I licked my lips, milliseconds from contact when the front door slammed open. We jumped away from each other, but instead of Opal coming through the front door, Vincenzo Moretti stormed in, liquored up and yelling,

"Where you at, Seppi, we got a problem!"

We glanced at each other and Vinny appeared in the kitchen doorway, red faced and clearly worked up about something.

"You know that broad you're looking out for? Well, they sent someone else."

Vinny pulled up a man's picture and when he turned the phone, I was peering over Seppi's shoulder to see a candid shot of Lance Arnault. You'll be happy to know, I managed not to shit my pants or pass out, so that's good. I played dumb and waited to see what he was going to say. Seppi went for his office, so Vinny followed him, and I followed Vinny. Seppi poured whiskey into his rocks glass, no ice, and swirled it around He slammed it back and poured another, his voice nothing like when our foreheads were touching,

"How the fuck did this happen!?"

My eyes bugged out of my head and I wondered if I'd deleted Lance's texts, or if I still had pictures of us. I was paranoid and neatened drapes that already looked good from outside. Seppi barked,

"Sit!"

I sat, and you'll be happy to know that I also shut up. Seppi inspected the picture, and Vinny had a couple more to show him. Seppi was connecting dots and filling in gaps. He glanced at Vinny briefly before going upstairs to get dressed. I didn't know where they were going but I wasn't invited. The two of them drove off into the night in Vinny's BMW, and I stayed by myself in the world of emotional baggage and muddy waters. And what I really mean is bubble-gut and the shits. I was destroying one of the downstairs bathrooms when Opal returned from the store with the cilantro.

She must have passed them on her way up the street because she was mumbling under her breath when she came through the door. She'd gotten more than cilantro, so I grabbed her bags and carried them to the kitchen. We put things away and she joined me at the counter. Opal didn't seem mad but she didn't seem happy. She sighed and pulled a stack of menus out of a drawer,

"Whatcha in the mood for?"

Opal fanned the stack of menus and I made my way through the pile. Chinese, Indian, Italian, Mexican, Asian, subs, burgers and fries. We Door Dashed authentic ramen bowls, egg rolls, and pork fried rice. I was walking on eggshells. Opal's biggest concern was my safety, and I was pretty sure that wherever Seppi had gone off to, it had something to do with me and my safety, and my perpetual talent for fucking things up.

We ate our ramen noodles, egg rolls, and pork fried rice. I smoked half a joint and Opal sipped bergamot tea, Seppi still wasn't home when I left. I figured he and Vinny were on a fact-finding mission where Lance was concerned, but maybe they'd whacked him. I pushed it out of my mind the best I could and didn't hear anything from Seppi the next day. I was worried, but I tried to hold it together because I would have heard from my sister if something bad happened. I sent Lance a text and he replied that he'd be in Jersey until the second week of February. At least he wasn't at the bottom of the lake. I'd been filling a void with Lance Arnault, I was only with him because he was hot and seemed mysterious. He was fine, it's not like he was a dick or anything, but there wasn't any real emotional connection. I wondered what the hell was going on, who Lance really was, and why Seppi and Vincenzo gave a shit.

I went about the business of slinging lattes at Muddy Waters, driving to the impressive office building of Isabella Rossi, and to the hippie-dippy goat farm of Calliope Cromwell. I spent my evenings getting high and petting my cat, or with my ear against the kitchen door, listening, as Kane played his guitar late at night. I lost track, but Alex hadn't been around in a while. The combination of no Alex and the late-night guitar playing told me they were taking another break. I was lonely and empty and almost went scratching at his door for some 'friends with benefits' action. I didn't mention it.

I thought about Lance. If he was sent to Bunman to see if he could find Sal, or what happened to him, he struck out. I was right in his bed, for crying out loud. Lance hadn't acted weird or seem to be sniffing around for info. Lance wasn't really looking for his uncle, and it was a big no-no that I'd been spending time with him, but I kept it to myself. No point in making things worse. Lance wouldn't be back for a month so I had a little wiggle room. I compartmentalized that shit into a little box in the back of my head where I push those things into the darkness, just out of reach.

I didn't push my panic button anymore because Seppi was busy with his restaurant, and I knew it. I went on the sun porch and glanced toward the new structure that would house Giuseppi's Italian Ristorante. You know, a place with authentic Naples cuisine and none of that pesky mafia energy. As I was standing on my sun porch, Seppi pulled in and parked behind the ristorante, I watched as he went through the back door. There was a construction pickup and a delivery truck in the alley, a man in a jumpsuit and gloves unloading wine glasses.

I shoved my feet in my Uggs and bounced down the stairs. I speed-walked passed my twenty-six-year-old piece of Swiss cheese and the mini mafia sedan. I swung through the back door of the ristorante to the aroma of fresh drywall and lumber. It took me a second to figure out the new layout but it was much like the old one. Seppi's office door stood open but he wasn't in it. I peeked in the kitchen and dining rooms. I didn't see him, so I sat in the chair across the desk from his. The leather armchair was expensive looking and I took in the smell of it as I ran my fingers over the stitches. My phone vibrated and it was Seppi. 'Where are you?' He was next door looking for me. I sent a picture of his empty chair and replied, 'The question is, where are you?'

Three minutes later, Giuseppi Moretti was sitting across from me with tension in his eyes. He poured whiskey into two rocks glasses and I should have popped an edible an hour ago. Seppi looked at me, I looked at him. His energy was making me nervous. He slid his phone across the desk and I picked it up, a picture of Lance Arnault staring back at me. I'm sure my face did something that gave me away and I slid the phone back. Seppi looked me in the eye and scanned me like a lie detector. I swallowed audibly. He knew. His voice did something it doesn't usually do with me,

"I am going to ask you once."

The tone and power in Seppi's voice made my asshole clench, even though I knew him by then. I knew him personally, he was all bark and no bite with me. I knew what he was going to ask before he asked it, and I was aware Seppi could snuff me out in the blink of an eye if he wanted to. My guts gurgled.

"Have you been spending time with this man, Amelia?"

Shit.

I looked back at him like a deer in the headlights and didn't say anything, what was the point? Seppi already knew the answer to the question. He tilted his head and considered his next move. Was he going to be gentle or intimidating? Just like a parent with evidence you broke the rules,

"I have some pictures would you like to see them?"

And right then, I knew for sure Seppi had a picture of me with Lance Arnault. I prayed it wasn't from when I was drunk and practically licking his face in the hallway of Paducci's Pub. Either way, it made me look like a traitor, or like I was playing games with him. I hadn't told Seppi I saw a stranger, even after he told me to. I was a traitor, and I was the one who killed Sal, so I was the one at risk, wasn't I? I hadn't done any of it on purpose. Seppi stared at me like he was going to give me one more chance to answer before showing me whatever picture he was looking at. I swallowed the new lump in my throat, the one that replaced the old one. I didn't like being the one Seppi was grilling like a lobster tail, my voice trembling as I spoke,

"Yes, I've been spending time with that man. No, I don't want to see the other pictures."

Seppi threw his phone to the desk and it made me jump. I bubbled up inside and my eyes filled with tears, a scared little girl getting caught doing something I shouldn't. Seppi's voice ramped up and if there had been anyone else in the building, they would have heard him yelling at me,

"He is here because *you* killed my father!"

Seppi moved closer, growling at me,

"I told you how important it was that it look like an accident! I told you his boss would send someone! I told you to tell me if you saw strangers around Bunman!"

There was disappointment in Seppi's eyes and his voice went up another notch. His words had sharp edges and they cut me as they landed,

"Not only did you neglect to tell me you saw someone new around Bunman, but you're FUCKING him!?"

Seppi glared at me, his eyes the darkest I'd ever seen them, and there was nothing gentle or protective in his voice. He threw his hands around as he yelled at me, I was surprised he hadn't pinned me to the wall with his body and a hand to my throat. He clenched his teeth, his voice making my nipples hard, but not for the usual reasons. His fist pounded the top of the desk, and my eyes flew up to his as he demanded answers,

"What the fuck are you thinking!? Are you *trying* to get yourself killed!? Are you purposely trying to self-destruct!?"

Seppi flew around the desk and barely stopped to take a breath, yelling, talking with his hands,

"Here I am, running whenever you need me, thinking I'm doing you a favor, trying to protect you!"

He scoffed at me,

"And here you are, fucking someone who was sent here because of YOU!"

People could probably hear him from the parking lot, he taunted me,

"Am I wasting my time!? Please tell me if I'm wasting my time!"

Seppi closed the gap between us and leaned in until our noses touched. The heat from his breath on my lips,

"Am I wasting my time on you, Dimples!? Because it feels like I'm wasting my time!"

It felt like I'd been punched in the gut. He went back to his side of the ring, momentarily. What was my problem? Why was I like that? I tried to steady my shaky voice, tears bubbling up in my throat.

"I just ran into him a couple times and we ended up seeing each other. I'm sorry I didn't tell you."

Seppi's eyes had fire in them, like when someone says they saw red,

"You have put all of us at risk!"

The anger rose as he paced, but there was something else in there with it. Was he jealous I'd been with someone else? He slammed his fancy office chair under the desk. Instinctively, I got to my feet, in preparation to run for my life. Seppi strode around the desk and walked me backward until my back hit the wall. My breath caught as he hooked my chin with his finger. Rougher than usual, Seppi's body pressed against mine, whiskey on his breath as he spoke,

"You're lining up to get yourself killed!"

He demanded,

"You'll tell me if you see him again, do you understand!?"

He brought his hand to my throat and squeezed. Jesus. Seppi moved his face closer to mine until we were nose to nose again, gritting his teeth,

"You understand me!?"

He squeezed a little more and I felt it in unmentionable places. I nodded and squeaked out,

"I understand."

When I swallowed, the tips of Seppi's fingers dug into the sides of my throat. He said,

"Good girl."

My knees went weak.

He was holding me against the wall with his body and I thought he might start to cry. The anger had morphed into something else and the pendulum swing was palpable. Seppi's body softened. His hand relaxed, and right then, he was baring his soul to me, even if he didn't mean to,

"Nothing can happen to you, do you understand me!?"

I nodded again,

"I'll be more careful."

Seppi cupped the side of my face and rubbed his thumb over my left dimple. With my back against the wall and his body pressing against mine, our eyes locked and I felt it everywhere. I had never wanted anyone more than I wanted him. We were breathing in unison; I was terrified and turned on at the same time. We were locked in the kind of eye contact that leads to a kiss and I swallowed another wave of tears,

"You're not wasting your time on me."

"I know."

Our foreheads touched again; our mouths agonizingly close. Aftershocks of arousal gripped my body, and I wondered if it did something for him to pin me against the wall. Seppi took a step back and looked down at me like he hoped I meant it. I slowed my breathing and regained control. Whatever that was, put things into perspective, and I think I needed the reminder. He was the head of the Moretti mob family, and I was just a broken little bitch.

CHAPTER 15
A CUTE HAT AND VINTAGE BAG

THE FOLLOWING MONDAY, I did my early morning shift at Muddy Waters, slinging lattes and giving the basic bitches their fancy drinks. Kane could tell I was preoccupied but I didn't care. And, I could tell by the way he was looking at me that Alex still wasn't around. Sorry, Charlie, I had more important things to do than mollycoddle some man-child. Kane seemed to 'forget' that he asked if I killed Sal, because he never brought it up again. I'm not complaining, I just found it strange. Although, maybe Seppi 'handled it' by telling Kane not to bring it up again or he'd end up at the bottom of Clover Lake.

I noticed a woman about my age sitting in the corner, hair stuffed in a cute ear flap hat that looked like a dog. She wore a wool sweater, well-loved jeans, and a pair of smart looking boots. Her nose was deep in what looked like a mystery novel. I noticed her bag was vintage leather and I bet it was thrifted. I tried to give her a once over without making it obvious. She stopped reading long enough to take a sip of her latte and a bite of her bagel. Before she jammed her nose back in the book, I asked about her amazing bag and complimented her cute hat. She asked me about Bunman, asked why I chose to settle there. She seemed cool. I told her I was Amelia, and she told me she was Helen. She looked like a Helen, but a cool one.

"Do you know anyone with a used car they're looking to sell, just something to get me around? My last car shit the bed and was horrible in the snow."

There was a twenty-six-year-old piece of all wheel drive Swiss cheese in my driveway that I'd be willing to part with for five-hundred bucks. Maybe.

"I have a maroon Subaru Legacy wagon I wouldn't mind selling."

I gestured toward the parking lot,

"It needs work but it's great in the snow and will get you from point A to point B, if you have extra duct tape and cable ties. It's right out back if you want to see it."

Helen smiled and Kane gave me the stink eye to stop fucking around and get back to work. Whatever, it was the slow time between breakfast and lunch. Helen and I went out the back door to the parking lot and I gave her the grand tour of the car's exterior in all its glory. Helen made a big deal about the mini mafia sedan and I told her it was mine. She loved it. Sorry, lady, that one's not for sale. It didn't even belong to me, it belonged to a mob boss. Helen commented on the vanity plate. I kept steering her back to the rusted-out station wagon and eventually she cupped her hands against the glass and looked inside. She made a face and threw her hands up,

"I really like it, but I don't know how to drive a standard. Thank you though, I appreciate you showing it to me."

I mean, how hard is it to learn how to drive stick?

"I can teach you if you change your mind, it's not that hard."

When Helen left, she gave me a wave and I hoped I'd see her again. She seemed like someone I'd get along with, and besides Sunny, I didn't really have any girlfriends in town. I finished my shift, took a shower, and made an effort when I picked my outfit. I pulled on some skinny jeans and dug through a messy pile of sweaters for one of my beloved thrift finds. I only wore that sweater when I knew I wasn't going to be drinking red wine or eating marinara. That sweater was a very expensive cream-colored sweater, and I thrifted it for fifty cents. It was one of my favorite things in the whole world and I hardly ever wore it because I didn't want to ruin it. I even put on mascara that day, finished up with lip gloss and some perfume.

I pulled on my Docs. It would be getting dark by the time I got out of therapy, so I dug around in my purse to make sure the new can of pepper spray was in there. Sometime soon I'd feel comfortable carrying my handgun, not yet.

I bounced down the stairs and out the back door, fired up the mini mafia sedan and then ran back to turn the porch light on. Lost in thought on my way to the impressive office building of Isabella Rossi, I wasn't in the mood to have my head shrunk that day. I smoked half a joint in the parking lot and went inside. I rode the elevator to the luxury office in the sky and checked in with Elaine. Fingered the fuck out of those magazines about shit I didn't care about. Passed Dr. Rossi in her doorway in a trail of Alien Elixir and weed. I plopped in the overstuffed chair.

We made eye contact and I didn't say anything right away. I could've talked about a couple of different things; knowing the baby probably wasn't Seppi's, the fact that my sister had one foot out the door. Finding out I got caught with the handsome stranger, my confusing feelings for Giuseppi Moretti.

"How are you doing, Amelia?"

I dropped my eyes to my lap and then stared out the window at pigeons. I pulled off my boots, tucked my knees up to my chest, and sobbed for a solid ten minutes. I had no idea what was happening to me. I looked over at Dr. Rossi with tears in my eyes and pulled a tissue from the box on the table next to me. I laughed because I was uncomfortable with my feelings,

"Apparently, I'm not great."

She sat with me while I cried. I was going to punch her in the face if she brought up meds again, but she didn't. She just let me sit in my shit; she was present while I fell apart, and that time, she didn't do anything to hold me together. I wondered if Seppi would approve of paying for a session, even if all I did was cry. I made another appointment with Elaine and she handed me the reminder card. I locked myself in the bathroom and splashed cold water on my face before patting it with a nonabsorbent paper towel. By the time I left, people were getting out of work and cars were filing out of the parking lot. I backed out of my space and entered the stream of mice following the maze back home. I didn't press my panic button, but I got off at the exit with the gazebo and the low wall and the water. I needed Seppi, but that was the whole problem. I almost pushed the button that made him come running, but I didn't.

I threw my cross-body bag over my head and locked the car as I walked away. A sedan pulled in a couple spaces from me. Church bells caught my attention. Then I saw a man walking his golden retriever near the woods. I'm telling you all this because a lot of different things caught my attention, and maybe I wasn't as aware of my surroundings as I should have been. I sat on the low wall and smoked half a joint as night finished falling. Cars drove through the little village and I sat on the low wall as night closed in, watching lights and listening to tires in the slush on the road. I wanted to take a picture of the way the streetlights reflected on the snow like diamonds, and realized my phone was on the passenger seat of my car. I didn't bother getting it.

I had a jolt of panic but could see the mini mafia sedan from where I sat. I was safe and would be fine, even if I was a hundred feet from my phone. There were people close by, I was alone, but not. I was around people, but not. The passenger door of the sedan opened and the dome light illuminated the inside of the car. The person in the passenger's seat had a hat just like Helen's and it made me wish we'd exchanged numbers. Sometimes you cross paths with people for a reason and I wondered if I'd see her again. Maybe we'd be friends. The couple got out of the car and I wondered if they had a dog, it was dark and I couldn't see details. I'd been crying so I didn't want to cross paths with anyone. I hopped off the wall and moved toward the gazebo as the couple made their way toward the low wall. I rolled my eyes when they changed course and took the walkway to the gazebo. Maybe I could just pretend I forgot something and turn around. The man said something to the woman with the hat like Helen's and she nodded. I moved my eyes from his face to hers and we locked eyes.

I smiled and waved at the woman excitedly, what were the chances I'd run into her?

"Hi, Helen!"

I pointed to the middle of my chest,

"Amelia, from earlier, the one with the car."

The tall, slender man moved in my direction so I stepped to the side to get out of his way. He gripped my upper arms and threw me against the base of the gazebo. It knocked the wind out of me a little but I tried not to panic. I had a new pepper spray, if I could get to it, I'd be okay. I barked,

"HEY!"

I looked the guy in the face, rooted around my bag, and yelled,

"What the fuck are you doing!?"

He shoved me again and I shoved him back, fuck that guy. I whipped out the pepper spray Lance had given me to replace the expired one. Nothing. I shook it and pressed the button again, maybe I'd done it wrong. Nothing. He must've gotten a dud, just my luck. The man grabbed my wrist and the pepper spray fell to the ground; I twisted my wrist and pulled my arm free. Helen wasn't helping. I ran into the darkness, close to the low wall. Helen pulled out a pocketknife and my mind raced as I ran away. I was forced into the woods beyond the park and the low wall and the gazebo. I was on a gravel path, so if I ran until I found someone walking their dog, I'd be okay.

My heart was beating in my ears, my breath was burning in my throat, I had to pee. The woman with the cute hat and vintage bag slashed at the back of the expensive sweater that only cost me fifty cents. She tore at the sweater I never wore because I didn't want to get red wine or marinara on it. The footsteps behind me closed in, my hyper-senses felt the contact a second before the man tackled me to the slush covered gravel path. I hit my chin and split my lip, pain shot through my leg as a jagged rock pierced through my jeans and tore my flesh. A wave of adrenaline and nausea, my bladder full, the cold of the snow on my skin, jolting me out of it. I cried, some solace in thinking of what Seppi would do when he found out,

"You're going to be sorry!"

The right side of my face was pinned against the slush covered gravel. The man pressed his knee into the middle of my back, he smelled of cheap cologne, cigarettes and beer. Helen cable tied my hands together behind my back. The man was putting too much weight on me. I made myself breathe in and breathe out, breathe in and breathe out. My panic rose, what if he pinned me to the ground and raped me like that boy? Would I survive something like that, twice? The man lowered himself over me, whispering in a breathy voice that gave me chills,

"Hi, Dimples."

He kissed me on the cheek, another wave of adrenaline flooding my body, hot acid in the back of my throat. My bladder gave way from the weight of him and hot urine clashed with the cold of the snow. I talk a big game, all fight and no flight, but there I was, paralyzed with fear. Helen pulled off my boots and tossed them in different directions. Right then, I realized the woman in the cute hat was really the red-haired lady in the pantsuit. Things went fast but they also went slow, my mind went a mile a minute. I showed her my old car, which was parked next to my new car, and she'd made a note of my vanity plate so they could follow me. The man pulled me up by the back of my torn and bloodied, expensive sweater that only cost me fifty cents. The front of me wet with melted snow and my own piss, I squeaked out,

"Why are you doing this!?"

The girl with the cute hat and vintage bag mocked me,

"Why are you doing this!?"

She punched me in the stomach and I doubled over, coughing, gulping for air. I straightened up and she punched me in the face. Blood streamed from my nose and I sucked it into my mouth as I gasped for air. Helen spit in my face,

"Tell Giuseppi I said hi."

She shoved me and I fell hard, my hands cable tied behind my back. Searing pain as I landed, something tearing through the palm of my hand. I sobbed into the snow and let the cold soothe my face. I hyperventilated and then went quiet, listening. When I was sure they were gone, I managed to get myself up, getting my bearings straight. I couldn't see anything out there unless it was in front of my face. I took a couple sock-footed steps on the slush-covered gravel and spotted something in the snow, it was the knife.

I dropped to my knees as gently as possible and laid on the ground, shimmying backward until I felt the cold metal of the knife against my hand. I laid there with my cheek in the snow as I concentrated. It took a long time because my hands were slippery with blood and snow, but I finally cut through the cable tie. I desperately pawed through my bag for the panic button. I pulled out my keyring, and the fob wasn't there. My mind blank, I felt helpless, I forgot I took the panic button off after Lance pushed it. Blood dripped onto the snow, and I had cuts all over the place, my left eye was swelling shut. I scooped a handful of snow and held it to my nose. I was shivering with my whole body, the piss turning to slush on the front of my pants. I spit out blood but I was swallowing a lot of it. I dumped my purse into the snow, and when I thought all hope was lost, the panic button fell out of the back pocket. I frantically grabbed it, pushed, and held it for three seconds.

CHAPTER 16
PROBLEM AND SOLUTION

I COULDN'T HEAR SEPPI, but he could hear me. I was screaming into the one-way speaker, praying he was there, frantic,

"Seppi!?"

The world was spinning and it felt like I was going to pass out. I dropped to the ground again, hyperventilating, squeaking through sobs, barely coherent, praying he could understand what I was saying,

"I'm hurt, Seppi!"

I swallowed hard, the words washed away with my tears,

"Please help me!"

He would call my phone but it was in the car. I didn't know if he was even there, I pressed the button again and held it forever. I couldn't breathe. I choked on the blood I'd swallowed and gagged on a blood clot before throwing up. Shivering on the ground next to my bloody vomit, face in the snow, sweater ripped to shreds, piss down the front of me, sobbing desperately into the panic button,

"HELP ME!"

And then I passed out.

I woke when I heard him, but he was far away and his voice sounded like it was coming through a tunnel. I tried to yell back but my throat was dry and my voice wouldn't work. What if Seppi couldn't find me? What if he left? I prayed, desperately, please find me, please find me, God, please let him find me. My name was getting louder, he was frantic, because at that point, he didn't know if I was alive. Seppi called to me with tears in his voice, there was nothing about him that screamed 'patriarch of a mob family.' Right then, he was something else entirely. His voice cracking with powerlessness,

"AMELIA!?"

I could see the light from his phone as he followed the GPS in my direction, I waved my hand when I saw him, raspy and weak, and I squeaked out,

"Here!"

Seppi rushed over and knelt in the slush next to me. He brushed the bloody hair away from my face, and his eyes filled with rage,

"Jesus, Amelia, what the fuck happened!? Who did this to you!?"

I looked up at him, pitifully, embarrassed, ashamed,

"I wet my pants."

I sobbed with relief that I wasn't going to die that night. He scooped me up and carried me out of the woods, my bloody face against the chest of his fancy wool coat, piss all over the front of me. The familiar smell of whiskey and Tobacco Vanille mixed with a hint of stress sweat. Seppi growled through clenched teeth,

"I am going to kill whoever did this to you!"

I had no doubt.

When we were at the Escalade, Seppi wrapped me in his coat and buckled me into the passenger seat. Sunny was on her way with Vinny to get my car. Seppi was clenching his jaw in the light of the dash. He had to pull over so I could throw up. We rolled through the gate of mafia mansion land and I covered my face with bloody curls so Gary wouldn't see me, but luckily it was the other guy. Seppi carried me to the front door and whispered quietly before putting me down,

"Your sister will worry."

He opened the front door and I crossed the threshold on my own. Opal glared at Seppi before running to me with tears in her eyes. She wrapped me in her arms and directed her venom at Seppi,

"You said you'd keep her safe!"

She backed away from me and gestured at my face,

"I won't tolerate this shit!"

Opal moved to him, jabbing her pointer finger into his sternum with each word,

"Do. Your. Fucking. Job."

And then she hauled off and slapped him across the face, muttering,

"You're worthless!"

Seppi just stood there, stunned, shaking his head. We made eye contact as he rubbed the growing hand print on his cheek. Opal spun around, pulled me up the stairs and started the shower. She hung a plush robe and towel on ornate hooks next to the shower, mumbling about how Seppi was a useless piece of shit. I attempted to run my fingers through curls that were somehow both wet from the snow and glued together with dried blood. I made another mental note to get six inches chopped off.

I removed my poor, battered, beautiful, cream-colored wool sweater that was expensive but only cost me fifty cents. I unhooked my torn bra and tossed it on top of the sweater. My wet socks came off inside out. I undid my ripped, piss covered jeans and pulled them off inside out along with my panties. The hot shower brought on a surge of deja vu about the first shower I took after being shot by Salvatore Moretti.

I scrubbed the blood out of my hair with Seppi's fancy shampoo and used one of the plush washcloths to scrub at the dried blood from my face with something heavenly. I was broken and beaten, working seventy-five-dollar conditioner through my curls, naked in one of Giuseppi Moretti's showers. I stood in front of an elaborately framed full-length mirror, my wounds on display, the ones on the inside and out. I had a fat lip, black eyes, my chin was split, and I had gashes in my legs and the palm of my hand. I wrapped myself in the robe and Seppi came in to close my wounds with steri-strips and bandages. Opal stormed off to his room to retrieve sweatpants and a hoodie, glaring at him as she passed, I was at the mercy of other people's emotions. I was pretty sure I'd brought all of it on myself and prepared for a reprimand.

Seppi left the room but I sensed that he was close by because I hadn't heard him go down the stairs. Wearing his sweats, I stared through the balcony doors into the darkness as I worked expensive curl cream through my hair. Lost in my thoughts, tears falling silently as I replayed the night in my head, it could have been so much worse and I knew it. I caught a reflection in the window and turned around to see Seppi standing in the doorway. He had fire in his eyes but I could see that even though Seppi was raging under the surface, he intended to be gentle with me.

He stepped into the room and put his hand out to me. I ran to him, my tears coming before he even had me wrapped in his arms. Protecting me from the demons in the woods and the ones in my head. Tears on the brink, he pulled them back, clearing his throat before he said,

"You hungry?"

I nodded in his arms. Seppi kissed the top of my head before releasing me and hooking my chin,

"Anything you want and it's yours."

My stomach lining was having a smashing good time eating itself. I glanced at the big fancy clock, it was late but Seppi objected,

"If you're hungry, you'll eat. Capiche?"

I blinked up at him like a startled doe and he led me down the back stairs where Opal was making me a cup of tea. I sat on a stool, my body stiff and aching. Opal slid a tin of edibles across the counter,

"I found them in the van, they'll be stale before I get a chance to use them."

I tossed two weed-filled wedges down the hatch and sipped some peppermint tea. Seppi tied on an apron and put his hands on his hips,

"What's it going to be this evening?"

I smiled a little and I could tell it made Seppi happy. He could make me anything my little heart desired and I knew just what I wanted,

"Blueberry Pancakes and bacon, please."

Seppi winked,

"Coming right up."

Opal and I sipped tea and nibbled on fruit as Giuseppi Moretti whipped up the best blueberry pancakes and bacon I've ever had. I mean, come on. We did the dishes after, and Opal found a spare toothbrush in the linen closet. We brushed our teeth in different sinks in her bathroom and then curled up on the sitting room sofa in front of the fire. Seppi joined us and the three of us just sat there enjoying the fact that I had not been raped or murdered by those fuck-wits who had most likely eaten their last supper.

A while later, Opal hugged me, kissed Seppi on the cheek, and disappeared up the stairs. The two of us sat there together on the sofa, our stocking feet on his fancy coffee table. Seppi used his home voice and not his work one,

"Come to me, Dimples."

Seppi put his arm around me as I nestled into his body with my knees curled to my chest. Only that time, I didn't curl into a ball because I was scared; I curled into a ball so I could cram every last inch of my soul into Giuseppi Moretti's cage. He caressed my arm with his thumb,

"I'm glad you're okay."

I nodded and looked over at him, my tears brimming, chin quivering. He didn't leave me to kill the woman with the cute hat and vintage bag, he stayed with me instead.

It didn't take long for the edibles and exhaustion to swallow me whole, sleep closing in like the grim reaper. I closed my eyes and let Seppi hold all my broken pieces together. When he thought I was asleep, he wrapped one of my ringlets around his finger. It felt intimate, like he wanted to take care of me, but not in the usual way. I was safe with his arm around me, the left side of my face resting on his chest. In fact, I'd never felt more cared for or protected, I'd never felt more loved, even though I didn't think he loved me. When it was obvious I was falling asleep, Seppi carried me up the stairs to the room next to his. I crawled under the covers and he sat there with me for a little while longer. After he thought I was asleep, he kissed my temple and kept his lips there as he whispered,

"Sweet dreams, Dimples."

I fell asleep with a warm heart that night, and at some point, Seppi left my room to go to his own. I woke the next morning and felt like I had been hit by a train. My body hurt and my left eye was swollen shut. The cut on my chin throbbed, my lip was split and I kept touching the scab with my tongue. As reality fell over me, I pushed the covers back and went into the bathroom to look in the mirror. I had no idea how I was going to work at the cafe anytime soon, there was no hiding that I had been beaten about the face, as they say. I stood there, spiraling, as I stared back at myself in that mirror. I'd been in Bunman for almost a year, and never in a million years would I have pictured whatever the hell you call all of that.

I made my way down the stairs and sipped a latte that both hurt and soothed my busted lip. There was a bowl of fresh berries, yogurt, and granola waiting for me, and my sister was making herself a smoothie. I dug through my battered cross-body bag for the thrifted flip-top tin and wandered into Seppi's office with my latte. Curled up in the expensive leather chair, I smoked half a joint. He slid a bottle of Ibuprofen across the desk and went to the kitchen to get me some orange juice. I knew we were going to have to talk about what happened but I didn't want to. I wanted to rewind time and go home instead of going to the park. My sister pulled the office door closed to give us some privacy. I'd wanted to be friends with the woman with the cute hat and vintage bag, I didn't want her to be the red-headed lady with the pantsuit.

"Vinny brought this for you, it was in the car."

Seppi slid my phone across the desk and waited for me to say something about the night before. Was I in trouble for forgetting my phone? I wasn't sure whether I was going to be reprimanded or mollycoddled. He didn't say anything, he didn't want to rush me, but eventually, I couldn't take the silence because it amplified the voices in my head. Seppi was assessing the situation with pain and anger in his eyes. My voice weak like a broken little girl who blamed herself for being hurt,

"I shouldn't have gone to the park after therapy but I just wanted to think."

Seppi went to say something but I put my hand up,

"I didn't push my button when I left therapy, I tried to be better, I tried not to bother you."

He came closer,

"Amelia..."

"But I should have just gone home."

I was sobbing, all curled in a ball in the big leather chair. He pulled me to my feet and held me in his arms in the spot we danced on Christmas Eve. I looked up at him,

"She spit at me and told me to tell you 'hi.' She punched me in the stomach and the face. There was this skinny guy who smelled like cheap cologne and cigarettes, he tackled me to the ground. Then he got on top of me and whispered in my ear. The weight of him made me pee my pants."

I cringed and continued,

"She cable tied my hands behind my back and took my boots. And before that, she slashed at my back with a pocketknife."

I was spiraling but it didn't matter, Seppi knew who hurt me. I continued, but he wasn't listening as much as he was daydreaming about killing Helen with his bare hands.

"This woman came into the cafe yesterday; she had a thrifted wool sweater, a cute hat and a vintage bag. She was looking for a used car that was good in the snow, so I showed her my Subaru. She asked questions about the Caddy, I just thought she liked my car. She was reading a book, I thought she was just a girl I met, and maybe someone I could be friends with. I don't really have many friends."

His face grew angry and his eyes grew even darker. I thought I was in trouble so I grew more frantic. I took a step back from Seppi, I was out of control and talking too fast,

"You said to watch out for the red-headed woman in the pantsuit, but she was wearing jeans, and I couldn't see her hair, it was tucked up in an ear flap hat that looked like a dog. I didn't know. I told her my name. You're not wasting your time on me, Seppi, I promise!"

My eyes overflowed as I sobbed, and I pleaded, "You're not wasting your time!"

Seppi met my gaze and his eyes were no longer dark and full of rage. I was sure he'd imagined killing them a million different ways, and I wondered what he was going to do to them. But, even if I didn't know how he'd do it, I was sure they would suffer before they went into the ground, and I was sure he would find it exquisite. Eventually, he reassured,

"I know."

I didn't say anything after that, and neither did he. We just sat there in the same room, in our own heads, filled with shit and death and demons. Just a broken little girl and a broken little boy, pretending to be a woman and a man. I could tell something bad was going to happen as Seppi sat at his desk, bathing in the darkness and fire, ruminating in it like acid. He gave off an energy I didn't like, but I was so exhausted that I fell asleep on the leather sofa in his office. I woke a couple hours later, covered with the blanket I liked so much. Vinny came by, and the men needed to talk, so I went to the kitchen. Once it was dark, they slipped into the night. I knew he was going to kill them but I put it in a little compartment in the back of my mind where those things went.

Seppi and Vinny came back a couple hours later and burned a bunch of clothes in the fire pit. I watched from the sliding glass doors as the cute hat went into the fire. Opal dragged me into the sitting room. I heard the sliding door and then showers running upstairs. The men came down, damp hair, clean sweats. Vinny kissed me on both cheeks and went into the night. Later in Seppi's office, he handed me Helen's vintage leather bag. It had some blood spots on it, but nothing I couldn't get out with a little peroxide.

CHAPTER 17
SHOWING HIS HAND

SEPPI AND I did a strange dance as the ties tightened, gripping my body like the tendrils of a Sea Witch. Some unspoken contract I'd signed by taking the car and the panic button, a slippery slope, a booby trap, paradise. My brain couldn't distinguish the burning heat of attraction from the adrenaline rush you get when it's time to run. The tongues of a thousand Devils, lapping at my skin like lava. I wrote in a journal and kept to myself most of the time. I told Seppi I wanted a hair cut, and a woman named Carol came on the third day. The black eye didn't faze her, she'd been in my shoes a time or two. She cut off six inches and added some layers, it came about an inch above my shoulders. It hadn't been that short in years and it looked cute, even if the rest of me was toast.

Every night, Seppi gestured me into his cage after Opal went upstairs for the night. I'd never felt more sheltered from the storm inside my head and healing body. As we sipped whiskey over perfectly square ice cubes, the two of us had a couple deep conversations. Some of those conversations made me realize, Giuseppi Moretti is everything you think of when you think of the mob. And curled up on that sofa in front of that fire, something told me it was only a matter of time.

I spent the week in the room next to Seppi's and slept like a baby. I let my guard down for the first time since childhood and slept on my back, above the covers, without worrying the Boogeyman would molest me in my sleep. It was one of those situations where something really bad brought me something really good. I'd fall asleep with the side of my face against his chest, listening to him breathe. Once again, I found refuge at the hands of someone who's killed more people than I can count. Even then, I knew he would never hurt me.

In all my spare time, I processed the mind-fucking I got from the woman with the cute hat and vintage bag. I mourned the beautiful, battered, cream-colored sweater that only cost me fifty cents. I took care of the black eyes and split lip. In a week, I'd be able to erase most of the mess on my face with concealer and foundation, as long as I didn't get too close to anyone. To be honest, the worst wounds were inside.

The following Monday, I left the land of mafia mansions and expensive luxury shower gel, and parked in the spot next to my twenty-six-year-old piece of Swiss cheese. I sat there staring across the lawn before I went up to my apartment. I hooked the vintage bag on the coat rack and got ready for work. Acid flooded my stomach when I realized it had been one week, and it was therapy day. Goddammit. I brought my curls to life, but only so I could use them to camouflage my face. I did my best with concealer, and foundation, and hated how it felt on my skin. Mascara, lip gloss, Alien Elixir, blah, blah, blah, pulling on a mask, you get the point.

I made my way downstairs and tied an apron around my waist. Ten minutes to spare and Kane was buzzing around with a bar rag over his shoulder, in no mood to talk, by the looks. I got to work brewing the house blend and filled the sink with hot soapy water. I did a lap to make sure all the tables had honey, raw sugar, and extra dark maple syrup. If I kept moving, maybe he wouldn't look too closely, I was in perpetual motion while going through the motions that day. Hiding in plain sight.

Work was fine, I was self-conscious about my face and couldn't wait to scrub the spackle off my skin. I served the basic bitches their fancy lattes, and listened to their bullshit small talk with a smile on my face. Most of them were so self-absorbed, I don't think they noticed my face. Kane stood next to me at one point and noticed the pancake makeup, he made a face but didn't say anything. Seppi had 'handled it' with him, and Kane knew he shouldn't ask any questions about why I needed six days off. He could see some green working its way through the concealer and foundation by the end of the day, and everyone could see where my lip had been split. I was preoccupied with wanting to wash my face. At one point, Kane put his hand on mine, and I pulled away. I wasn't falling for his bullshit again. And nothing about Kane made me feel like when I was in Seppi's cage, the one with the tendrils and vines. The one who held me gently, and suffocated me all at the same time. Kane only liked me when Alex was away, or they had been fighting, or they were taking a break. He could get his beard buttered somewhere else. Yes, I said beard, no pun intended.

I hung my apron at the end of my shift and went upstairs to decide if I was going to wear my mask to the impressive office of Isabella Rossi. Standing in front of the mirror in the bathroom, I scrubbed my face, I couldn't breathe with that shit on my skin. I took a good look, made sure I had every stitch of makeup washed off, and then patted in some serum. I didn't bother with mascara or lip gloss, put on some Carmex, and went into my room to figure out what to wear. I threw on my favorite jeans with Seppi's hoodie and spritzed on some Alien Elixir. I kissed Indie, threw on my coat, and shouldered my new vintage bag.

I fired up the mini mafia sedan, set off for hell, and smoked half a joint in the parking lot before going inside. I checked in with Elaine, fuck the garbage magazines. I picked at the skin next to my thumb even though I would regret it later. Isabella Rossi opened the door and I passed her in a trail of Alien Elixir and weed, dragging my emotional baggage behind me. I plopped in the overstuffed chair and waited for her to settle in and look at me. She tried not to make a shocked face when she saw everything I had going on, my lip was healing, but it was still a little swollen. My left eyelid was regular size, but the bruises around both eyes were all kinds of greens, yellows, and a little purple. The tiny cuts were better, but obvious. My chin was still bruised, and I was sporting a glorious scab. I crossed my legs and looked her in the eye,

"If you ask me how I am, I'm going to lose my shit."

I paused and made a circle with my pointer finger at my face,

"I think it's obvious."

Isabella Rossi was smart, she didn't react, she sat there looking at me, calmly. I knew her fingers were itching to write something insightful with that expensive fucking pen of hers. I wondered if Seppi had already told her, or maybe she was really that professional, or maybe nothing fazed her.

"Would you like to talk about what happened?"

I wanted her to know, but I didn't want to tell her. The whole thing was bullshit, I would never feel safe going to the park with the gazebo and the low rock wall, and the water. I was preoccupied with the fact that it was getting darker by the second, and I'd have to walk to my car after my session. I sat there in the houndstooth sports jacket and suede loafers with the tassels that belonged to people who were whacked by the Morettis. I was wasting her time,

"When I left last week, I went to a park and was attacked by someone I met at work earlier that day, a woman I thought I could be friends with. I thought she was a lot like me and maybe we could be friends, only it turned out she was playing me."

Dr. Rossi's interest was piqued,

"Playing you?"

"Yup. And so was the guy I was seeing. Playing me like a fiddle."

I wanted to punch someone, but at the same time, I noticed my fingers were loosely laced together in my lap. Something was happening inside; I was getting pissed, but in a subdued, quiet way, in the way serial killers probably do. The way where you think of all the people who wronged you, and you picture them dead, or picture causing them pain in one way or another, causing them the same kind of pain they caused you. I glanced out the window again briefly to see if it was dark yet, and then returned my eyes to Dr. Rossi,

"I met this guy and started seeing him, he was only in Bunman to figure out what happened to Salvatore Moretti."

Dr. Rossi's eyes got wide for a split second before she reigned it in. I continued,

"Last Monday, this cool woman came into the cafe, so I chatted with her. I even showed her my old car because she said she needed something that was good in the snow. She was wearing a thrifted sweater and had a vintage leather bag. She was a lot like me, and I imagined becoming friends. Maybe we could go to thrift stores together, and I'd have someone who was mine, and not someone I've known my whole life, or someone connected to the cafe, or the Morettis."

"That sounds nice."

"Doesn't it!? Yeah, well, buckle up. I came here, and when I left, I went to a park to sit by the water and think. I pointed in the general direction,

"In Tuttle, the one with the low wall and gazebo."

She nodded.

"A car pulled in next to me, and as it turns out, it was my new bestie, with some guy that smelled like skunky beer, shitty cologne, and second hand cigarettes. They proceeded to kick the shit out of me, cable tie my wrists together, and steal my boots. They left me out in the woods, bleeding in the snow."

I put my finger up,

"Oh, and I pissed my pants."

It didn't seem like I was talking about myself,

"I pushed my button and Seppi found me, he brought me to his house and I stayed there until this morning."

I hesitated but was sick of hiding,

"He protects me in a way no one else ever has, not even my own mother. I know without a doubt that he will save me, protect me, avenge me. You should have seen the fire in his eyes when he found me out there, all beaten and bloody...his 'Dimples,' as he calls me."

She already knew the answer to the question,

"What did he do when he found out someone hurt you?"

I didn't say anything, but we made eye contact, and she knew what I meant; she knew they were dead and I subconsciously dropped my eyes to the bag. Dr. Rossi took the opportunity to reiterate that sometimes getting rid of people is no different than taking out the trash. I felt a wave of confidence,

"Honestly, if he'd let me, I probably could've killed that bitch myself."

She seemed pleased, I think she smiled a little,

"How does it make you feel to say that?"

My body tingled as I imagined wrapping my fingers around Helen's throat. Digging my thumbs into her windpipe as she tried to scream. Staying silent as she begged me to let go, watching the light go out of her eyes. My cheeks flushed,

"It makes me feel good."

I squeezed my thighs together and picked at the arm of the chair,

"Something is brewing inside of me, the scales are tipping, the runt is kicking her way to the top of the pile."

I made eye contact with her again,

"I've snapped, lady."

She restrained a laugh and waited, I was on a roll and she wasn't about to stop me with silly questions,

"It's been my whole life really, but that night in the woods with Sal did something to me, nurtured some deep seething anger. I could've run away, you know. If I'd taken a couple steps into the woods, I would have disappeared into the darkness."

I took a deep breath and noticed my heart was beating in my ears,

"But I didn't. I asked myself if I wanted to hide like a broken little bitch, or if I wanted to kill that mother fucker for all the pain he caused people. There was no other choice, so I gripped that shovel and my focus narrowed, my vision became more acute."

My mind flashed back to that night, and I shivered as goosebumps climbed my extremities. I thought about stepping out of the tree line and swinging that shovel, contacting his head, *thunk*. The bullet tearing through my shoulder, the adrenaline rush that quieted the pain. The second, more desperate swing of the shovel, *thunk*. Watching him stumble, the blood splattering across my cheek in a fine warm mist. That last charge of emotions...pain, fear, shame, worthlessness, rejection...*thunk*. I swallowed the lump in my throat and glanced out the window, night was falling,

"There wasn't any other option, it's like you said, it was a kill or be killed situation. It's too bad I was in that position, but I did what I had to do, and it was him or me. I'm a good person...a caring person, and he was just some narcissistic fuck who existed to hurt people."

I curled my knees up to my chest and cried until the end of my session. I made another appointment and got a reminder card from Elaine. Locked in the bathroom, I threw cold water at my eyes and patted my healing face with nonabsorbent paper towels. I stood there looking at myself under the horrible fluorescent lights, frozen. There was no way I was going to be able to take the elevator, or walk up the alley to the parking lot, or get in my dark car, or drive home. Well, folks, I think that's called PTSD.

I paced the hall and waited until the elevator was empty. Through the windows in the lobby, I could see darkness on the other side of the glass. I joined a group of four women and stayed close until we got to the parking lot. The women stopped to talk, and I made a beeline to the mini mafia sedan, gripping the can of pepper spray I picked up at a Walgreens on the way there. I got in my car and locked the doors. Deep breaths, I reminded myself I was safe. Calm. I put my foot on the clutch and pushed the ignition. I joined the line of mice following the maze home. Once I was on the highway, I became almost paralyzed with fear. I white-knuckled it with one hand while the other pushed the panic button and held it for three seconds.

When he called me, I touched the screen and Seppi's voice came through the speakers, he knew I'd just gotten out of my session with Isabella Rossi, he knew exactly where I was, and he knew I wasn't in the woods somewhere bleeding,

"Amelia, I can't come right now, I'm handling something. Opal's home, I'll tell her you're coming. You're okay."

And then he was gone.

What the fuck was that!?

I pitched the panic button to the floor on the passenger side and drove home. Fuck everyone, and especially fuck Giuseppi Moretti. I pulled behind Muddy Waters to see Kane and Lola in the back yard. Kane waved and I waited for him. He kissed me on the cheek and then scanned my makeup-free face with concern. He moved things around in his head and adjusted his tone,

"What happened to you, Amelia?"

I looked up at him,

"It's complicated."

Kane tucked a loose curl behind my ear, and I should have known right then, I was about to make some possibly questionable decisions. Kane invited me over, and once I peed and fed Indie, I went tap-tap-tapping at his chamber door. We sat on his porch to share tequila and a joint. I put my feet on the rattan table and glanced at him, told him some of it but not all of it,

"I went to that park in Tuttle and this couple mugged me. I got roughed up pretty good. It was really bad for a couple days and I couldn't barista looking like that."

I teared up a little and pushed it away, but Kane looked at me with his dark chocolate eyes and something happened to my insides. There was love in there somewhere and I needed it. He leaned forward and tucked another loose curl behind my ear, and you know what that did. My breath caught in my throat. I knew he wanted to know more, but didn't ask,

"Wanna go to dinner?"

I wasn't expecting that, and it snapped me out of my dark chocolate trance. I was kind of hungry, but my face was a mess. Kane didn't seem to feel like he needed to hide me. I didn't answer right away so he tried again,

"We could order pizza and listen to records."

Kane called the place at the other end of the block, ordered the same thing we always used to get, pepperoni pizza and a piece of chocolate cake for dessert. We bundled up and walked to the pizza place. Our pinkies hooked as we made footprints in the snow. Snowflakes fell around us and cars made tire tracks as they passed. He went in to get the pizza and cake, and we made our way back home.

We sat on his couch, eating pizza and sipping tequila, listening to Tom Petty and The Eagles while we enjoyed each other's company. It always felt comfortable with Kane, it felt vanilla-safe and I forgot about Alex. I brought the pizza box and plates into the kitchen and Kane retrieved dessert. We sat there with two forks, sharing chocolate cake out of the box, and I wondered if we were thinking the same thing. I washed the dishes and wiped off the counter but couldn't gauge his vibe so I tested the waters,

"Hey, I'm going to get going."

But, Kane closed the gap, tucked a loose curl behind my ear, and my eyes fell shut. Our foreheads met as he pulled me closer and I smelled his six-dollar coconut conditioner. We jumped when the back door slammed against the exterior wall of the building,

"Amelia!?"

We locked eyes and froze as Giuseppi Moretti screamed my name again, more desperately,

"AMELIA!?"

I swung Kane's door open to see Seppi running his fingers along the top of the door frame, in search of a key,

"It isn't locked."

Seppi spun around and looked from me, to Kane, and back to me,

"Jesus Christ, Amelia!"

I ran into the hall, frantic,

"Did something happen to my sister!?"

Confused,

"What!? No."

He put his hands on my shoulders,

"Are you OK!?"

I scrunched my eyebrows together, patted myself on the chest, and pretended to be taking my own pulse,

"Yeah, doing pretty good, actually. What are you doing here?"

Seppi was clearly frustrated or hurt, maybe both. He clamped his fingers around my arm and dragged me into my apartment. I put my finger up to let Kane know I'd be right back, and Seppi slammed the door. He pinched the bridge of his nose and paced around the kitchen, relief and something else in his voice,

"I thought something happened to you, Amelia!"

I had no idea what he was talking about. I shook my head and went palms up, I couldn't help but sound annoyed,

"I'm fine."

I gestured across the hall, the weed and tequila talking,

"If you don't mind, I was kind of on a date or something."

The color rose in his cheeks and his eyes grew dark. I stood there like a deer in the headlights, staring at the mob boss in my kitchen. I braced for impact when he came toward me, but he was gentle and held me to his chest. Seppi smelled of whiskey, stress sweat, and Tobacco Vanille. I rested my cheek against his expensive tailored shirt and listened to his heart as it dropped out of panic-mode. My curls got caught up in Seppi's stubble, his body shaking the way it does when you're crying, I held him tight as his tears rolled down the back of my neck.

I'd pushed my panic button, and since Seppi couldn't come to me, he told me to go to his house. And then I didn't. Which was fine, until he got home and my car wasn't in his driveway. Opal told him I probably went home to get high, eat garbage, and cry myself to sleep. He'd been calling and texting but my phone was on my coffee table and I had been across the hall. It had been one week since Seppi carried me out of the woods, and apparently, it had been traumatic to hear me sob and choke over a one-way speaker. I'm sure the whole thing made him feel incredibly angry, and desperately helpless. I exhaled and looked up at him with tears in my eyes. I was full of anger, pain, and remorse, I was tempted to touch his face, but didn't,

"I'm sorry, Seppi. I needed *you*, not my sister."

Feelings stirred in his eyes, deep feelings, for me. He was cracking but tried to hold the pieces together. He dropped his eyes and moved toward the door. As he opened it,

"I needed to see for myself that you were okay."

Seppi gestured toward Kane's door but wouldn't look at it, he looked at the floor instead. His voice sounded as if I had physically hurt him, but I hadn't,

"Go back to whatever you were doing, have a good rest of your night, Dimples."

Seppi disappeared into the hall, leather-soled footsteps descending the stairs. The storm door slapped shut and it took my breath away. I shoved my feet into my Uggs, and took off after him. When I burst through the backdoor, Seppi spun around and I ran to him. He wrapped me in his arms and I returned the favor. We stood like that for a long time, a broken little girl and a broken little boy, holding each other's pieces together. I smelled weed, and when I glanced up at the sun porch, Kane was looking down at us as he smoked a joint. Crap.

CHAPTER 18
THE NEW GIRL

BETWEEN DR. ROSSI, Giuseppi Moretti, and Calliope Cromwell, I'd been thoroughly convinced it was time to get comfortable carrying a handgun. My mind was swirling with old stuff and new stuff. I worked my shifts at Muddy Waters, and served the basic bitches their fancy lattes. I went through the motions and, most days, I made my way to Cal's goat farm shooting range homestead, and dreamt of a day when I would have that kind of peace. Living my best life in some fixer upper farmhouse in the middle of nowhere, far away from the fear and the bullshit. Far away from the masks and the shame and the wildlife refuge. Far away from my mother and those boys, that bathroom floor, and those panties with the day of the week embroidered on them.

I went up the old wooden steps to the porch, and I could smell sage and weed before I got to the door. Cal waved me in, and we spent a long time just talking in a room filled with hanging plants and fairy lights. We talked about things I don't usually talk about with anyone. She started to feel like a mother to me, but a mother who cared and who wanted me to be safe. Not like the mother I had, nothing like the mother I had. This woman had been through some shit, and made it to the other side. She had compassion and deep understanding. She was someone who had been pushed, maybe it was a kill or be killed situation, maybe it was something else. She had done things to save herself, and she wanted to teach me to do the same. Our talks did more to prepare me to shoot a gun than target practice and timed drills ever could. It's easy to pull a trigger with your finger, but it isn't so easy to pull it with your mind. It takes that little switch to flip, the one that tells you it's kill or be killed. The one that gives your brain permission to move the finger you have hovering over the trigger. The one that bypasses compassion for others and sets aside fear, the one that takes control.

I did a lot of reading about guns and women who use guns. I became obsessed with training videos and spent an hour a day doing timed drills to see how quickly I could reach for my gun and kill an assailant if I was attacked. It was becoming like second nature, I was building muscle memory and getting more confident. I knew exactly where to strap on the holster. I knew exactly where the hem of my shirt lay. I was aware of my surroundings in a different way than before. I was hyper-aware of the things around me. I made a mental note of makes, models, and license plate numbers. I scanned faces. I started to feel like I could competently protect myself, if necessary. I started carrying my gun in the bottom of my purse along with my pepper spray, and sometimes it was against my skin in a holster under my ratty vintage overalls.

Seppi knew I was meeting with Cal frequently, and that I was getting more comfortable with my handgun. He was preoccupied with the restaurant, so maybe it was a good thing I was learning how to protect myself. After all, what if I really needed him and he blew me off like he did the last time? What if I really needed him and he didn't come? I couldn't rely on anyone. Seppi was the one who left me out in the woods with his father, I couldn't expect him to protect me. So far, he hadn't done anything but swoop in after the fact and clean up the messes.

I managed to avoid Kane for a little while but eventually, we were alone after the cafe closed one day. I don't know what I was worried about, he wasn't anyone. He was just some dumb barista with dark chocolate eyes and an acoustic guitar. I had no idea what he thought was going on between me and Seppi. But, I knew enough not to go back to Kane's apartment the night Seppi showed up. I realized it could have been anything, but we stood too close for too long and I knew that no matter what, it wasn't just an innocent hug. I knew it, Seppi knew it, and Kane knew it too.

I expected Kane to ask me questions, but he didn't. He moved to me and tucked a curl behind my ear. I swallowed the lump in my throat and looked up at him. I felt wanted and cared for and loved. He scooped my head with his hand and pushed me up against the counter. We stood in the semi-darkness, kissing in the kitchen of Muddy Waters. He lifted me to the counter and stood between my legs, I looked up at him and our mouths came together again. Kane pulled me to him, and I wrapped my legs around his waist as we moved toward the dining room. Piece by piece, we lost our clothes as we kissed. We messed around on the leather sofa in front of the fake fireplace before grabbing our clothes and continuing our activities in Kane's bed.

We laid there sharing a joint and some tequila, and I was exactly where I needed to be. I was safe with Kane, there weren't bullets zinging through the trees and I wasn't worried he would inadvertently put me in harm's way. The underlying sense of panic receded and I let myself relax. I let Seppi and Opal do their dysfunctional thing, and I kept my nose to the grindstone. I worked at the café and practiced shooting with Cal. I felt like the stuff with Lance was a long time ago and the dust had settled. I had almost forgotten about the woman with the cute hat and vintage bag who was really the red-headed lady with the pantsuit. Almost.

My sessions with Dr. Rossi were more of the same, I was in a holding pattern while I waited for something big to happen. I needed to choose which monkey-wrench to use when I opened the next can of worms. She never seemed shocked by anything I said and made sure I knew I could say anything. Either way, I stopped talking about Seppi and stayed away from discussing my love life. I focused on taking out the trash, and doing the world a favor, and sometimes its kill or be killed. She'd look at me in her button up shirt, tailored pants, expensive leather pumps, and never had judgment in her eyes.

My time with Cal was deep and emotional, and I wanted to be like her someday. She was an independent woman who knew who she was and what she wanted. She knew what she was capable of and how to handle herself. Calliope Cromwell was always one step ahead. She was aware of her surroundings and always had some sort of weapon within reach. She told me stories about women like me, women who had to save themselves from strangers, from husbands, from fathers, from exes. Women who needed to kill or be killed, and I was one of them, I was part of that club whether I liked it or not. A club of broken little girls who wanted nothing more than to feel whole.

It does something to you mentally when you realize you're capable of murder. Sure, we all say it, we all say we know we could do it if we had to, but there's doubt. There's this little bit of doubt that creeps in, and you wonder if you'd flounder in the heat of the moment. You wonder if you'd freeze and just stand there while someone killed you. I can tell you that in the moment, when you're in that position, when it's kill or be killed, a deep animal instinct takes over and you go into autopilot. Your past and your present, your strengths, and your weaknesses, they all come together in a perfect storm, you grip the handle of that shovel, and swing for dear life, *thunk*.

I didn't push my panic button after the time he wouldn't come. Fuck that. It was in the bottom of my purse or on the floor of my car, I didn't know, and I didn't care. No point pushing it if he wasn't going to come. Let's see how he liked it when I took care of shit on my own, and didn't need him to come running for every little spider and snake and ass-kicking in the woods. Mentally, sometimes I felt like I was losing my grip, and other times I felt like my mind was quieter than it had been in a decade. I was in control and helpless all at the same time. A couple times a week, I'd pick up one of the pill bottles on top of the microwave and think about taking my meds. I'd write in a journal and take walks in the cemetery, but mostly I kept that shit inside. I'm talking, the really dark shit, the shit I thought about when I was alone so no one would judge me. I'd stare at the ceiling and think about how it felt to kill Sal. Sometimes I hoped I'd get to feel it again, the release that came when he fell to the ground was almost sexual.

I was in that murky mental spot with the dark corners and the demons as I threw my curls into a messy bun and sipped one of Kane's maple oat lattes. I put on jeans and a black Muddy Waters T-shirt before spritzing on my Alien Elixir and bouncing down the stairs to the cafe. I ground the espresso and the house blend. I plugged in the fairy lights and watered the plants in the windows, with their vines moving from hook to hook along the ceiling. I turned on the lights and unlocked the door, I thought it was going to be a normal day. Kane and I planned to go to the Hibachi place on the mountain with his sister and her boyfriend. I was excited to see his sister, Constance, she was a bad-ass and I wondered what type of man such a woman would attract. The last time I went to the Hibachi place was the night my sister met Seppi. I had a pang of something in my guts and in my heart.

Business as usual with the basic bitches and their fancy lattes. The regulars and the banter and the enabling of the caffeine addicts. Kane poked his head in the kitchen,

"I have an interview coming in shortly, when she gets here, could you show her to my office? Thanks. Her name is Gretchen, she goes to the university."

I waved at him, and he went back to his office while I wrapped paninis for a pickup order. Marlaina was manning the counter and there was a lull in the late morning rush. During a lap around the dining room to pick up plates and wipe up crumbs, the door opened and a woman walked in. I did an ocular pat-down and ascertained that she was me about three years ago, but less broken around the edges. That woman was a more athletic version, twenty pounds lighter, a little perkier. Where my hair was frantic ringlets, hers was a cute pixie. Where I had dimples, she had freckles. Her eyes were dark brown, and her lashes were black. Her teeth were straight and white, always the first thing I notice about a person. When she smiled, her entire face lit up. Her name was Gretchen Rodrigue. Crap.

Marlaina told the woman that Kane was waiting for her in his office, and I took a detour from the tables to show her the way. I glanced over at Gretchen as we walked the twenty feet to Kane's door, she smelled like warm vanilla and a little bit of patchouli. Kane waved to me as Gretchen went into his office. I tried to eavesdrop as I wiped tables, but he closed the door most of the way. We needed another barista, but it didn't need to be her. Or maybe she liked girls, that would be good. I busied myself with cleaning and lunch prep, and noticed the woman was smiling when she came out of Kane's office. She waved to us as she pushed through the door,

"See you tomorrow!"

Crap.

Okay, it was no big deal. Just because she's adorable doesn't mean anything. And anyway, she was a child. Suddenly, I was feeling self-conscious and like everyone could see the zit starting to grow on my chin. Another two hours and I'd be home getting high, just two more hours. Then we'd meet Constance and her boyfriend at the Hibachi place on the mountain.

Kane came behind the counter,

"We've finally got some more help, she's starting tomorrow. Gretchen seems sweet and she's a literature major at the university. She's got a couple summers worth of experience and she's eager to get started. Thank you for busting your asses lately, I appreciate it, I'll order you lunch from the pizza place later this week."

Kane retreated to the world of paperwork and window plants that desperately need to be watered. I filled lunch orders with my mind spinning. I was experiencing this yin and yang of emotions and feelings, there was a black and white quality to the situation. Not like a yes or no type of thing, that's not what I'm talking about. But I was not only on the fence about a lot of things, I was also halfway out the door with every little complication. I was accustomed to the bullshit with Alex, but if that little pixie-headed twat started making fuck-me eyes at Kane, I'd pack my shit and find somewhere else to call home.

I missed Seppi, and not even in a way that crossed any lines. I just missed being around him, and hearing his voice, and smelling his cologne. But I'd allowed myself to catch feelings for Kane again, and I was hyper vigilant and jealous about the innocent college girl who hopefully wasn't into guys. I didn't have anything to prove.

CHAPTER 19
THE EVENT PLANNER

WE CLIMBED INTO Kane's vintage Bronco and made our way to the Hibachi place on the mountain. We sat at the grill and sipped drinks as we chatted. That time, I didn't worry that the chef would toss a flaming hot shrimp at my face that would deposit a grease spot on my shirt before tumbling into my crotch. My phone vibrated; I had a message from my sister, who had taken a picture of me from the other side of the room. I turned around and waved before sliding out of my seat and going to Opal's table. We hugged, and she gestured to the other side of the table,

"He just went to the bathroom."

Which was 'coincidentally' where I was now headed. Their appetizers arrived, and I made my way down the hall to the bathroom. Stepping slowly, I was hoping the door to the men's room would open. I prayed Seppi would come strolling out with his whiskey breath and Tobacco Vanille. I kind of junior-highed it, stopping at a bulletin board to carefully read a poster for an event that happened a month ago. I gave up after thirty-seconds, and as I was reaching for the lady's room door, the men's room opened and out came Giuseppi Moretti. His eyes lit up and he winked as he kissed me on both cheeks, warmth spreading like wildfire through my body, straight to my who-ha. I took in the scent of him in that brief moment of closeness, in the sexy, intimate version of his voice, his hand on the small of my back,

"It's nice to see you."

Seppi flicked his eyebrow ever so slightly,

"I've missed you, Dimples."

He went back to his table, and I went into the lady's room and stood there. I felt like I had been punched in the gut. I was there with my sort of boyfriend, having a good evening, but seeing Seppi made my heart hurt. When I returned to my table, someone was sitting in my seat next to Kane, it was Gretchen. Okay, well, I'd been in the bathroom, but I was back. I approached my seat and she waved at me excitedly as she flashed her cute fucking smile. I wanted to tell her, 'No, that's my seat!' I got closer so she'd get the point, but she continued talking to Kane. What the fuck was happening? After forever, she touched his arm as she got up. Excuse me!?

Gretchen smiled at me before joining a gaggle of women at a booth in the corner. A couple of the women, clearly drunk, pointed over at Kane and gushed obnoxiously. The chunky ginger one slapped Gretchen's arm, and mouthed, 'Wow, he's hot!' Gretchen smiled back at them and I rolled my eyes. I just wanted a nice evening without any drama, and the whole fucking town was there. Jesus. I was pretty sure the adorable pixie-headed bitch was going to try to weasel her way into Kane's bed, or at least into his pants. I made a mental note to leave a hair tie and some perfume in his nightstand.

I stewed. Not a fleeting thought that Gretchen might be a problem, but I wouldn't worry about it until she gave me a reason to worry about it. I'm talking like, right then, I had a disdain for that woman, right to my core. I know now that I should have listened to my gut. Where did that stupid little bitch get off coming into the cafe, and maybe someday making fuck-me eyes at my sort of boyfriend, who already had another girlfriend? I didn't have any interest in competing with two women, and it took the wind out of my sails to think about it. Was I losing my damn mind? I needed to slow my roll. I didn't even have a reason to think Kane found Gretchen attractive, and like I said before, maybe she was into girls.

I trained Wretched, I mean Gretchen. She was focused, experienced, and already knew the ropes. She was charming with the basic bitches, and they loved the fancy lattes she made for them. Gretchen actually seemed to give a shit. I mean, I gave a shit too, but in more of a 'it would be great to get through the day without killing myself' kind of thing, and not a 'let's try really hard to make people happy' kind of thing. Kane didn't seem to be flirting with Gretchen, and she didn't seem to be trying to lick his face. So far, so good. I have no idea why I was so insecure, well besides the obvious reasons.

While that was all going on, the new and improved Giuseppi's Italian Ristorante was getting closer to its opening night. Apparently, when you're in the mob, you can get things built in a hurry, especially if it scratches clean a couple debts. Seppi said he was going to be at the ristorante, late morning, and wanted to meet with me. I was excited to see him, and curious why he wanted to see me. That man could crush me so easily and didn't even know it, but I hadn't yet realized it would have been just as easy for me to crush him. Since there were three of us working the cafe, Kane said I could run next door for a few minutes to meet with Seppi, in the lull between breakfast and lunch.

I made myself a latte and set off across the parking lot, brushing coffee grounds from my apron before I swung through the back door to the new and improved Giuseppi's Italian Ristorante. The vision was coming together, it was a world away from the smoldering embers. The new place reminded me of the old place, but with better ambiance and a more authentic feel. I peeked in Seppi's office and knocked on the door casing, he waved me in. He kissed me on both cheeks, and I took in the scent of him, the warmth of his lips, the scratch of his salt and pepper stubble,

"How are you, Dimples?"

I glanced away so he wouldn't know I was lying, "I'm fine."

He gestured and I sat in the leather armchair across the desk from him, I didn't realize I was at the cusp of the inner sanctum. Seppi poured two whiskies over perfectly square ice cubes and set one down in front of me. His eyes were pulling me into the abyss, sometimes the darkness inside of him felt like a refuge from the darkness inside of myself. Sometimes, if someone's darkness is that much darker than yours, your darkness seems like light. Seppi's stormy eyes, full of all he had done and seen and felt, spoke to me in those moments. I made a sound low in my throat, and nibbled at my bottom lip, which had finally healed. Gauging the vibe; it didn't seem like I was in trouble. I hadn't spoken to Lance, so it wasn't that. I hadn't seen anyone new, so it wasn't that. I hadn't pushed my panic button for a stupid reason, so it wasn't that. I was anxious but wasn't sure why. I jumped when he broke the silence, his voice deep, all business,

"I plan to reopen on Valentine's Day, and would like to extend you an offer."

Giuseppi Moretti wanted to extend me an offer? Not knowing if I should be excited or terrified, I stared into my glass and nervously swirled Seppi's expensive whiskey around with the perfectly square ice cubes. My leg jiggled and my stomach did somersaults. When I glanced up at him, he was smiling with his eyes, head tilted a little, like he was amused with me for one reason or another,

"I would like you to join the team as my Event Planner."

I made a face, and he put his hand up,

"This would be a wise move for you, Dimples."

I felt like we were playing a game of chess, and I wondered about his next move, my curiosity piqued. What would it be like, to be that close to him all the time? I imagined him, pinning me against the wall with his body, or getting the chance to rub whatever he had inside of those expensive tailored pants. Swallowing the lump in my throat, I tried to get a hold of myself, nodding at Seppi to continue.

He gestured across the alley,

"You've got more to offer than what you can do at that hole in the wall over there."

I followed Seppi's eyes to the wall and back, he continued,

"There's a substantial difference between pulling espresso and being a part of my team. I'm offering you a valuable opportunity here, Amelia. And I can guarantee this job will open doors for you."

He spoke with his hands,

"What is your salary at Muddy Waters?"

I shrugged and picked at the skin next to my thumb,

"Umm, I don't really get a salary, it's minimum wage, and tips, but I have rental income, so it's plenty."

He leaned forward,

"The Event Planner position would provide you with a more professional role, and a great deal of responsibility. The salary is seventy-five thousand, to start."

I stared at him as if I was looking through the bottom of a pair of bifocals,

"You're going to pay me seventy-five thousand dollars a year to be your Event Planner?"

My mouth was hanging open, he sweetened the deal, even though it wasn't necessary,

"You'd be working closely with me, which would afford you the benefit of additional protection."

Seppi read my face and I blinked up at him like a doe-eyed idiot. He reassured,

"I have no doubt you'll be a wonderful addition to the family."

The family!? Was I his little sister now!? A distant cousin who needed a favor!? And because I can never take anything at face value, I was immediately conflicted. We all know at this point that I was fighting my feelings for him, but I knew it wasn't time to do anything about it. And we all know I had feelings for Kane a little bit too, but Alex was orbiting in the periphery, and what about Gretchen? If I was over at the ristorante, who would make sure Kane wasn't screwing Alex or Wretched, I mean Gretchen? If I was over at Muddy Waters, would I miss a valuable career opportunity? What if that Event Planner job opened doors for me, and what if it finally made me feel like a woman. But we all know it was more than that, accepting that Event Planner job would mean spending a lot more time with Seppi, and I didn't know if I could handle that, not really. I was just some dumb broken bitch, and he was the head of a mob family, I didn't even rate in the same hemisphere.

Seppi put his hand on my lower back and escorted me to the office across the hall. He flipped on the light, gesturing around the room, cream-colored walls and white trim. If I took the job, I would be all but signing up for the mob in one way or another. I was already involved, but working in that building, across the hall from an actual mob boss, would mean I'd know everything that was going on. If that was my new office, then I'd be sharing space with him, intimate space. The inner sanctum. It would mean I'd have the password to the back room, one of the good ones who did bad things sometimes.

I knew some of this was my sister's idea because, in her eyes, if Seppi was watching over me, maybe I'd stay out of trouble. I wanted to be in Opal's place, in a bed down the hall from him, so I could sleep through the night without fear of the Boogeyman. But, if I was in that house long enough, I would crawl into bed with him in the middle of the night, so I could sleep with my body against his. I didn't tell her that, but I thought it. I plopped in the cream-colored leather desk chair and spun around like a little girl in a candy store, Seppi smiling with his eyes as he leaned against the door frame.

The bathroom was stocked with plush towels and fancy soaps, like the ones at his house. A crystal bottle of whiskey and a little etched glass jar of edibles sat on the vanity. The leather sofa was a cream-colored version of the one across the hall. A round maple coffee table, topped with a lidded glass jar full of fancy trail mix and an expensive looking candle in a frosted jar. There was a glass-front mini fridge filled with bubbly water and Culture Pop. I plopped on the sofa and Seppi sat next to me. He put his hand on my knee and patted it, electricity shooting to my privates.

"You know your sister worries about you, the closer I keep you, the happier she'll be."

I wondered if she knew how ironic that was, keeping me close was making me happier too. I was trying really hard not to be the bad guy, the one who crossed the line, the one who broke the boundary, but this was going to make it difficult. Opal wasn't staying, but I was trying to stay in my lane. Whenever I spent time around Seppi, I craved more, it's hard to explain. Our connection grew deeper whenever we shared space, and by then, I was aware there were strings attached, but being close to him allowed me to let my guard down most of the time. We would learn subtle things about each other, we would pick up on nuances and quirks. Seppi was waiting for me to say something, anything, but I was lost in my mind, and my heart. Glancing over at him, I flicked my eyebrows and smiled with my whole face,

"I'll do it!"

He tried to keep himself right, but I noticed a twinkle in his eyes. He seemed happy that I'd be across the hall. He hopped up and clapped his hands together,

"Good then, I'm looking forward to it. You'll have to give your notice today; I'll need you as soon as possible. I want you to know what you're doing before we open; I already have people reaching out about retirement and anniversary parties."

Seppi winked at me and retreated to the world of whiskey and Cuban cigars. As an afterthought,

"Dimples."

I poked my head in, assuming he would tell me he was just kidding,

"Yeah?"

"You'll need something more professional than ripped overalls and dirty sneakers."

I made a face, but he was right.

"I will make you an appointment with my tailor, and will provide you with what you need."

What!? My head was spinning when my watch jiggled, it was Kane, 'In the weeds over here.' I left the world of gabagool and returned to the world of capicola, going through the motions while I shared space with Wretched, I mean Gretchen. I wondered what I would look like in some sort of tailored pantsuit, something made just for me. After my shift, I tapped on Kane's door and he gestured me in. Sitting in the wobbly secondhand chair across the desk from him, I told him I was leaving. The timing wasn't great, we were finally fully staffed. I watched Kane's eyes, and it seemed like he was both upset, and kind of relieved. He insisted I stay on the payroll in case I wanted to cover a shift sometime. I knew it wasn't going to happen any time soon, and I think he knew it too. Telling him I was leaving didn't change things right away because things wouldn't change until after I left.

Kane was insecure about Seppi and I knew why. It started last year, when Kane found out we shared lunch sometimes. Even way back then, before the connection and the history and the panic button, before all that, Kane was still a little jealous of Giuseppi Moretti. Kane was a long-haired hippie with an acoustic guitar, and Seppi was the real deal, the big cheese, the one you fight in the boss battle. Kane couldn't compare, but sometimes, I didn't need him to. Sometimes, I chose the one with the dark chocolate eyes and the record collection.

The next couple times we made love, I knew I needed to cherish it, I knew there was going to be a last time, or at least it felt that way. There's no way we would survive a world where I worked for Giuseppi Moretti. The close quarters, the late nights, the whiskey over perfectly square ice cubes, the Tobacco Vanille. That was the beginning of the end for Kane Buchanan. Not literally, but our time as bed fellows was winding down. Once I inevitably crossed the line with Seppi, there would be no turning back. Kane tucked a curl behind my ear and it brought me to tears. Was I doing the right thing? Did I choose Kane? Was he safer? Yes. Was he the one? I didn't know. I flashed back to seeing Alex for the first time, finding her hair tie and perfume in his nightstand.

I thought about the first time I saw Kane, the time he winked at me and I thought he was winking at someone else. He wondered what had gotten into me. I kissed him more passionately, and made love to him more feverishly. I needed to get him out of my system, but he didn't know it. And maybe I didn't know it either, but I should have known it. People in that town knew their place, and you needed to be somebody to go up against Giuseppi Moretti, and that was the truth even before he was king. But now that Giuseppi Moretti was the one everyone answered to, Kane Buchanan didn't stand a chance.

CHAPTER 20
THE BEGINNING OF THE END

THE NEXT TWO WEEKS flew by and I was doing double duty. I'd work my shifts at the cafe, clean up, get into some of the clothes Seppi bought for me, and go to the restaurant. Things were coming together, and I was making connections already. I was spending time with Cal, but not as much, and I missed her. I remembered the times I went shooting at Kane's buddy's house, and it made me sad to know that part of my life was going to be over sooner than later. Kane didn't seem interested in Wretched, I mean Gretchen. She worked a couple days a week and everyone loved her, she was the younger, cuter, softer version of me, without the rough edges and the scars.

I had a better understanding of Seppi's job, not the one at the restaurant, the one where he was top dog. I met people, heard conversations, learned things I can't talk about. All those men knew I could be trusted, they didn't stop talking about bad things when I was around. Maybe they knew I had been spoken to about discretion. One night, while those men shared whiskey with Seppi, I leaned in the door and waved on my way by. I was sure every one of those men were packing heat, both literally and figuratively. I suddenly had more than one set of eyes looking at my tits, my curls and my dimples, and it kind of turned me on. But those men knew I was sort of off limits, I was untouchable, or at least that's how it was starting to feel.

I mean, think about where I was a year ago, the morning I filled up at a little gas station along Route 7 on my way to Bunman. The morning when I waltzed into Muddy Waters and had no idea what was coming. The men trickled out over the next little while and I was alone in the inner sanctum with Giuseppi Moretti. After the last man went into the night, Seppi's voice came low and sexy from across the hall, an entire sentence in one word,

"Dimples."

I spun around in my chair, went to Seppi's office, and sat across the desk from him again. He slid a rocks glass to my side with a heavy-handed shot of whiskey over some of his perfectly square ice cubes.

He crossed his loafered feet on the edge of the desk and lit a Cuban. I dug a joint out of my purse and joined him. Our eyes met, we clinked glasses across the desk, and enjoyed our poison as we swallowed fire. I imagined holding his head to my breasts and taking in the scent of him as I held him there. I imagined pushing his papers to the floor and screwing him on that expensive hardwood desk. I didn't do any of those things, but I was alone with him in the lair, the inner sanctum, the VIP lounge, the first glimpse of our new routine.

He let the power go to his head sometimes, whether he meant to or not, and I liked it. I got to watch him go from marionette to master of puppets. I got just as drunk on his authority as I did on his whiskey. The underlying feelings I had for him had been pushed to the side and changed into something else. I was the one who was closest to the soft parts, the daggers, the secrets, and the demons. I watched Seppi talk to the ones like him and I learned how he negotiated. I listened to his words, but even more importantly, I observed his body language, his expressions, the inflection of his voice. I watched as he steered conversations and served ultimatums. I learned my role and made more connections. I practiced with my gun, got comfortable, and carried it all the time. I didn't need my panic button, I walked around like I was untouchable.

I spent time with Kane, but things were changing. My mind was always preoccupied, thinking about things, keeping secrets, staying in the inner sanctum. There was a level of perpetual hyper-vigilance, a deep awareness. I knew where my handgun was at all times. I looked over my shoulder and made eye contact with people walking toward me on the sidewalk. I made mental notes of faces, and sensed subtle changes in my environment. It was my new norm to spend evenings at the restaurant, working on administrative things, helping manage the final stretch before the finish line. It was also my new norm to sip expensive whiskey across the desk from Giuseppi Moretti at the end of the night. I was carrying myself with confidence and knew what I was doing. I strutted around town like I had a pair, if anyone messed with me, they'd have hell to pay at the bottom of the lake.

I finally had the balls to walk alone at night, and sometimes I'd make a loop around town and stroll through the cemetery. It was my quiet time, my peaceful time, the time when my mind was clear. Most people wouldn't have the guts to do what I did. And then one night as I strolled through the cemetery, a car pulled in. I hid behind a tree and watched as a man stopped at the end of a row and put something into one of the cement planters behind a grave. And then he left. I waited a couple minutes and then looped around the path and lit up the planter with my phone. Nestled inside the cement urn was a gallon Ziploc bag, half filled with banded stacks of one-hundred-dollar bills.

I looked both ways and shoved the baggy in my coat. As I was zipping it up, headlights swung into the entrance and made their way toward the grave with the planter. I ran along a stream and up a hill at the tree line. I hid behind an ancient maple and followed the headlights with my eyes as they drove to the planter. I held my breath. The dark sedan came to rest in front of the planter and the first guy hopped out. The first guy walked around the front of the car and swiped around inside the planter. He threw his hands up in the air and shouted something. The driver got out of the car and joined the first guy, which is precisely when they noticed my footprints. I went for my gun, which was strapped to my stomach inside of the shirt that was zipped inside of my coat.

I yanked frantically at the zipper and it stopped after two inches, the baggie jammed in the threads. I tugged frantically at the zipper as the men stormed in my direction. They stopped, turned around and went back to the planter. They checked the planter again, turned back around, and followed the footsteps. I worked my arms out of the sleeves and threw the coat over my head. The men were getting closer, coming up the hill. Fifty feet away at that point. I lifted the hem of my shirt in one fluid motion and pulled the gun. I could see shapes in the moonlight against the snow. I found my voice as I held the gun out in front of me and pointed at the chest area of one of the men. My voice trembled with adrenaline,

"STOP!"

They stopped and realized it was just a stupid girl. The one on the right smacked the one on the left, this was going to be like taking candy from a baby,

"You have something that belongs to us. Why don't you give us what's ours, and we'll let you go home to your cat."

I was offended, and how did he know I had a cat. Anyway, that asshole had no idea I was aiming a gun at his chest. And I couldn't really tell if I was aiming at his chest, but that's what I was hoping for. The safety was off. The gun was out in front of me. My hands were shaking, but I kept my breathing steady and my heart wasn't beating in my ears. I was in control of the situation for the first time in my life, or maybe the second.

"If you come any closer, I'll shoot!"

They laughed at me, both of them. Oh yeah? I shot the gun in the air,

"I'm not kidding assholes! Come any closer and I'll shoot!"

They turned around and started running back to the car. Thank God. When they were at the bottom of the hill, I slid down the trunk of the big maple, sitting on my coat and the bag of money. And then I heard car doors, but the engine didn't start. I leaned over and peeked around the tree to see the two of them running up the hill again, with what looked like guns. I fought with my arms and my legs and scraped my hands against the bark as I tried to stand. My jelly legs failed me. They were thirty feet away and getting closer. I held the gun out in front of me, the safety off. My voice trembled through my tears,

"I'll shoot!"

They didn't pause, they just kept coming, here goes nothing. I could only see shapes in the dark as the light of the moon reflected on the snow. I squeezed the trigger at the objects moving toward me. Nothing. They laughed. I pulled the trigger again and that one landed, that one changed things a little. The first guy fell as his leg gave out beneath him. The driver stopped in his tracks and grabbed the one who fell,

"Let's go, come on!"

The driver desperately dragged the first guy toward the car. The first guy realized he was leaving a trail of blood in the snow, and started to panic. The driver yelled at the first guy to get in the car. They got in the car and sped around the twists and turns. I waited until the taillights disappeared up Maple Street, and then I waited a little longer. I sat there shivering from the cold and the adrenaline, as those assholes went to wherever people like that go when they get shot in the leg in a cemetery at eleven o'clock at night. I holstered the handgun, wrapped my coat around the zipper bag, and speed walked home without looking back. Indie meowed at me from the sink as I stood in the shower until the hot water ran out, adrenaline receded as I washed away the cooties of the day. I didn't mention it to anyone and I slept like a baby. I didn't even wonder if the guy was okay, fuck him. And in the morning, while I drank a latte and smoked half a joint on my sun porch, I counted my hundred-dollar bills.

CHAPTER 21
MASTER OF PUPPETS

THERE I WAS, this bad bitch, too good to work at Muddy Waters, packing heat in line at the grocery store. On top of my shit in the luxury office of Isabella Rossi. Keeping my boundaries with Seppi, even though we were sharing close quarters. I was learning from him, watching him, mimicking him, soaking it all in, I was a blank slate. Seppi carried himself differently and I was there for it, he was getting full of himself right in front of my eyes. I wondered if Opal saw that side of him, the side that sat at that desk. I knew the business and the personal, and my mind wandered into places it shouldn't, especially when I was lonely. It was one thing, people warning me that Giuseppi Moretti was in the mob. It was something else entirely, to know what he smelled like at the end of the day, to be the one he shared his whiskey with. It was intimate to share his close quarters, almost as intimate as sharing a bed.

I did what Seppi wanted; I did whatever he said. I was a good little girl, with ringlets to die for, and those goddamn dimples. I sat across the desk from him in his office, at the end of a long day of tying up loose ends, the ones before the finish line that was really the starting line. I was the one he talked to about the things my sister couldn't know about, the things she wouldn't approve of. I knew classified information, his secrets and my own. I didn't tell Seppi I shot that guy, and I didn't tell him about the money. I was allowed to have my own secrets; he didn't need to know everything, and there wasn't anything wrong with that.

As the time ticked down to the finish line, I was dressing more professionally, and that included some tailored aesthetic that showed a little leg, and a lot of cleavage. I had guys, I'm talking guys with money, and power, and any woman they wanted, looking at my tits and making fuck-me eyes at me in Seppi's office. And one night, I would be the right amount of high, or the right amount of lonely, and I'd blow one of those guys in his big SUV, or sports car. What a shit storm that would create, and I was giddy to see Seppi's face when his buddy told him what I'd done.

Then, one night, about a week before the big night, Seppi and a couple of his associates were lounging around his office, drinking whiskey and puffing on Cubans. The group of Italian mobsters were listening to exactly what I thought they'd be listening to. Out of curiosity and boredom, I wandered across the hall, in my stocking feet and my couple of unbuttoned buttons. Seppi's eyes fell to my cleavage. He winked at me as he sipped his whiskey and I felt it everywhere. I nervously scanned the room and one of the guys was totally my type, sort of like if Kane was in the mafia. Mysterious type with a professionally groomed Viking beard. He was hot and dark, tall for an Italian. That man was over six feet and lean, not stocky like Seppi. He had dark wavy hair, and hypnotic eyes that bordered on black. It has been over a decade, but I can still remember Luciano's eyes, my God. He seemed like a good one who did bad things, and sometimes I wonder if it would have gone anywhere between us if things had been different.

I bet when Luciano 'Mozart' Cavallaro got his hair cut, it cost him hundreds of dollars and he left a good tip. Someone like that wasn't messing around with Master Cuts, or some salon in the mall. Luciano smelled expensive, his dark eyes had a softness about them, and he wasn't that much older than me. He had been looking at me, and I had been looking at him. I wondered if Luciano brought that Mozart energy to the bedroom. I blushed, even though I was pretty sure the nickname had something to do with piano wire neck ties. Luciano put his hand out to me and Seppi clenched his jaw as he watched. We danced, Luciano in his expensive leather loafers, and me in my stocking feet. He twirled me and dipped me, and I felt like one of those girls in the old movies, the girls with the long cigarettes, only I'm partial to a joint.

Luciano was exotic and sexy; he drove a fancy Porsche Cayenne and hangered a private jet. I was rubbing shoulders with men like that, worlds above a barista with a man bun, an espresso machine, and a skinny blonde with perky tits on the back burner. I could have fucked that guy if I wanted to, even if there would have been hell to pay. I was moving up in the world, moving up on the food chain, hanging out in the inner sanctum, allowed full access to the bat cave. I had somehow fooled everyone into thinking I could handle it. So far, not a single person had given me the side-eye as I strolled around in the office of a mob boss in my stocking feet. Looking back, maybe he was molding me like putty in his hands, but I had somehow convinced Giuseppi Moretti that I was of value to him. Listen, I'm not stupid, I knew there was a chance this whole thing was bullshit and I was just a play thing. And because I desperately needed access to him so I wouldn't lose my mind, I was willing to take whatever I could get.

I was clinking glasses with men who had whacked people, men with millions of dollars, men who were untouchable. Those men were way out of my league, but I was passing, and 'Mozart' Cavallaro was hitting on me for sure. Maybe it paid to show my cleavage and my legs, it made me feel like a woman, instead of some frump in a pair of ratty vintage overalls. Maybe the overalls were my chrysalis, and maybe I was emerging, some bad-ass bitch in the mafia. Our fingers laced together and he pulled me close as we danced to familiar Sicilian music I hadn't heard since the restaurant burned down.

The night I danced with Luciano, shit kind of hit the fan a little bit. Once everyone cleared out, I peed, shrugged into my thrifted wool pea coat, and grabbed my purse. I stuck my head in Seppi's office to let him know I was leaving, but he wasn't in there. I made my way to the dining room and found Seppi behind the bar, gripping his empty rocks glass. He was out in the wild, away from the protection of the inner sanctum, and it felt like we were on even ground. I thought about plucking the glass from his hand, getting close enough that I could smell his skin, and the whiskey on his breath. But, when I took a good look at him, it was obvious he was bubbling under the surface. He was frozen in place, holding his breath, and it made me nervous. Seppi's nostrils flared and he threw his glass at the wall so hard that it exploded into a million pieces. Minuscule shards of glass rained down to the floor like glitter.

My breath caught in my throat when Seppi's body slammed into mine like a ton of bricks. He growled, and my back hit the wall. I eyeballed him, unsure what he was doing, or thinking. He narrowed his eyes at me and clenched his jaw. His hand flew up to my throat, my purse falling to the floor. He got in my face,

"What the fuck do you think you're doing!?"

I blinked up at him, and wasn't sure if he was hitting on me or reprimanding me for something. He was making me sweat in my 'dry clean only' pea coat. He growled,

"If you're going to be a distraction, then I'll need to do something about that! Capiche!?"

I teared up and it startled me when he barked,

"Don't start with me Amelia!"

I opened my mouth to reply, and he cut me off, raging in my face, spit flying,

"DON'T!"

He dropped his hand, but held me against the wall with his body a little longer. It was more than that, it wasn't about me being a distraction to Luciano, it was about Seppi having to watch it. Maybe he was bringing big brother vibes, but I was almost positive it was more than that. I was pretty sure he was jealous that I was twirling, and dancing, and showing my dimples and cleavage to some hot rich guy that was closer to twenty-five than forty. Luciano wasn't some dumb barista with a man bun and an acoustic guitar, he had a fancy Porsche Cayenne and a private jet. Luciano smelled expensive and could have whisked me away to an all-inclusive in the Caribbean, if he wanted.

What was Seppi's problem, anyway? I guess that's when I realized the puppet master was pissed he couldn't control me, or my dimples, or what I did with my cleavage. I was rubbing shoulders with the big boys and I was a loose cannon. Eventually, I'd get drunk and climb into a backseat or fall into a bed. Fine, but that too-big-for-his-britches wasn't going to twat-block me while he was playing house with my sister. Seppi shifted his weight and took a step back, he'd pushed me just a little bit too far, and he knew it. I narrowed my eyes at him, buttoned my coat, and retrieved my purse. I glared at Seppi and turned for the backdoor, fuck him. He put his hand out to me, but I stormed away without looking back. Seppi sighed loudly from down the hall as I pushed through the back door into the night, his voice defeated and pleading, calling after me,

"Dimples."

I let his words hang in the air as the door latched behind me. I was seething, Giuseppi Moretti needed to be taken down a peg or two, I don't play his bullshit games. He puts his pants on one leg at a time, just like everyone else. He wasn't anything special, not really. If Seppi was going to act like that, then maybe I didn't feel the way I thought I did, maybe he was just some guy I knew. And maybe I'd call Luciano Cavallaro and see if he wanted a blow job in the back seat of his fancy Porsche Cayenne.

Seven days and counting until the finish line and things were coming together. Fancy tables and chairs were moved into the dining rooms, upstairs and down. The final touches were done on trim and fixtures and decor. Almost time for wine deliveries and stocking the kitchen shelves. Seppi was starting from scratch with most of the kitchen staff, and some of the servers. Opal would hostess until she bailed. She was buzzing around, a little over six months pregnant, over the morning sickness and crippling fatigue, not quite ready to start nesting.

I was pissed when I woke up the next morning, What had gotten into Seppi? Who did he think he was, pushing me against the wall, telling me I'm a distraction. I didn't see him bringing his buddy Mozart out behind the dumpster for a piano lesson, no pun intended. Seppi might have been the big shit around there, but he wasn't going to treat me like that. Someone tapped on the front door, so I hopped up and ran to see who it was. A man waved at me from the other side of the glass and shouted with a gritty Italian accent,

"I'm here for an interview with Mr. Moretti."

I rolled my eyes, Mr. Moretti, what a fucking joke. There was a good chance this guy was going to smell like cigarettes, weed, and cheap cologne. I unlocked the door and pushed it open. The guy was probably thirty, a little rough around the edges, but he cleaned up nice. As I thought, he smelled like left-handed cigarettes and knock off cologne, but he had a nice smile. Guido Leone was there to speak with Mr. Moretti about one of the prep chef positions and looked like a chef to me, but what do I know? I retrieved a cup of black coffee for Guido, and left him to poke around the kitchen. I leaned into Seppi's office and snapped my fingers at him like an asshole. He glanced in my direction like he was expecting me to say something witty or entertaining, I did neither of those things. But instead, I acted like a complete fucking bitch,

"Hey Geppetto, your marionette is here for his interview."

I spun around and marched into my office. I returned a couple of phone calls, and one of them was to 'Mozart' Cavallaro. Maybe I was getting too big for *my* britches. I had people coming in to look at the space for upcoming events. I had future brides booking tastings and meetings with the Event Planner, and I was the Event Planner. I was the one who booked the shit, and rubbed the shoulders, and greased the elbows, and whatever else I was told to do. And I did it well. Maybe Seppi was right, maybe I had more to offer, maybe I was ready to be a bad bitch.

I answered the back door for a delivery, smoked half a joint in the parking lot, sat on the couch in my office, digging through some fancy trail mix for the dark chocolate covered blueberries. I heard the guy leave, and it sounded like Seppi hired him. Good, maybe Seppi would calm the fuck down. The kitchen was going to be fine. And there was a steady flow of single moms, and college girls, to wait tables with smiles on their faces while showing a little cleavage. The ones with the fancy fake nails, who smelled like cigarettes, Victoria's Secret body spray, and spearmint gum. A dime a dozen. I imagined running a business like that was a revolving door of mediocrity.

My office door swung open and bounced off the stopper as Seppi charged in. My feet were crossed on the coffee table, dark chocolate covered blueberries in my mouth. He towered over me and growled through clenched teeth,

"Get up!"

I'd had just about enough of his bullshit. I moved the mouthful around and scrunched my eyebrows at him before shoving my hand in the jar to retrieve another blueberry. His hands were flying around and he was all worked up. He shouted down at me,

"I'm not asking!"

Seppi plucked the jar from my hands and slammed it onto the coffee table. I cheeked the mouthful, smacked his arm, and yelled up at him,

"HEY!"

He swept my legs from the coffee table and pulled me to my feet by my shoulders. I rolled my eyes, swallowed the mouthful, and scrunched my eyebrows at him again. Seppi let go of my shoulders and threw his hands around some more,

"Why did you call me Geppetto!? Is that some kind of joke!? Is that supposed to be funny!?"

I shrugged, pointing at him with my palm up, like I was stating the obvious,

"Aren't you the puppet master around here, now?"

Seppi just stared back at me with his mouth hanging open, and while I had his attention,

"Last night, you made it clear that you're under the impression you get to tell me, what I can, and cannot, do with my body. You even went so far as to put your hands on me in some assertion of your dominance, like you own me."

I paused and got closer, locking eyes with him,

"I can dance with whoever I want to dance with, I'm not some fire hydrant you can piss on."

I tapped the side of my head like a light bulb went off,

"I've got it! I bet you're overcompensating for something. Does your dick not work, or something!?"

Seppi flicked his brows, hands on hips, our eyes locked together,

"My dick works just fine."

Well, he won that round, because I didn't really want to think about what he was doing with his dick, since he wasn't doing it with me. I matched his energy, hands on hips,

"Hey, Mr. Big Shot Mob Boss Moretti, isn't that what they call you, now that you're the big cheese!?"

I waved him away with all of his bullshit,

"Jesus, get over yourself."

Seppi stared back at me blankly, so I clarified,

"You're acting like a possessive asshole!"

I lifted my arms and legs like a marionette, and broke into an improvised rendition of a little song I like to call, 'I'm a little wooden girl, a little wooden girl.' I couldn't tell if he was pissed off, or just completely flabbergasted that some dumb broken bitch would call him out on the carpet for his bullshit. He was clenching his fists, red faced, and I was over his holier than thou attitude. I was also remarkably high, fuck it,

"Oh really!? What are you going to do now, tough guy, whack my ass and dump me in the lake!?"

I stared him down, leaning in with my hands on my hips,

"Try it, I dare you!"

I wound up for the grand finale, like I was stating the obvious,

"You're a chip off the old block, aren't you?"

I laced my fingers together in front of my heart, smiled, and pretended I was feeling sentimental for Salvatore Moretti,

"Your father would be so proud!"

And that was it, that's what did it, just like pulling the plug from a drain, emotions crashed in like a tidal wave, because he knew it was true. He just stared back at me and I watched as the anger turned into pain. Seppi kind of just slunk away, but it was more like he just completely deflated. I followed him with my eyes as he went back to his office and I wasn't far behind. He stood at his bar with a thousand-yard stare, working the stopper out of a bottle of Johnny Walker Blue. I crossed the threshold and saw the side of Seppi he saved for me. The anger I pent up was subsiding, along with the feelings of rejection. He was busy with the renovations, and the longing deep inside of me wasn't being fed. There I was, alone with him again, our feelings raw and rough and out of sorts. I pushed the door shut and could see that he was figuring out if I was there to give him a pep talk or a blow job. I plucked the glass from his hand before he even had a chance to take a sip, I tossed it back and put the empty glass on the bar. He locked eyes with me, his voice full of feelings. I was in his personal space and hadn't been invited, he flicked his eyebrows at me again,

"Whatcha doing, Dimples?"

I wrapped him in *my* cage for a change, hugging his waist, the cold of his Glock against my arm. He wrapped his arms around me and rested his chin on the top of my head as I replied, equally breathy, almost a whisper,

"Reciprocating."

It was the first time I'd gone to him, and he kind of just melted in my arms. Somewhere along the way,

Giuseppi Moretti had dropped his masks and all of his armor. He spoke, but the words tripped over his feelings,

"I appreciate you."

And somewhere along the way, I had become the one who held his broken pieces together, even if I didn't know it yet. I moved away from him before we crossed any lines. I sat on the sofa and motioned for him to sit on the floor in front of me. He picked up his whiskey and came to me, pushing his shoes off, sitting cross-legged on the floor in front of me with his back turned.

I tucked my legs on either side of him and put my hands on his shoulders as he sat on the fancy rug in his expensive tailored pants. I rubbed the base of Seppi's skull with my thumbs and moved my way to his shoulders. When I scratched my nose, I could smell his cologne on my fingers. I worked on a knot and he lowered the back of his head to the lap of my thrifted Burberry trousers. His eyes fell closed, and he made a sexual sound low in his throat, I didn't mention it. Seppi stayed like that as I rubbed his shoulders, his temples, his neck. I wanted to release the tension, lift the weight of the world from his shoulders in the only way I knew how. Neither of us said anything, and I wondered if it said something about our relationship, the way Seppi came charging in like a bomb about to explode, the way I just completely defused him. Right then, I felt like maybe Seppi wasn't the boss of me, even if he was the boss of everyone else. When he turned around, his eyes were softer than they had been in a long time, he looked raw and genuinely vulnerable. He put his hand on my knee and I felt it in places I shouldn't,

"Thank you, no one has ever done that for me before."

No one had ever massaged Seppi's shoulders before? No one else had tried to lighten the load? I was the only one who gave that man anything in return, and I guess I should have known then that eventually we'd cross a line, even if it was just with our hearts. Maybe I was deluding myself, but it felt like something to me, something deep that I had never felt with anyone else. Seppi slid his feet into his oxfords and pulled me to my feet. Our eyes connected, I glanced away and then glanced back. He held me in his arms, his voice vibrating under my ear,

"I'm not trying to control you, Dimples."

I pulled back, so I could look him in the eye as he said whatever he needed to say,

"What I'm saying is, I'm sorry. You're right, and I know it. You're on the inside because you can hold your own, and I can trust you."

But his eyes did something personal,

"I trust all of my associates with my life, but I don't trust a single one of them with you."

We hugged again, but that time it felt like I was reassuring *him*, letting him know I knew what he meant, even though I didn't. Just for a moment, I had Giuseppi Moretti wrapped in my cage. I protected him from his demons that day, and maybe I was also protecting him from what was going on in his heart. His phone rang,

"Yes."

It was a woman.

"I'll be right there."

Seppi put his phone on the desk,

"Opal is here."

He went out the back door and I stood there for a minute or two, trying to compute what had just happened. I was pretty sure Seppi was saying he didn't want to see me with anyone else. Maybe he was, and maybe he wasn't. I pulled my shit together and went out the back door to help carry in some fancy-pants art my sister found for the restaurant. Seppi made eye contact with me, flicked an eyebrow, and closed himself in his office. I considered locking myself in my bathroom to rub one out, and wondered if Seppi was having the same problem.

CHAPTER 22
HERO OF THE DAY

MY SISTER FIGURED out where she wanted the paintings, and someone would be hanging them in the morning. But since Opal was a bit of a control freak, she was doing it herself five minutes later. Seppi was in his corner and I was in mine, I even had my office door closed most of the way. I had my nose to the grindstone when I got a text from Kane, 'You've got company over here.' And then, 'I'm just the messenger.' I made a face at my phone and shrugged as I poked my head in Seppi's office,

"I'm running next door, apparently there's someone over there looking for me."

I went palms up and he waved me away. I bounced out the backdoor of the soon-to-be Giuseppi's Italian Ristorante and through the backdoor of Muddy

Waters. I glanced at my twenty-six-year-old piece of Swiss cheese on the way by, blissfully unaware of the impending doom. I waved at Wretched, I mean Gretchen, and the look on Kane's face told me I wasn't going to like this very much. Things went in slow motion as I rounded the corner, into the space with the leather sofas and realistic fake fireplace. I stopped in my tracks when I saw Max and Marta Birch standing in front of me. Crap.

I pulled the mask out of my back pocket, shook off the dust bunnies, and pulled it over my head like a trash bag. I couldn't breathe. I zipped the costume into place with one fluid motion, transforming into a good little girl who hadn't been broken into a million pieces. My dad picked me up off the floor with a hug,

"Hi Boo-Boo Bear!"

I hugged my mother, and it was half-ass like a floppy fish. I mean, what was the point? Sometimes she would hug me, but do it in a forceful way, and then throw me away from her body. I called that one 'The Catch and Release,' which I guess was fitting for a floppy fish. But I was glad to see my dad, even though it wasn't really worth it if I had to see her. I hoped maybe someday he'd leave her, but I knew he was too nice for that. I took a deep breath, swallowed all the hatred I had for my mother, and made sure my voice sounded genuine,

"It's so good to see you, come next door to see the restaurant."

Kane nodded like I did a good job; I finger waved and rolled my eyes as I went for the door. My parents followed me from Muddy Waters to Giuseppi's Italian Ristorante, we went passed my twenty-six-year-old piece of Swiss cheese and the mini mafia sedan on the way. We passed the Escalade and Opal's champagne colored Volvo. There was no way to warn anyone, and there was no way Opal knew about this. I pulled the back door open and gestured my parents across the threshold. What do they say about wildly narcissistic mothers? Once you invite them in, the garlic won't work? That's fine, I'll just go right for the stake through the heart.

My mother helped herself, and just found her way, since she knew everything about everything and apparently the rules didn't apply to her. She entered the world of Authentic Naples cuisine with big time mafia energy, whether anyone liked it or not. Opal passed through the dining room, blissfully ignorant, looking for another nail or something else to stand on while she put up her commissioned fancy-pants art. Opal stopped in her tracks when she caught site of our mother. She did a better job than I did of dusting off her mask, and I wondered if she did timed drills in her spare time. She hugged our dad, and he picked her right up off the floor,

"Look at you, Opie, you're glowing!"

My mother hugged Opal but it was disingenuous and I rolled my eyes as she made floppy fish arms. Seppi strolled out of his office with an empty espresso mug, humming to something by Frank Sinatra. For a moment, he was completely fucking clueless. I know the exact moment he saw her because he came to a halt. Seppi wasn't intimidated by many people, but I think he was intimidated by Marta Birch. He liked our dad, but had good enough intuition to know our mother needed to be tossed off a cliff with rocks in her panties. I wondered why they were in Bunman and where they were planning to stay.

My dad shook Seppi's hand, but Seppi pulled him in and kissed him on both cheeks. Maxwell Birch excitedly declared,

"We've come for the grand opening, we wouldn't miss it for anything!"

My dad felt that way, but I had doubts my mother gave a shit since it wasn't about her. I smiled at him, and when I glanced back at my mother, she was very obviously judging one of the paintings. Let me make something very clear, that woman wouldn't know a good piece of art if it bit her in the ass. My mother procured her art and home decor from the collection of mass produced bullshit at her local TJMaxx. Ask me how I really feel.

And what the fuck were we supposed to do to entertain them? Seppi was going to be busy at the restaurant until late, and it wasn't his job, as the head of a mob family, to drop everything and host my parents. I wanted to slam a double of whiskey and a fistful of gummies. My sister and I stood there looking at each other like we were going to rock-paper-scissors to see who was going to deal with our parents that night. Fuck it,

"You guys are welcome to stay at my place, it's right next door, I have plenty of room."

My mother kept a straight face for a beat, and then barked with laughter, swatting at me like an asshole,

"For a minute there, I thought you were serious."

She continued to carry on about what a comedian I was, and I wanted to punch her in the throat. I wanted to make some super-secret hand gesture to Seppi that it was time to whack her. I thought about telling her that I cultivated my keen sense of humor as a fun little side effect of stuffing all the trauma she ignored. In my spare time, as a child, I enjoyed playing dress-up with our considerable collection of closet skeletons. I even made them costumes for each holiday, I wish I was kidding. My mother moved toward my sister, like the two of them were close. Opal moved her eyes to mine and raised one eyebrow, her 'throw me a rope' look. And then she looked back at the high and mighty, Marta Birch. Our mother's voice was sweet as pie, because she wanted something from her eldest daughter,

"Opal has plenty of room at her house for a pop-in."

My mother touched Opal's arm and I cringed on her behalf. I was thinking, you mean, there's plenty of room at Giuseppi Moretti's mafia mansion, not my sister's, his. It was Seppi's house, and Marta Birch was inviting herself over. Knowing Seppi, he was going to say it was fine. Anything to keep Opal happy as long as she was under his roof. The timing wasn't great, for so many reasons.

Opal planned to make an escape and I told my parents I'd finish up and then lead them to the land of mafia mansions and impromptu visits. They had been to Seppi's before but needed to slow their roll. Opal mouthed 'thank you' as she gathered up her things. I was going to try to give her some lead time to do a sweep for dirty underwear and dust bunnies. If there's one thing Marta Birch was serious about, it was dust bunnies. I mean, the most important thing was that the curtains looked good from the outside, but after that, it was dust bunnies. Opal needed time before our parents arrived in the land of mafia mansions and speed-cleaning pregnant women who can't swallow fire or smoke a fatty.

I leaned into Seppi's office and pretended to blow my brains out, he shook his head. I went palms up and rolled my eyes. He smiled at me and winked. I need to press pause here, because there are only a handful of things a man can do that will make me weak in the knees. That was the precise moment I realized that, under the right circumstances, getting winked at by Giuseppi Moretti was one of those things. Good to know. I lead my parent's out the back door of the new and improved Giuseppi's Italian Ristorante, and watched them get into their nineteen-year-old Toyota Corolla. I fired up the mini mafia sedan and they followed me up the alley. We made our way to the gate and I grimaced at Gary,

"This strange couple has been following me for ten minutes, and I think they're up to no good, I don't think you should let them in."

He glanced at their license plate and then at the clipboard of approved guests. He met my eyes,

"Aren't those your parents?"

I went palms up,

"What's your point?"

He shook his head and the gate swung open,

"See if I bring you any more cookies."

Gary chuckled and waved me away. I entered the land of mafia mansions, and people who overstay their welcome before they pull in the fucking driveway. I parked in Seppi's spot and my dad pulled in next to me. I helped my mother retrieve her QVC rolling luggage filled with QVC clothes and fake diamonds. I wondered how long until she'd be rooting around in the wine cellar. The real one, the one with expensive bottles of wine that had corks instead of screw caps or spigots. My mother wouldn't even know what she was looking at down there, her wine came in a box with a little faucet that you can stand on the edge of the counter. Or, if you're classy, right on the top shelf of the fridge next to the skim milk and pulp-free orange juice. Right next to the left-over Lean Cuisines and the low sodium V8.

I'll give the Readers' Digest version of the night. It was filled with poorly veiled insults and criticisms. Our dad tried to smooth things over, change the subject, keep it positive, but my mother had a knack for being a buzzkill. Opal only had one meltdown, and you'll be happy to know that I didn't run off to one of the many spacious closets to hug my knees. As everyone else stood around the island picking at fancy cheeses and local uncured meats, I snuck out to the patio to sip whiskey with Seppi as he built a fire in the brick oven. I swung my feet from my perch on the stainless-steel counter and chewed on an ice cube, gesturing toward the house,

"I mean what the fuck, she's such a waste of space. What do you think my dad sees in her?"

Seppi glanced inside as my mother snooped through his cabinets and smacked a cube of cheese out of my dad's hand. I read her lips as she scolded, 'you'll spoil your dinner, Maxwell!' Seppi bit his bottom lip and gave me the eyebrows,

"Maybe she's dynamite in the sack."

I pinched the bridge of my nose and shook my head

"Gross!"

I tossed back the rest of my whiskey, hopped off the counter and stomped toward the house in disgust, mumbling under my breath about how Seppi could go fuck himself. As I reached for the sliding glass door, Seppi exclaimed,

"I mean, look at her!"

So, I did. He added,

"Now, there's a woman who can gobble a dick."

I didn't turn around, I just muttered,

"Come on."

Seppi barked with laughter as I flipped him off over both shoulders. He was doubled over by the light of the brick oven when I closed the door. We shared a dinner of gourmet brick oven pizzas and tossed salad at the same table I covered with vomit on Christmas Eve. I served the rest of a vanilla cake I found on the counter, but would have preferred chocolate. When I got ready to leave, Opal thanked me for providing a distraction. I'd soon find out she wasn't just talking about doing a once-over for dust bunnies. Seppi kissed me on both cheeks and it felt more intimate that time, maybe he wished he could have come with me. I looped around the carport to see the four of them standing in the front room and I had a serious case of FOMO.

I slept like shit, and five days until the finish line. I walked in to see Seppi's associate, Franco. I hadn't seen him since, well, you know. He kissed me on both cheeks and said it was nice to see me. I crossed the threshold into my office to see a pair of feet on the coffee table. My heart skipped a beat when I realized the feet were attached to Marco Masiello. I squealed and ran over to him. Marco sprung up, scooped me into his arms, and lifted me off the floor. He kissed me and my feelings came out of hibernation, he said,

"Your hair looks cute like this!"

I smiled and my mind flashed to our first night together, it seemed like a long time ago and yesterday, all at once. He said,

"All hands-on deck for the grand opening and I got a call!"

He seemed happy about it. And, I was happy because maybe I'd get to dip Marco in gravy and sop him up with a biscuit. I grabbed his hand and giggled as I strolled into Seppi's office with Marco trailing behind me. I smiled ear to ear and squeezed Marco,

"Can you believe it!?"

Seppi wasn't jazzed about how excited I was to see Marco but I brushed it off. I kissed Marco on the cheek and returned to the world of last-minute inspections and deliveries of fancy olive oil and pasta. The aroma of Mama Moretti's marinara filled the ristorante, and the realization that I was a part of it all brought tears to my eyes. I finally had connections in life, a little bit of authority, someone looking over my shoulder. I tossed some cardboard in the bin out back and noticed someone sitting on the back steps of the cafe. I did the old Michael Myers head tilt and went to investigate.

Sitting there looking pathetic was Wretched, I mean Gretchen. I plopped down next to her on the steps and put my hand in the middle of her back. I had worked with her for a couple weeks and she really did seem like a sweet girl. I remembered how it felt when I was in college, how things that seem little now, seemed big, or how I was homesick, even though my mother was a bitch. Maybe she broke up with her boyfriend or got an F on a paper.

"Hey, what's wrong?"

Gretchen wiped her big brown eyes and glanced over at me, she looked like a wounded doe. Pathetic and defeated as she twisted a tear-soaked napkin into a rope,

"My roommate moved out, and I don't know how I'm going to pay the rent. The landlord is a battle-ax bitch who doesn't give exceptions."

When I was in college, I lived in a dorm, I wasn't one of the cool kids who had an apartment with their friends. I was sure at least one of the new servers would flake, or have a sick kid, or be too high to do their job. It was all hands-on deck, and Seppi wouldn't get mad if I brought on one more girl for the grand opening.

"Listen, the restaurant is going to be opening in less than a week, and if you're as good with Giuseppi's customers as you are with the ones over here, I'm sure he'll give you a permanent job as one of his servers."

Gretchen's tears dried up almost immediately and it felt like I'd saved the day. I used my connections to make the world a better place for some doe-eyed twat, I did the girl a favor. I felt like a big shot as I reached my hand out to her,

"Come on."

The construction smells had been completely replaced with the smells of marinara and a test batch of garlic knots. Maybe Gretchen got over the rumors she'd heard about Seppi, maybe she realized he isn't that scary. Everyone was devouring apps and entrees and desserts as the new chefs played in the kitchen. Opening night would come soon and things needed to be perfect. Seppi was chatting with Franco, Marco, and a delivery man. I told Seppi I hired a server and he gave me a thumbs up as he nonchalantly signed an invoice with a seventy-five-dollar pen. I guess I was allowed to hire people. I had to pinch myself. I gave Gretchen the grand tour and she blended in with the crowd. Cute, young, personable kid with a nice smile, someone who gave a shit if people were happy and wasn't just trying to make it through the day without deep-throating a shot gun. When I went back to my office, Opal had Gretchen tucked up neatly under her wing, like the mother hen she was becoming. It's funny how things work out, and I was finally able to help someone.

CHAPTER 23
RIDE THE LIGHTNING

I RETIRED FROM my day of saving the world for a college kid. I strolled into my apartment to Marco sitting on my futon in sweatpants and an old-school Giuseppi's t-shirt, Indie purring as she rubbed against his hand, what a strange couple days it had been. I showered and stood on the cold hardwood floor in my bare feet, raking curl cream through my ringlets. I brushed my teeth and spritzed myself with vanilla body spray, in preparation for date night. I wandered out to the living room and plopped down next to someone who had seen me naked before. To recap, for anyone who wasn't around back then, here's the Cliff's Notes version. I met Marco Masiello when he came into my aunt's gift shop looking for handyman work. Long story short, we ended up dating. Marco was this Italian stallion with olive skin and dark hair. Beautiful eyes and lips, rough around the edges in all the right places. He had been a kid who got involved with the mafia when he was fifteen years old. Somehow wrapped up with the Moretti family when he was in ninth grade. I assume he stole something, or owed someone something and had to work off a debt. Slippery slope.

You create alliances and become involved in a brotherhood of protection. You're a fifteen-year-old kid with a handgun and you have mobsters letting you drink whiskey and smoke Cubans in a dark back room somewhere. You feel like you're really part of something. Marco would go to school the morning after helping dispose of a body. He'd sit across the table from his Mama, eating her homemade manicotti, knowing he'd be driving a duffle bag of laundered money to an overgrown drive-in movie theater once she went to bed. Other kids would have twenties, Marco would have hundred-dollar bills. When you're a kid with a single Mama and you don't fit in, finding a place in the mob is like being adopted into a family of powerful uncles.

Marco touched my face; I looked up at him and our eyes met. I squeezed his leg. I tried to look inside to see where he'd been since he left, and wondered if there were other girls in his bed while I was daydreaming about Seppi. I wondered if Marco was thinking of me the first time I pushed my panic button after therapy. Was Marco thinking of me the night I got my ass kicked in the woods by the woman with the cute hat and vintage bag? I wondered if Marco was going to stay, or if he was just a tourist, but it didn't really matter. I was lonely and old feelings were coming back. I didn't do anything about it that night, but it felt good to be close to him again.

Four days until the finish line that was really the starting line. Marinara and roasted garlic in the air, I sat in the leather armchair across from Giuseppi Moretti. My eyes were undressing him, unbuckling the black leather belt he had threaded through his expensive tailored pants. The top two buttons of his shirt were open, cuffs rolled up a couple times. The way he was sitting, I could see part of the tattoo on his chest, a phoenix rising from the flames. He had salt and pepper five o'clock shadow, smelled like whiskey, Cubans, and Tobacco Vanille. He stared at the melting ice in his empty glass, swimming around in his own head. I swallowed a mouthful of whiskey and lit a joint before breaking the silence,

"Penny for your thoughts."

Seppi moved his eyes to mine and held my gaze briefly before flicking his eyebrow. A lightning bolt went straight to my panties and I squeezed my thighs together. I made a sound low in my throat and I'm pretty sure he heard it. It had gotten to the point that my body reacted when I heard his voice, but here I was clamping my thighs together, and he hadn't even said anything. It was just him. Something about the way he flicked his eyebrow seemed sexual. If I had my way, I would've pulled him out of that chair and walked him backwards until *his* back hit the wall. I'd have kissed his neck and inhaled the scent of him, I would have pulled that belt out of those loops and taken care of whatever he has inside of those expensive tailored pants. I wouldn't know where to start with him if I had the chance, and I'd make sure he had a story to tell. Holding his gaze, I flicked my eyebrows in return, and I'm pretty sure we were talking about the same thing.

Marco, Franco, Opal, Mary, Guido, some guy named Carlo, Wretched, I mean Gretchen, me, Seppi, a girl named Holly, and another girl named Sue. The kitchen guys left for a restaurant supply place to get their fancy chef's jackets and hats, and whatever else chefs and kitchen staff need. Mama Moretti was standing over a gigantic pot of marinara she planned to transfer to the walk-in, once it cooled. I went over and put my arm around her shoulder, things were coming together, and we could almost see the finish line. I could almost taste it, the marinara, and the experience of watching Seppi reopen his Italian ristorante. The one with authentic Naples cuisine and most definitely some pretty shady mafia vibes. I would watch him give handshakes and cheek kisses on opening night, watch him rub elbows with old friends and new ones. I'd watch my mother get her nose rubbed in figurative shit as she saw how important I was around there. To top it off, Opal marched across the hall, stood in front of Seppi with her hands on her hips, and told him she didn't like Gretchen. His only response was,

"Who!?"

So, that was the end of that conversation, like Giuseppi Moretti had time to worry about stupid shit like whether Opal liked the help. Opal shrugged it off, blamed it on hormones. When I went back to my office, Gretchen was in there waiting for me. She was admiring the built-in bookshelf and I surprised her when I walked in. I felt bad because Gretchen was so anxious and stressed out and I hadn't meant to startle her. We shared a joint behind the restaurant and she seemed to feel better after. We talked a little more and she told me about her ex. I told her about mine, the one with the whore and the love child. I told her that's why I came back to Bunman a year ago. We talked about life and about how life doesn't always turn out like you'd hoped. Gretchen dug a baggie out of her apron and handed me a couple yellow gummies. Opal leaned out the back door and waved at Gretchen to come back in. Gretchen found her way to the dining room for an AED training the new staff were getting as part of the on-boarding process. I went back to my office and tossed the yellow gummies into the jar on my vanity, to get lost in the shuffle.

My cell phone rang, and it was Marco,

"Hi! How's your day going? Did you get your chef costume."

Marco was getting all sentimental or something, I think he was panicking that he was back in Bunman. I could tell he was looking for some reassurance, some proof that I hadn't been sucked into the world he had tried to escape. Marco was quiet for a long time and as soon as he started to tell me why he was upset, Seppi tapped on the door frame, pointed at me and then pointed toward his office. I didn't mean to, but I cut Marco off mid-sentence,

"I have to go."

I could tell Marco was hurt,

"Oh, okay. That's fine, I have to go, too."

There had been a huge misunderstanding, and I wanted to fix it. Seppi snapped his fingers,

"Let's go, Dimples."

I whispered to Marco,

"We'll talk later."

I hung up and felt a pang of something in my stomach. For the record, things weren't the same with Marco after that, and it was a simple misunderstanding. As I was crossing the hall from my office to Seppi's, Opal came marching toward me with tears in her eyes. She grabbed my arm and dragged me back into my office. As Opal was slamming my office door closed, I saw Seppi go palms up in the hallway. My sister stood there, hands on hips,

"I can't with her!"

No idea who she was talking about,

"Who, Gretchen? The tall one? The one with the fake tits who's a whore?"

Opal waved me away,

"I'm over that, I'm talking about our mother. What the fuck is wrong with her!?"

Okay, at least I knew what I was working with. I took a deep breath, and we moved over to the couch. I got Opal a bottle of bubbly water and a Kleenex, rubbed her shoulders. I waited.

"Well, first off, she opened a twenty-five-hundred-dollar bottle of wine last night and I don't know how to tell Seppi."

I made a face,

"That's not great."

She looked like I hadn't heard anything yet,

"There she was, drunk on a bottle of wine worth more than her car, red cheeks, no filter, like less than usual."

I rolled my eyes.

"She was going on and on about Seppi, and my track record for 'hippie losers and potheads.' She told me I should hold on to him for dear life, as she guzzled expensive wine out of his fancy glasses. I mean, what the fuck!? Who tells their daughter to stay with someone because they have good wine?"

That wasn't exactly what my mother meant but it was close enough. Here was this free spirit, this butterfly who needed to flap those wings of hers, with a baby in a growing chrysalis, and she was already aching for the road. If our mother knew Opal at all, she would know that she would never be happy as a mob wife with a two carat Tiffany & Co and a Porsche 911 in the garage. Opal would never be happy with the separation between her life and his, her dreams and his. That was bad enough, and it was even worse because Opal didn't really want to be there in the first place. But for our mother to tell her she should stay with Seppi because of his money and power, really rubbed Opal the wrong way.

"That's not great, but what did you expect, she's keeping true to her brand of bullshit. Is that what you're upset about right now? I saw you earlier and you were fine, so to speak. I mean as far as our mother was concerned."

Opal held her phone out so I could read the conversation between she and our mother. My eyes scanned the messages and my face got hot at the same time my stomach started to twist and turn and feel icky. Did my mother text Opal to apologize for drinking a bottle of wine that was worth more than her car? Nope. Did she text to thank them for providing a place to stay for the week leading up to the grand opening? A week that was hectic, non-stop, and stressful enough without Marta Birch coming into town to drink expensive wine and throw insults like confetti. No apology or thank you. But she did message Opal to tell her, she thought I was blowing Seppi. Well, my mother was fancy and said, 'performing fellatio.'

Wow, nice. I read and re-read, 'How do you think she got that car?'

Wow. I was tempted to find my mother and tell her I got the car because Opal insisted on it after I was in a high-speed car chase with Salvatore Moretti in a stolen BMW. Nothing was going on between me and Seppi, not really. But I knew that if crossing an emotional line was considered infidelity, Seppi was in questionable territory. In my defense, I knew my sister was leaving, but she hadn't left yet, even though she was sleeping down the hall. And then I wondered how they were pulling that off with our parents staying there,

"How are you managing to sleep on the other side of the house with the two of them staying there?"

Opal shook her head and pinched the bridge of her nose,

"I'm not."

I scrunched my eyebrows and shook my head for clarification, she clarified,

"When I raced home ahead of them, I gathered all my shit and put it back in his room, made the other room back up, and pretended everything was fine between us. What the hell else was I supposed to do?"

Okay, well that wasn't great. Not only was I having to deal with my parents, I had to think about Opal sleeping next to Seppi. I pinched the bridge of my nose too, but knew Opal didn't understand why.

"It's so fucked up. But, Seppi told me to take the bed, and he's been sleeping downstairs, on the sofa in his office. He tells them he's staying up late to work. They go to bed relatively early since there's a whirlpool tub and living room in the guest suite, and then Seppi sleeps in his office. He gets up before they do, makes a pot of coffee and then comes upstairs to shit, shower, and shave. They are none the wiser."

Opal paused,

"They couldn't have stayed with you!?"

I threw my hands up,

"What are you talking about!? I offered, and that cunty old bag thought I was making a fucking joke!"

Opal waved me away,

"I know, I know. I'm sorry, it's not your fault."

I put my hands on my hips,

"Let me get this straight."

I gestured across the hall,

"The patriarch of a mob family is getting ready to reopen his restaurant, is beyond stressed out, is hosting our crazy fucking mother, *and* has to sleep on the sofa in his office!? Are you fucking kidding me!?"

Was everyone in the world taking advantage of him and giving nothing in return? No consideration? No compassion? No minuscule amount of concern or interest in making Seppi feel taken care of, or provided for, or loved? Drinking a twenty-five-hundred-dollar bottle of wine, making it so Seppi had to sleep on a sofa. Opal threw her hands up,

"Yeah, I get it, they're fucking everything up, what am I supposed to do about it!?"

It wasn't long before we were yelling at each other. That's when Seppi knocked and opened the door. We turned our heads and barked, in unison,

"WHAT!?"

He threw his hands up in surrender,

"Geez!"

What the hell was happening? Marco was upset about whatever he was upset about, Seppi was stressed and tense and waiting for me in his office, my sister was pissed or sad or jealous or some combination. Gretchen was turning out to be a sweetheart. Mama Moretti was happier than a pig in shit, stirring her marinara. I even shared a joint with her out back. Eventually I made my way into Seppi's office and plopped down in the big leather armchair across the desk from him. Our eyes met and it was clear that neither of us knew what the fuck was going on around there.

It had only been a couple hours since the moment we shared in his office, but the day had caught up with him, and not in a good way. That was the first time I saw Giuseppi Moretti look like hell. He had stubble, dark circles under his eyes, he smelled like whiskey, Cubans, Tobacco Vanille, and a hint of stress sweat. I wanted to tell Seppi, he should go do some yoga, but I knew I would get laughed right out of the room. Thanks everyone, I'll be here all night. It was like déjà vu; Seppi swirled the remnants of whiskey and perfectly square ice cubes around the bottom of his rocks glass. We were trapped in a revolving door of waking and sleeping, of weed, Cubans, and glasses of whiskey that never have a chance to water-down. But apparently, Seppi was only doing the waking part and not so much the sleeping. We were in this perpetual state of stress, the impending return to life before the fire, but bigger and better and closer. Seppi was lost in his thoughts and I didn't jump in. We sat there in silence and I saw a single tear fall but didn't mention it. I did what he always did to me,

"Tell me what you need, so I can give it to you."

Seppi moved his eyes to mine and nodded ever so slightly. I was the only one in the world who made Giuseppi Moretti feel safe enough to remove his armor, and maybe that's what I did to get the car. Word to the wise, giving a man a blow job isn't nearly as sexy as giving him a safe place to fall apart when the weight of the world is on his shoulders.

CHAPTER 24
MEAT AND POTATOES

THREE DAYS to the finish line, and Isabella Rossi moved my appointment from Monday to Wednesday. I felt good for the first time in a long time. I showered, took care of my ringlets, put on mascara, lipstick, and Alien Elixir. My appointment was in the morning, so when I parked behind the impressive office building of Isabella Rossi, it was eight fifty-three. My morning 'latte joint' hadn't worn all the way off yet so I didn't even smoke one in the parking lot before going inside. Checked in with Elaine, picked up a new magazine I found on the table. I felt pretty damn good.

I strolled into her office with a smile on my face and plopped down gingerly in the overstuffed chair. Dr. Rossi sat and smiled back at me, in a reserved, clinical kind of way that felt disingenuous. I felt good and wasn't even on meds, the therapy must have been working. I took a deep breath and let it out, the weight of the world lifting from my shoulders.

"Good morning, Amelia. How are you doing today?"

I didn't sass or throw sarcasm in her face. I smiled and said I was doing well. Told her I was settling into my new job at Giuseppi's, and it was almost the finish line that was really the starting line. I told her I was making connections and took a college kid under my wing. My parents were in town and it wasn't even ticking on my radar. Out with the horrendous bullshit, in with the good shit. Maybe I was finally getting that fresh start I was looking for. I had my shit together, and in another week I'd be booking receptions and retirement parties. I'd be orbiting in the same solar system as Seppi, and even then, that was the most important thing.

I had some serious feelings for him, and I was pretty sure he had at least some sort of feelings for me. We had some sort of trauma bond. A naïve bitch with a motormouth and too many questions was the one Seppi felt safe with. Sometimes the two broken pieces find each other in the bottom of the box. Sometimes you're part of a puzzle and you find the piece that fits next to yours. I knew Marco was temporary, which was good, because I had big feelings for his boss. I knew the king of the hill had feelings, and five o'clock shadow. I also knew he smelled like whiskey, Cubans, and Tobacco Vanille.

I felt good that day, all things considered. I touched on things with my mother, but felt like I was so busy that I wasn't dwelling on their visit. It felt like I had priorities, and worrying about my mother wasn't one of them. Even if she drank an exorbitantly expensive bottle of Seppi's wine, and thought I was 'performing fellatio,' I didn't let it bother me. Dr. Rossi seemed pleased. I told her I was carrying my handgun and could protect myself if I needed to, even if I didn't tell her I knew from experience. When I made my next appointment, I almost felt like I didn't need to come back, but I made the appointment anyway. I waved at Elaine and at a man in the hall. I didn't lock myself in the restroom or splash water on my eyes, or pat my face dry with a nonabsorbent paper towel. I rode the elevator like a big girl, didn't hesitate when I got to the street, made it to my car, hopped on the highway and didn't push my panic button.

Nosing the mini mafia sedan into the driveway between Muddy Waters and Giuseppi's Italian Ristorante, I passed Opal's Volvo and a new Escalade that was a fancier version of Seppi's. I parked next to my twenty-six-year-old piece of Swiss cheese and thought about taking her for a spin sometime. I circled the new Escalade parked in Seppi's spot, it was hot looking. Black metallic paint, matte black rims, even the Cadillac emblems on the front and back were matte black, maybe it belonged to 'Mozart' Cavallaro. I went to my office to dump my bag and coat, and took the remnants of a maple oat latte on a walk to find my sister. Opal was sitting at a table, unpacking menus. I slid in across from her and she looked exhausted. I didn't ask if it was because of our mother, she'd tell me when she was ready.

I sat with her as she did what she was doing, scanning the new space from the perspective of a patron. I wondered if someone would sit in that seat when they went on a first date, or a last date. I had the profound realization that people made memories at places like that, and I was going to be a part of it. I was looking at a picture that someone would be looking at when they got engaged, or got their heart broken. Opal snapped me back to reality, sniffing the grass for the right place to shit,

"Oh, Dad called me."

I glanced over at her as she humped up,

"They want to take us out for dinner tonight."

I rolled my eyes and went palms up, whining,

"What for?"

She shrugged.

Whatever. I'd get my shit done, please the king, and go to dinner with my dysfunctional fucking family. Three nights until the finish line. I spent some time staring at the wall in my office. I had a fleeting thought that something was wrong with one of our parents and hoped it was our mother.

I wondered why they were taking us out for dinner instead of wanting to eat in the land of mafia mansions and expensive bottles of wine. I did busy work as I drowned my sorrows with the smells of fancy desserts. I ate warm Italian lemon cookies dipped in icing, even though I was told to wait until the cookies cooled. I had a bite of tiramisu that was even better than the old recipe. Cannoli, panna cotta, panforte. I whipped up a latte on the brand new, and very fancy espresso machine. The wand steamed milk like a dream and I made perfect leaves on the surface of the perfect crema. Someone needed to give it a maiden voyage, and I knew what I was doing more than anyone else over there. I delivered lattes to everyone else I could find, and an herbal tea for my sister.

I strutted around like my shit didn't stink. Guido and Carlo and Franco and Marco, all dancing in the kitchen with Mama Moretti, as she smiled ear to ear. I tore into a day-old garlic knot and made my way to Seppi's office. He put his finger up, he was on the phone. I asked if he wanted me to go and he shook his head. He told the person 'that sounds good' and ended the call. Seppi flicked his chin at me, stood up, and poured whiskey into two glasses over perfectly square ice cubes. We clinked glasses and I leaned against the back of the sofa, he sat on the edge of his desk. I moved my eyes to his, and felt something bounce between us. Clean shave, shower gel, Tobacco Vanille, must have caught him before a couple puffs of a Cuban. I wanted to bury my face in his chest and inhale. Dark pants, white shirt, top buttons unbuttoned. Gold chain around his neck, dark Italian eyebrows, expensive shoes with leather soles. I wondered if maybe the sexy Escalade was his,

"Is that your mob boss aesthetic out there in the parking lot?"

He left the glass behind, shrugged into his leather jacket, and nodded toward my office. I grabbed my purse and coat on the way out the door and pulled myself into the passenger seat of his brand new rig. Seppi nosed the Escalade onto Maple Street and drove to the lake. We sat on a low rock wall by the water, Seppi smoked half a Cuban, I smoked half a joint. He needed to get out of his cage for a while but didn't want to do it alone. Maybe he needed me to fend off the demons while he came up for air. I moved my eyes to his silhouette as he lost himself in the mountains, and that was the first time I thought I might want to be with him. I glanced over my shoulder at the Escalade and wanted to make out with him in the big back seat. I didn't ask why I was the one he turned to when he needed a break from reality, I didn't ask why the broken little girl with the ringlets and the magnificent dimples was his refuge. I just sat with him and appreciated the proximity, appreciated that I could smell the cigar smoke on his fingers as he talked with his hands.

Seppi asked about Marco, and I sugar-coated it before changing the subject. I told him my parents wanted to take me and Opal for dinner, and he made a face. He probably didn't want to have to spend the night making her feel better. I understood. We made our way back to the car, but for a minute, I had been sitting at Clover Lake with Giuseppi Moretti. I wondered if Seppi thought of me that way, if he thought it was a big deal that he was sitting there next to me. Probably not, but you never know.

We went back into town and Opal hadn't even noticed we were gone, busy organizing and making things look just right. I was busy wondering what our parents were going to tell us. My mother was not a 'celebrate a milestone' kind of person, so that dinner would be a way to dilute some sort of bomb. Medical issue, divorce, a move to Abu Dhabi. Although, I didn't think either of them looked sick, I knew for sure they would never get a divorce, and I didn't think either of them had a passport.

My little mind spiraled but not as spirally as it might have spiraled a couple months ago. No meds, but I was feeling good. I pulled it off, I was in control. Dinner with my parents in four hours, and I was sure my hair, my clothes, or my personality was going to be the butt of criticism. From her, not him. Significant others were not invited, but both of ours were working anyway, if you consider Marco my significant anything. I wondered what the big deal was. Maybe for the first time ever our mother wanted to celebrate us, our lives, our accomplishments, our milestones. Maybe for the first time in our lives, she was going to act like she cared. With our luck, our dad had cancer and he'd be dead in six months. But maybe they just wanted to thank us for being such amazing displays of their parental tutelage and genes. Maybe the apples didn't fall too far from the tree.

I wondered where we were going and picked everyone up in the mini mafia sedan. Opal in the front with me and our parents in the back. My mother mumbled about how I got the car, and my father shushed her. I made a face at my sister, and she giggled. We arrived at a place on the mountain with a water wheel and a ski slope. There was valet parking, it was a fancy place, they wouldn't sell boxed chardonnay. There were luxury SUVs and other cars like the mini mafia sedan. I didn't see any twenty-six-year-old Subaru wagons in that parking lot. I handed the keys over to a good-looking college kid and the four of us went inside. The place smelled like warm popovers, expensive seafood, and fat, juicy steaks. The dining room and bar were full of families on vacation from places that don't get snow. And they'd probably drop their expensive outerwear off at a Goodwill on their way out of town.

We were seated and I wondered what the occasion was. Once we settled in, my dad and I got Southern Comfort on the rocks. My mother got a glass of expensive wine, but not as expensive as Seppi's. Opal had seltzer with lime. Before long, the energy shifted. There was anxiety and excitement and apprehension floating around like an impending storm. It's like when you watch those videos of tornadoes, when everything comes together in a perfect storm, and everything starts spinning. My father leaned into his liquid courage and broke the ice,

"We wanted to talk with you about a big change we're making in our lives."

Maybe they were changing the color of the dining room or maybe my mother decided to buy a different kind of toothpaste. I'd leaned forward, on pins and needles, waiting for the ball the drop in the middle of that table.

"You've both settled in Bunman, five hours from us."

My dad moved his eyes to my sister,

"And you're having a baby."

He gestured between himself and our mother,

"We're going to be grandparents!"

I was annoyed and agitated. Yup, that's how it works when your kid has a kid. Brilliant. And thank you, Captain Obvious. Opal shifted nervously; she saw it coming before I did. I think she tried to warn me, to throw herself out in front of the train but wasn't fast enough.

"Your mother and I have decided to sell our house in Roundelay, and move back to Bunman."

And with that, I spit a perfectly good mouthful of Southern Comfort across the table. My mother dabbed at it frantically with a cloth napkin as I clenched my jaw. And they hadn't better be planning on staying in mafia mansion land while they hunted for a new house. Besides, the market was shit, maybe they wouldn't sell their house, or find a new one, for like fifteen years. My sister and I held hands under the table, it felt like we were little girls, and it felt like we were in trouble. My dad added, proudly,

"We've already started the process with our place, and tomorrow we're looking at a few properties near Aunt Maggie's."

That sounded a little too close to our old stomping ground for my liking. It was bad enough being back in Bunman, but now *they* were moving there too!? Did I really need any more reminders of my old life? The life where bad things happened, and all of it was just swept under the carpet? I had a mind to pull the metaphorical carpet out from under the whole thing. It was nonsense. They'd never do it, not in this market. We made it through the rest of dinner without a single insult or criticism, maybe my mother sensed the energy coming from our side of the table. I ordered a double of Southern Comfort and the expensive shrimp scampi. Opal got the chicken piccata, my mother got the fish, and my dad got the meat and potatoes.

CHAPTER 25
FROM THE OUTSIDE

AT THAT POINT, so much happened in such a short amount of time. I'm going to try to remember all the details and tell it in a way that makes sense. Since you're probably wondering what happened with our parents, I'll just go ahead and tell you the next part of that story. The next day, my parents looked at three houses, all in, or around, the neighborhood where my Aunt Maggie lived. My father wanted to live near his sister, and I wondered if she knew anything about it. Maggie wasn't a fan of my mother, and she wasn't afraid to say it. One of the houses was a raised ranch like my aunt's, right down the street. Apparently, the back yard was too small and the basement smelled damp. Scratch that one off the list. The second one was a Cape Cod style home on a small hill with a fire pit and a cute back yard but that one was too close to the street. No dice. The third house was beautiful, there was a wrap-around porch, two bay garage, nice back yard, a lot like our old house. They were excited and couldn't wait to show us. Things went fast so I'm going to try to get everything in order, but it doesn't really matter, the ending will be the same either way.

They made an offer that day and it was accepted by dinner time. Yes, I'm serious. When does that ever happen? The seller was motivated, and the price was right, and my parents loved the neighborhood, they said the house was perfect and we'd love it the second we saw it. Cool, I thought that sounded nice. Maybe they would move and my mother would get lost on her way to the store and not come back for twenty years. I was kind of excited for them but also on edge because I knew what it was going to mean to have them living there.

It was going to mean my mommy issues would come front and center and I was going to have to confront some things I didn't want to confront. I knew my sister was going to have to battle with my mother and receive unsolicited advice, as well as pop-ins by our father when he wanted to hold the baby. Boundaries would need to be set right away; a precedence would need to be set. If Opal ended up staying, they were going to have to realize they couldn't just show up uninvited, in the land of mafia mansions and cute little footie pajamas. They couldn't just roll up in their

Toyota Corolla and tell Gary they had a free pass to come and go as they pleased.

That evening, Thursday evening, my sister drove her fancy champagne colored Volvo. I sat in the back with my dad as we took our trip to see their new house. It felt like old times, really. It felt like when opal had her license, and I didn't, and my parents would let her drive, and I'd sit in the back with my dad. My mother would sit in the front seat and holler out 'MAILBOX!' whenever my sister passed a mailbox. My mother would stomp on the passenger side floor and grab the dashboard. She would gasp and say 'shit' and clutch her fake pearls. It was a bit of a shit show. But that day, my sister had been driving for a decade and she wasn't driving a beat-up sedan. We made our way as a family to see our parents' new house in their old town.

I knew my father was the one who suggested it. I knew my mother would never relocate her life for the likes of her children or her children's children, she wasn't that kind of mother. Marta Birch was the kind of mother who had no idea what her kids liked or what their dreams were. She had no idea about what we liked because she was too busy worrying about herself and the box of wine with the spigot and her latest package from QVC. It made me think of a year when she bought so much stuff that she received a holiday card signed by all the hosts. She acted like they were her friends. She got a card from salespeople and displayed it proudly on her fridge but returned a ceramic wax melter I made for her one Mother's Day in college. Priorities, that woman had her priorities and none of them had to do with her children, or her husband, or anyone else she should have cared about.

I would eventually fall into a routine of meeting my dad at a diner, at a Dunkin' for coffee and donuts, or he'd swing by and take me for a steak dinner and a maple creemee. I loved my dad and I was looking forward to having him around. I tried to focus on the glass half full, but it was pretty hard while I was trapped in a car with my mother's wine breath and black heart. I hated her. And now she was going to move to the place I ran to for my fresh start, my new beginning. Maybe she would fall off a cliff. Maybe she would realize she loved me. Maybe she'd say she was sorry for throwing me to the wolves and then sweeping it under the carpet. Maybe she would tell me she was proud, and knew I didn't perform fellatio on Giuseppi Moretti to get my car. Maybe she would respect me.

My mother directed our course and I had a growing dread in my soul as we neared our old neighborhood. I saw my elementary school and the corner store where I bought candy. I saw where I would wait for the bus and remembered something I did as a child to sooth myself. When I was feeling especially anxious or alone or like I needed to know everything was going to be okay, I'd run home from the bus stop. I'd run my little heart out all the way home and I'd tell myself that if I got to the maple tree at the end of the driveway before the next car went by, everything would be okay. And I made sure I always made it to the tree before the next car. I made sure. And so, I knew everything was going to be okay, I was going to be okay, because I made it to the maple tree before the next car. Only, sometimes I wasn't okay. Sometimes the pile that had been swept under the carpet was so tall that I couldn't see to the other side of the dinner table. I was trapped and claustrophobic. My wounds, the ones on the inside and out, bleeding and itching and healing and dying.

I knew where we were going and I was sure my parents thought they had pulled a fast one. I knew my father had no idea what he had done, or how much he had hurt me by doing it. He didn't know what happened when I was little. My mother smiled her smug little smile, didn't care about me or my feelings. She didn't care about those boys or that bathroom floor or the panties with the day of the week embroidered on them. We drove by the house where it happened and I felt sick to my stomach. My eyes were tight, and my shoulders ached. It was like things were going in slow motion, my sister looked at me in the rear-view mirror and there was nothing either of us could do about it.

My mother pointed right, and we pulled over in front of our childhood home. Maybe we were just visiting but I knew better than that. I knew they had done it. My father was probably proud of himself. My mother probably had no clue how much that house triggered me. I know everyone is fucked up, but some people are better at hiding it. I'm a heart on my sleeve kind of girl. Just a girl with ringlets and magnificent dimples and her heart on her sleeve. The house I went home to after the older boy pinned me to the bathroom floor and had his way with me. When I left that day, I ran through the cornfield connecting our houses with my underwear in my pocket. We sat there watching the people eat at the dining room table and I wondered if those kids were as miserable as we were. I wondered why they were moving and where they were going. As if my dad knew what I was thinking,

"They're moving to New York; the father got a new job at SUNY Albany teaching accounting."

Good people, well-off, educated. There was a boy and a girl, they looked like a happy family from outside of the dollhouse. We played nice but what the actual fuck. I kicked the back of Opal's seat, and she cleared her throat to tell me to knock it off. I decided to just have Opal take me back to Seppi's, he was coming home for dinner and then I'd get a ride back into town with him. My mind was full and empty at the same time. I knew my parents had different motives. I don't even know what my mother's motive would have been for moving back there, but my dad meant well and loved us and was going to be a Popop. Let me add that our dad didn't look down on Opal for wanting to live in a van down by the river. Our dad loved us, and that was it, that was the only saving grace in all of this.

Once we got back to the land of mafia mansions and reheated leftovers, I made my parents a nibble board and set my mother up with some not expensive wine, but it still had a cork because, I mean, it was Giuseppi Moretti's house. Anyway, while they were settled in the front room with their snacks and my mother had her wine, I was finally able to talk with Opal. As if rehearsed, when I returned to the kitchen, we looked at each other with wide eyes, went palms up, and mouthed, 'what the fuck!?' I felt bad she couldn't sip some whiskey or join me outside for a joint, but she'd be back there in another four months or something. We were getting so close to the finish line that was really the starting line, that I could taste it, and it tasted like marinara, tiramisu, and trauma.

When Seppi showed up for dinner, he had Marco in tow. I knew it was Marco's idea, and not Seppi's. Seppi barreled through Marco to get to me, what the hell was happening? Marco didn't even get to say hi before Seppi dragged me into his office and shut his door.

"Sit."

I sat.

"Where did you find that girl?"

"Gretchen?"

"Yeah."

"She came into Muddy Waters for a barista job. She's a college kid at the university and her roommate just moved out of their apartment, so she needed a side-hustle. She's harmless. I'll admit I was a little jealous of her at first but, she's fine. Why?"

Seppi retrieved two rocks glasses with perfectly square ice cubes and poured us each a shot of whiskey. He slid mine across the desk. Seppi didn't sit, he paced. He wasn't necessarily making me nervous, but he wasn't instilling much confidence either. His voice was low,

"She was poking around in your office earlier, I don't think she knows I caught her, and I want to keep it that way, for now."

A squirt of adrenaline fired off. His voice wasn't as quiet this time,

"Trust is nonnegotiable, I won't tolerate members of my staff snooping around in my business. Depending on the level of over-step, I can do anything from fire someone to put them in the ground."

I made a face and got goosebumps; I didn't like to think about what he could do to people who crossed him. I hoped I never crossed him. I swallowed the lump in my throat. I had seen Gretchen in my office, too. Honestly, I thought she just wanted to be friends, and tried to run into me or be in the same place at the same time. I didn't worry about my purse, which was whatever, I never carried cash, and if Gretchen needed a joint that bad, then whatever. Anything Moretti related was under lock and key, I wasn't stupid, and I didn't want to end up at the bottom of Clover Lake.

"I'll keep an eye on her, but I think she just wants me to take her under my wing. She's a dumb college kid."

Even then, I wasn't entirely sure I could trust her, but either way, she was a college kid who needed a waitressing job, not some plant from deep in the recesses of the mob. Seppi was just being hyper-vigilant because he had a lot going on, and didn't have time to worry about me. I knew not to communicate with Lance, and I knew I needed to let Seppi know if anyone suspicious came around. I was aware of my surroundings, always had a loaded gun on, or near, my person and knew there was a lot at stake if I fucked up. I reassured Seppi and it made me feel powerful to be the one in the inner sanctum, to be the one sharing whiskey and a private conversation while everyone else waited outside.

Seppi nodded his head toward the door, and I stood. He kissed me on both cheeks before we returned to reality, and I felt like he kissed me a little closer to my lips than he needed to. I didn't mention it. I left the office in front of Seppi and sat next to Marco on a stool at the counter. Marco leaned over and kissed me on the cheek, Seppi kissed Opal on top of the head. Nobody asked any questions. We just fell into a conversation about nothing, and sat around the counter on stools eating leftovers with my parents.

I had a mouthful of lasagna when I realized I hadn't introduced Marco to my parents. What was wrong with me? I guess he probably introduced himself when I was in the office with Seppi. And it felt like an awkward time to introduce someone, so I didn't. I hoped he wasn't hurt. Marco knew some of the shit with my mother and maybe he knew it didn't matter what she thought of us. I hoped he didn't find out that my mother thought I performed fellatio on Seppi to get the car. I bet it intrigued my mother that I was locked in his office just now, maybe she thought I had to earn my dinner, too.

Marco seemed quiet and looked tired. After we ate, the three of us returned to the land of chicken parmigiana and moderately priced Cabernet Sauvignon. I sat in the back and smoked half a joint, because I could. I pushed my shoes off, slouched down, and put the bottoms of my feet on the back of Marco's seat. Seppi's five o'clock shadow was illuminated by the lights of the dash. The weed mixed with the smells of new leather seats, Alien Elixir, Tobacco Vanille, and Marco's warm spices and musk. It was this clash of some kind, there was a past and present quality to it. When we got to the restaurant, Marco and I lingered in the parking lot after Seppi went inside,

"Your mother thinks there's something going on between the two of you. I introduced myself to your parents and told them we're seeing each other. Your mother all but spit her wine in my face."

What the hell. I was on fact finding and damage control duty, acting casual,

"What did you say to that?"

Marco shrugged with his shoulders and his face,

"I didn't really know what to say, that's how she replied after I told her we were seeing each other."

I smacked my forehead with my palm, what was wrong with that woman? Keep your assumptions to yourself, you dumb bitch. That's what I wish he had said, but that would have made eating leftovers together a little awkward. Jesus Christ.

"Marco, I apologize for how she is, and I'm sorry I was pulled away before I could introduce you."

It was time for me to find out if he was wondering if she was right, but I didn't have to wait long, Marco chuckled like someone told him a joke,

"You and Giuseppi Moretti, that's funny."

That was funny?

I watched Marco be amused with himself,

"I mean seriously, does your mother have any idea who he is?"

Marco was nearly bent over, crying as he wheezed about the thought of me being with Giuseppi Moretti. I was a little offended, but I didn't mention it, I laughed it off and we went inside. Between the misunderstanding on the phone, and whatever the fuck that was, I was kind of over the whole Marco thing, I just didn't have time to deal with it right then. I formalized some final details, two more days until the finish line that was really the starting line. The next day was the last full day of finishing touches and trial runs. The last day before life returned to normal, the last day before my fresh start.

CHAPTER 26
BOLOGNESE

IT WAS ALMOST the finish line that was really the starting line. All hands on deck. Seppi, Opal, me, Mama Moretti, Marco, Franco, Guido, Carlo, Gretchen, Holly, and Sue. Seppi held a celebration brunch to thank everyone for their hard work. When you work for Giuseppi Moretti, you're part of the family, which brings with it certain perks. I scanned the room and it seemed like I was the only one who thought that sharing space with him was one of those perks. We drank mimosas, ate fancy French toast sticks and home fried potatoes. I made lattes for everyone, and we sipped them while eating tiramisu with the new forks. I had an edible or two on board, on top of the mimosas, and was feeling my feelings toward Seppi.

He swung his foot as he sipped his drink, complete with an orange wedge and champagne-sugar on the rim. Our eyes connected briefly, and he winked at me before looking away. It was a casual gesture, but electricity shot to my nether region and I made a sound low in my throat. It's like when you're in high school and you have your sights set on some hot guy who sees you as nothing more than a face in the crowd. The energy building in my chest almost took my breath away. Looking back, I know Seppi was feeling a lot of the same things, even though he was better at hiding it. And I'm not talking about something sexual, I'm talking about when someone is good for your soul, and I knew by then that I was good for his. I was the one person who dismissed his ego and didn't care who he was to anyone else. The one who saw the shields come down behind closed doors and let a 'larger than life' be vulnerable, it felt even more intimate than if we had been intimate.

The next day was going to be insane, but I didn't know the half of it. In fact, the next thirty-six hours or so, would be something like I'd never experienced before. I focused on the promise of a full house and then some. There would be marinara and garlic knots in the air and people clinking glasses. It wasn't going to be a regular night; it was an open house with extra appetizer and drink specials, live music, and no reservations. People would be coming in and out, sitting at the bar and mingling, dancing to the music and working up an appetite. It would be one for the record books and I was going to be part of it. The energy was increasing, there was a low level of anxiety in every one of us, even Giuseppi Moretti. I had my arm around Mary's shoulder as we sat at the bar, singing along with Frank Sinatra. The whole thing was surreal, like some cut-scene from a movie before the shit hits the fan. Everyone else had a mimosa, but Mary had a Bloody Mary, and I thought that was ironic. I took in the essence of her, Chanel No. 5, a hint of her long skinny cigarettes, tomato juice and celery on her breath. Her classy aesthetic, her blue eyes, her expensive jewelry, and bright white smile.

My insides hummed with anticipation and I knew I wouldn't sleep that night, the night before the finish line that was really the starting line. The time when I would get to see Seppi open his new restaurant, the place with authentic Naples cuisine and all that dark mafia energy. When there were no distractions, I felt my soul calling to his in a way I had never experienced. We were in his office at one point, I was just sitting on the arm of the couch and he was leaning against the bar. Casual, no big deal. Our eyes met and another bolt of lightning went straight to my lady bits. I looked away and tried to think about something more appropriate than wanting to make out with Giuseppi Moretti.

Seppi put his glass down and came to me, which didn't help to quell the thoughts swirling in my mind, or in other places for that matter. My body was vibrating and I wondered if he could see it through my clothes. Seppi squeezed my hand and I squeezed back, a gesture of appreciation that I was along for the ride. I glanced up at him and our eyes connected, the world ceased to spin, time stopped. Think about it from my perspective, think about the day I rolled into that town and everyone warned me about that man. Here I was alone with him, so close I could feel the warmth radiating from his body and the energy he brought to the table. I wondered what that man was like in bed, wondered if he made sure his partner finished first. Wondered if I would ever get the opportunity to spend time with him, off the clock. He took another step closer and there was static when he touched my left dimple with his thumb. My eyes fell shut and I leaned into his palm with my cheek. I daydreamed about kissing him but knew I would explode if our tongues ever touched.

There was a rapid knock at the door,

"Amelia? Are you in there?"

We were pulled back to reality, time started ticking again, the world continued to spin. Seppi opened the door to my sister, in a flurry of tears and anger. We went to my office, and she slammed the door,

"What the fuck is wrong with her!?"

I shook my head and she paced around which made me do the same. Opal had gotten into it with our mother, who had called her a 'gold-digger' and a 'whore.' Anger rose as I listened to her cry like she did when we were little. I hated my mother and thought maybe someday I'd do the world a favor. It made me smile a little. I sat there like an absolute lunatic, smiling as I daydreamed about tossing my mother's body into the lake. Opal plopped on the couch and dumped some fancy trail mix onto a cloth napkin,

"I'm losing my fucking mind."

I sat next to her and grabbed the jar, digging around for a couple dark chocolate covered blueberries. She scrunched her eyebrows at me,

"That's really gross, did you even wash your hands?"

I shrugged and snaked my fingers to the bottom of the jar. I tossed a couple blueberries in my mouth,

"What can I do to help?"

She shook her head and cheeked her mouthful, sarcastically,

"Do you still have that shovel?"

I shook my head, I was uncomfortable talking about the shovel,

"I broke the handle."

She made a face of disgust,

"I wasn't serious."

I knew that. I changed the subject,

"They'll be leaving soon, and then you'll be free of them until the next major holiday."

"Wrong."

She pointed at her swollen belly. I reasoned,

"Okay, but they won't stay long if you've just had a baby, right?"

She pinched the bridge of her nose and let out a big sigh,

"I am losing my mind in that house."

"The mafia mansion?"

"Could you please stop calling it that!?"

"Well, that's what it is."

She gestured at me, exasperated,

"Whatever, I hate that fucking house! You'd think that since it's, you know, a fucking mansion, that I'd be able to get five seconds of fucking peace!"

Jesus.

"I have to go sit in my van to get any time to myself. And I'm trying my best to play the fake fucking bullshit until our parents leave, but I can't take it anymore."

She stood and went to the sink to throw water at her face,

"It's like one of these things is not like the other, and no one has noticed! I fucking hate it there!"

I pushed the bathroom door shut to create a sound barrier, but it was too late and there was a tap at my office door. I closed her in the bathroom, on the verge of losing my own mind when I swung the door open to Seppi. As politely as possible,

"Yes?"

He scanned the interior of my office and his eyes landed on the bathroom door, I put my hand on his arm but almost put it on his waist,

"She's just got a lot going on, she'll be okay."

I knew by the look in his eyes that I was preaching to the choir, and that he knew I was full of shit. He leaned in, a friend right then, not a mob boss and I knew it,

"One more day, that's all I need, I can't deal with this right now."

I nodded and went back to Opal. Everything would be fine, it had to be. I popped an edible and rinsed it down with some whiskey straight out of the bottle on my vanity. I got her calmed down and sent her on her way, I had shit to take care of. Business as usual, I held my head high and made everyone proud. Gretchen seemed to be doing better, seemed less anxious, we had taken her under our wings when she needed it. She wanted to be friends, and tried to be in the same place at the same time. I knew she would be in my life until the end, for some reason, I knew. Maybe we would be best friends and our kids would play while we drank White Claws. You know what they say, 'ain't no laws when you're drinking claws.' But even at that point, I preferred Giuseppi Moretti's Johnny Walker Blue and perfectly square ice cubes.

Seppi was ready to be back at the helm, back in the swing of things, and Opal was ready for life somewhere besides mafia mansion land. I was ready to show Seppi I could be trusted and relied on, that I had his back just as much as he had mine. I was a naïve little bitch, a broken little bitch, but I had grown, and I was in control. I would do anything necessary to make the night go off without a hitch. I could manage the crowd and keep a smile on my face. I'd have to manage the little things, the guy who got too drunk, the couple making out in a booth while the live music played. I'd have to keep my sister sane, and maybe Seppi too, but I was ready.

I wondered what it was going to be like, how life would be once the restaurant opened. My only experience with that place was as someone who'd come in from next door for a meatball sub and a complimentary tiramisu. I was someone who'd go to Giuseppi's on a date with Kane, and get hard nips when Seppi kissed me on both cheeks during his orbit of the room. I was on the inside looking out, instead of the other way around. Only this wasn't a dollhouse, this was an Italian Ristorante owned by Giuseppi Motherfucking Moretti. I was on *his* side of the glass, I was across the hall, I was the one who shared his whiskey.

The back door banged open and in came Vincenzo Moretti. You're thinking, oh yeah, I forgot about Vinny. Yeah, me too. So, he came banging in with a fat lip, a black eye, and a bloody nose. Seppi was on the phone and didn't look up as I steered Vinny into his bathroom. I flipped on the light and assessed the situation, not great, the night before opening night. He washed his face, and I tended to his wounds. Seppi was late to the party and gestured at his brother with his eyes wide,

"What the fuck happened to you!?"

Vinny moved his eyes to Seppi's in the mirror,

"What the fuck does it look like!? I got my ass kicked!"

I scrunched my face at Seppi like he was asking a stupid question. Antibiotic ointment, band aids, paper stitches, what the hell? Seppi brought his brother a double of vodka, and a look of concern,

"Look, I'm not trying to be insensitive here, but I'm opening the restaurant tomorrow night, and you're supposed to be front of house."

"Seppi, I know, I'm sorry."

Seppi threw his hands around as he yelled, his voice echoing off the marble surfaces,

"You can't very well welcome people through the doors with your face looking like Bolognese!"

And then his brakes came on,

"Wait, who the fuck kicked your ass?"

Vinny made a face like Seppi wasn't going to like the answer. I shook my head and waited for whatever was coming. There was a pause and I didn't know what it meant, but Seppi did,

"Oh, for Christ's sake."

I was on pins and needles, what was I missing?

Seppi pinched the bridge of his nose and gestured for me to follow him. I trailed behind him while Vinny refilled his vodka. Seppi sat and gestured toward the chair across the desk from him,

"Dimples."

I sat. Vinny tossed back the vodka and twisted a tissue, spinning it around in his nostril. I mean, come on, what the fuck was all this!? I shook my head at Seppi with my eyes wide and my palms up,

"Yeah, and? Are you going to need me to greet people, now? You know I'm not good at shmoozing."

I gestured at Vinny,

"I'm not charismatic, or whatever."

Seppi tipped back the remnants of his whiskey and chewed on a perfectly square ice cube, making eye contact with me, testing the waters one last time before doing a cannonball of sorts,

"I need a favor, Dimples."

CHAPTER 27
ON THIN ICE

I KNEW WHAT WAS COMING before the words came out of his mouth. I don't know how, I just knew. I pinched the bridge of my nose and waited for confirmation. All business,

"You're gonna go with Vin."

I crossed my arms, annoyed at the prospect of some sort of mob bullshit,

"Why?"

They made eye contact and then Seppi looked back at me,

"Vin needs help with something."

I tried to change reality,

"Like, he has to drop his car off for repairs and needs a ride back?"

Seppi shook his head,

"No."

I tried again,

"Like, I need to help him pick up a last-minute shipment of fancy olive oil at the fancy olive oil store?"

Seppi was sick of my bullshit, I was on thin ice, and there was most likely a warm body getting cold in Vinny's trunk. Seppi knew I knew, but he said it anyway,

"You're gonna help Vin ditch a stiff."

That's exactly what I thought he was going to say. I'm just some dumb-ass, not some highly trained member of the mob. My heart pounded in my ears and my stomach tossed and turned as another shot of adrenaline fired through my system. I was looking down a tunnel and the walls were closing in as I tried not to crap my pants. But then my emotions did something, went somewhere else, it was nothing personal, it was just a job. Seppi leaned back and retrieved a bubbly water from his mini fridge. He twisted the cap and slid the bottle across the desk to me. I held it in both hands, jiggling my foot, body trembling. I wasn't cut out for that shit and he knew it. He gave me a chance to take a couple sips, a second to let reality set in. But I didn't sip the bubbly water, I just rose from the chair and stood there, frozen in place. Seppi gestured toward the bottle,

"It'll settle your stomach."

I took a tentative sip of the bubbly water as Seppi rounded the desk, my butt hole threatening to complicate things. Seppi stood in front of me for a second and then put his hands on my shoulders. He assessed me one last time before committing and then kissed me on both cheeks. Seppi leaned in and spoke quietly, intimately,

"You're a good girl, Dimples."

A jolt of electricity fought between my nipples and my nether region. That favor would be my initiation in some strange way, not that I'd asked for it. That's how I'd prove I could be trusted and didn't need to be at the bottom of the lake. I followed Vinny through the back door and got in his passenger seat for the first time. He retrieved a bag of miscellaneous black clothing and I fished around until I found things that fit. I tossed an edible down the hatch and Vinny handed over a silver flask. I swallowed fire and then changed into sweatpants, a beat-up Giuseppi's Italian Ristorante hoodie, and sneakers that were three sizes too big. The hoodie didn't smell like the one I slept with every night, it smelled like a hamper and had something crusty on it. Picking at the crust with my fingernail,

"What is this on here?"

He shrugged nonchalantly and without moving his eyes from the road,

"I dunno, probably blood."

I was sorry I asked and dug around my bag for some sanitizer. Before long, Vinny hopped out and unhooked a rope with orange flags hanging down, he nosed his BMW down a narrow gravel road that led to the quarry. It was like we had discussed it, or like I had done it before. In the end it was just like dancing, and I took his lead. Overcast and dark, a storm rolling in, and I could relate. I pictured some balding middle-aged asshole, frantically scanning the shelves at a drug store for a heart-shaped box of shitty chocolates, and here I was at the precipice of hell. A plain-Jane in mom jeans and an ugly tunic was at the fragrance counter, picking out expensive cologne for her husband while he fucked his secretary and I was preparing to see another dead guy.

There was nobody else around, but I could tell we were in a place high school kids went to drink beer and get awkward hand jobs. Vinny nosed the car into a pull off and cut the lights. I got out and pulled on the heavy coveralls he'd handed me, I had to roll them up three times at the bottom. It was six forty-six, the night before the finish line that was really the starting line. Chills ran down my spine, someone could get killed out there and nobody would ever know, I didn't realize the irony at the time. We were parked next to the water and I'm not talking a riverbed or a pond, I'm talking, water that seemed like it went to the bottom of the earth. I helped Vinny lift the body out of the trunk. Not a big guy, but big enough because he was dead weight, no pun intended. I asked where we were going but he didn't say anything.

There was a railing and a very old metal ladder deep in the marble walls. There was an edge where a slope had formed from snow that melted and refroze on warm days and cold nights over the winter. I stood there with my eyes adjusting to the darkness and Vinny handed me the flashlight. I shined it on the makeshift ice chute, and he slid the body onto the ice, it caught a little speed, but stopped about twenty feet in. Vinny climbed down the rickety one-hundred-and-fifty-year-old ladder. I froze at the top and he looked up at me, mumbling something about knowing it was a mistake to send me along. I held my breath and made my way down the fucking five-thousand-year-old rickety piece of shit ladder. Vinny adjusted the plastic so we could each take a corner. I noticed the first few flakes of the storm and hoped this wouldn't take long.

We dragged the body into a little alcove in the quarry wall you wouldn't know was there, unless you knew it was there. You couldn't see it from where any sane person would stand. And within that alcove in the marble wall, there was a pocket where the water wasn't frozen. Son of a bitch. The hole was about the size of a person. I didn't know if the hole was natural, or man made, and it didn't matter, the guy in the plastic was going in either way. I was fine with it. I knew what it was like to get my ass kicked, to get punched in the face. It would have felt wonderful to kill that bitch with the cute hat and vintage bag, the one who was really the red-headed lady with the pant suit.

I couldn't see everything, but I saw enough that I shifted into autopilot. Vinny needed help pushing the guy to the open spot in the ice, that was a two-person job because we had to be on all fours. I'd never done anything like that before but knew it was a weight distribution thing. When we got close, we laid on our bellies and pushed the body toward the hole, a little at a time. It felt like we were getting too close, but what do I know? One more push and the stiff rolled awkwardly off the tarp, a sneaker catching on the lip of the ice. We laid flat on our bellies and Vinny held my feet as I worked my way to the edge. I pushed the sneaker over the lip and the body sunk out of sight, tiny bubbles rising to the surface. I shivered as the body descended into the deep, dark, frigid water, I couldn't imagine.

I shimmied away from the edge; I could hear it and feel it all at the same time as the ice gave way underneath me. Vinny pulled me back as fast as he could, but it wasn't fast enough. The ice fell out from under me and I plunged into the frigid water, the sneakers coming off in Vinny's hands. My body flipped some switches, and I was breathing in a frantic way, hyperventilating, I flailed and I panicked. Vinny reached for me but couldn't get any closer and he was panicking. If something happened to me, Seppi would kill him. And if Seppi didn't, my sister would. And let's not forget that Vinny was in a relationship with my childhood best friend, who would kill him if nobody else did.

I tried to control my breathing but it was physically impossible, I felt like I was drowning in reverse. My breaths weren't deep enough to sustain me and I was starting to feel sparkly. I groped for the ice, broke off another piece, went under again. Vinny hadn't prepared for this situation; he didn't have a plan, the wet coveralls were going to be the death of me. Vinny snapped out of it and scurried frantically to the wall, up the shitty fucking ladder,

"Hang on, Amelia, I'll get you!"

It seemed like he was gone forever before I heard boots on the rungs. Vinny slid across the ice on his knees with a ten-foot tree branch in front of him. He laid flat and pushed the branch to the opening, his voice quaking with adrenaline and fear,

"Grab it!"

My body felt funny. Blubbering, tears and snot running from my wet face, my words chopped up by violent shivers,

"I can't feel my fingers!"

His voice was shaking, pleading,

"You'll die, Amelia! Grab it!"

A split-second passed as I tried to get my body to move the way I wanted it to, he grew impatient,

"FUCKING GRAB IT!"

I grabbed the branch with my frozen numb fingers and held on for dear life. I had to do it, or I'd end up dead in the water with the dead guy.

"Hold on, please hold on, I've got you, you're going to be okay! You're okay, I've got you!"

Vinny was frantic, panicking and convincing himself, just as much as he was convincing me. He pulled the branch, and I held on so tight. If I didn't hold on, I would be dead in the water, with the dead guy, with the sneakers and the bullet hole. My life flashed before my eyes and I didn't want to go out like that. Little by little, Vinny dragged me out of the ice-cold water, the wet coveralls sticking to the ice. He hugged me to his chest,

"Oh, thank God!"

Vinny threw me over his shoulder, adrenaline coursing through his veins as he climbed the rickety ladder, two rungs at a time. He was going to be on thin ice with his brother, no pun intended. Vinny gave me a once over and unzipped the coveralls, peeling them from my shoulders,

"Get out of your clothes, you need to get your body temperature back up!"

Seconds later, I was in front of Vinny in my bra and panties, body shaking uncontrollably, curls frozen, lips blue. He grabbed his wool trench from the back seat and buttoned me into it. He was muttering to himself, making me nervous. I curled up on the heated seat in nothing but my wet underwear, bra, and Vincenzo Moretti's trench. He dug around in the bag and handed me a pair of socks. If I had died down there, Vinny could have left me and no one would have known. A chill ran down my spine, even though I was already frozen. How was he going to explain this to Seppi? The ride was silent except for the intermittent,

"You're okay, I've got you."

Vinny lit one of Sunny's hand-rolled cigarettes and offered me one. I hadn't smoked since high school, but I pulled a cigarette out of the box. At a stop sign, he lit my cigarette and then his own. I took a drag and the nicotine made me light-headed. Vinny was mumbling, trying to talk himself down, I felt bad for the guy,

"I'm going to be okay."

He didn't say anything, he just shook his head and smoked his cigarette. Vinny went through a drive thru for a black coffee and large fry. As we waited to pull onto the main drag, my nostrils over the mouth-hole sniffing coffee-scented steam, Vinny said,

"I don't know where to go."

He couldn't deliver me back to the restaurant in my wet bra and panties, his wool trench, and a random pair of black socks, right? Well, that's exactly what he did. I think he held his breath all the way back to the restaurant. He parked on the far side of Seppi's fancy Escalade and left me in the car with the heat blasting. He banged through the back door with his face looking like Bolognese. Seconds later, Seppi was screaming at Vinny with panic in his voice, unable to be strong where I was concerned,

"Jesus Christ, Vin, she could have been killed!"

Seppi scooped me into his arms and transferred me to the passenger seat of the Escalade. Where were we going? He certainly couldn't take me to his house like that; my parents were there. Well, that's exactly what he did, he took me to the land of mafia mansions and puzzled looks on faces. He skidded into the driveway going too fast and carried me to the door. It was past dinner time, and I figured my parents would be sitting in the front room sipping night caps. With any luck, they had already gone to their room for the night. Seppi didn't seem to care one bit, after all, it was his house, and he could do whatever the fuck he wanted. We crossed the threshold, and I slid into my sisters Uggs. He steered me to the kitchen, where he started the real-looking fake fireplace and turned on the tea kettle. Opal crossed the threshold carrying the remnants of a charcuterie board, and stopped in her tracks when she saw me, she couldn't hold herself together. She slammed the board down, olive pits and toothpicks rolling across the counter, hands flying around, eyes wide,

"WHAT THE FUCK!?"

She ran over and gave me a once-over. Any affection turned into hatred for Giuseppi Moretti. She moved to him with fire in her eyes, smacking the shit out of him. He tried to talk her down,

"Opal, stop, she's okay!"

He grabbed her wrists and looked her in the eye, she seemed to come to her senses for a second, before twisting her right wrist free. She gestured at me in Vinny's wool trench and her shearling boots, curls drenched and dripping onto my shoulders. She swung her arm back, slapped Seppi across the face, and that's when I knew it was over between them. Our mother crossed the threshold and put her wine glass on the counter before reversing course. I'm sure she was standing around the corner listening to the whole thing, and I don't think any of us gave a shit at that point. Who the fuck cares? I was grateful my dad was in the shower, because he would have been inconsolable if he ever saw me that way, or knew what I had gotten myself caught up in. My breathing returned to normal but I probably should've gone to the emergency room. There was a knock at the door and a man named Roger entered the foyer.

"Amelia, this is my next-door neighbor, he's a doctor, he's going to make sure you're okay."

I wondered what debt that man was scratching clean by being the house call doctor to the Morettis. Opal took me upstairs and Roger followed. I wondered if Chinese people liked pork fried rice and egg rolls and then realized how many calories I probably burned while I was in the ice-cold water with the dead guy. I knew Seppi was right outside the door. Roger took my blood pressure, temperature, blood sugar, and oxygen. He listened to my lungs and asked me some questions. Looked in my eyes with a tiny flashlight. When Roger left, I was in a warm shower, not hot. My sister threw plush towels and a bathrobe in the dryer down the hall. When the water hit my face, I lost it. I mean, fucking lost it. I was standing there like frozen chicken you're trying to thaw in time for dinner. Things had changed, I had helped dispose of a body, and I'd almost died again, no big deal, and I knew it wasn't the last time I'd help Vincenzo Moretti dump a body.

When I was sufficiently thawed, I dried off with the warm towels and wrapped myself in the bathrobe. I pulled on some of Seppi's sweats and worked curl cream through my ringlets, examining myself in the mirror. No visible bruises, no need for a bandage, the curtains looked good from the outside. I had some tea and a little bit of whiskey, and Seppi said he'd bring me back into town. My sister would have some sharp words for him when he got home later. She hugged me for a long time before I left and I didn't bother saying good-bye to my parents. The ride into town was silent. I was drowning in my feelings, choking on rage, flailing around in my heart. I'd gotten what I thought I wanted, hadn't I? Wasn't this entire thing about getting closer to Seppi?

I was making a mental list of the things I would shove in a backpack if I decided to leave town. Could I justify running for the hills in the expensive car he paid for, or would I need to take my twenty-six-year-old piece of Swiss cheese? As Seppi nosed the Escalade up the alley, all the feelings I thought I had for him kind of just went somewhere else when I realized the reality of the situation, the reality of their lives. It wasn't even just about me, Sunny was with a man who runs out to get a gallon of milk but manages to whack and dump a man while he's at it. Seppi put it in park, and I could tell he wanted to say something but I wasn't in the mood,

"I need my purse, and I can't go in there like this."

Seppi jogged inside and a minute later he was back in the driver's seat, handing over my purse and phone, I didn't even look over at him.

"Amelia..."

I was done with the bullshit. Done with the triggers. Done with the roller coaster of emotions. Done with Giuseppi Motherfucking Moretti. He reached out for me as I opened the door, but I slid to the gravel and didn't look back,

"See ya tomorrow."

Seppi sat there as I went up the back steps in my sister's boots, and he probably waited until the lights came on in my apartment. I wondered what he would say when he went back into the restaurant, Marco was in there somewhere and would be coming over soon. I didn't know if he would know what happened, but I wasn't going to tell him. I changed into some of my own pajamas, and buried Seppi's sweats at the bottom of my hamper. I plugged in my heated throw and stood in front of the fridge smoking a joint. I was famished. Not long after, there was a tap at the door, part of me wondered if it was Seppi. I swung the door open to Marco carrying a pepperoni pizza and a chocolate cake with fudge frosting. He kissed me on the cheek and I hoped I didn't feel cold to him. You know, like I almost died in the water with a dead guy with sneakers and a bullet hole. In between mouthfuls of pizza, Marco took a swig of beer, and let out a big sigh as he crossed his feet on the coffee table,

"Thank God it's Friday."

"Yeah."

I nodded but didn't really feel that way, as acid churned in my gut. I realized the next day, was the day, the day we had been working toward. I sat there digesting pizza next to Marco Masiello, with Seppi sweats at the bottom of my hamper. Maybe Seppi had been testing me before the big day, maybe he wanted to know for sure that he hadn't been wasting his time. All that aside, I had a normal night, once my core temperature returned to ninety-eight point six degrees. Marco was none the wiser and I kind of liked it that way.

CHAPTER 28
OH, HOW YOU'VE GROWN

IF YOU'VE LOST TRACK or forgot, or I didn't mention it, opening night was on Valentine's Day. So, there was going to be a flood of couples flocking to Giuseppi's Italian Ristorante on top of the usual crowd. When we woke up, me and Marco did some down the pants stuff, so I crossed that one off my to-do list before my feet hit the floor. I analyzed my feelings for Marco and realized whatever that was, wasn't going anywhere, it just felt familiar and we had chemistry. I'd deal with that some other time, he was going to be staying with a buddy after that anyway so, out of sight, out of mind. I think we both came to the same conclusion at the same time. We knew our way around each other's trauma, and each other's bodies. Maybe that's what we both needed right then.

He leaned on the counter as I made coffees, a latte for me and a pour over for Marco. We moved to the sun porch, he smoked a cigarette, and I smoked half a joint. We simultaneously blew streams of smoke into the cold air, ahh, Valentine's Day, commercial holiday of companies like Hallmark and Kay Jewelers. I was never really into the theatrics of it all, the mushy, squishy, romance of it all. The dozen long-stemmed roses and diamond pendant from the 'forever mine' collection, the sexy lingerie and candle lit dinner, it was never my thing. But when I woke up that morning, I had no idea I'd have a new disdain for Valentine's Day by the end of the night. We heard tires on gravel and the Escalade emerged from between the buildings. I hollered down to Seppi from the sun porch, as he emerged,

"Happy opening day, Boss!"

Seppi glanced up and gestured with his travel mug. Marco gave Seppi a wave, and I did devil horns with my fingers, stuck my tongue out like an eighties rocker, and rolled my eyes at myself. As the back door closed behind him, I could see Seppi shaking his head. I wasn't sure if he was shaking his head because I made devil horns at him, or because I had clearly spent the night with Marco. What was wrong with me? I felt pretty good, considering what transpired the previous night. Somehow, I kept my shit together. I hadn't flooded Seppi's phone with a million texts or push my panic button because I didn't know what to do or how to feel, I didn't need to be rescued. I'm pretty sure I had stuffed all that shit into one of those filing cabinets in the back of my mind where I keep that shit.

I wondered if Marco would ever know what happened the night before but knew it didn't matter. Returning to Bunman had triggered him, and he was already threatening to run back into his shell. He said my place was too 'close to it' and that's why he decided to stay with a friend instead. But I knew it meant something about his feelings for me, and I was okay with it. In all honesty, I didn't have the time, or the patience, to mollycoddle him. I glanced over as he sat there with his feet up on the shitty sun porch coffee table, scrolling through his Instagram, draining the last sip of his coffee. My feelings for Seppi made it difficult to feel things for Marco. It was like the scales had tipped while he was living in New Hampshire, it was like I outgrew him. Back then, I saw him as a bad boy, and now, just a minion. Maybe it was the corpse disposal or the hypothermia or the already present PTSD, but I was shutting down where Marco was concerned.

I went through the motions though; we made it to the finish line that was really the starting line. It seemed like opening day would never come but it also felt like the place burnt down yesterday. The concept of time can be a mind-fuck. The niceties, the phony smiles and fake hellos that were coming, were a mind-fuck. The drastic change in my identity and feelings and purpose were also a mind-fuck. Other than that, the day started like any other. I put my hair in a braid with a couple loose curls framing my face. I didn't wear the outfit or makeup I planned for that night, but I was pulled together and professional when I waltzed in the backdoor of the restaurant with a buzz, and one of Kane's maple oat lattes. I only went down to get a latte from Kane because I wanted him to see me in something besides ratty vintage overalls and dingy white Chuck Taylors. I wanted to rub it in his face that he blew it with me, even though it was me who lost interest because of the drama, his, not mine.

I moved through the backdoor of the ristorante to the aroma of Mama Moretti's marinara, and espresso. As I approached my office, I smelled diced onions, roasting garlic, and Italian bread in the oven. There was a hum of energy and voices, I felt like I found my people, I belonged there, maybe that was the fresh start I had been looking for. I crossed the threshold into Seppi's office and slammed into his chest like a brick wall, stumbling backward across the hall, glad I didn't drop my latte.

"Dimples!"

Seppi lunged forward, his hand flying up to the door frame of my office. The back of my head landed against the back of Seppi's hand, our eyes locked for a second, his mouth centimeters from mine.

He flicked an eyebrow and smiled,

"Morning."

Seppi kissed me on the lips like it was no big deal and continued toward the kitchen. I just stood there and watched him walk away with my back against the door frame. Once the flush drained from my cheeks, I took a second to absorb everything going on around me. The calm before the storm, the chaos on the periphery, the anxiety, the energy. The scent of marinara and tiramisu, espresso and stale cigarettes on someone's clothes, spearmint gum, roasted garlic and olive oil. It was profound really, that I was in the same orbit as Giuseppi Moretti. I closed my eyes and took a deep breath, held it for a few seconds, and let it out in a slow steady exhale. I was startled by a chipper voice behind me,

"Hi Amelia!"

Gretchen came bouncing through with a smile on her face. She kissed me on the cheek as she danced by. Everyone had a part to play, and Gretchen was playing hers. She wanted to make me proud, nestled under my wing. I watched as she went in the same direction as Seppi. I heard my sister laughing with Mary and made my way to the chaos. Guido, Marco, Franco, Carlo, Mary, Opal, Seppi, and Gretchen. Holly and Sue would be there later. Vinny was sitting at home with his busted face that looked like Bolognese, and his guilt about almost getting me killed. I don't think Sunny ever found out. Nobody told me, but I knew which secrets to keep. I could handle myself, I had Seppi's back just as much as he had mine. I was right where I needed to be.

Kane put together a congratulatory tray of pastries, so I went to retrieve it. When I came through the front door of the ristorante, I got a preview of what it would be like that night. Valentine's Day night, a night when people would make memories with their significant others, and I'd get to see Giuseppi Moretti open his doors for the first time. I'd get to watch his eyes smile, smell the whiskey and Tobacco Vanille, I'd get to see him wearing a tux. I scanned the room, one of the last moments of calm I felt that day. Everyone was nibbling on Kane's pastries, sipping lattes, and working at a bowl of marinara with chunks of warm Italian bread. Everything was going to go off without a hitch and I was going to be part of it.

Mary held me close and kissed me on both cheeks, she told me she was proud of me. I blinked away tears as she returned to the kitchen. I had a flash of the night I killed Sal and wondered what it was like to be married to him forever, to be in prison for someone else's crimes. To roll over and play dead in order to stay alive. I thought about the connection I built with her before it happened, and how much closer we were 'after the fact.' Mary regarded me as a hero in some ways, little old broken me was her hero. Seppi was grateful but felt guilty. He was still struggling with not being there to protect me but I wasn't mad about it, he was human. And there was no rule book for something like that, it was kill or be killed and no one could have predicted it.

My eyes moved to Marco, and feelings flooded in when I thought about the night he almost died. I swallowed the lump in my throat and thought about rushing over to him, but I didn't. My feelings for him were fleeting, unpredictable, and drastic. I'd go from zero to sixty and back again over the course of the day. I watched Gretchen laugh with Opal and knew she was going to be in our lives until the end, sometimes things work out like that. You cross paths with someone by chance and it changes the course of your life, and theirs. Carlo ran the kitchen like a well-oiled machine and everyone took their places backstage.

It was finally the night everyone would see the performance. The night I'd watch Seppi rub shoulders and shake hands and give cheek kisses to old friends and new ones. The night I'd see Seppi in action, the night I'd get to prove I had his back as much as he had mine. Seppi was speaking with Guido and glanced over at me,

"Dimples."

I glanced over.

"Grab my phone, it's in my office."

I did as I was asked, and set off to retrieve Seppi's phone from the office. Good little girl, I went down the hall to the inner sanctum. I had just been sent on an errand by a mob boss, no big deal. I was in the back room, the bat cave, the VIP Lounge. I scanned the top of Seppi's desk, the bar, the coffee table, and then started opening drawers. Not in the big one, but the smaller one to the right of the big one, I found Seppi's phone sitting next to the holstered Glock he usually wore on his right hip. Maybe he was distracted that day because of everything going on, or maybe he was confident the day would go off without a hitch. Either way, I'd wear my Sig Sauer that night, just in case. I delivered Seppi's phone, but he was distracted and we didn't make eye contact. It hurt me a little, I was looking for a connection and he was busy being distracted the day he made it to the finish line.

It was late morning and things seemed to be like ducks in a row. It seemed like things were going better than anyone could have expected. The girls knew the night's specials and what to wear, and how to carry themselves. They knew the expectations, and the importance of opening night...for a performance, for a musician, for a restaurant...the curtain would go up in six hours. They all knew who they were working for, and being employed by Giuseppi Moretti carried a level of validation and protection. But, it also carried a level of fear. Everyone was doing what they were supposed to, everyone knew what was at stake and the energy was palpable. I retreated to my office to return some phone calls and regain my peace as the finish line approached.

I tossed an edible down the hatch and washed it down with some whiskey. I plopped on the sofa with my feet up, digging through fancy trail mix for the dark chocolate covered blueberries, not even twenty-four hours after helping dispose of my first body. I almost died in the ice-cold water, with a dead body, with sneakers and a bullet hole. I focused on sucking dark chocolate from shriveled up wild blueberries and biting them in half with my front teeth. The back of my head rested on the cushion and my eyes closed in the calm before the storm. My phone vibrated and the screen lit up, but it was all the way across the room on my desk and I wasn't wearing my watch. Goddammit. I plunked the glass jar on the table and dragged myself off the couch, almost freezing to death was quite exhausting, my muscles ached from the violent shivering my body had done to keep me alive. I tapped the screen of my phone, there was a text from Seppi, 'Come to my office.' You don't have to tell me twice.

I did as I was told and crossed the hall, closing the office door behind me. Seppi rose from his chair and went to the bar, pouring whiskey into two rocks glasses over perfectly square ice cubes, he handed one of them to me. We clinked glasses and Seppi winked at me, which set my body on fire. There he went with the winking again, and there I went getting weak in the knees. We swallowed fire and our eyes connected, Seppi leaned against the bar and swirled whiskey around the bottom of his glass. It seemed like he was finding the right words to say. I knew he had a lot on his mind now that he made it to the finish line. He seemed to be feeling his feelings and I didn't mention it. His voice was full of emotion, and it caught me off guard. He said my name in a different way than he had before, it was just my name, but it was an entire sentence,

"Amelia."

It was serious if he wasn't calling me, Dimples. Seppi swallowed the lump in his throat and when he looked up, our eyes connected again but only for a second before he looked away,

"I just wanted to thank you."

It was like the wind had been knocked out of me, I took a deep breath to right myself, and pointed to the middle of my chest,

"Thank, ME!?"

Seppi moved closer and removed the glass from my hand, put it next to his. I was leaning against the back of the couch, sort of sitting, sort of standing. He came to me and our bodies touched, the side of my face against his buttons. I listened to his breathing and his heart beating, his pulse slowed as we stood there like that. I had the power to calm him, even the day he made it to the finish line that was really the starting line. He held my head to his chest like I was something precious and I had to fight back the emotions rising within me, I felt like I mattered. Seppi stepped back and hooked a finger under my chin so he could tilt my face toward his. Our eyes met again, and I swallowed a tidal wave of feelings. Seppi had me where he wanted me and his voice had something new in it,

"I value you, Dimples"

I didn't know what to say to that, or what to do with the idea that Giuseppi Moretti valued me. I was a nobody in the grand scheme of things, just some broken little girl, but people in the mafia protected their valuables.

"You've grown so much in the last year, and I've noticed. I just wanted to tell you, I'm happy you're a part of the family."

So, there I was, my heart pounding as I stood with Seppi's finger under my chin, looking him in the eye. I was deeply flattered, and deeply hurt at the same time. I was grateful that man, that powerful man, considered me family, and that I had proven myself, I had some value to him. But I felt like someone was sitting on my chest when I thought about how much more I felt for him than that. I wondered if it had all been in my mind. The encounters, the near kisses, the panic button. Maybe I was blowing it all out of proportion. He was a man who could have any woman, and maybe he was screwing people I didn't know about. I was probably like a little sister to him. There was no way the patriarch of a mob family felt anything like that for me. A broken little bitch, a naïve little bitch with magnificent curls and those goddamn dimples.

I convinced myself I was happy with whatever I could get. Reminded myself I was grateful to have him in my life, to be the one with a panic button, to be the one who shared his whiskey. Seppi took both of my hands and rubbed the backs with his thumbs. I swallowed hard when our eyes met. It was that thing again where I swam in his eyes, and he swam in mine. Someday. Someday, I'd have the balls to kiss that man in a way that would tell him how I felt. Maybe all I'd ever be is a person in his life. But I'd be the person with the panic button, who shared his whiskey, and I'd be happy with that. We didn't get interrupted that time, and I think we said a lot with our eyes as we stood there alone in his office, in the final stretch before the finish line.

CHAPTER 29
RUNNING ON EMPTY

LATER, I found myself back in Seppi's office. He looked tired, and I understood why. He had his own things to worry about and I knew he worried about me. It probably kept him up the night before, the excitement of opening night, the realization I could have died at the quarry. I wondered what Vinny would have told him, maybe he would have lied, to save face. Seppi wasn't stupid and Vinny would have had hell to pay if something happened to me. I just sat there with Seppi for a while, watching him from across his desk as he pondered life. I leaned my weary head against the back of the expensive leather armchair and let my mind go to other places. Sometimes I think it's a trauma response to be able to completely lose myself in fantasy, and sometimes I think it's normal.

I thought back to the first time I saw Seppi. I'd been warned that he was in the mob. For a while, I walked the fine line of lust and fear, in the knowledge he could kill me or make me cum in the blink of an eye. I thought about the time he pinned me against the wall in the basement, and the first time he called me Dimples. I remembered sitting with Seppi at the lake the previous summer as he cried. The presence, the energy, the respect he commanded. But I never played that game, I didn't care about that, I never let his rank, or his money intimidate me, I never let him get the upper hand, even though I looked up to him. I felt like Seppi was saving me from myself, but I felt like I was saving him in some ways too. He would come to my rescue with a handgun, and I'd come to his, with patience and presence and the way I'd calm his heart. I'm not sure who had more power.

The last year flew by in my mind, a highlight reel of sorts. And there in the final stretch before the finish line that was really the starting line, I sat with my head in my hands and Seppi asked,

"What's the matter, Dimples?"

But I think he knew the whole thing the night before was catching up to me. There's no good way to debrief something like that. I didn't know how to process the fact that I went with his brother to dispose of a body. I saw the guy, he had a bullet hole in his forehead, but I pretended I didn't see it. I pretended it was a mannequin or a crash test dummy, all dressed up with weights tied around its waist. I knew what kind of sneakers the guy was wearing when he died. Seppi was waiting for some sort of answer to his question. This wasn't a hair-trigger response, I'd been thinking about it for a while, but my eyes brimmed with tears just the same,

"It isn't working out for me here."

His eyes met mine, and I saw a little panic in there somewhere. He didn't say anything in reply, and I think he was holding his breath. I glanced out the window,

"I can't really handle all of this. I moved here to get away from my mother and now she's here. And then on top of it, I've gotten myself caught up in whatever happened last night. I've been thinking about going somewhere else, anyway. And, umm, well, that whole thing kind of pushed my other leg over the fence."

Seppi seemed sad and goosebumps spread across my body as I recalled the jolt of fear I had when the ice cracked. I was hyperventilating and almost threw up. He slid a bottle of bubbly water across the desk to me but kept his distance, I think he was afraid my panic would be contagious, the feeling of losing control. I was exhausted physically and mentally and I think he was too, because I knew he had volumes to say about me leaving. We moved on to surface chit chat about opening night, and eventually, I told him I had something to do. When I returned to the dining room, Opal was sniffling to herself at a table by the window. I sat next to her and watched her fall apart, I put my hand on hers,

"What's wrong?"

Opal really started crying then, those big fat tears, I could tell it was a lot of things and not just getting in a fight with our mother, or being at her wits end with mafia mansion land. Maybe she was hormonal. But she reminded me of the same thing she said a couple months ago,

"I'm not doing this anymore."

Crap.

Right then, Seppi had both of us, but we were both planning to run for the hills. Opal, to be a free-spirit, and me, to get away from my mother and stiffs that needed to be dumped. Our parents were selling their house and moving back to Bunman for their daughters, who had new lives. Opal had a baby on the way, and none of it was what anyone thought, it was only a matter of time. Opal wiped her nose with her sleeve,

"I need to speak with you, in private."

I glanced at the time, did some mental math, and grabbed my keys. I stuck my head in Seppi's office and told him we would be right back, he waved me away,

"Keep track of the time, Dimples."

We weren't gone very long, but I wondered if it crossed his mind we might just leave town and never look back. Seconds later a text from Seppi flashed onto my console, 'Make sure you come back,' Opal and I glanced at each other. We went to a place that served tea and biscuits and hot bowls of soup, we sat in the back and looked like any two women stopping by, except we were discussing Giuseppi Moretti. He had given her an elaborate opal ring, and she spun it around on her finger before putting it on the table. I panicked that she would forget it there and knew it probably cost thousands of dollars. Opal didn't care about that, but she put the ring back on her finger, probably for the same reason,

"I told him I'd stay until this restaurant stuff is over but I'm having a hard time holding it together, especially with our parents staying there."

I wondered how long it would be until our parents would go back home to pack up the sentimental things and the stuff from QVC. Our dad with the memories of his daughters and our mother with her fake diamond rings. I knew Opal was right and I knew it wouldn't be long before she hit the road.

"There's something else."

She slid her hand into the pocket of her purse and pushed a folded piece of paper across the table. I scrunched my face, and she said,

"Just open it."

I unfolded the piece of paper and frantically scanned a report from a lab. It was dated a couple weeks earlier so whatever this was, she'd known for a while. I never know how to read these things,

"Are you okay!!? Is there something wrong with the baby!?"

She teared up a little,

"Read it."

I read it. Oh, shit. You might be wondering what that was all about. Was she sick? Was there something wrong with the baby? Was it twins? No to all of those, but it was somehow even worse.

"I think I knew all along but I was scared and lied to myself, and then it seemed like the truth."

The suspense was killing me. She sipped her tea to buy some time,

"The baby isn't Seppi's."

Even though we all knew it was a possibility, the floor fell out from under me and the walls closed in. My heart was pounding in my throat, and I had to slow my breathing. The feelings flooded in like a tidal wave, my sister would be leaving and there was nothing holding her there anymore, not really. I took a deep breath and held it for a few seconds before letting it out slowly to get myself out of the panic. That was the day we reached the finish line that was really the starting line. Only it turns out, it really was the finish line, for the two of them. I guess I knew all along that it was going to go like that in the end. Opal sat there crying a little but had already had time to cry about it, at that point, she was thrashing against the bars of her cage, going insane.

"I'm going to need to stay at your place for a while, I need time to figure shit out. Auggie will be back next month."

Our parents were moving back to Bunman for nothing. Opal would be gone and so would the baby. She wasn't going to be a mob wife, and she wasn't going to have to give up the feeling of the sand under her feet or the water over her toes. And I had all but decided to find some place else entirely, somewhere I didn't know a soul. I had a pang of regret when I thought about leaving Seppi and I swung one leg back over the fence, we'd have to deal with all of that another day, this wasn't the time. I wondered if he knew about the baby, and Opal could see what I was thinking,

"I told him a while ago, I just didn't know how to tell you, because you know this means I'm leaving."

I compartmentalized all of it into little boxes in the back of my mind, in a place just out of reach. I took Opal's hands; she'd been in Bunman far too long. She had only promised to wait until the restaurant was reopened, and it was opening night. We went back, and I pretended I hadn't helped dispose of a body the night before. I pretended I hadn't almost died, and I pretended I hadn't just found out the baby wasn't Seppi's. And lastly, I pretended my sister wasn't going to leave. I pulled up my big girl panties, and swallowed the lump in my throat before returning to the belly of the beast, acidic and churning with fire. All was well as time ticked down, everything was running smoothly.

Seppi was sitting in his chair sipping whiskey from a rocks glass over perfectly square ice cubes. Opal told him she was going home to rest for a while and he didn't object. She would be back with our parents, and needed to change into something that didn't have snot on the sleeve. I glanced at Seppi and wished he was the one going home to take a nap.

The well-oiled machine chugged along toward the finish line that was really the starting line. I stood in Seppi's doorway and watched him think he was alone. He collected his thoughts or gave himself a pep-talk, or realized his power as he sat there, the king of the hill. Maybe he knew I was there, but he let me think I was clever, he let me think I had the upper hand. I went out the back door as Gretchen was coming in, we waved at each other as we crossed paths. I smoked half a joint and returned to my sofa, my coffee table, and my dark chocolate covered blueberries. At that point, I was also eating pieces of dried mango because I was running out of the blueberries. It was almost time and everything was going as planned or better. I closed my eyes again and took it all in, marinara and garlic and the weed in my hair. Seppi's booming voice broke the Zen,

"What do you mean, we're out of propane!?"

Carlo was reasoning with Seppi, but he wasn't having it. He was angry, maybe angrier than I'd ever heard him. Seppi slammed his fists on the stainless-steel counter and voices began to elevate, so I jogged down the hall carrying my jar of fancy trail mix that only had a couple dark chocolate covered blueberries left. I leaned on the entryway to the kitchen and watched the chaos ensue. Two hours before opening and we were out of propane, it couldn't get much worse than that. Seppi tried to calm himself, but it wasn't working. I told him I'd call the gas company, and he followed behind me as I went to his office. I clicked the door shut and stood in front of the desk,

"Everything's going to be okay; I promise."

I was going to fix it; I wasn't bullshitting him. He slid a business card in my direction. I grabbed the card, plopped in his chair, and used his desk phone. Then I used what I had learned from him, how to be sweet but also in control. Ten minutes later, Gladys had radioed to a driver, to detour from their route for an emergency delivery of propane to Giuseppi's Italian Ristorante. I offered Gladys a complimentary dinner for two that night and exhaled. Seppi paced,

"I'm not going to feel better until those stoves are on."

I gave Seppi some space, it seemed like he needed it. I smelled a tinge of stress sweat in the pits of my shirt, so I started over. I took a shower, worked curl cream through my hair and did my makeup. I did the winged liner and mascara. I did the gold hoops and Alien Elixir. I went to the closet in my bra and panties, staring at the brand-new tailored pantsuit. The thing cost about a thousand dollars, and it made me look like a million bucks. The heeled leather boots really pulled it together. I clipped the Sig Sauer to my waistband and once I shrugged into the suit jacket, you couldn't even see the bump from the gun. You never know, these days. Drunk people can get out of hand and I felt better knowing I could take matters into my own hands if I had to. My gun was even loaded.

The gas company was there before I was back at the restaurant. The guy said someone had turned off the gas line and that the tank was practically full. I thought about how I passed Gretchen coming in, as I was going out. I laughed it off, my mind playing games with me because of the stress. After all, not twenty-four hours earlier, I helped dispose of a body and almost died of hypothermia. I was running on empty but strode through the back door like my shit didn't stink. Just kidding, I had bubble-gut and stunk up my bathroom about five minutes after I got there. But once I was done with that nonsense, I strutted my expensive pantsuit-covered ass right out to the front of the house. It was almost time.

CHAPTER 30
THE FINISH LINE THAT WAS REALLY THE STARTING LINE

THE BAND WARMED UP and the heat was rising. Seppi had used the shower in his office bathroom and was getting into his tuxedo. I voyeured on him from across the hall as he buttoned into the crisp white shirt. Seppi's vest and bow tie were draped over the back of the sofa, his grandfather's cuff links were in a box on the desk. He had a clean shave, and he smelled like shower gel, deodorant, and Tobacco Vanille. Seppi was a sharp dressed man, ready to take the helm. I wanted to lick his face, and other things for that matter. That moment was surreal, that is when I realized that if I stayed in Bunman, there was no turning back, and I didn't think I could handle it. I wasn't cut out for that shit, I wasn't cut out to dump bodies.

Forty-five minutes to go-time as Seppi shrugged into his vest and put on Nunzio's cuff links. I hung my suit jacket over the chair at my desk and leaned on Seppi's door frame, watching as he worked his magic with the bow tie; I was in heat. He caught movement in the tall wood framed mirror and our eyes met, it was the first time he took a good look at me in my opening night aesthetic. I was wearing an expensive bra, and the tailored white button up shirt clung to my breasts. The black Italian leather boots were sexy and made me feel like a bad bitch. Eyeliner, mascara, and wine-colored lipstick. Alien Elixir spritzed on my throat and pulse points, the Sig Sauer holstered at my hip. My vibe was doing something for him and I knew it. It was like I had completed the transformation, I had finally broken free of my chrysalis, the one made of ripped overalls and dirty sneakers.

The girls were slicked back, pushed up, and smelled like Victoria's Secret body spray, cigarettes, and spearmint gum. It was almost time. Seppi kissed me on the cheek before unlocking the door. It wasn't like when you see people swarming a Walmart on Black Friday, but I was a little nervous at the amount of people. So many people cramming themselves into the dining rooms and the dance floor of Giuseppi's Italian Ristorante. The string quartet was serenading the guests and people sipped glasses of complimentary champagne. The kitchen staff were on top of their game and people filled their bellies as they tossed money at the bartender. The volume rose, and at times, it felt like the walls were closing in. There were too many people. Too many conversations going on at once. The more alcohol people drank, the higher the volume. I watched Seppi make his way around the room over and over and over. My dad hugged me and kissed me on the cheek,

"You look beautiful, Boo-Boo Bear."

My mother gave me a floppy fish hug before they nestled into a booth and started devouring free bread and champagne. Seppi shook hands and kiss cheeks, I lost track of him a couple times but he'd always come back around in his orbit of the room. Things felt hectic, Seppi was probably upstairs, but I panicked. I heard a commotion and watched as a spilled bottle of wine dripped onto the brand-new carpet. I caught movement and swung my head around to see two men fighting outside the front door. I let the spilled wine go and made my way to the front. I pushed the door open and barked,

"HEY!"

The men stared at me and spoke in unison, "What!?"

I pulled my suit jacket back to reveal the butt of the Sig Sauer. Hands on hips in the thousand-dollar pantsuit that made me look like a million bucks, calm and like I was in control,

"Look, assholes, unless you want to end up in the ground, you might want to go jerk each other off somewhere else."

I turned around and the door closed behind me, the two men stood there staring. I spun around and lunged at the door, both of them jumped and then jogged away. I dove back into the belly of the beast and did another visual. I asked Opal if she had seen Seppi and she pointed to the other side of the room. I made my way to the other side of the room and couldn't see him; he was probably sitting at one of the booths with someone he knew. I waded my way through the sea of people, too many people to be in there at once. I stood on my tiptoes in the expensive leather boots and scanned all the faces. Seppi was a grown man who was the head of a mob family, not some twenty-something with a twenty-six-year-old piece of Swiss cheese, he could handle himself. But I worked my way through the sea of people and opened his office door. The bathroom was dark, and the room was empty. I backed out and pulled the door shut. When I turned around, I ran right into Wretched, I mean, Gretchen,

"Hey, have you seen Seppi?"

Gretchen was out of breath and a little off kilter, she needed a break. It looked like she was having a panic attack, probably from all the people crowding in the dining room and at the bar. She told me she saw Seppi over there and pointed in the direction I had just come from. Gretchen went into the hallway bathroom, and I went back to my task of checking up on the head of the Moretti mob family. I swam my way through the sea of people and still couldn't find him. I checked upstairs and down. I was sidetracked by people and conversations. Time went by and I knew he was there somewhere; that was his big night. I tried not to worry, I tried to keep things under control and make him proud. But, eventually, enough was enough. My sister wasn't worried, she was going from table to table, she was being pulled every which way. I ran into Gretchen again on her way to the kitchen and she snagged my arm,

"Help me grab a couple of things."

I followed her and she pulled the walk-in open. I went in and she turned to someone and hollered,

"I'll be right there!"

I picked up a hotel pan full of salad and when I was almost to the door, Gretchen's hand slipped and the door slammed shut. I was in pitch darkness. I had a jolt of adrenaline but I could push the glowing emergency release for the door if Gretchen got sidetracked and didn't open the door right away. My mind wasn't spinning yet but I was triggered by the cold, twenty-four hours after the last time. It wasn't the darkness or the claustrophobia, it was the cold. Gretchen would open the door in a second. I needed to chill; no pun intended. But I couldn't wait. I put the pan on the shelf and slammed my palm down on the emergency release for the door. Nothing happened. I panicked and felt like I was suffocating. There was music playing, glasses were clinking, corks were popping, there were too many people talking. Everyone was everywhere and no one would notice I was missing. I started to put it all together, the timing, the chance encounters with all three of them. Lance, Helen, Gretchen, one right after another.

Lance and Helen had been more subtle, really, but Gretchen wasn't as smooth. The way I caught her in my office, always in the right place at the right time, a little too sweet. Wretched pushed all the right buttons and crawled under my wing. I wondered if she shut off the gas. I pounded but no one could hear me, and I knew it. I slammed against the door, over and over; she must have blocked it with something. Be calm, Amelia, someone will need to get in here sooner or later, you're going to be okay. But then I remembered I hadn't seen Seppi in a while and I panicked.

My stomach gurgled and I hyperventilated. I was throwing things at the door, I was crying and frantic, I was going into flight mode and couldn't get out of my cold dark hell. I screamed inside of my head and slammed against the bars of my cage. Maybe I would have been fine for a while, but the world closed in around me and everything clicked into place. I was a naïve little bitch, a gullible, desperate bitch. All the times Seppi tried to rescue me, I'd made my own bed, and now I was sleeping in it. I grabbed the hotel pan full of salad and slammed it against the door.

I screamed as lettuce rained down around my feet,

"HELP!"

I threw the pan to the floor and slammed myself against the door, it gave a little that time,

"HELP! Someone let me out!"

I slammed against the door again, whatever was holding it shut was moving a little. I slammed my body against the door one more time and my sister pulled it open. She seemed frantic,

"What are you doing!?"

I rushed out and started spewing nonsense in her direction. Telling her I couldn't find Seppi, and that Wretched wasn't who she said she was. That's when I finally saw concern in Opal's eyes. Not when I'd been asking if she knew where Seppi was for the last hour, but right then. That's when she realized something might have happened, when she realized we were involved, in whatever this was. I was pissed and wanted to grab Wretched by her cute little pixie cut so I could slam her head against a cinder block wall a couple times for good measure.

"Where's Seppi!?"

Opal looked at me like a deer in the headlights. I grabbed her shoulders and looked her in the eye, I raised my frantic voice another octave,

"Where is Giuseppi!?"

She went pale and had to sit down. She couldn't handle that shit; she wasn't cut out to be a mob wife. The only thing keeping me from completely falling apart, was knowing that I had caused every bit of it. I hadn't played by the rules, I hadn't trusted that Seppi would make it happen, he said it needed to look like an accident. I took it into my own hands, I was a broken little bitch. It didn't look like an accident when I smashed Sal in the head with a shovel. Seppi warned me that would happen, but I thought the dust had settled.

I ignored the warning signs; I ignored the red flags. I didn't listen when Seppi told me to watch out for new people, I didn't listen to my gut. My stupid broken guts that couldn't see things coming from a mile away like most people can. Too trusting, too helpful, too naïve, and now I put Seppi in harm's way. I squeaked as I pleaded. I shook Opal as the string quartet played in the background and people clinked their glasses of moderately priced Cabernet Sauvignon. I had tears in my voice, pleading,

"WHERE IS HE!?"

I could tell Opal was coming back to reality,

"A guy came in and I thought it was a friend."

I gestured for her to keep going, she just kind of mumbled,

"Oh my God."

She stared at the wall. I shook her,

"What happened!? Who was he with!?"

She swallowed the tears in her throat,

"Umm, the guy put his arm around Seppi's shoulder, and they went toward his office, I thought they were friends."

My mind raced. I hadn't seen anyone strange; I hadn't noticed anyone who didn't belong there. I didn't know all of the Moretti's associates, but I knew Seppi, and he wouldn't draw attention to it if something happened, he needed the night to go off without a hitch. I left Opal and rushed into Seppi's office, empty. I pushed through the back door and the Escalade was where he left it. I panicked and needed to find him. How would I find him? I raced back inside and got my phone out of the office, stumbled with my pass code twice before getting it unlocked and scrolling through pictures. I ran back and shoved my phone in Opal's face, she was right where I left her,

"Was it this guy!?"

Opal nodded and stared at the wall some more. The floor fell out from under me and the walls were closing in. The night was going off without a hitch, no one noticed Seppi was gone. Where was Wretched? I needed to get to Seppi, where would Lance take him? And then it dawned on me. I dumped my purse on the desk and the panic button wasn't there. I pulled my phone out and opened the app, the panic button was on the move. Wretched must've had it in her purse. Or maybe Lance had it. Either way, the GPS would lead me closer to Seppi, I was sure.

I'm going to take a time out here. Let's appreciate the absolute shit show unfolding, on a night that was supposed to be something else entirely. I was walking the walk, I mean, if you could have seen that fucking suit, you'd understand. Something about it made me feel like I was worth something, like I had something to offer, that I wasn't just some broken little girl. But right then, I had fucked up so badly that I'd have no other choice but to apologize profusely and make a graceful exit. I had single-handedly ruined everything just by existing.

CHAPTER 31
SWEATING BULLETS

I THREW MYSELF behind the wheel of the mini mafia sedan, kicking up gravel as I backed out of my spot, skidding to a stop where the sidewalk crossed the alley. I raced into the night without a single clue what I would do next. But action was a distraction and I couldn't sit still, waiting to see if Seppi would be able to take care of himself. He was in that situation because of me, and all my stupid decisions, he had never been anything but protective. I had a gut feeling the panic button was heading toward the warehouse on the other side of town, the one where I didn't think anyone would hear someone shoot a gun. Some sense of responsibility lured me away from the safety of Giuseppi's Italian Ristorante.

Whoever had the panic button was en route to their destination, and if they were going to the warehouse, they'd be there ten minutes before me. If Gretchen was the one who stole my panic button, I wondered if she knew it was tracking her location. My mind spiraled, had 'doing the world a favor' put the only person who had ever accepted me, in harm's way? At that moment, it didn't faze me that Seppi might not feel the same, it didn't matter. I realized I might never see him again. A wave of nausea and tears crashed over me, I pushed it away. I tried to control my breathing, otherwise I would go into a full-on panic and Seppi wasn't there to rescue me that time.

Why were those people going after *him*, *I* was the one who did it, *I* was the one who killed Sal. I called Vinny and screamed into the phone, even though it was hooked up to the car,

"Someone took your brother!"

Vinny had no idea what I was talking about, maybe he was a little high, or maybe I'd ripped him from a deep sleep,

"What are you talking about!?"

Adrenaline fired and I went into action-mode,

"SOMEONE TOOK YOUR BROTHER!"

Silence, Vinny still didn't get it,

"Isn't he at the restaurant!?"

I let out an exasperated sigh, I didn't have time to explain it to him. I was on the highway doing ninety. I was in shock I guess, the reality of the situation setting in, my voice trembled with tears, but for a second, I didn't let any of them fall,

"I think Gretchen took my panic button and I'm tracking it; I don't think she realizes the thing has a GPS! I'm pretty sure she's going to a warehouse on the other side of town!"

"What the fuck are you talking about!? What warehouse!? Are you high!?"

I frantically screamed through sobs,

"HELP!"

I didn't have time for Vinny's nonsense. I gave him the approximate address before I ended the call and went back to tracking the panic button. He would be at least ten minutes behind me, but he would bring reinforcements. I'd have to handle the situation on my own, and the thought of it made me want to vomit, a wave of acid flooding the back of my throat. What if I didn't make it in time? What if Seppi had come to a horrible end because of me? I'd made so many stupid decisions and would never forgive myself if something happened to him. Seppi spent his entire life in the mob, he'd been in so many dangerous situations and what if *my* stupid decisions got him killed. I couldn't let myself go there, especially if I wanted to have any semblance of control. I raged inside at the injustice of losing someone who meant so much to me, to lose someone who held all my broken pieces together. I reasoned, I had no proof Seppi was dead, no evidence it had already happened.

But what if, what if Lance beat Seppi with one of those rusty crowbars? What if Lance stood over him and laughed as he put a couple bullets between Seppi's dark, stormy eyes. What if he was bleeding out on that dirty cement floor? Another wave of nausea churned in my stomach, my heart pounded in my ears, the dark tunnels growing narrower. I shook my head and focused, preparing myself to see Seppi, once I saw his dead body, I'd be a force to be reckoned with, I'd have nothing to lose. My mind flashed to the dead guy with the bullet hole and the sneakers, what if that guy had been somebody's Seppi? What the hell was I mixed up in, and what the hell had I done? I opened the windows and sucked in cold air to prevent myself from vomiting. There was a dance of adrenaline and powerlessness, of strength and fear, of fight and flight together, not just one or the other.

A hundred and ten on the highway, I sped through the night in the thousand-dollar pantsuit that made me look like a million bucks. When I got close, I cut the lights and rolled to a stop, out of sight. I flipped off the switch for the dome light and eased out of the mini mafia sedan, it was starting to snow. I crept from tree to tree in silence, stopping near the bags of cement I'd used as a target, and that's when I saw her. Wretched was focused on the trunk of her car and wasn't paying attention to her surroundings. I had the upper hand; she was distracted by whatever she was doing. I snuck along the periphery, under the cover of darkness, in my expensive Italian leather boots. Wretched wasn't worried about someone coming along, not all the way out there.

Advancing with my back against the exterior of the warehouse, my suit jacket snagged as I slid along the cinder block wall in the darkness. When I saw what Wretched was doing, another surge of adrenaline and hot acid flooded my throat. She was lining the trunk of her car with a large piece of thick plastic. I wasn't stupid, I knew what that meant. I wanted to run away but I didn't, I swallowed the acid in the back of my throat and pushed away the elephant sitting on my chest. Her car was running, driver side door wide open, the stereo blasting Bad Medicine by Bon Jovi. The casual manner with which she went about her business, told me I was too late. It took everything I had to fight the acid, dry heaves, and urge to vomit. The night Seppi made it to the finish line; really had been the finish line. I prepared myself for the worst, as my heart pounded in my ears and my vision narrowed into a dark tunnel. I shook it off the best I could, slamming against a wall of anger, injustice, and pain, I wanted to fucking kill someone.

It took running away from home to lead me to someone who made me feel whole. I kicked myself for not telling Seppi how I felt, but I guess I was finally just realizing myself that I loved him. And really, it didn't matter if he felt the same, that wasn't the point. After all I'd been through, and the example I had, I never thought I'd be capable of loving someone so deeply, and I never thought I would feel that safe in someone's cage. I didn't think I would ever meet someone who'd make me feel the way Seppi did.

And then something snapped, it wasn't fair! That wretched bitch might not have been the one who killed him, but it didn't matter, I was vicariously avenging Seppi's death either way. Venom coursed through my veins and all my demons swung out of their cages in unison. A wave of darkness and anger engulfed me like a Venus fly trap, closing its daggered claws into a cage around me. I thrashed against the bars; my heart being ripped to shreds. Tears crept in, the smells of whiskey, cigars, and Tobacco Vanille, forever some traumatic sense memory after that. I pushed back another wave of nausea.

I needed to lash out, to make someone pay for stealing that man away from the world, for stealing him away from me. I knew I was too late, the unhurried way Wretched worked in her trunk, he was probably dead before she even got there. She hummed to the radio as she prepared the trunk for Seppi's dead body and I fucking lost it, I went off the rails. I could have used my gun, but I wanted to use my bare hands on that bitch, I needed it. My eyes narrowed and I wrapped the ends of a burgundy wool scarf around my hands, silently emerging from the darkness. With one fluid motion, I hooked her throat with the scarf and yanked, throwing her off balance. She fell into me, the smooth leather soles of my boots sliding over the snow-covered gravel. My back hit the ground, and I gasped for air as she landed on top of me. I bucked and she slid onto the ground, snow sparkling around us like diamonds as I desperately scrambled to my feet. I wrestled with her in that thousand-dollar pantsuit that made me look like a million bucks.

She shoved me and I slipped again, landing on the ground, hard, a jagged rock piercing my left elbow, another shot of adrenaline firing off to soothe the pain. Wretched swung her leg in an attempt to kick me. I groped the air, grabbed her boot, and yanked. Her feet pointed to the sky and her back slammed to the ground. Maybe she hadn't been the one who pulled the trigger, but it didn't matter. She had lied to me; she was a wolf in cute clothing. I scrambled to my knees and straddled a girl I knew I'd know until the end. Squeezing her sides like I was riding a bull for eight seconds, I could feel her gun pressing against the inside of my left thigh, and wasn't surprised later, that it left a bruise. Things had come full-circle, I was in another kill or be killed situation, but I knew I was capable of it that time. I wrapped my fingers around her throat and dug my thumbs into her windpipe, she thrashed and squeaked as she tried to get air. Fuck her.

She grew desperate, but before her lights went out, she slammed her fist into my left ear. I lost my balance and tumbled onto the ground beside her, my ear ringing, disoriented. She scrambled to her feet and I swung my leg in a semi-circle, catching one of her ankles, I watched as her feet came out from under her again. Thud. That time, she hit her head on the lip of her trunk and I saw blood. At first, it didn't seem to faze her, as she crawled toward me, clawing at me. I wondered if she'd forgotten about her gun, I was holding myself up by my elbows and couldn't reach for mine. She caught my foot and pulled me closer, my white button up and suit jacket riding up in the back, slush and gravel digging into my back. We were both on the ground, but I was on my back, my right calf clamped in her left armpit, her face wild, she had the upper hand. As her hand was in motion to the butt of her cute little handgun, I pulled my left knee up to my chest and slammed the bottom of my fancy boot into her face. Something cracked. Gretchen dropped the gun, stunned, hands to her face, groping her nose and mouth as blood streamed to the new fallen snow. She hissed,

"You, bitch!"

Her two front teeth were broken at an angle, there was gravel and dirty snow on her face from the bottom of my boot. While she was disoriented and holding her mouth, I pulled her up by the collar and punched her in the face, hard, to the sound of Sweating Bullets by Megadeth. Fitting, I know. With every ounce of energy, anger, and venom I had left, I propelled the butt of my right palm in an arc, connecting in an upward thrust that landed under her bloody nostrils. I learned that move in a self-defense class, a way to incapacitate a potential rapist, but it worked on dumb bitches too. Her eyes rolled into the back of her head, and she went lights out. As she fell, I pushed her into the plastic-lined trunk. Click.

Three minutes had passed since I got there, but it seemed like an eternity. No time to catch my breath or give in to the urge to vomit, I jogged to the tall metal door; it was open several feet. I was in the dark, but the inside was illuminated with fluorescent lights, I spotted Seppi's motionless legs on that cold, dirty, cement floor, his head obscured by a workbench. My heart pounded against my ribs in a way that shook my entire body. Lance was yelling and pacing, gun hanging from the fingers of his right hand. He wasn't making any sense, maybe he had lost his mind. My eyes were trying to flood with hot tears, but I swallowed them back, I couldn't have emotions blurring my vision or my judgment at a time like that.

But what if he wasn't dead? What if I wasn't too late? What if there was still a chance? He was Giuseppi Motherfucking Moretti, and that situation was way beyond my pay grade. Even though I was terrified, I pulled myself back to reality. I fumbled around with my holster but what if I missed? Maybe I could distract Lance, shift his attention away from Seppi. If Seppi was still alive, maybe he'd have a chance to defend himself, and I was the person Lance really wanted; I was the one who killed Salvatore Moretti. I didn't feel panic or fear, as my demons swooped down with their smoke and flames, licking at my body with darkness and fire. An odd sense of calm fell over me, if Seppi was dead, I had nothing to lose. I shifted my position and could see Seppi's face, he was alive. There was a hint of fear in his eyes, but he maintained a level of control as he stayed perfectly still on that cold, dirty floor. It was like running from the bus stop to the maple tree at the end of the driveway, if I could distract Lance, Seppi would make a move, and everything would be okay.

I gripped a slush-covered rock and threw it through the open door of the warehouse as a distraction. That rock was flying at the speed of light, I wasn't messing around. And since my aim was absolute dog shit, the rock ricocheted off the metal door frame into my nose, and the right side of my face. The rock banged loudly when it hit the metal, Lance's attention swinging in my direction. I yelled out in pain, blood pouring from my nose, it all happened so fast. Lance advanced, he had fifty feet to go. Seppi scrambled to his feet, and I moved around to keep Lance's attention, forcing myself to make eye contact with a monster. I can't describe it any other way, his eyes were wild, he didn't look like the man I knew,

"I knew you'd come, you stupid bitch! So predictable. And now I get to kill two birds with one stone, how fucking poetic."

Lance paused, he was completely off his rocker, and there was white powder under his nose. Posturing like he was super-human, he thought he held all the power in the exchange,

"The only reason I didn't kill you sooner was because you were so fucking easy to play with."

Lance tilted his head back, his arms out straight like a scarecrow, gun dangling from the fingers of his right hand, he screamed at the ceiling,

"WHOOOOORE!"

Ten seconds had passed, and Lance's focus narrowed as he strolled closer,

"I played you like a fiddle, whore, it was like a game of cat and mouse."

My heart pounded in my ears. I shook my head and bumbled around for my gun. Lance was getting closer, but he wasn't in any hurry, what did he have to worry about? How could he say those things? There I was, seconds from dying, and I was thinking about the fact that I was a whore. I was a broken little bitch who no one ever loved, not even my own mother. I wrapped my fingers around the handle of the Sig Sauer and did like I had practiced a hundred times. I drew, aimed, and fired. Ping. The bullet flew far left, hitting the opposite wall. Lance barked in laughter, in the way a serial killer would laugh. He clamped his gun in his armpit and golf-clapped at me,

"Bravo, WHORE!"

Manhandling his handgun some more,

"I'm going to enjoy watching you die."

I blinked my swollen eyes, blurry with dirt and tears. I squeezed the trigger again, the bullet zinging past Lance's head, pinging off the ceiling. Who was I kidding, I shouldn't have come. I was shaking so badly, there was no way I'd hit him, and I knew it. I was going to die out there and I had never gotten to tell Seppi I loved him, it couldn't end like that, I couldn't die like that. It wasn't fair. A little girl who had panties with the day of the week embroidered on them, then a woman in a thousand-dollar pantsuit that makes her look like a million bucks, dying before experiencing what it's like to tell someone she loves them. A little girl on a bathroom floor and then a woman dying in a parking lot on the other side of town. My entire life boiled down to that, had I done anything that mattered? Would anyone

miss me when I was gone?

The rest of that part happened in quick succession, in a matter of seconds. Lance raised his gun and squeezed off two shots, I dove to the right, but one of the bullets bit into my left cheek, I screamed and dove to the ground. Seppi raged like an animal, unsure how badly I'd been hurt, and I knew what was coming. Lance started to turn around, so I waved my arms and screamed to get his attention,

"HEY!"

He swung his head back to me, curled in my little ball, a sitting duck, killing me would be like shooting a fish in a barrel. I screamed,

"KILL ME! NOT HIM! KILL ME!"

The couple seconds of hesitation on Lance's part, gave Seppi the time he needed. Lance gripped his gun again, closing the gap, almost to the door,

"Are you ready to die, whore?"

Seppi lunged, screaming in guttural desperation, "NOOOOO!"

There was darkness and fire in Seppi's eyes as he swung the crowbar in an arc, landing on top of Lance's head. Blood sprayed; bone cracked. Lance crumpled to the floor and made gurgling sounds, he started to convulse, I almost threw up. I wondered if he was punishing Lance's bullets, or the fact that he had called me a whore. Vinny's BMW skidded to a stop ten feet from where I sat. Seppi didn't look up, he remained focused on Lance's crumpled body. That one blow had done the job, but Seppi wasn't finished. Vinny ran to me, and turned my face to his chest so I wouldn't see. Seppi swung the crowbar again and again and again, and even though I couldn't see it, the sounds are burnt into my memory. Seppi's primal grunts with each swing, the sounds of bone and wetness, a warm spray of blood cascading over me as the crowbar swung. With a shaky finger I pointed,

"Gretchen is in the trunk."

Vinny was so matter of fact,

"Is she dead?"

I went palms up; I didn't think so. Maybe she was coming around, I didn't know, I had never knocked anyone out before. Vinny took the keys out of the ignition, went to the back of the car, and picked her gun up off the ground. My vision narrowed, darkness closing in, a ringing in my ears. The crowbar clanked as it landed on cement, Seppi ran to me. Vinny had keys in his left hand, the gun in his right. He popped the trunk and as it swung open, he said,

"Hi!"

Gretchen's hand reached up to him and he shot her in the head. He tossed the gun in on top of her and slammed the trunk. Seppi knelt in the gravel next to me and covered my eyes, but it was too late for that. Hot acid flooded the back of my throat again, a wave of nausea and deeper darkness circling the periphery. A car skidded to a stop next to Vinny's, a man I didn't know, took the keys to Gretchen's car and drove away with her body. Vinny stepped over Lance's body and assessed the situation, it was all business, just another day at the office.

Seppi helped me up and we stood there, my right ear against his chest, his heart pounding a mile a minute. His monsters retreated into the shadows as my demons climbed back into their cages. I was nothing more than a broken little girl, battered and bloody in that thousand-dollar pantsuit that made me look like a million bucks. I was dirty and covered with blood, two inches to the right and I would have been dead. Even though I'd been shot, I had dodged another bullet, and I knew it. When you get the chance to say the thing you thought you'd never get to say, you say it.

My face bled all over Seppi's tuxedo shirt as we stood there, and he completely lost it. I had seen him cry before, but I had never seen him cry quite like that, it was more like weeping. He made this desperate, high-pitched whining sound with his sobs, his body couldn't cry as hard as he wanted it to. The two of us were wrapped together in that slushy gravel parking lot with diamonds falling around us. Right then, Giuseppi Moretti wasn't a mob boss, he was something else entirely, and I could see in his eyes that he was breaking.

As the adrenaline receded, I cried so hard I almost threw up. I was covered in dirt and bruises and blood, mine and someone else's. My body aching, my face swollen, blood dripping onto my tailored white button up shirt. I was wet and cold and covered in blood in that parking lot on the other side of town. Vinny laid a tarp on the cement floor next to Lance's body as another car slid to a stop. Franco emerged from a Lincoln Navigator and nodded to Seppi as he jogged by. Vinny and Franco moved Lance and his bashed skull onto the tarp and dropped him like a sack of shit. The two of them had it covered, they would make it all go away.

Seppi gently hooked my chin with his finger, tilting my face toward his. My breath caught in my throat when our eyes met. Through the dirt and blood and tears, electricity flowed through his fingers. A tidal wave of emotions crashed over me as Seppi moved his eyes to my cheek, his voice was hard to decipher, a sound of disappointment or sad sentimentality,

"Your dimple."

I swallowed hard, dirty tears blurring the vision in my swollen eyes. I reached for my cheek, and he stopped me, his voice desperate and trembling with retreating adrenaline,

"Don't touch it."

I moved my eyes to his, as blood dripped from my face, eyes swollen, my legs made of jelly. I knew he was going to tell me that every bit of what happened, was my fault. I needed to be reprimanded for ignoring the red flags, maybe I deserved to be at the bottom of Clover Lake. I made so many stupid decisions, I hated myself and understood why my own mother didn't love me. My voice raspy and weak,

"I am so sorry, Seppi!"

He started to say something, but I put my hand up to stop him, tears of desperation running through the riverbeds of clean skin on my cheeks. I swallowed and tried not to lose my words in the tears,

"All of this is my fault! I keep doing stupid shit, and you keep saving me. I wanted to show you I could return the favor."

Seppi reached out to me, but I pulled away, my tears turning to self-deprecation,

"Who am I kidding? I don't belong here."

Our eyes met, my voice trembling with tears and the aftershocks of a million jolts of adrenaline, snot dripping from the end of my nose,

"I'm sorry you wasted your time on me, Seppi."

I dropped my eyes to the parking lot,

"I am just so sorry."

I was broken in every way. My mind, body, and soul were crushed, my heart had broken into a million pieces, and I had done it to myself. The version of me who had loved someone, had failed miserably. The version of me who protected the broken little girl, was bloody, battered, and in a million pieces. So, I stood there in my costume and decided once and for all, to try again some other place. I was never going to get the fresh start I was looking for, not in Bunman. I turned and walked away, and he let me.

Well, he let me, and then he didn't.

Seppi jogged after me,

"Amelia, wait."

I turned to him; he was ten feet away. We just stood there looking at each other, and then he said,

"I love you."

I blinked back at him, a new wave of tears replacing the old one, weak and shaky,

"What?"

He took a step closer,

"Remember the night in the woods?"

I nodded but didn't know why he was asking.

"I've known since then."

I crumpled to the ground as my legs gave out beneath me. All the times I'd looked at Seppi and wondered if he felt the same, every time my body felt electricity in his presence. That night in the woods, maybe he'd wanted to kiss me, but he hadn't, because that's not what I needed. He knelt there in his tuxedo, and Grandpa Russo's cuff links. Seppi rubbed my back in that slush covered parking lot on the other side of town, diamonds falling around us, and then he kissed me. It was tender and broken, blood and dirt, wounds, and demons getting in the way, but our mouths came together gently and our tongues touched.

There was no time to cherish the moment, everything was happening too fast. Vinny followed Franco into the night with Lance's body. Moments later, Seppi was buckling me into the passenger seat of my car. I was dizzy and my head was pounding, the pain in my face was making me nauseous. He kicked up a patch of gravel as he sped toward home, I hadn't said it back. Seppi wrapped his hand around mine,

"Everything is going to be okay; I promise."

But it wasn't. What did that even mean? He in his tuxedo, me in the thousand-dollar pantsuit that made me look like a million bucks. I unzipped my boots and curled my knees up to my chest, hugging them as I cried. Seppi called his mother, it was all business, she was accustomed to that type of call for decades,

"There was a situation. Amelia and I are safe, but we won't be returning to the restaurant tonight."

Mary Moretti didn't skip a beat,

"I have everything under control here, no one has noticed you're gone, I keep telling people they just missed you."

"Thank you, mom."

The call ended.

What was happening?

I needed a hot shower and some stitches. I needed some whiskey and some weed. I needed to say it back, but that wasn't the time or place. Seppi raced to the land of mafia mansions and blood splattered thousand-dollar pantsuits that make you look like a million bucks. Roger met us at the door. Seppi's big night, the night he returned to the helm, the finish line that was really the starting line. I had never been through something so chaotic, even the night at the refuge wasn't like that. That night made things clear, that night reminded me life is too short. Maybe that night, things happened exactly as they were meant to.

Nothing would ever be the same again, the cat was out of the bag, the cards were on the table. Things went in slow motion as Roger cleaned my wounds and stitched up my face, right through my left dimple. The front door slammed against the wall. Seconds later, Opal appeared with fire in her eyes, she rushed over to me, I looked like hell,

"What happened!?"

"I got shot."

She spun around to Seppi, who was covered in other people's blood,

"And what the hell happened to *you*!?"

He shook his head,

"I'm good."

Opal moved to Seppi and slapped him across the face, her teeth clenched as she yelled up at him,

"You're *good*!?"

Opal got in his face and pointed in my direction,

"You're fucking GOOD!?"

I knew she was leaving. She geared up one more time,

"Two days in a row, you son of a bitch! You're one job is to keep her safe, you're fucking worthless!"

She had no idea he'd saved my life, and I don't think, in her eyes, it really mattered anymore. Seppi reached for Opal's hand, she pulled away, crisscrossed her arms in front of her and threw them to her sides,

"I'm done!"

Seppi nodded because he wasn't surprised, she'd agreed to wait until after opening night, but it had been a struggle for both of them. She spit in Seppi's direction and I could see that it hurt him. That was the last time Opal would be in that house. She wrapped me in her arms and pulled back to give me a once over, I was a mess. Roger was done with my exam and the stitches. Seppi came to me and I wanted him to, but Opal's venom flew out at him. Through clenched teeth,

"Get the fuck out of here, you worthless piece of shit!"

She kicked him out and slammed the door. Opal was in mama-hen mode, she was strong and angry and wanted to take control of the situation. Just like the night before, she hung a towel and bath robe next to the shower door. I let the suit jacket fall to the floor and unbuttoned the tailored white button up shirt that was covered in blood. I watched myself in the full-length mirror, standing there in my fancy bra and panties. Opal held me to her chest, and I broke down when I felt the baby kick. What if I had missed becoming an aunt? I couldn't contain it, all my wounds were open, the ones on the inside and out.

"You're going to be okay; I'll sit with you."

Opal sat on the lid of the toilet while I washed the pain away. I sudsed up my hair three times with too much shampoo, and scrubbed the dried blood out of my hair. I washed my face, being careful with the bruises and the clear dressing over the stitches in my cheek. This was not how it was supposed to go, the night Seppi reached the finish line that was really the starting line.

Once I was wrapped in the bathrobe, my sister took my hands, I knew what she was going to say before she said it. I bit my bottom lip and held my breath. But before Opal said anything, she led me to the full-length mirror and made me take a good look. It was bad. The right side of my face was full of cuts and scratches, my eyes were black and almost swollen shut. The left side of my face was cut up, and you know how it went with my dimple. It might seem vain, but my face was never the same after that night. My wounds were creeping from the inside to the outside and I was trading my masks for scars. Opal teared up but I could see she was sure of herself and what she was going to say,

"He knows the baby isn't his, there's no reason for me to stay. This isn't my life."

She was right, that was never what she wanted. Maybe she wouldn't run far, maybe she just needed to get away from mafia mansion land. I could tell Opal wanted to say something else, she was trying to find the words, and I knew whatever it was, she had given it a lot of thought,

"He loves you, Amelia."

My tears returned and I opened my mouth to protest but she knew better. She put her hand up,

"We've talked about it."

Opal waved it away,

"Even if that wasn't the case."

She pointed at my face,

"Even if I could've put up with all this mob bullshit, this isn't my life, and you know it."

I tried to convince her she was wrong even if she wasn't,

"Opal, I..."

She touched my arm,

"I'm not upset that I'm leaving, I'm upset that I stayed."

My knees got all squishy and wobbly and she led me to the bedroom. I sat on the end of the bed while she packed her bags. Most of the clothes in that closet were designer and she'd never wear them again. Opal left the jewelry and keys to the Volvo in a basket on Seppi's dresser. She moved things from the designer handbag, into her old reliable patchwork tote. She didn't care that my parents would wonder where she went. I followed Opal down the stairs, and she went out the door to her van. I stood in the foyer, awkwardly holding the handle of Opal's rolling luggage. Seppi was waiting there, freshly showered, in sweatpants and a hoodie, on the night he reached the finish line that was really the starting line. He held me to his chest and this thing between us was to be continued. Our eyes met, but it was different that time. That was our first Valentine's Day, the night he saved my life. Seppi gently cupped the side of my face, and our mouths came together one more time. That kiss was tender and warm, and the electricity went to my heart instead of my panties. In a strange way, killing had become our love language and deep inside where my demons played, I knew he had done the world a favor.

THE
TIES THAT BIND
SOUNDTRACK

1. Maybe - The Flying Tigers
2. Dangerous Game - Klergy & Beginning
3. Y'all Want a Single - Korn
4. Wicked Ones - Dorothy
5. I Put A Spell On You - CCR
6. So Much to Say - Dave Matthews Band
7. The Way You Look Tonight - Frank Sinatra
8. Cut You In - Jerry Cantrell
9. Take It Easy - Eagles
10. How Villains Are Made - Madalen Duke
11. Fly Me Courageous - Drivin N Cryin
12. Bag of Tricks - Isle of Q
13. You Can Run - Adam Jones
14. Black Sea - Natasha Blume
15. Haunted - Adona
16. Blood In the Water - Joanna Jones as The Dame
17. Small Words - Speak No Evil
18. Wicked Game - Daisy Gray

ABOUT THE AUTHOR

VANESSA FELL IN LOVE with writing in the third grade and spent hours typing stories on an old Smith Corona. After pursuing degrees in Sociology, Nursing, and Education, Vanessa returned to writing. She became obsessed with Sue Grafton in the mid-nineties and was inspired to create an equally relatable female main character.

A survivor of childhood trauma, Vanessa is no stranger to battling her own demons. The unapologetically broken main character in this series will feel like an old friend you'd meet for coffee or a glass of well-aged whiskey around the fire. Vanessa's no-filter writing style cultivates an immediate familiarity and connection to the people and places in a world that's shrouded in ruthlessness, mental demons, and self-medication.

This series is planned to have at least ten titles. Vanessa is currently writing a gritty southern novel about a woman on the run, and a young adult fiction about not fitting in.